I0768532

The Daughter of Danray

Copyright © 2024 by Natalia Hernandez

This is a work of fiction. All characters and events portrayed in this novel are fictitious. Any resemblance to real people or events is purely coincidental.

TITLE: The Daughter of Danray

AUTHOR: Natalia Hernandez

ON-SALE DATE: OCT 17, 2024

Print ISBN: 979-8-9865983-9-0

Digital ISBN: 979-8-9865983-8-3

Book Cover Design by ebooklaunch.com

Map Art by: Chaim Holtjer

For more information, including content warnings, please visit:

www.NataliaHernandezAuthor.com

No portion of this book may be reproduced in any form without written permission from the publisher or author, except as permitted by U.S. copyright law.

NATALIA HERNANDEZ

THE DAUGHTER OF DANRAY

NATALIA HERNANDEZ

TIERRAMADRI
N
Cassalan
The Northern Tribes
Gulen
Carlen
The Borders
Miramar
Andala
Mages University
Pelgar
Dovingen Temple
Capitol
Andalon Palace
chaim 2022

For anyone battling their own monstros:
You are stronger than you know.

CONTENTS

CHAPTER 1

RAWL

R awl gave a firm flick of his wrist, urging the old horse to pick up his speed. The steed's response was a lazy flip of his tail, idly attempting to swat the buzzing flies from around his hindquarters. The hum of insect wings was almost melodic, accentuated by the chirps and whistles of nearby birds and punctuated by the slow *clop, clop, clop* of the ancient stallion's hooves against the paved road.

Despite the animal's advanced age, the horse—who Rawl had secretly named *Viejo*—became a dependable companion throughout their journey, pulling their small wooden cart with relative ease. He was, however, prone to veering off course to eat any patch of grass that they came across, delaying them if Rawl didn't hold him in line. This didn't leave the archer much time to rest, as it was imperative that they reach their destination as swiftly as possible. He couldn't blame the old beast, as the oats Rawl purchased in the last populated village dwindled quickly, and the creature was expending much more energy than he was used to by pulling the rickety cart. But time was of the essence, and Rawl couldn't let him graze nearly as often as he would have liked.

The day was warm, as most of them had been since leaving the Borders. The further they traveled south, the more the scenery shifted from the cooler, brown-and-yellow mountainous terrain to the more verdant forests of Rawl's youth. Even the sounds changed throughout their journey. All around him, he could hear the rustling of trees and bushes, the noise rounder and fuller and somehow *wetter* than the crisp crinkling of fallen leaves and dry grass that they passed through in the north. Over time, the grunts, snorts, and clucking of livestock transformed into the screeches of monkeys and squawks of macaws.

But now, even those sounds were beginning to change.

The Great Andalan Road lay long and winding ahead of them. It cut through the thick expanse of forest like an angry river of rock, dividing the lawless chaos of the wild with a bold and declarative marker of *civilization*.

Rawl thought he rather preferred the former.

He had been raised in the woods, after all. His people, the Padir, were a nomadic tribe of forest folk, and Rawl had spent the better part of his life climbing trees, hunting, trapping, foraging for food, and sleeping under the open night sky. So-called "civilization" made his teeth hurt. But that was exactly where he journeyed. Towards the pinnacle of civilization, the Andalan capital, and more specifically their shining jewel, the Mage University.

They couldn't reach it soon enough. Rawl's muscles ached, and he tried blinking the sand away from his gritty eyes. Rolling his knotted shoulders, he risked a quick glance behind him to the bottom of the transport cart, suppressing a wince at the sight. Alric, his companion and friend, lay bound and gagged on the hard wooden floor. The image pained him every time he witnessed it, despite the fact that it was Rawl himself who had placed him there.

The Mage Madness, which had overcome him during a battle in Tureene, continued to course through Alric's blood. The illness mottled his skin, painting murky red rivulets over his flesh, as if his very veins were flowing with lava. After nearly a week of travel, the errant sparks of magia that often crackled from his friend with wild abandon struck Rawl more times than he could count. During their journey, the mage had tackled Rawl from the cart, bitten him twice, and stabbed the poor archer once. Luckily, the blade had missed anything important, though narrowly.

But Alric was still alive.

That was all Rawl cared about, keeping Alric alive. It had become a mantra of sorts, a reassurance, a promise.

He is still alive.

Rawl repeated it to himself over and over as they traveled through the rain, as the cart's wheels got stuck in mud. Every time that Alric attacked him, each time he had to gag and bind his friend, dose him with sedatives or physically subdue him, he repeated the words.

At least he's still alive.

The truth was that Rawl could handle the elements, the attacks, and the verbal abuse with far more ease than the unadulterated hate in the mage's eyes every time he managed to keep him in check. Seeing his companion, his friend, his ... Seeing *Alric* look at him like he loathed the very sight of him broke something within Rawl's chest, and he knew he could not mend that break until he found a way to cure the mage of his affliction.

But at least he's still alive, the archer repeated to himself desperately.

Rawl had no idea how long most mages could survive after being affected with Mage Madness, as it was routine to kill the aggrieved mage upon discovery of the affliction. Mages with the madness were erratic, unpredictable, and very, very dangerous. Something about the tainted blood increased their magical ability; right before it killed them.

Rawl knew Alric would not last much longer in the state that he was in. His skin, where not painted with the ugly red marks of corrupted magia, was beginning to turn pale and gray. His usually beautiful face was now drawn and gaunt, sweat incessantly pouring from him, plastering his clothing to his body and his thick black hair against his temples and neck. Rawl had taken to giving the mage water hourly, sometimes pouring it down his throat by force to counteract the dehydration. It was working; for now. But Rawl knew he needed to get Alric to the Mage University as quickly as possible.

"Not long now," Rawl called back to Alric as they continued down the Great Andalan Road. It was risky to use such a well-transited path, but it was the quickest way to the coast, and to the university.

Rawl knew that Alric could not answer. He was the one who placed the gag on the mage, after all. But he had taken to speaking to Alric as if the man he cared so much for was still in there, somewhere.

Rawl had to believe he was.

"Soon enough we will find the Altamar road and take it west to the coast. That's where the Mage University is."

Rawl laughed ruefully. "Well, I don't have to tell you that. It's where you studied, after all."

He heard Alric struggling against his bindings, and his body tensed.

"You never did tell me much about your time there," he continued, as if nothing was wrong. "If I were a betting man—which you know I am—I'd wager that you were even more prim and proper there than you were ..."

Rawl hesitated. "Than you *are* now," he continued.

A low growl sounded from the bottom of the cart, making the hair on Rawl's arms stand up, but he did his best to shake off his unease.

"I bet you never missed a single lecture, were the favorite of all the instructors, and an even more insufferable know-it-all in your youth." He smiled a little, thinking of a young Alric, even thinner and gawkier than he was now, a full head of unkempt hair flopping over his eyes, and a thin strip of peach fuzz over his upper lip.

"Did you go to fiestas?" Rawl asked him, not expecting an answer. He tried to picture Alric with a cerveza in one hand, talking to a pretty dark-haired girl. "I can't imagine it," he added a little dreamily.

A low rumble broke Rawl out of his fantasies, and he jolted up from the cart bench, straining his eyes to see past a looming bend in the road. The old horse startled at the abrupt action, hopping anxiously from one leg to the other.

The rumbling grew louder.

"Coño," Rawl muttered, pulling the horse to a full stop before vaulting to the back of the cart. The reverberations intensified as the very ground beneath them seemed to shake as the noise grew stronger. Unless the dioses themselves had taken to walking the earth, there was only one thing that could cause such a commotion.

The Andalan army.

Alric's eyes, tinged with red, burned through the archer as he fished out a vial of sedative from his pants pocket. Grimacing, Rawl realized he had precious few of the tinctures left.

Let it be enough, he internally pleaded.

Rawl squatted by the mage and braced himself. This was always the worst part. He would rather be stabbed again, ten times over, than endure what was coming next, but he knew he had no choice.

Rawl removed the gag from Alric's mouth.

"You will not win, you weak, insignificant insect. I could crush you with the heel of my boot and give it no more thought than an eagle picking off a tick," Alric immediately seethed.

Rawl ignored the abuse, though internally he winced. Hearing such vile words come from a mouth that he had kissed made the wound cut deeper. He struggled to keep Alric's head down, yanking his hand away just before the mage could sink his teeth into his fingers. With his other hand, he pulled the stopper out of the vial with his own teeth, then cupped Alric's face in a parody of affection, pinching his fingers towards each other to keep the mage's mouth open. Alric thrashed beneath him, gargling more insults and slurs as Rawl quickly poured the sedative down his throat. Alric attempted to spit it out, but Rawl was prepared, covering his mouth and pinching his nose until the mage had no choice but to swallow it down, eyes glaring daggers at him all the while.

"Make no mistake, forest rat," Alric growled when Rawl pulled away. "I will kill you. I will escape these bonds and burn you with my magia until your skin peels and crackles, and your flesh falls from your bones."

Rawl struggled with the gag, attempting to stop the words that drove splinters through his heart with every ire-fueled syllable.

"Even then, I will not stop. You will be less than ash. You will be the specks of dust in sunlight that no one will ever see, because I will drag you to the Night Wood and leave you in infinite darkness for all of eternity."

His voice was softer now, his words slurring as the sedative began taking effect.

"Even your afterlife will be an endless, sunless void." His voice trailed and his body grew limp. "Unending pain," he murmured, before falling into sleep.

Though regret pulsed through his body with every beat of his heart, Rawl gently placed the gag back in the mage's mouth, making sure he was breathing normally before draping his body with a heavy cloak. Then he quickly arranged more furs and goods around Alric's slumbering form before climbing back onto the front bench, doing his best to feign casual nonchalance.

It was time to sneak past the Andalan army.

CHAPTER 2
NOVA

Nova stepped through the archway into the inner sanctum of the Danrayen Temple and heard the soft grinding of stone as the grand doors shut behind her. In an instant, she was plunged into shadow.

Nova tightened her grip on the blades in her fists, concerned over the dampness she was already beginning to feel in her palms.

Nova stood motionless for a long moment, allowing her body to adjust to the new environment. Outside the walls of the sanctum, in the temple garden, the day was hot and bright, the sun goddess Tz'ola's rays wrapping the land with her comforting blanket of warmth. Inside the sacred room, the air was much cooler, and the quick contrast in temperature caused goose pimples to erupt on the exposed flesh of her arms.

Nova took deep, steady breaths in through her nose and out through her mouth as her eyes became accustomed to the darkness. After a few moments, she realized that the sanctum wasn't as devoid of light as she had thought. Several sconces lined the walls of the long room, bathing it in a warm, honeyed glow.

Honeyed, she realized, because gold encapsulated the entire space. Just like the towering statue of the goddess Danray, which loomed above her outside, the metal constituted the entirety of the sanctum. Even the sconces holding the flames were made of gold.

Nova hesitated, not knowing whether to explore the room further or remain exactly where she was, holding her guard.

Nova didn't know much about the Trial of Danray, other than the few whispered rumors and speculations she had overheard while she was an initiate at the temple. As girls, she and her friends would try to guess what the Trial would consist of.

Would they be a series of tests, like when the priestesses ran them through drills? There were several competitions amongst the young trainees several times a year, allowing each girl to highlight their individual strengths and talents.

Perhaps it was a trial of loyalty? A series of scenarios meant to test how dedicated they were to the path of the goddess.

Would there be written examinations? Was the inner sanctum just another classroom, an uncomfortable desk waiting for them with parchment and paper?

The last seemed the least likely scenario, as every time a young woman passed the Trial, they emerged sweaty, tired, and often injured. Some of those injuries were mild, like the scratches that Damika experienced. Others were much more serious in nature, like the ones her friend Raidea had sustained.

Some girls didn't make it out of the Trial at all.

No, Nova was certain that whatever waited for her in that room was meant to challenge her combat abilities, not test her on whether she could construct a well-written argument.

As a young girl, Nova never imagined that one day she would be in the sanctum, taking the Trial. She lived in the temple under false pretenses, not a true Danrayen initiate, but a traitor to the crown in hiding. Even the name that she gave herself then—Phanessa—was a fabrication. Back then, she was certain that she had no right to take the Trial, no matter how hard she worked, no matter how much warrior training that she received, because she was not truly one of them.

At least, that is what she had believed. When High Priestess Adira told Nova that she had proven herself as true a warrior as the other young women, she had been stunned. When it was suggested that she take the Trial to earn her place among them, she almost believed herself to be dreaming. But here she stood, determined to take her place as a true Danrayen Warrior.

Or die trying.

Nova lifted her chin and stalked determinedly to the center of the room. If this was to be her test, let it begin.

At first, nothing happened. Nova suddenly became worried that nothing *would* happen. That, after everything, the High Priestess had been wrong after all, and she would have to leave the sanctum, defeated not by the Trial, but by the knowledge that her initial assessment had been right all along. That she did not belong amongst the ranks of the Danrayens. That she was not one of them, and never would be.

Slowly, however, Nova noticed that the floor beneath her feet began to move. At first, she thought it was a trick of the light. Then, she believed it to be her frayed nerves playing tricks on her imagination. But when the yellow ground began to ripple, as if it had become a giant shimmering pond of molten metal, she quickly began stepping backwards, trying to find anything that she could vault herself onto if necessary. Frantically, she scanned her surroundings but didn't see anything. The entire room was completely vacant of any furniture that might provide assistance. Just as she was turning towards a wall, determined to suspend herself on the sconces, the liquid began collecting in the very center of the room, swirling like a furious tempest.

Nova threw her hand out in front of her face, concerned that droplets of the material would fling out errantly, and for some reason, she was sure that she did not want any of the strange substance touching her. But the swirling mass stayed collected, pulling up more and more from the floor in crashing waves twisting around a singular point. More and more of the floor drew itself into the center of the room, until finally, it collected, forming a golden statue towering in the space before her. Shaped like a woman, the sculpture showed an outline of hair, breasts, a tight waist with curved hips and thighs, but without clear definition. As if a sculptor had just begun giving the material form but hadn't yet brought their creation to life. Nova took a step forward, but an enormous flash of light suddenly blinded her. The gold of the room became a blistering, all-encompassing white, and Nova was suddenly sure that she would lose her sight forever. Even behind her eyelids, the light permeated. She cried out, flinging her arm across her brow and sinking to the ground to hide her face.

Then, the light was gone, and Nova remained panting against the cool floor. She knew she needed to open her eyes, but she didn't dare. Whether it was fear of what she might see, or that she might not see anything at all, she did not know.

You are vulnerable, a voice whispered in her head. *You are open prey for whatever else might be in here!*

The voice sounded like her friend Petra.

You cannot stay on the ground, Rojya, the voice continued sweetly, now sounding like Rawl in her head.

You can do this, Alric told her firmly in her mind.

You were ready for this Trial far before I was, Raidea said, the voice so full of teasing mischief that tears prickled behind Nova's eyes to hear it. She would never hear her friend outside of her own mind again.

We believe in you, Taruka promised.

Stand, meft royan, Axchel whispered.

Stand, soldier!

It was Damika's barking order that had her finally lifting her chin. Years of practice in obeying her friend's commands overrode her body, and she dragged a leg forward, flexing her knee and readying herself to spring upwards against whatever danger may await. She tensed, blinking back the moisture in her eyes to be ready to attack—but instead, froze in place.

The feminine statue was gone. Before her was a stunningly beautiful woman in a long, flowing golden robe.

She was tall, at least six feet, and her dark brown skin glowed with touches of radiant amber. She was strong, with arms and thighs neatly defined by thick ropes of muscle that were visible, even as she stood still.

The woman's face was the definition of lovely. It was a perfect oval shape, with high, prominent cheekbones and dark piercing eyes. Her nose was strong and straight, but her lips were by far her most overwhelming feature. They were both full and wide, and the color of a deep burgundy wine.

It wasn't until Nova noticed her hair—massive waves of curling chestnut ringlets that tumbled out from her scalp and across her back—that she realized that the statuesque woman wasn't a woman at all. She recognized that hair. She had seen the same wild tresses every morning for ten long years, every time she exited the temple bedchambers to begin her day. Every single morning for a decade, Nova had stared up at the very same face before her now, raising a clenched fist towards her visage and drawing her thumb back to touch the hollow of her collarbone in respect.

Respect towards the goddess, Danray.

Instead of leaping up as she planned, Nova instead tucked her body back down, resting on her knees once more and bowing her head in supplication. She hastily tucked her daggers away while her heart thundered hard in her chest, at her throat, and in her ears. The sound of it was so deafening that she felt it would burst at any moment.

"Goddess," she gasped.

"Rise, mija," a voice said, warm and deep, as if panela coated her throat.

Nova's entire body was trembling so hard, she wasn't sure that she was going to be able to obey her goddess's command. Lurching, she did her best to stand, knees knocking against one another. She kept her gaze down, unsure of the proper protocol when gazing upon one of the dioses.

When she'd spoken to the Flowers of Prophecy, she'd trained for a full decade in all the rites and procedures and etiquette involved with addressing them before she was allowed anywhere near their presence—and they were only messengers of the dioses! How was she meant to act in front of a goddess?

"Do not be afraid. Let me look at you, child," she heard the goddess say.

Still trembling, Nova forced herself to lift her chin.

The goddess's face was open, kind, and the smile on her face shocked Nova. It was large and wide, showing off perfectly straight white teeth and more than a bit of gum. It surprised her that such a very human-looking smile belonged to the goddess. Instead of diminishing from her perfection, however, it only seemed to add to it. And while everything about her was clearly apt for a goddess of battle and transition, it took Nova aback to see how much warmth radiated from her. It only served to disarm her further.

"Why did you not come for your Trial sooner, mija?" the goddess asked her.

Nova swallowed against the dryness in her mouth. "Lo siento, diosa," she apologized. "I did not know it was mine to take."

The goddess tsked lightly, pacing the golden room as lightly as a large cat, her golden robe trailing behind her and rippling where it touched the ground.

"You trained at my temple, ate at my table, learned under my priestesses. Why would you think that the Trial would not also be open to you?"

While Nova's trembling had mostly subsided, a tremor still ran through her at the question.

"I thought I was only a guest. Less than a guest—an imposter. I never imagined that I could have been chosen to walk this path, had life not lead me down another first."

The goddess hummed, still walking her slow, languid circle around her.

"And now?" she asked Nova.

Nova straightened, throwing her shoulders back and raising her chin, not in defiance, but with determination. "Now, I would like the chance to prove that I am worthy of it. Of the path, and of your patronage. Of being a Danrayen Warrior. Your warrior."

With a giddy rush, she realized that she meant every word. Gone were the days where she doubted her strength or her worth. She was no longer the scared child that was sent to hide in the temple. She was not the wary initiate, fearful that someone would discover her secrets at any moment. She had proven to herself that she was capable of so much more than she believed possible. Now, she was ready to prove to the goddess that she was ready to walk in her path.

"So, you have come to take the Trial at last." It was not a question, but Nova nodded anyway. "And do you know what the Trial entails?" she asked.

"No, my goddess. Only that it will test me on my combat ability," Nova answered, stiffening.

"On your combat ability," the goddess repeated, as if considering the words.

"On my, my fighting skills," Nova ventured again. "My ability to be a true warrior."

"And what makes a true warrior?" the goddess asked.

Nova started, a memory slamming into her mind unbidden. Long ago, Mamá had asked her a similar question. At the time, she had used Damika as the model for what she thought made a great warrior. But Mamá told her that a true warrior stood for more than those who could fight or handle their weapons with great precision. That the path was not simply about how skilled one was in battle, and that Danrayen Warriors were so much more than soldiers skilled in combat. She explained that being a true warrior was just as much about caring for the wellbeing of others, healing the sick and wounded, and the protection of those less fortunate than it was battling against great foes.

Nova frowned. "I—" she began, then hesitated. It was one thing to hear such things from Mamá, but did Danray believe them as well?

The goddess finally stopped her pacing, staring directly into Nova's eyes.

"My daughter, you passed the Trial long before stepping through this sanctum."

Nova felt her jaw drop, and she knew that she was staring at the goddess with her mouth gaping open like a fish.

"Qué?" she blurted out without thinking. While Nova most assuredly did not want to argue with a literal goddess, she couldn't help but ask. "But I-I never—" she stuttered.

"Let me show you," Danray said through her wide smile, and the room faded from view.

Nova plunged into the middle of a forest, trees and bushes around her topped with bits of frost. She gasped and her breath created a puff of smoke in the air. She scanned her surroundings. It looked like the northern Andalan forest, right as the weather began turning cold. But that was impossible. She was miles away, and when she stepped into the sanctum, it had been early spring across Andala, not the dawn of winter.

She opened her mouth to call out for the goddess and heard a loud crashing through the brush. Nova whirled, watching in amazement as a very familiar scene unfolded in front of her.

It was Rawl, the day she first met him, in his hunter-green cloak, hood pulled up over his face. He was running through the frost-covered grass until he reached the base of a thick tree. Nova watched as he scrambled up its rough trunk, almost impossibly fast, as two monstros of the Night Wood followed him in chase, close behind. Fear gripped Nova around the neck, and she instinctively reached for her throwing knives, but before she could reach them, a loud voice called out in the glen.

"Aim for the eyes!" it—*she* shouted. She watched herself spring forward to help Rawl, and then Alric quickly followed.

The memory faded, and the swirling gold fog opened on yet another.

Again, Nova recognized herself, this time fighting against flesh peddlers determined to capture her and her friends. She saw as they all scrambled into the hanging carriage, suspended along a deep canyon that would carry them away from the threat. Then, almost as if in slow motion, she watched the younger version of herself throwing a knife to cut through the ropes which suspended it, plummeting the rest of her party to safety, leaving only herself in the grasp of the traffickers.

The fog lifted to surround her once more, then cleared, showing Nova standing in front of Axchel, large and looming, imposing in his red Cassalain uniform. The scene showed her making the choice to free him from his binds, even though he was the "enemy."

As quickly as it had started, the memories faded and Nova found herself back in the temple sanctum, staring at the goddess.

"But ..." Nova faltered, dazed. "You are the goddess of battle ... those moments are not of battle. Some of them led to battle, but what you showed me ..."

"What is the ultimate aim of battle?" the goddess asked her, no longer smiling.

Nova hesitated, thinking. It was not a question that she had ever pondered before. "To win the war?" she ventured.

Danray's eyes sharpened. "I am the goddess of battle, not of war. Battles are needed. Battles are necessary. Battles keep us from becoming stagnant. They allow us to protect ourselves, and they facilitate our growth."

Nova saw her jaw tense, then felt a shiver of apprehension down her spine.

"War?" the goddess continued. "War is needless. It is wasteful. My warriors do not train for *war*." Despite the strength in her words, Danray's voice remained calm. "Why fight, mija? Why risk your life, your body, your soul? What is the aim?" she pressed.

"For peace," Nova answered quietly. Understanding warmed her chest like a shot of tequila, fast and honest. "For peace," she repeated, more confidently this time.

Danray smiled down at her and the vision was so lovely Nova had to look away, blinking away tears.

"For peace," Danray confirmed. "Every one of those moments of compassion, of friendship, of mercy, brings us closer to peace. It is the ultimate aim of all Danrayen Warriors. The ultimate aim for all who fight in my name."

Danray looked around the room thoughtfully. "You are correct that the Trials that happen here often require fighting. And I do require most of my daughters to prove themselves to me in this room before I accept them as my warriors. But a battle is not always fought externally. They sometimes happen within. My warriors will come across immeasurable difficulties, terrible trials, and impossible decisions. And throughout it all, they must not give up. They must not falter. A warrior is not judged by the sharpness of her blade, but by the courage in her heart. That courage looks different for every one of the women who steps inside my temple. You proved yours to me long ago, since that first moment in the forest. It matters not that it didn't happen within these walls. You are a Danrayen Warrior, and I am proud to call you my daughter."

The tears Nova had blinked away returned in full force, forming two small rivers on her cheeks.

"And now," Danray said, becoming very serious. "I need you more than ever." Nova knelt, purpose radiating through her entire being.

"What would you have me do, Mother? I am yours to command," she promised.

Chapter 3

Damika

Damika paced in front of the sanctum, periodically glancing at its closed doors. She'd long since trampled the grass beneath her feet, but she was too nervous to feel sorry for it. Her gaze shifted up to the enormous golden statue of Danray, guarding the room in which her friend now ran her Trial.

Danray, she pleaded for what felt like the hundredth time in the past hour. *Protect her.*

It wasn't that she didn't believe in Nessa's ability. She always knew that she would make a fearsome warrior. She always assumed that her childhood friend would someday realize it for herself as well. But she hadn't expected that Nessa would leave the temple before the Trial, or that she would earn her confidence, not as a Daughter of Danray, but out roaming Tierramadri as a symbolic leader of rebellion.

Damika once imagined Nessa performing great acts and heroic feats. However, she'd assumed that they would be doing them together. Side by side.

Damika also worried, only slightly, that Nessa's time away from the temple might have left her vulnerable to the Trial. She had proven, time and time again on the road, that she had grown into a formidable warrior. Gone was the quiet, meek girl who was once so quick to defer to others. Disappeared was the young woman who tripped over her own feet and dropped her weapons at the slightest scare. She was bold, and self-assured, and so confident in her path.

Damika once felt the same. Now she envied Nessa's conviction.

Despite all of her friend's accomplishments, however, Damika worried that her time outside of the temple had also served to distance Nessa from Danray. She didn't want the goddess to test her anymore severely then she did her other initiates, just because she had left before earning the title of Danrayen Warrior.

"Does it always take this long?" Damika heard a young voice ask behind her, and her shoulders stiffened.

"I don't know," Axchel's deeper voice answered the boy—Churan.

Resentment churned in Damika's belly. *They shouldn't even be here,* she thought bitterly. The Temple of Danray only allowed men to enter by invitation, and she didn't know of a single instance where they were permitted to bear witness to a Trial.

Is that the reason you resent their presence? A voice in her head asked her. *Because they are male? Or because the large soldier kissed Nessa before she walked into the sanctum?*

Damika brusquely brushed the thought aside, turning on her heel to continue pacing. It was an absurd thought in any case, she knew that she had no claim to Nessa.

And yet, she could not deny that the knowledge did not lessen the certainty that she felt in her heart. A certainty which screamed to her that, no matter how much time passed, no matter the arguments or disagreements of the past, and no matter the uncertainty of the future, she and Nessa remained connected. That they belonged in one another's lives, in some capacity or other.

Damika just didn't see where there was room for the Cassalain in that scenario.

Again, she looked towards the sanctum doors, which remained stubbornly closed.

The Trial does often take a long time, she answered the boy's question in her head, mostly to reassure herself. *Mine was several hours long, though it felt like only moments.*

When Damika had taken her Trial, the gardens had been full of initiates, young girls of the temple, priestesses, and full Danrayen Warriors alike. Damika was the youngest initiate to ever take the Trial, so it drew in quite the crowd. Some had even traveled great distances to be present, should she succeed. But when she exited the sanctum, Damika had barely noticed them at all. All she saw were her friends, their faces full of quickly dissipating worry and fierce pride. It was their opinions she had cared about, not the cheering crowd.

Damika didn't get to see any of her friends' Trials, as she left the temple the day after her ceremony to begin her first mission.

To hunt down the traitor to the crown, and therefore her sworn enemy, the missing Name-Bearer.

And now here she was, praying that her "enemy" exited the sanctum safely.

She heard the grinding of stone before she saw the doors move, and she was up the sanctum steps before Nessa even had a chance to slip out. She felt others following her, but she ignored their presence, gripping Nessa right above her elbows and scanning her body for injuries.

"Are you all right? Are you hurt?" she asked her. She couldn't see any blood, but sometimes the injuries were internal. Sometimes, girls took hours or even days to be able to speak, struck by the shock of the Trials.

"Nessa," she started, when the Cassalain soldier appeared by her side.

"Meft royan," he said softly, and something pinched Damika hard in the chest as Nessa's eyes met his.

"I am well," she answered him, placing a hand on his arm. Damika dropped her hands to avoid accidentally touching the man. She made herself swallow her resentment as Nessa focused back on her a moment later.

"I am fine," she insisted. She didn't look fine, she looked dazed.

"Are you sure?" Damika asked her quietly, stepping forward to try to block out the soldier. To his credit, he moved out of hearing range. "I know the Trial can be a lot. It's all right if you need a moment."

"I passed," Nessa said softly. A small smile stretched her lips. "I passed."

A fierce pride pulsed through Damika's veins. She felt she breathed it in, her chest felt so swollen with it.

"You are a Danrayen Warrior?" she asked her, a grin splitting her face.

Nessa nodded. Just as Damika was about to throw her arms around her, to lift her off the ground and spin her with glee—dioses be damned about what the others thought of it—Mamá appeared by their sides. Her face was drawn and weary. For a moment, a pang of guilt knocked Damika straight in the chest. She had been so concerned for Nessa that she had momentarily forgotten that Adira had passed on.

But she wasn't prepared to think about Adira, or who she was to her. It was too much.

Mamá stepped forward to hug Nessa, who buried her face in Mamá's shoulder.

"Come," Mamá told her, wrapping an arm around her waist. "It has been a long day. Let us get you settled in your room."

They walked away from Damika, and Nessa didn't even look back.

A few hours later, with a full belly, freshly bathed and changed, Damika tucked into her bed. But no matter how clean and comfortable she felt, sleep eluded her. She tossed and turned, kicking off her covers, only to grab them back up again. She twisted from her back to her side, then flipped her head to lie where her feet had been, resting her legs on the wall behind her headboard.

Nothing worked.

Finally, she sat up, placing her feet on the floor and her elbows on her knees.

High Priestess Adira had been her mother.

And now she was dead.

Damika had always loved the High Priestess. Loved and respected her in the way that a student loved a teacher, and a soldier could love their general; if they were a good one. While Damika was raised with a healthy respect for the Andalan monarchy, if she was being honest with herself, her true allegiance had always been to the Danrayen Order. And Adira was the head of that order for as long as Damika had been their member. She was everything that Damika strived to be.

But she had lied to her. Damika clenched her fists and pressed them against her eyes. She had *abandoned* her. She had borne her but not raised her, had not wanted her. The High Priestess gave her up, so that Adira could pursue the path that now Damika was meant to follow. Mamá, who had been the closest thing to a mother that Damika had ever known, had also kept secrets from her. And not only had they not told her the secret of her birth, but they had kept Nessa's true identity hidden from her as well. They all had.

Damika stood and stalked from one end of the room to the other, unable to stand still.

What did it mean that three of the women she loved more than anyone else had not thought her trustworthy enough to confide in?

And now they expected her to simply slip into the role of the High Priestess, all because a woman who did not care enough for her to keep her decided it was the best choice for her precious order. Even in death, she prioritized her position over her daughter.

It wasn't as if she had never thought about becoming High Priestess. Of course she had. Out of all the young Danrayen initiates, she had always shown the most promise out of anyone in her age group. It wasn't bragging to claim to be the best at something, if it was fact. She was one of the best fighters in the order. Individually, there were others with more skill than her. Taruka was far more practiced with a bow, and Nessa was always better at hunting. Other girls had a mind for strategy, or apt for riding. But collectively, Damika was good at all of them. As a whole, she had always been much better than the others. She'd known that. And so had the priestesses.

Her instructors wanted her to become a Danrayen Rider immediately after her Trial. It was an immense honor. Not only would she be the youngest initiate to take and pass the Trial of Danray, but she would have been the youngest member of the Danrayen elite forces. If the Danrayen Warriors were respected, the Danrayen Riders were revered. But she wanted to carve out her path first, to have a chance to help the people of Tierramadri on her own terms, before conforming to the life of a soldier.

She thought there would be time. That she would return to the temple, already a hero, with many successes under her name. Then she could join the Riders, rising in ranks amongst them. Only after, when her body began slowing, would she move back into the temple to become a priestess, training the next generation of initiates in the path of Danray. And yes, if she was honest, that is when she imagined that she would ascend as High Priestess.

Not now. Not so young! Who was she to be responsible, not only for herself or a small contingent of warriors, but for an entire order? How was she going to keep from disappointing them all? How was she expected to lead the priestesses, which held more age and wisdom than herself? Or command the generals with more battle experience? How would she mentor the young girls who would look to her for guidance? What if she failed them all?

What if she failed her goddess?

Damika threw on her training clothes and grabbed her Danrayen blade, slipping out into the darkness.

There would be no sleep for her that night.

Chapter 4

Rawl

A thin trickle of sweat carved a path from Rawl's temple to his chin as he approached the marching Andalan army. He couldn't see any soldiers yet, but based on the size of the dust cloud they were kicking up, it was clear there was at least a cavalry unit. After a few moments, the first few soldiers came into his line of sight, followed by troops of Andalan soldiers on horseback, confirming his theory. Rawl veered the carriage as far off the main road as he felt comfortable with, out of the way of the approaching army without appearing like he was attempting to hide from them. Viejo, at least, was happy for the break and immediately began nibbling on a patch of high-stalked grass.

As the soldiers drew closer, Rawl resisted the urge to glance back at Alric, hidden underneath the pile of furs. As surreptitiously as he could, he wiped away the sweat on his face and brow with a handkerchief, then adopted a neutral gaze, praying to whatever dioses would listen that the army would ignore him and continue their march north.

It seemed that neither luck nor the dioses were on his side, as a small group of officers stopped suddenly, forming a clustered group to stare pointedly at him. At the same time, he heard a low groan from the back of the cart, and Rawl's blood ran cold. The sedatives he'd dosed Alric with during their journey had begun losing their potency almost immediately. It seemed that, as the Mage Madness grew in strength, it burned off the effects of the medication faster. Still, he hadn't expected Alric to come out of his stupor this quickly.

Rawl ignored the instinct to bolt, deliberately loosening his grip on the reins, his fingers releasing stiffly from the tension. Then, before he could so much as flex his fingers, he watched in horror as one of the officers nodded to the other two, turning his horse to make his way towards the cart.

"Buenos dias!" the soldier called out in greeting when he reached Rawl. The archer didn't fail to notice that the soldier's hand rested on the hilt of his sword, despite his jovial greeting. Rawl bared his teeth in what he hoped would pass for a smile.

"Greetings to you," he replied respectfully. "Heading to the Borders?"

"That is none of your concern, civilian," the officer replied, and Rawl inwardly groaned. He was one of *those* soldiers.

"Of course," Rawl replied, as easily as he could.

"And what is your business on the Andalan Road?" the soldier asked.

Rawl startled a bit when another low moan sounded from beneath the furs.

Please don't let Alric be heard, he prayed.

"Traveling to visit my sister at the Mage University," Rawl answered. The archer had learned from an early age that, when lying, it was best to stick as close to the truth as possible. Another sound drifted from the back of the cart. "I haven't seen her in quite a few years," Rawl continued, louder than necessary, attempting to muffle Alric. "So, I'm quite anxious to be on my way."

The soldier frowned and glanced back at the pile of furs which hid the mage from sight. "That is a lot of goods for someone simply visiting their sister," he remarked. "Are you certain you are not selling your wares? Because it is the law that you need royal permission to sell on the Great Andalan Road," he added pompously.

Rawl clenched his fists around the reins again but kept his smile easy and loose on his face. "I am not selling anything, I assure you," he said in his most trustworthy voice. "Those are just gifts for my sister and her friends."

The soldier narrowed his eyes. "Where are you from? You don't look Andalan."

Rawl gritted his teeth, then counted to three before answering. "I am not from the Andalan capital, if that is what you were referring to. We have been traveling from Tureene."

"*We?*" the soldier immediately barked, gripping his sword and glancing around as if an assailant was about to jump out of the bushes. "What do you mean 'we?' Are you not traveling alone?"

Stupido, Rawl thought to himself. It was a stupid, careless mistake. A slip of the tongue. If the journey had not been so exhausting, he would never have made such a foolish blunder. Then, to make matters infinitely worse, a whimper sounded from the back of the carriage. This time, the soldier couldn't help but hear.

"Show yourself!" he shouted, pointing his sword at the pile of furs. Rawl's heart jumped and lodged itself in his throat.

"Señor," he tried, but the soldier swung his sword around, inches from Rawl's throat. He instinctively threw up his hands, dropping the reins. Viejo didn't even notice, but simply continued to munch on the springy grass.

"There is no one else," Rawl lied as calmly as he could, though his heart beat against the hollow of his throat. "I meant we, as in my horse and myself." Alric moaned again, and the soldier swung back around to the furs.

Dioses, Rawl prayed. *Padir, Danray, Mamajove, Mamamedia, Mamavieja, Trucar*, he begged, naming off as many gods as he could remember. *If I have ever been in your favor, please help me now.*

The soldier began to dismount his horse, violence in his eyes as a noise more like a yowl than a moan arose from underneath the pile of cloth. When the man's feet hit the ground, a skinny gray cat slinked from underneath a ratty cloak, bending into a long, claw-baring stretch.

The soldier stopped, clearly stunned.

"Oh, and my cat, of course," Rawl quickly lied, sending a quick thank you to the gods for hearing his prayer.

The soldier hesitated, looking confused. "Lift up the furs," he demanded finally, motioning to the pile with his sword. Any relief Rawl had felt at the cat's distraction instantly evaporated.

"Señor, I promise you; it is just myself and the animals, there is nothing more—"

"Lift them!" the soldier barked again, getting closer.

Rawl turned and swung his legs over the bench as slowly as he could, doing his best to make it look like he wasn't stalling at all. His bow lay hidden on the opposite end of Alric and the clothing, but even if he could reach it in time, the cavalry still marched strong behind them. He was outnumbered, and there was no way that Viejo could outrun them all. But once the soldier realized that he was hiding a mage, and not only a mage, but a mage with Mage Madness, they would arrest him and kill Alric.

No, Rawl decided. *If we are to die, we die together.*

He reached his arm towards his bow when a voice called out from the road, "Vamos Ramon, we need to keep moving!"

The soldier near Rawl hesitated, glancing again towards the pile of cloth.

"Ahora, Ramon!" the officer called out again.

The soldier glared at Rawl, but quickly remounted his horse. Without another word, he turned and galloped back towards the cavalry, whose numbers were disappearing towards the north. Rawl stared until the last of the soldiers were out of sight, then collapsed on the carriage floor, overwhelmed with relief.

Just in time for Alric to kick him in the jaw.

CHAPTER 5
NOVA

The morning after her Trial, Nova found Axchel and Churan in the meal hall. She rushed them through their tortillas and queso fresco so she could speak to them in private.

"I have much to tell you," Nova told them once she was sure that they were alone.

"Is it about the Trial?" Churan asked, his words fast and clipped as they always were when the boy was excited. "One of the Danrayen initiates told me that you are not supposed to talk about what happens in the Trial. I mean, not *you* specifically, but anyone who takes the Trial. 'It is between them and our goddess,' she said. But you would know that, of course, because you grew up here! I can't imagine you as a little girl," his head swiveled around, taking in the temple grounds and the statue of Danray. "But it seems like a wonderful place to live! I watched some of the girls training yesterday, when you were with the High Priestess. I heard that she died, I am so sorry for that. Were you close to her?"

Before Nova had a moment to respond to his question, he carried on. "But as I said, I watched some of them training and they are wonderful! So very skilled, and many of the girls look younger and smaller than me! But no doubt that they could best me in fighting, no doubt at all. Would you teach me how to fight?" he asked Nova, then looked at Axchel. "You, too! You could teach me Danrayen fighting and soldier fighting! It seems to me that having two forms of fighting would be better than one, wouldn't it?"

Axchel calmly placed a large hand over the boy's shoulder, and Churan subdued. He grinned ruefully at the two of them, but stopped talking.

"We were both worried about you," Axchel admitted sheepishly. "After your Trial, you were led away so quickly, we weren't sure if you were well. But we did not want to interfere with your customs. Even so, we worried, and as you can see, that has created a bit of nervous energy."

"It was quite the day," Nova conceded. "Are you two all right? You were on your own for longer than I intended, and I am sorry for that."

Axchel nodded. "We have been very well," he assured her. Despite his words, Nova thought that she could see some tightness around his eyes and mouth. In her periphery, she could make out clusters of Danrayen initiates, staring and whispering. Men were not often allowed behind the temple walls, and it seemed that, unlike the refugees, Axchel and Churan somehow gained full access to the grounds. Nova knew that would make them curiosities at best for some of her sisters. She hoped that they would treat her friends with courtesy and respect.

Nova didn't realize that she was frowning at a group of young, whispering girls until Axchel's fingers turned her chin to look at him. She jerked her head away, embarrassed to be touched in such a way by a man, especially in front of other Danrayens.

She felt a pang of guilt at Axchel's expression, but couldn't fully regret the action. She had just proven her merit by passing the Danrayen Trial. She did not want her accomplishments overshadowed by idle gossip.

She also, however, did not want any of her sisters to make Axchel and Churan's stay in the temple uncomfortable.

"The Danrayens are not used to men inside the temple," she tried to explain. "You are welcome, but ..." her voice trailed off as her gaze drifted to the whispering girls once more.

"Your people have been very kind," Axchel assured her. "We have had food and water, and a young initiate explained the attack to the nearby village."

"Pelgar," Churan added helpfully.

Axchel nodded. "There are many who escaped the attack, but even more who did not. I tried to help care for the wounded, but I was not permitted."

Nova's stomach twisted with embarrassment. "The Danrayens are a particular sect. We are a tight-knit group, and protective of our own. I am sure it was not meant as an insult, only—"

"I did not take offense to it," Axchel interrupted to assure her. "They do not yet know me. I am aware that trust is often hard won, especially by those who are most worthy of it. Instead, as the boy said, we watched some training for a while." The soldier's lips twitched up in a small smile. "He's not wrong. The children here are very talented."

It was strange to hear the Danrayen initiates referred to as children. He was right, of course, they were, but she had never quite felt like a child here. Nor had she seen her friends as children, either. They were always young Danrayens, and she was content to pretend to be just like them. At the time, they had seen themselves as very wise and serious, but children they had been, despite their irregular upbringing.

"They also assigned us a room, over there," Churan added, pointing towards a wing of the temple buildings where Nova knew the guest rooms were located. "I thought that we would have to sleep with the displaced people, but Sofia said Axchel would find it easier to keep me safe over there."

"She was right," Nova answered, making a mental note to thank Mamá later. It seemed Churan, at least, was not feeling any discomfort from the whispers and stares. She hoped that, after a few days, the women would grow used to her companions.

"How are you?" Axchel asked her. "Your time has been more eventful than ours." He made it seem like a joke, but Nova could hear the concern behind his words.

"My High Priestess died," she said, devoid of emotion. She had thought the knowledge of it, and the goddess's words, would have kept her up the night prior. Instead, she had slept like the dead, waking groggy and disoriented but refreshed. The grief for Adira had yet to find her.

Perhaps I am in shock, she mused. The priestesses taught them the effects of traumatic events during her time at the temple, as Danrayen Warriors were likely to experience many of them. She knew the grief was there, churning dangerously underneath the surface. It would hit her eventually, but her body did not seem to have space for it at present.

"Adira," she continued. "She knew who I was and offered me refuge in her temple and among her initiates, anyway."

"I'm sorry," Axchel said simply, and it was just enough.

"I passed my Trial," she said, knowing that it was an abrupt change in topic, but found she did not care. Axchel's expression softened.

"Of course," he responded.

It was not "Of course, I was there when you exited the sanctum," Nova realized. It was "Of course you did. There was never any doubt." The back of her eyes prickled sharply, and she suddenly felt ashamed that the death of Adira had yet to cause her tears, but Axchel's words had.

"You said you had something to tell us?" Axchel reminded her gently, and Nova worked to bring her emotions under control.

She bit her lip, then took a deep breath. Before she had fallen into her deep, dreamless sleep, Nova had made the decision that she would not hide anything from her people. She had also realized that she viewed both Churan and Axchel as "her people." But although she believed in her decision, a lifetime of training made her hesitate to tell them what it was she needed to share.

"You are correct that Danrayens are not permitted to speak of their Trials to anyone else," she told Churan. "No Danrayen would consider talking about their Trial, nor would she be comfortable hearing about anyone else's. But there are things that you need to know ..." she smiled conspiratorially as a thought hit her. "And you two are not Danrayen."

Churan practically vibrated with excitement. "I love secrets!" he whispered loudly.

Nova and Axchel exchanged an amused look over the boy's head.

"We would be honored to hear about your Trial," Axchel said, and Nova quickly sobered.

"I saw the goddess," she said. "Danray." Nova barely gave them a moment to look shocked before pressing on. "And she spoke to me."

"What would you have me do, Mother? I am yours to command," *Nova asked her, both knees pressed against the cold floor. From the corner of her eye, she saw the goddess wave a hand, and liquid gold pulled from the ground beneath her, forming a bench. Danray sat, and then motioned for Nova to do the same.*

Nova picked herself off the floor and perched on the edge of the bench tentatively. When they were both standing, the goddess practically towered over her. It felt sacrilegious, somehow, to be seated at equal level with her.

"You have been given a difficult task, mija. Made even more difficult by the forces that now work against you," the goddess said.

Nova's braid had swung over her shoulder, and she played with the ends of her hair nervously. "Do you mean Lord Guerro?"

"And more," the goddess replied. "You have always been one of my order, one of my daughters. But in this, I cannot help you. The creatures that now roam freely among our land should never have been born. I do not say this lightly, child. But they are an abomination. They are an enemy far greater than any you have faced before, and their numbers are far greater than you believe. Even with the full force of my daughters against them, they will not be defeated."

Nova's mouth hung open in shock. Danrayen Warriors were the fiercest soldiers in all of Andala. Possibly all of Tierramadri. None were their equal. A handful of them could turn the tides of battle. All of them together were nearly unstoppable. To think that there was a force greater than the entire contingent of warrior women was unimaginable to her.

"What can we do?" Nova asked her.

"A bundle of flowers must be picked, draw their forces close.

Beware the thorns that prick your fingers, for enemy will turn friend, and friend will turn foe.

A watery grave bears a weapon that delivers light, but its wielder will fall into darkness.

The wilted crown will bloom anew when the jacaranda learns to trust the rose."

Nova looked at her goddess, aghast.

"I don't know what that means," she said, her voice a desperate plea.

"You will, mija," Danray told her, gifting her with another dazzling smile. "You will."

And then she was gone, leaving Nova sitting alone on the cool metal. She would have sat there longer, bewildered by the entire encounter, but the bench had slowly begun melting back into the floor, forcing her to stand. Once she had, Nova realized that the only thing left to do was leave the inner sanctum.

As a true Danrayen Warrior.

Nova let her voice trail off at the end of her story. Axchel wore the same stoic expression that he usually held, but Churan's eyes were narrow, two dark slashes across his boyish face.

"Another prophecy," he grumbled. Nova understood his reticence. She herself had had quite enough of prophecy.

"But what does it mean?" he continued.

"I'm not sure," Nova admitted. "Some of it seems straightforward, but the rest is murky."

"'Enemy will turn friend and friend will turn foe,'" Axchel mused. "Is she warning you of a betrayal? But by whom? Your Danrayen sisters may not be quite aligned with our mission, but they seem dependable. Though I will admit, I do not have the same confidence in them as I do in Rawl and Alric."

Nova was grateful that Axchel had added Alric to the number of those he trusted, despite them not knowing whether the mage was all right. Nova quickly shoved that thought away, as she had every time her traitorous mind tried to get her to think of her friend. She refused to believe that he was anything other than alive and well. The less that she thought of him, the easier that was to do.

"The bundle of flowers—could the goddess have meant our allies?" she ventured. "Those who believe in the Flower's prophecy? Perhaps it means that we need to call whatever allies Churan may have together?"

"Maybe it means that we are better together than apart," Churan agreed. "A bunch is a group, after all."

"A warning to stick together?" Axchel added.

"What could the weapon that she referred to be?" Churan wondered out loud.

Nova felt a rush of irritation. "Why couldn't she just have spoken plainly?" she griped, referring, of course, to the goddess.

Axchel's lips twitched in that small smile of his. "I cannot claim ever having spoken to one of the dioses in person before," he admitted. "But I do not think they are well known for their candor."

Nova sighed. He was right, of course. There were countless stories of the dioses meddling in the lives of mortals, and they were always tricky and secretive. Nova assumed it was just a trait of divinity.

Churan was muttering under his breath, repeating the prophecy over and over to himself. It made Nova smile, lifting some of the heaviness that had settled in her heart. She didn't have to do this alone.

"Come," she told them both. "We have a council meeting to attend." She had found the missive under her door when she had finally woken that morning. She knew the invitation was for her alone, but at that moment, she found she had made another decision.

"We?" Axchel asked, as Churan bounced on his heels at the prospect.

"Yes," Nova confirmed confidently. "It is not common, but the Danrayens have allowed men into their council before. We have had to, in order to consult with other captains and generals about the war, or various threats to Andala. We journeyed here together, and whatever is discussed within those walls involves us all."

Axchel looked at her with an expression that sent a strange thrill up Nova's spine. To her surprise, Churan took her hand in his.

"Let's go then," he beamed, and it was enough for Nova to know she had made the right decision.

Chapter 6

Nova

Nova had never been in the council room before, but she knew where it was. All initiates did, because it was strictly off limits to anyone not invited within its walls. Churan dropped her hand after only a few steps to run and explore around corners and doors, unsatisfied with her slower pace.

Axchel kept stride beside her, not speaking, but offering her quiet company and support. He amazed Nova. A man that had once made her feel wary and afraid now provided her with both comfort and strength.

When they reached the council room, Mamá and Damika waited for them outside, beside the large doors. Damika's eyes flicked over the Cassalain and the boy.

"Do you need someone to show you back to the guest quarters?" she asked. Nova was sure that Dami thought her voice was polite, but she heard the irritation behind her tone.

"They will join me," Nova answered her firmly, and watched as Damika's lips pressed into a straight line.

"Men are not often permitted in the council room," Mamá hesitated.

"Not often, but nor are they prohibited," Nova answered.

"Even if men have been allowed, *he* is just a boy!" Damika exclaimed, motioning to Churan. "A child has no place in a council room!"

"He is a child," Nova conceded. "Which is exactly why he *will* be in that room. Not I, nor anyone else, will make decisions on this child's behalf." She met Damika's eye over Churan's head. "Enough decisions have been made on behalf of the children of prophecies without their say."

Then she looked back down, stooping to place a hand on Churan's shoulder. Addressing him directly, Nova ignored all others around her. "You are a child of prophecy, but you are not bound by it. So long as I live, you will be free to make your own choices."

Churan's eyes were very wide in his head, the fuzzy bit of brown growth over his upper lip vibrating with tension.

Axchel stepped to Churan's other side and placed his own hand on the boy's opposite shoulder, closing the boy between himself and Nova.

"And so long as I live, I will make sure your choices are respected," he vowed.

The bump in Churan's throat jumped erratically as his eyes became glassy, not with tears, but with emotion. He simply nodded solemnly at the two of them, then turned to face Damika.

Damika's eyes flicked over Nova, then Axchel, and finally down to Churan before rising her icy stare back up again. Nova wondered what they looked like to her at that moment. Was she seeing a friend and fellow Danrayen? Or were they a separate unit, allies now, but still outside of those Damika trusted implicitly?

Finally, Damika shrugged, turning to Mamá. "Can you have someone bring Taruka here as soon as she returns? We will need her council as well."

"Taruka and Petra traveled back with you?" Mamá asked hopefully.

With a pang, Nova realized that with all the commotion, they had not had the chance to let her know that Taruka had headed to Pelgar, or that Petra had remained in Tureene.

Or that the reason Petra had stayed with her family was in order to bury Raidea.

She and Damika exchanged a pained expression.

"Why don't you three go in and get settled," Damika said, motioning to the council room doors. "Mamá and I will join you shortly."

Nova watched as Damika led Mamá away, but when she saw Mamá stop, throwing a hand over her mouth and beginning to cry, she quickly crossed into the open room. She didn't have the heart to witness more grief, not while she still held her own at bay.

"She is already more of a leader than she believes," Axchel mentioned, jerking his head back towards Damika. He then took a quiet moment to absorb the grandness of the room, finally sitting down on one of the oversized chairs within it. There were thirteen of them in total, all circling a large and sturdy oval-shaped table.

Nova crossed to sit in the chair next to him, then paused. The chair at the top of the table, placed at the far-side of the room, was no more large or ornate than the others. There was nothing that would distinguish it from the rest of the chairs, and yet its placement, just behind the large windows and framed by Tz'ola's light, made it clear that it was where the High Priestess should sit.

Nova crossed the room and deliberately sat on the chair to its left. She would not pretend to be Damika's right-hand warrior, but she needed to show that she had as much of a say in what happened in that room as anyone else.

"Damika has always been a leader," she answered, finally answering Axchel's earlier comment. "She just never wanted to be tied to this place any more than she already was. At least, not so young. She wanted many years of adventures before returning."

"Do you think she will agree to be High Priestess?" he asked her.

"Yes," Nova answered without hesitation. Damika didn't know how to do anything other than excel. She would accept her role sooner or later. Her people needed her, and Damika never turned away from someone in need. Nova knew that better than anyone.

Churan was pacing the room, browsing through the large wooden bookcases stuffed with books and scrolls and tomes. He picked up a leather-bound novel from a pile, sneezing several times in succession as the action dispelled a poof of dust. He made his way to the windows, his gaze turning sour as he looked down at the scene below. Nova twisted her neck to follow his sight, only to grimace herself.

It wasn't that she had forgotten the temple was serving as a refugee camp for the people of Pelgar. It was simply that she was not accustomed to seeing the fields as anything but training grounds. She had half-expected to see a throng of young women with swords, axes, and bows, battling against practice dummies, shooting arrows into moving targets, or sparring with one another. Instead, there were neat rows of russet tents, overflowing with injured men and women. From her vantage point, Nova could see the red of blood seeping from bandaged wounds, people with missing limbs sprawled on makeshift cots, and children streaked with dirt and tears.

There were so many people, too many people, and yet not nearly enough. Nova knew that for every person who had made it to the temple in time, there were several that had not been able to make the journey. It was not flesh peddlers or bandits which raided Pelgar. The villagers did not have to battle against men, but monstros. It was a miracle there were as many of them alive as there were. Nova knew that they had the Danrayens to thank for that. But what of all the other towns and villages who did not have the luxury of living a stone's throw away from trained and seasoned warriors? What of them?

"We will find a way to end this," she told Churan. Her voice was soft in volume, but hard in resolve. He dragged his eyes away and met hers, nodding. Then he crossed behind her chair, resuming his perusal of the room. He stopped at the enormous map of Tierramadri, covering the majority of the room's left wall. The map stretched up high towards the ceiling, beautifully illustrated and marked with important places like the Andalan Palace, the Mage University, the Danrayen Temple, and the Borders. Further up was a surprisingly detailed depiction of Cassalan, information likely gathered over many years and pieced together little by little. Above that were the Northern Tribes. The paper of the map thinned where someone had drawn their borders, removed them, then redrawn again. Churan lifted on his toes, attempting to touch a tribal name, but he was not yet tall enough to reach it. He dropped back down with an audible exhale.

There was noise in the corridor before several people entered the room at once. Damika, with a red-eyed Mamá. General Vashti, Head Priestess of Battle and leader of the Danrayen Riders, strode in wearing her full battle armor. Although she'd not been the head priestess's best pupil, Nova found that she was delighted to see the woman once again. After her came Priestess Ovidia, the priestess in charge of all wildlife in the temple. All animals within the temple walls were under her charge, including the horses meant for battle. The beasts trained almost as rigorously as the young Danrayen girls. She was so skilled with their schooling that even some generals of the Andalan army came to have their mounts trained by her.

Priestess Ianuaria followed shortly, and Nova resisted the urge to leap from her chair to give the healer a hug. Ianuaria was never the warmest of women, but Nova had a lot of affection for her. Her slow progression at fighting meant that she had spent a lot of time in the temple infirmary as a child, nursing a multitude of injuries. And after Raidea's difficult Trial, Ianuaria allowed Nova to spend all of her free time in her sickroom as she recovered. There had even been an extra cot placed next to her friend's bed, and Nova had always suspected that the action was Ianuaria's doing. The Temple Mage, Nuna, soon entered with the Priestess of Temple Strategy, Sinchi. They looked at Nova and the men curiously, but quietly took their seats.

Relief crashed through Nova as Taruka was led inside by a young Danrayen initiate with frizzy brown hair. She was the last to enter, and the girl closed the doors behind her, leaving the rest of them within the privacy of the room.

It was obvious that Taruka had come straight there from her visit to Pelgar. She was still in her same travel clothes, but now there was more dirt and grime than before. A splattering of blood ran across the sleeves of her tunic, though not over her arms, so Nova guessed someone had at least allowed her to wash her hands before joining them. And if she smelled? Well, they were all warriors, and no one would bat an eye at such a trivial thing.

That made eleven of them. Two seats remained open, and Nova had no doubt that Petra would occupy one on her return.

That left the thirteenth empty.

Nova refused to think of the people who could have sat in that position. Adira, of course. Alric. Rawl. Raidea.

Nova pressed her lips into a thin line and turned her gaze away from the empty seat.

Mamá led Damika around the long table, motioning her to the head chair that Nova had noticed earlier. Damika visibly balked at the position, and the implication, but sat. Mamá sat on her right, and Nova wondered if that was her place when Adira had been High

Priestess as well. She and Damika had just learned that their warm and loving mother-figure was a lot more than she seemed. In fact, she was a master spy for the Danrayens, weaving an intricate web of networks all across Tierramadri. Nova still found it difficult to think of the small, round woman—who had never even taken her Trial—as one of the most formidable and well-connected people in the realm. But she also imagined that most of the women in the room would find it hard to believe that she was the missing Name-Bearer.

It seemed that they all had secrets.

Finally, the entire room sat, Damika at the head with Nova and Mamá at her sides. On Nova's side, Churan and Axchel sat. On Mamás 'right sat General Vashti, then Priestesses Ianuaria, Ovidia, Sinchi and Mage Nuna. Taruka took her place next to Axchel, which secretly pleased Nova. If there were to be two empty seats that day, she wouldn't have liked the implication if the one next to her Cassalain ally was one of them.

Damika looked around the room at the familiar faces, then opened her mouth. After a second, she closed it again and swallowed hard. She turned to Mamá, her eyes pleading.

Mamá stood, placing a hand on Damika's forearm as she did so.

"Adira is dead," she said without preamble.

Only Taruka reacted audibly, a small gasp escaping from behind her raised fist. The rest of the room looked somber but resolved. It was clear that the other priestesses knew that her death had been inevitable. Axchel and Churan had not known her well enough to understand the full depth of the loss felt by the room, not just to the women, but also to the Temple and Order of Danray.

"How?" Taruka croaked out, face dry of tears, but with a tempest of grief raging behind her eyes.

"The Night Wood attack," Mamá responded. "We lost twenty-three Danrayens, including Adira."

A fist of anger and sickness punched Nova in the stomach. *Twenty-three.* How many of them had been full Danrayens, and how many had still been girls?

"Those deaths were nothing compared to the losses of the people in Pelgar. We anticipate that at least two-thirds of the villagers were killed. That is, unless there are survivors that managed to hide, in their homes or in the woods. We can discuss sending a rescue mission," Mamá continued.

Taruka shook her head, looking even more stricken than before, which Nova would not have believed possible.

"I was just there," she said, her voice hoarse with repressed emotion. "I couldn't even reach the village itself. I only got as close as the river. It is completely overrun with monstros. More than I ever thought possible. The village is burning, and there is no way in or out. I tried. I thought I saw someone fighting, but with the amount of monstros …" She shook her head again. "There … there would be no survivors."

Mamá nodded, looking grim, but not surprised.

General Vashti was looking between Nova and Damika, eyes narrowed and assessing.

"I have questions," she said in her usual commanding tone. Then she focused her gaze on Axchel and Churan. "*Many* questions."

"There is much you all need to know," Mamá said, sitting back down.

Then she began to speak. She told the tale of her childhood friendship with Adira. Of the prophecy that promised any child that came from Adira's womb would have a great Affinity. She told them of Adira's pregnancy, and what the goddess Danray had foretold. She spoke of Lord Guerro, and how his men had hunted them. Of the child that was born, and later brought to the temple to train. Of Adira's deathbed revelation that Damika was that child.

Ianuaria expelled a long breath, and general Vashti opened her mouth as if to speak, but Mamá lifted her hand to cut her off.

"There is more."

She then shifted to Nova's story, of her time as the Name-Bearer, and the prophecy that had forever altered her life. She explained that Adira had known, had made the choice to believe the Flowers and protect Nova.

When she could tell no more, Nova jumped in, explaining her quest with Alric to find the Unnamed Prince. When all eyes turned to Churan, he was already sitting straight and somber, effortlessly slipping out of his true, childlike personality into the mysterious and stoic persona that he had cultivated in his time with the Northern Tribes.

Axchel's expression was less schooled, a small crease appearing between his brows at the open scrutiny of the boy.

"We need to get him to the Flowers," Nova finally finished, her body feeling like she had run miles. Telling her story, so soon after the shock of her Trial, had thoroughly exhausted her. All she wanted was a long bath and an even longer nap, but there was much still to be done.

The room was quiet for a long moment, the air charged with the weight of the decisions yet to come.

"This is a lot to take in," Priestess Ovidia said simply, Ianuaria nodding beside her.

"You mentioned that Lord Guerro had been hunting Adira because of the prophecy," General Vashti said, glancing at Damika. "The prophecy about her child. Is this the same Lord Guerro who whispers in Queen Issalia's ear now? The one rumored to be Princess Zerlina's father?"

Mamá nodded. "The very same. It seems he has never ceased his quest to sire a powerful child. And we know he succeeded at least once—with Kichka."

Nova winced. Kichka had been her childhood tormentor, a beautiful and powerful Danrayen initiate blessed with magia.

"It seems that the dioses have been weaving this tapestry since before many of us were born," Ianuaria mused. "It will take some time to step back far enough to make sense of it," she added.

Nova bristled at her words. "We don't have time to step back! Night Wood creatures are invading our lands. They are killing our people. Lord Guerro has somehow found a way to sit, if not *on* the throne, then right next to it, and who knows what further havoc he will wreak? We need to bring Churan to the Flowers. Peace is promised with his Naming. If I can get there to perform the Naming Rite, then we have a chance at stopping all of this. It may be our *only* chance at stopping it."

General Vashti was shaking her head before Nova even finished speaking. "We have problems of our own to contend with here. Do you not see what is happening inside of our very walls? The people of Pelgar are depending on us to protect them. We cannot spare the warriors needed to escort a Cassalain, a child, and a traitor to the crown to the capital so that they can break into the Andalan Palace."

A rush of heat flashed through Nova's body, but before she could answer, Damika was on her feet.

"She is *not* a traitor to the crown. The *crown* is the traitor, disregarding the voice of the Flowers, who are the messengers of the dioses. They ally with untrustworthy men, like Lord Guerro. Men who surround themselves with dark brujas. Men who seem to be responsible for the Night Wood attacks."

Damika's hard eyes scanned the room. "Nessa has been fighting this war before most of us even knew there was a battle that needed to be fought. She has been willing to shape her entire life around this mission, and we owe it to her to help."

"We need to focus on our problems at home before we can commit to helping any other cause!" General Vashti argued.

"Then I formally petition the council for Danrayen aid. I call a Summoning," Nova replied.

Vashti shot her a look filled with contempt. "You must be a Danrayen Warrior in order to call a Summoning. And you must formally request it of the Danrayen High Priestess. You are not a Danrayen, nor do we have a High Priestess."

"Nessa completed her Trial this morning," Mamá said, causing Vashti's eyebrows to shoot up. "Adira sanctioned it right before she passed. Phanessa is officially one of us."

"We still don't have a High Priestess," Vashti shot back quickly.

With a deep sigh, Damika stood.

"Actually ..."

Chapter 7

Rawl

By the time the Mage University finally, *blessedly* rolled into sight, the tincture had completely worn off of Alric and he was straining and struggling against his binds once more. Crackling red sparks of energy burst from him like a spitting bonfire, and Rawl prayed to Padir that the carriage would not catch fire. Viejo grew more and more agitated, and it was taking all of Rawl's strength to keep his course steady. They were almost at the university gates when Rawl finally pulled them to the side of the road.

There were only two of the sedatives left, and he was not going to take any chances. Rawl had to use both if he wanted to smuggle Alric into the university under everyone's noses and find his sister before the other mages discovered him. Further, he needed to find her before the other mages had a chance to realize that he was smuggling in a mage afflicted with the madness. He knew that they would not hesitate to kill Alric if they figured out the truth.

Rawl was not going to let that happen.

Wiping away the sweat on his brow with his forearm—and doing his best to ignore the trickle that was making its way from the nape of his neck to his back—he jumped into the bed of the cart, warily regarding his ailing friend.

Alric's hair was beginning to stand on end from the staticky magia emanating from his body. Throughout their journey, the whites of his eyes had become more and more saturated with red veins, and now the entire space seemed completely red around the mage's dark pupils. The wine-stained veins had started stretching from his eyes to the tops of his cheekbones as well, painting his skin like a gruesome alternative to freckles.

When Alric noticed he had Rawl's attention, his assault intensified, the red sparks and crackling energy directed straight towards the archer. Rawl yowled and leaped back as they began stinging his exposed flesh. Alric growled behind his gag, spit dripping from the sides of the cloth where his lips pulled tight against his teeth. His entire body vibrated with the force of wanting to free himself. A spark of crimson magia caught on Rawl's robe, igniting a smokey patch of fire.

"Coño," Rawl muttered, patting the patch furiously to put it out. It left a hard, crusty singe, making the fabric crack off right into his palm as he examined it.

I liked that tunic, he thought bitterly.

Rawl scowled at the man, desperately trying to find any semblance of his true self underneath the burning rage of his madness. He found none, but he would be damned before he lost all hope. Regretfully, Rawl picked up his bow. Alric trailed the movement with his ruby eyes, flicking his gaze to Rawl's own. His lids narrowed, sneering behind the gag, as if daring Rawl to go through with it.

Go on, then, the look said. *You don't have it in you to kill me.*

Without allowing himself a second of hesitation, Rawl swung his bow around in a sideways arc, slamming the wooden end hard against Alric's temple. The mage's eyes rolled back in his head, and he slumped heavily against the furs. The crackling of his magia stopped.

Rawl jumped forward, pressing his trembling fingers against Alric's neck. The pounding of his own heart made it difficult for him to feel Alric's pulse, but after a few deep breaths—*there. There it was.* Fluttering and erratic, but still beating. Rawl let out a small whimper of relief.

Alive, he thought. *Still alive.*

Rawl gingerly pushed the hair from Alric's face, wincing at the chichón already forming on his brow. He hated having to strike him in that way, but Rawl knew he wouldn't have been able to administer the elixir again, not without a struggle. Alric's madness was getting too strong, and they couldn't afford to lose a single drop. They needed help, *now*.

Rawl eased the gag from Alric, wincing as the mage's cracked lips began bleeding with the motion. He wanted to rub them with salve, to take a washcloth and clean the mage's cuts, rub ointment on the angry red welts his bindings had left on his wrists and ankles. He wanted to wash Alric's dirty, matted hair, then carefully brush out the tangles. He wanted this nightmare to end.

Pulling the stoppers out of both bottles, Rawl poured one, then the other, into Alric's mouth, making sure the mage swallowed them down without choking. Then, his heart full of regret, he eased the gag back into place, and hid Alric under the cloth once more. The gray cat, who had been watching the entire interaction from a safe distance, jumped back into the cart bed and began nestling under the furs with Alric.

"You look out for him, eh, amigito?" he murmured affectionately at him. He wouldn't dare give the cat a name. He knew he was just as likely to disappear forever than stay with them, such was the way of felines. But he felt a rush of affection for the creature all the same, for saving them from the soldiers, but also for managing to stay close to Alric when he could not.

Once he successfully hid Alric, Rawl led Viejo back onto the road and towards the towering gates of the university. The horse was much calmer once Alric's power wasn't sizzling in the air, and he trotted happily towards the grounds.

Rawl knew, from oral accounts and Mila's occasional letters, that the Mage University was an impressive sight, but nothing could have prepared him for the towering structure looming on the horizon. It looked immense from afar, and only grew bigger the closer that Rawl got. He felt like an ant next to a tree.

The tower appeared carved from glistening black marble, jutting out proudly from the ground. No. Not just the ground, Rawl noticed. The structure stood between the rocky cliffs bordering the roaring ocean and the very sea itself. The building seemed carved right out of the rock face, appearing ancient, bold, and powerful. In fact, if someone told Rawl that the tower existed first, and that the cliffs and ocean had grown around it, Rawl would have been hard-pressed not to believe them.

Eyes wide and lips parted in awe, the archer watched the rolling sea pummel the sides of the tower again and again. Mighty waves crashed against the cool polished stone, cresting over in wild torrents of saltwater and foam. Some of the waves splashed as high as halfway up the structure, and Rawl found it a miracle that it did not sway with every strike. Rawl also couldn't help but wonder just how far down into the water the tower went, and how anyone could live and work in the lower levels without fear of being swept out to sea and drowning.

But that is mages for you, he thought, shaking off his stupor. *There is madness in mages, after all.* He winced at the last thought, proof of the adage passed out cold in the back of his cart.

"Alto!" a voice called out as he reached the enormous gates of the university, open and inviting despite the warning in the authoritative voice that called for him to stop. On either side of the steel gates were long imposing walls, making the area appear more like the entrance to a fortress rather than a place of learning.

"Alto, I say!" the voice called out again.

Rawl stifled an urge to roll his eyes. *Pompous mages.*

"Hola, amigo!" he answered back, scanning the land to see where the disembodied voice had come from. "I mean no harm and come in the peace of Padir."

Padir, his patron god, was often mischievous and tricky, so his "peace" wasn't as benevolent as other gods, but they had a strict code of non-violence unless attacked first, or if found in imminent danger. Rawl hoped that the voice wasn't *too* familiar with the Padir ways and would accept the sentiment, nonetheless.

"Padir?" he heard, and saw movement above his line of sight, high towards the top of the gates. Rawl shielded his eyes from the light to look up, managing to catch a flash of light hair before a head ducked down the other side of the wall. "Stay right there!" it called out.

It took a few moments for the person to make their way down the long expanse of the wall. While he waited, Rawl's eyes scanned the length of it, noticing that it curved in a half-moon formation all the way around the tower, reaching the cliff face and tumultuous ocean.

When the person was finally visible, Rawl's eyebrows shot up to hide behind the mass of curly hair that flopped over his forehead.

It was a man, and he was *enormous.*

He was taller than Alric and wider than Axchel, which was saying something on both counts. Everything about him seemed big. He had large, wide eyes which were a light brown color resting under wide eyebrows. The same light brown dusted the hair on the top of his head, though his roots were darker, giving Rawl the impression of butter spread over toast. The man's nose was large and broad but fit his face well. His lips were full and surprisingly turned up into a shy smile.

The shyness of it took Rawl aback. He had expected the man to come down in anger, or at least suspicion. Guards always seemed eager to flaunt their power and position, and he had been ready to disarm the brute with easy smiles, a cheerful demeanor, and, if necessary, an attitude that suggested he may be simple. But instead, the man's open nature disarmed him.

"Hello friend," the man said, lifting a large, meaty palm in salutation. "Did you say you come in the peace of Padir?"

Was that delight in his voice? Rawl thought.

"I did ..." he said cautiously, still eyeing the man's tremendous hands. They really were just gigantic, like two oversized hams on the ends of thick tree branches. He imagined being struck by one of them and felt his breakfast turn over dangerously in his stomach. If he could not convince the large stranger to lead him discreetly to his sister, both he and Alric were in grave danger.

"Are you a Padir?" the man asked, his tone hopeful. Then he flushed. "I mean, a member of the Padir tribe?"

Rawl hesitated. Growing up as a nomadic ruffian, he had very quickly developed the skill of reading people and their intentions. As a boy, he knew what men were dangerous to children like him, and who could be trusted. He learned what store owners were most likely to set aside their day's leftovers to distribute to street children. He could tell an easy mark for pickpocketing, and what tender-hearted ladies he could spin a tale of woe for.

My instincts, he thought, *have been finely honed.*

And yet, he could not get a grasp on the man before him. Everything about his physical presence screamed danger. This was the type of man that you crossed the street to avoid, the kind you gave a wide berth to in the alehouse. You never made bets, accepted loans, or asked favors of a man like this. And you most definitely did not want to get on his bad side.

And yet, nothing in Rawl's gut was warning him away. Other than the visceral reaction of standing in front of what may as well have been a giant to him, nothing about his demeanor encouraged Rawl to be on guard.

Well, you're still alive after all this time for something, Rawl thought. *Your instincts haven't steered you wrong yet, so you may as well trust yourself.*

If his gut reactions were going to fail him, this would be a spectacularly bad time.

"I am a follower of Padir," Rawl affirmed. "My name is Rawl, and I come here on urgent business."

The giant's face erupted into the warmest, sweetest smile Rawl had ever encountered in his life, and he almost took a step back at the unexpected warmth that it generated.

"Rawl! You're Rawl!" he said, and before Rawl had even a second to react, the man lunged forward and hauled him up in his two meaty arms.

"Unnngh!" Rawl had time to cry out, just before the behemoth hauled him against the hard pillar of stone that was his body.

No one that big should be able to move that fast, Rawl thought, dazed. *If he had wanted to kill me, I would already be dead.* He expelled a confused grunt from his lungs, but not from the strength of the man's grip. If anything, he held Rawl as gently as if cradling a babe.

The man squeezed Rawl just a tiny bit more firmly—in what the archer was just realizing was the giant's version of a hug—before letting him go. It wasn't until his feet hit the ground that Rawl realized that the man had bodily lifted him into the air. He sucked in a deep, rattling breath, mostly in surprise that he had gotten through it uninjured. Clearly, the man knew his own strength, but was careful to not abuse it.

"Oh, she will be so pleased. So pleased!" the man said, positively beaming at the thoroughly ruffled Rawl.

"She?" Rawl puffed out.

Suddenly, all the color drained from the man's face.

"Oh no, I didn't even think! I suppose you are not the only Rawl to be a member of the Padir tribe. Maybe it's a special name, a symbolic name to the Padir! There may be so many Rawl's of the Padir, and I am just being ignorant. Just because you are here at the university doesn't mean that you are her brother!"

"Her brother?" Rawl gasped as soon as he could get a word in. "Are you talking about Filomila?"

The expression on the man's face changed so abruptly that Rawl had the fleeting sensation that he had been standing in the shade and was now directly underneath Tz'ola's rays.

"You *are* him! You're Filomila's brother, aren't you?" he cried.

Thank you, Padir, Rawl silently prayed.

"I am," he confirmed. "And I need to see her, but I need to see her privately. I would rather that the instructors not know that I am here yet."

Or ever, he thought.

"Of course! Of course!" the big man said, his grin never wavering. "Anything for Mila's brother. My name is Andu, by the way."

The man held out his colossal hand, and Rawl suppressed a wince as he reached out to grasp it. Thankfully, the shake was firm but painless, and over quickly.

"We do have a small problem, though," Andu said, and Rawl's heart sank.

Looking out towards the ocean, Andu's smile finally fell.

"Mila, well ... she's Drowning."

CHAPTER 8
NOVA

A fter Damika's admission that she was considering the position of High Priestess, the council had erupted into chaos. Most of the priestesses argued that Damika was far too young and inexperienced to take up such a mantle. Mamá had reminded them all that it was Adira's dying wish, and choosing her successor was her right. The others argued that there had always been a vote, which Mamá considered symbolic.

Damika had remained silent through it all.

After many mind-numbing hours, the council meeting adjourned. It was clear that they would not find common ground that day. It was frustrating. The faster that they could agree, the faster that Nova could bring Churan to the Flowers and fulfill the prophecy. She was not filled with an abundance of patience now that she was so close to her goal. However, the goddess had advised her to make and keep her allies; if she was interpreting the prophecy correctly. That meant that they needed to remain at the temple for at least a while longer while the priestesses resolved the issue of succession.

Axchel took Churan on a walk around the grounds to burn off the boy's pent-up energy. The boy's behavior while in the council room impressed Nova. He remained the same composed, even-tempered leader he had shown himself to be during his time with the Northern Tribes.

Before they left, Mage Nuna promised to resume the magia training that Alric had started, which would keep the boy occupied in the days to come. She reminded them all that sorcery was different from the magia in which mages trained, but that she would do her best by him. Nova knew that Axchel would not leave Churan's side during his lessons, and she was relieved that she would not have to think of ways to keep them busy as she navigated her new role as a Danrayen Warrior.

Lost in her own thoughts, Nova drifted back to her new room in the priestess wing of the temple.

It felt strange to occupy a place she'd grown up revering as a child. When she was young, she never would have imagined sleeping amongst the priestesses. Now, she couldn't imagine sleeping in the dormitories, between all the hopeful young initiates.

Her room was bigger than the room she'd occupied in the palace; the only room to have been hers alone. Adorned much more warmly, this room contained a bed that could comfortably fit two people, with a blanket of pale terracotta and burnt sienna. There was a square woven rug of a golden brown over the clean wooden floors, and a large carved dresser made of blonde wood. Rather than having to travel down to the communal baths, there was a curved tub waiting for her, already filled with water. The steam rose in delicate ringlets just above its surface.

Nova was sure that she would fall into a deep sleep after her bath. The day had been long and emotional, and she felt rung out; like a well-worn tunic, fraying at the seams. And yet, when she lay down on the comfortable bed in fresh nightclothes, sleep eluded her. Her mind kept replaying the events of the last few weeks, ever since Damika and the others had found them. She mourned for Raidea, her sweet friend that she had only just had the opportunity to see again. They hadn't even had a chance to learn about the new shape of each other's lives before Raidea had lost hers.

She thought about Adira, one of the few people in Tierramadri who had known her secret. She may not have been an everyday presence in Nova's life, but she was a powerful one. A respected one. She had kept Nova safe, allowing her to build the skills that she needed to see her quest through. Nova owed her so much and would never have the opportunity to repay her.

Once it began, her mind wouldn't stop, and it propelled her to another memory that she was not yet ready to face.

Flashes of Alric, unconscious and ill, in the grips of Mage Madness. An ailment that Nova knew had no known cure.

She threw back her covers, and with them, her thoughts of Alric and Rawl. Slipping on her shoes, she rushed out the door. She needed air. She needed space. The walls were crowding in on her and she needed to *breathe,* dioses-damn it. Before she realized what she was doing, her body brought her back to the same garden where she and Damika were earlier. The one where the two of them had sat in their youth before Damika left the temple.

Before Damika had left her.

"You couldn't sleep either?"

Nova didn't have to turn to know who the voice belonged to. It didn't even surprise her that she was in the garden. Her heart rate and breathing finally slowed back down to normal as Nova turned to look at Damika.

She was not in her bedclothes, but fully dressed in her leathers and armor. Nova could see several weapons on her person, including the sword of Danray on her back.

"Si," Nova said, crossing towards her. "Me too ... but why do you look like you are preparing for battle?"

Damika looked startled, then glanced down at her blades and clothing. "I was going to go train," she finally answered. "Since I couldn't sleep."

Nova frowned. She didn't see why Damika would be so armed just for training, but assumed the warrior had her reasons. She sat on one of the garden benches, and after a moment, Damika joined her.

In the softness of the evening, they could hear the murmurs of people from afar. The temple had never been so full, and the garden was not the quiet sanctuary that it once was. Luckily, they were well enough removed from the center fields that the noise was a pleasant murmur rather than a disruption.

They sat like that for a while, the slight night breeze rustling the leaves and plants around them, kicking up the faint smells of the blooming buds. It didn't disturb Nova as it once might have, but she knew that she would never love the scent of flowers.

"That council meeting ..." Nova trailed, finally breaking the silence.

Damika barked out a rueful laugh, rubbing the back of her neck. "It didn't exactly go as planned, did it?"

"Oh, there was a plan?" Nova quipped, and Damika grinned at her. The first real smile she had given her since they had reunited.

"No, I don't suppose that we had enough time for a plan, did we?" she responded.

"A lot was thrown on us rather suddenly," Nova admitted. She bit her lip. "On you, more than on me. Do you want—"

Damika shook her head. "I'm not ready to talk about it."

Nova understood. There were things that she wasn't ready to talk about, either. Things that made the bottom of her heart feel weighed down with lead.

"Everyone will be more open-minded tomorrow, after a night to process everything. It was all too much, too quickly. We haven't even had a chance to mourn." Damika's eyes squinted shut, carving tiny creases at their corners. Nova knew that she was thinking of both Raidea and Adira, as well as all the other Danrayens who had lost their lives in the raid.

Nova knew that she should probably add Alric to the list of those for her to mourn, but that was one of those things she wasn't ready to face. Like before, she shoved the thought of him away.

"Will you really accept the position?" Nova asked. It seemed inevitable to her that Damika would end up as High Priestess, but she knew that her childhood friend had strong reservations and conflicting feelings.

Damika raised an eyebrow at her. Nova hated how, even after all the years apart, she understood the action just as clearly as if Damika had spoken.

I thought we agreed not to talk about it now.

Nova rolled her eyes. "What should we talk about, then? Since it seems neither of us will be getting any sleep anytime soon."

A look Nova *couldn't* decipher flickered across Damika's face.

"We could talk about that kiss," she finally answered.

Nova flushed. In a moment of anger and resentment, she had kissed Damika. They had been performing the Dance of Danray, as they had so many times before, and in the heat of the moment, both her anger and her nostalgia had mingled and gone to her head. She had been so desperate to breach the rift between them, to prove to her that, no matter what Damika might have thought about her disappearance and her deception, a part of them still held the same two girls who had loved each other in their youth. It was a moment of pure impulse, and Nova wasn't certain it was the wisest one.

"It was a mistake," Nova admitted softly. Damika whirled to look at her, but Nova kept her gaze on her hands, cracking her knuckles. "I got caught up in the moment. It had been so long since I had seen you, and I had been thinking about you for years. And then suddenly, you're there! You are right in front of me, but you held a sword at my neck, and you looked at me with nothing but anger and hatred. I was so angry and disappointed, and all of those feelings got confused. And with the adrenaline of the dance, I acted without thinking, and it was wrong."

She made herself meet Damika's gaze. "Lo siento."

"No, I'm sorry," Damika said quickly. "I was so confused. I'm still so confused." Nova looked down again, but Damika grabbed her hand. "Not about *you*. I understand now what you did. Why you hid. There has just been so much change. I feel like the ground is spinning underneath me and I have no idea where I'll land once it stops."

"We're not the same people that we were when we were last here," Nova said, motioning to the bench. "And I understand why you doubted me. I understand that so much of your life was spent in preparation for a worthy act on behalf of the crown. Then, your entire upbringing led you to believe that I truly was the traitor they branded me to be. And I *did* lie to you all. So, I can understand why you would doubt." Her lips pressed into a thin line. "But I'm still so angry about it," she admitted.

Damika looked neither sorry nor defensive. She simply nodded. "I'm still angry too," she said, to Nova's surprise. "I believe you. I believe you now, but I'm still upset that, in all those years, you never felt like you could trust me."

"I did trust you!" Nova argued. "I trusted you with my life!"

"Just not with the truth," Damika answered softly.

Nova didn't say anything. There was nothing that she *could* say.

"So, whether or not I have a right to be, I'm angry too," Damika continued.

Nova sighed, and nodded, releasing Damika's hand. "I know," she said.

After an awkward pause, Damika cleared her throat. "So, where does that leave us?"

Nova stopped fidgeting and straightened. "We can be angry," she said seriously. "But now is the time to trust one another. Both of us. There are things that we cannot face alone."

"I can trust you again, if you promise not to keep secrets again." Damika said.

"You know all my secrets now," Nova agreed. To her surprise, Damika laughed.

"Somehow, I don't believe that's true. But the secrets that won't affect our mission are yours to keep." She looked at Nova with a serious expression. "What must I do in order to make you trust in me again?"

Nova shrugged helplessly. "I believe that you believe me now. As long as you keep your promise to help Churan, then you have my trust."

There was a long, loaded pause.

"I would also have your friendship," Damika whispered softly.

Nova couldn't help the ghost of a smile that flickered on her lips.

"I would like that too," she answered.

Nova brought her own legs up on the bench, crossing them to mirror Damika's pose. She leaned back on her arms and tilted her face up to the moonlight. Despite all the uncertainty and sorrow, in that moment, she felt lighter than she had in a long time.

"That wasn't the kiss I was talking about."

Nova turned her head to look at Damika, puzzled.

It was hard to see in the dark, and against the dark bronze of Damika's skin, but she looked like she was blushing.

"When you kissed me, in Tureene, that wasn't the kiss I meant. I meant the kiss that the Cassalain soldier gave you before your Trial."

"Axchel," Nova automatically corrected, and felt disappointed to see Damika grimace. She hid the expression quickly and shrugged, all practiced nonchalance.

"It looked like more than a 'good luck' kiss," she mused, and then it was Nova's turn to blush.

"Well?" Damika pressed. "Aren't you going to tell me?"

"I am glad that we are friends again, Dami," Nova answered, feeling a small thrill to call her by her nickname once more. "But I don't think we are the type of friends that talk about such things."

Damika bit her lips. "No, I suppose we aren't."

Then, at the same time, they burst into grins.

"Raidea would get it out of you," Damika smirked.

"She wouldn't leave me be until I had told her everything, and then made up at least three additional stories when mine didn't suit her imagination well enough," Nova giggled.

"So, there is more to tell, then?" Damika prodded, but Nova simply shoved at her shoulder. Then Nova's breath hitched, and she began to cry.

"I can't believe she's gone," she choked out between soft sobs.

Damika didn't try to comfort her, which she appreciated. She simply sat there, her own eyes glassy and pained. They sat together, side by side, long into the night, long after Nova's tears ran dry. They sat until the first rays of Tz'ola's crown peeked over the horizon, finding a small measure of solace in one another's company.

CHAPTER 9
RAWL

Once inside the university gates, Andu found another student and waved him to them. The boy nearly stumbled on his over-sized mage-in-training robes to make his way over to the big man as quickly as he could.

Andu, for his part, was not wearing robes, but a gray sleeveless shirt that brought even more attention to his massive arms, and dark-colored trousers that hit just below his knee. It was a warm day, but even so, the breeze that came from the ocean created a chill in the air, but the goliath showed no discomfort.

Rawl vaguely recalled a letter his sister had written a few years after joining the university, delighted that she "no longer needed to wear the dusty mage robes." He hadn't thought much of it at the time, but now assumed that only the younger years needed to don the uniform.

"Take this horse and cart to the stables, make sure the old boy is fed, watered, and brushed down," he instructed the boy when he reached them. His voice was kind, but he spoke in a tone that bore no argument.

"Eh, about the cart ..." Rawl hedged.

"You need the cart?" Andu asked, unhitching Viejo and handing him to the eager student. "Just take the horse then." And the boy was gone, Viejo happily in tow.

Rawl supposed he shouldn't have been shocked when Andu lifted the wooden beams of the cart himself and began rolling it down the paved path, but he felt his mouth drop open. As for Andu, he seemed completely oblivious to the incredible feat of strength he was demonstrating. Rawl scrambled to keep up with him as they made their way to the east side of the university tower.

"Mila should finish Drowning within the hour," Andu said, glancing up at the position of the sun above them and then scanning the angle of the tower shadow for confirmation.

When Andu had told Rawl that Mila was *Drowning*, he thought that he would keel over right then and there from the panic. The fact that the man had delivered the news so casually had simply reaffirmed that Rawl had been an idiot for trusting him, and that the brute was every last bit as dangerous as he seemed. But when Andu had noticed Rawl's stricken expression, and how he gripped the side of the horse cart to keep from tumbling over, he had instantly understood his error.

"No, no!" Andu had cried out, grabbing Rawl by the shoulders before he could pass out. "*Drowning* is what we call utilizing the water magia that controls the waves and tides! She is not in danger, I swear it!"

Slowly, Rawl's breath had evened, and his heart rate slowed back to a normal pace.

"We say it so often here, I didn't consider how it would sound to you. I apologize," the big man had said, sounding horribly remorseful.

It took a while longer before Rawl had felt settled enough to cross into the Mage University property, but Andu had been patient and gentle. Rawl couldn't help wondering who the man was to his baby sister.

When the two of them reached the building, Andu led Rawl to a rusty iron door, half hidden by curling tendrils of emerald vines.

"There is a workspace underneath the tower that Mila and I discovered by accident last year. We can work on our magia there for days, undisturbed, if we need to!" he told him.

Rawl felt his brows pinch in the middle at the image of his sister alone with *any* man for days at a time, but quickly schooled the thought away. Mila may still have been a young woman when she left for the university, but by now she was a full-grown adult. Her life and her decisions were her own.

Andu opened the door, and despite it looking as if it hadn't been used in years, it swung open without a single creak. His surprise must have shown on his face, because Andu grinned at him.

"Magia," he whispered dramatically by way of explanation, and Rawl couldn't help but grin back.

That smile quickly fell, however, as the big man waved him forward. Rawl glanced back at the cart. Andu seemed to be a friend to Mila, but just how far did that friendship extend?

"You see, the thing is ..." Rawl struggled to find the words. "I came here for help. That is, I am hoping that Mila can help."

The futility of his mission, his trip, and his hopes came crashing down on him all at once. Rawl felt his shoulders slump, and his heart seemed to sink in his chest like a stone. Prickles of heat assaulted the flesh behind his eyes, but he could not even form tears. What if he had come all this way for nothing?

A warm hand clasped his shoulder, the large fingers spanning from collarbone to the top of his biceps. Dejected, Rawl lifted his eyes to meet Andu's.

"You are the thing that Mila loves more than anything in this world," Andu told him solemnly. "If she can help, she will. And if I can help her to help you, I will too. You have my word."

Rawl felt pressure against his shins and noticed that the cat, forgotten until then, had left the warm comfort of the furs to twine around his ankles. He could feel the soft rumbling vibrations of his purr resonate through his bones. A tiny seedling of hope blossomed in Rawl's chest.

"He's in the cart," he blurted out. "He—Alric. Alric is in the cart. Sedated. He was a mage here. He studied here once. He's in the cart, and he needs our help."

To his credit, Andu didn't even blink. He simply moved to the pile of furs, lifting them off in bundles until he revealed Alric's unconscious form. A soft gasp escaped his lips when he saw the ghoulish bruising and lighting-style veins that marred the mage's skin, and he took an almost imperceptible step back. He glanced at Rawl, but whatever he saw in the archer's face must have steeled his resolve, because he clenched his jaw and gave him a short nod. Andu reached in and picked the unconscious mage up as easily as if he were a babe and motioned for Rawl to cross through the hidden door.

Together they entered and made their way down a long staircase to the underground caverns of the Mage University.

CHAPTER 10

RAWL

Andu found a long length of what he called "binding rope" and used it to secure Alric to a chair once Rawl expressed that it would be better if they confined Alric before he woke up. Again, the large man did not question him, but worked to be as helpful as possible. The magia in the rope, he promised, would be more than strong enough to keep his friend from hurting himself or others. Then Andu left to leave word with Mila, telling her to meet him in "their spot" when she was done with the Drowning.

When he returned, he had three large plates of food balanced precariously between his hands and forearms. Rawl, who had been gazing dejectedly at Alric, watching the slow rise and fall of the mage's chest with an obsessive fervor, sprung up to help him.

"Gracias," Andu said, relinquishing two of his plates to Rawl and dragging over a low wooden table for them to sit at. Watching the giant fold himself down to the floor was an interesting experience. His massive limbs and bulging muscles made the seemingly simple act far less graceful than it would have been for some. When he finally managed, with a small *hhmph*, it surprised Rawl that the ground itself did not shake with the force of his bulk hitting the floor.

"One is for your friend there," Andu said, motioning first to a still unconscious Alric, and then to the food. Shoving a platanito frito in his mouth, he chewed vigorously before adding, "When he wakes up," through a mouthful of food.

Rawl pushed his white rice, beans, chicken and platanos around on his plate with his fork. "He hasn't been eating much," he confessed, his appetite withering. "I don't—" he paused to swallow past the lump in his throat. "I don't know how much longer he can last like this."

Andu set his plate down. "Even I can tell that whatever ails your companion is magical in nature. That means that you have brought him to the very best place that he can be right now. You have delivered him, safe and whole, to his best chance. And as I promised before, I will do everything in my power to help in any way that I can."

Rawl blinked at the man, the stranger that was so quickly becoming a friend. If this was Mila's suitor, he would be glad to welcome him to their family.

"Gracias," he muttered, the emotion embarrassing him. He picked up his fork again and forced a small bite of arroz and frijol into his mouth. It was good, and he kept it down, so he did it again. Before he knew it, his plate was empty and Rawl was feeling more fortified than he had been in weeks.

Rawl glanced again at Alric, who was still not stirring. He felt his brow pull down into a frown. He had hoped the double dose of tincture would work to keep him immobile until they reached the Mage University, but at the rate that Alric had been burning it off, it surprised him that he wasn't yet awake.

Before he could decide to check on the mage—and possibly try to attempt to rouse him—a resounding crash reverberated across the stone walls of the university's underground. Rawl whirled to look at Andu, who was feeding the cat bits of shredded chicken from their meal. Surprisingly, the man met Rawl's gaze with an excited grin.

"That'll be her, then," he said.

"Her?" Rawl started, before a blur of copper skin and hair collided into his chest.

"Rawlly! Rawlly, Rawlly Rawlly!" Mila cried out, her voice muffled against his sternum, before she pulled back to pepper his face with kisses; just as she had when they were little. It had always made him laugh, this little thing, like a baby bird pecking at his cheeks and brow, lips pursed into a solemn little beak.

But the woman before him was so little like the child he remembered. Gone were the gangly limbs and awkward poses. Gone were the baby fat cheeks and sticky, pudgy hands. Instead, she had grown into a beautiful young woman, her hair a mirror of his own brown and gold, tumbling in waves that stopped right at her chin. The spattering of freckles that they shared seemed more pronounced, likely from her time spent outdoors. Her eyes, however, her eyes were unmistakably Filomila. His baby sister.

Rawl threw his arms around her and lifted her off the ground. His side, where Alric had managed to stab him, screamed in protest, his scab opening and a thin trickle of warm wetness crawling down towards his waistband. He ignored it all, spinning his sister around in a circle before setting her down again. When her feet hit the floor, he still did not let go. She smelled like vanilla and saltwater and so much like home that it overwhelmed him with longing, nostalgia, and love. A great big laugh bubbled up from his stomach and erupted from his lips. He laughed and laughed and laughed until suddenly his laughs turned to crying. His breath caught in his throat, and he sobbed, his face buried in the crook of his sister's neck, his forehead resting heavily on her shoulder. She didn't stop him. She didn't ask what was wrong. She merely held him and rocked him back and forth, smoothing the hair on the back of his head and humming a tune low in her throat.

When his sobs had quieted some, he recognized the tune as the one their mother used to sing to them when they were ill.

Pulling back, Rawl wiped his eyes ruefully and managed to give her a watery smile.

"You grew up," he stated, obviously.

She grinned, showcasing her crooked front teeth, and for some reason the familiar sight soothed him even more than her embrace had.

"That tends to happen to children as they get older," she teased.

"Terrible habit," he tried to joke back.

"Someone ought to do something about it," she quipped.

They smiled at one another, a true smile from Rawl this time.

"Not that I am not delighted to see you, hermano, but what are you doing here? And why all the secrecy?" Mila finally asked him.

Before Rawl could open his mouth to answer, a sinister voice slunk from across the room. The voice was so laced with malice that the words themselves seemed to slither across the floor, over the walls, dangling above their heads. The space around them suddenly felt much, much colder.

"Well, well," the thing that was once Alric said. "Isn't this just touching?"

He hissed each "s" like a snake as he spoke. Alric didn't struggle against his bindings, but he did lean forward, eyes bloodshot red and skin crackling with the power of his unruly magia.

"The sister? Don't tell me you've brought me to the university!" Alric threw back his head and laughed, the sound hoarse and humorless.

"Did you think that the instructors could save you?" he demanded, staring straight at Rawl. He made himself meet the mage's eyes, refusing to cower away.

It's Alric, he told himself. *Somewhere in there, Alric still lives.*

"They won't save you. No one will. I have more power than all the mages here combined! There is no one who can match me! I will escape and I will have my vengeance. You will die more painfully than you could ever imagine." His inky black hair fell in front of his burning eyes and Rawl had the wild impulse to smooth it back from his face, as if his friend were not threatening his life at that very moment.

"I will make you suffer, forest rat. I will make you rue the day you met me. And I will start ..." his gaze finally broke from Rawl's and slinked over to Mila, who was standing mouth agape with shock. "With *her*," he finished.

Rawl leaped forward on instinct, years of defending and protecting his little sister overtaking everything else. Mila caught him by the arm, pulling him back just as a bolt of electric fire burst from Alric and landed in the space Rawl had just been standing in. He watched the flames dance and slowly fade on the cold stone floor.

"Mage Madness," Filomila whispered.

Rawl shut his eyes.

"Rawl, why would you bring someone with Mage Madness here? You know there is no cure!" Mila demanded.

"There must be!" Rawl cried desperately, whirling around to face her. "There must be a way! There must be something we can do!"

His eyes returned to Alric, who was sitting slumped over in the chair. The outburst of his magia warring against the magia in his bonds seemed to have exhausted him.

"There is only one way," Mila answered firmly, looking from Rawl to Alric, and back again. "We have to end this."

Rawl sprang forward and bodily placed himself between his sister and the man he loved.

"No," he said simply, but fiercely.

"Rawl," Mila started.

"No," Rawl repeated, harder this time.

"Rawlly," Mila's face softened with sympathy, but the intent behind her eyes was clear.

She wanted to kill Alric.

"I won't let you," Rawl said. He wasn't sure how he was going to stop her. He wasn't even sure if he *could* stop her. She had always been particularly blessed with magia. But he would try.

Mila sighed heavily. "Rawlly, you have to understand. There is no cure for this. It's not like they haven't tried. This is the Mage University, *of course* they have tried! Do you know how many students are lost to the madness each year? Too many! Do you think the instructors haven't tried everything? Do you think this hasn't been studied?"

Rawl looked away from her, biting the inside of his lip so hard the tangy, metallic taste of blood flooded his mouth. He shook his head.

"It is the kindest thing for him," Mila continued. "He is already so far gone ... he will burn himself from the inside out with the force of the corruption."

Rawl stood there, staring at the scorched ground in front of him as if the ash would somehow give him an answer. Was his sister, right? Was he just prolonging Alric's suffering because he couldn't let him go?

He had known that there was no cure for Mage Madness. He knew long before he saw Alric's stone break. He knew it even as he begged Nova and Damika to let him try to save him. He knew it during the long, impossibly hard trip from Tureene to the Mage University. But he had thought that if he could just get him here, get him to the end of their journey safely, then somehow it would have been enough. Somehow, the answer would appear. Because he had fought for it. Because he had earned it.

But Rawl knew that life didn't work that way, and that ultimately, all he had been was a fool.

"He can't be saved," Mila said softly.

I know, Rawl thought. He opened his mouth to say it, but before he could, Andu spoke.

"We could try."

Rawl jerked his neck to look at the man. He'd waited, respectfully quiet as he and his sister reconnected, and then fought. Now he stepped forward.

Mila frowned at him. "You know it's not possible," she said irritably.

"What I know is that you are the most gifted mage in an age." Then he paused. "That rhymed!" he said with a delighted grin.

"Focus, Andu," Mila said, her tone suggesting that this was not the first time she had uttered those words.

"Right," Andu replied. "You are so much more powerful than any of us are, and much more clever, too. The instructors are skilled and practiced mages, but they are also stuck in the past. You have new ideas and new ways of thinking."

"Ways that are constantly shut down by those same instructors!" Mila argued.

"Exactly! They aren't ready to see your brilliance. They aren't ready to change. But you are. You are already there. Maybe you can think of something that they couldn't."

"I don't know, Andu," Mila sighed, running her hand through her cropped curls. Then she shook her head. "It's too dangerous."

"Mila," Andu pleaded, his eyes so full of longing that Rawl's throat closed to hear it. "He loves him. Can't you see that? Your brother is in love with him."

Mila snapped her gaze to Rawl, who nodded slowly, but unapologetically.

Yes, he was in love with Alric.

They were all quiet for a long while, Alric's ragged breathing in the corner the only sound. Finally, Mila squared her shoulders and took a deep breath.

"We can try."

CHAPTER 11
DAMIKA

Damika made her way to the council room slowly.

Despite the sleepless night, she was feeling as awake and alert as if she'd found a full night's rest. She knew that her reconciliation with Nessa was part of the reason. The other, however, was pure anxiety.

Damika still had no idea what she was going to tell the council. Was she ready to accept the position of High Priestess? And even if she was, would they accept her in it?

By the time she reached the council doors, the rest of the members were already inside. There was a heavy tension filling the air, and a deliberate silence. She could see the Cassalain and the boy sitting to the right of the room, their shoulders leaning in towards one another, as if pulled by an inexplicable force. Damika doubted that they realized that they were doing it, but the message was clear; they were allies. A unit. On the other side of the table, General Vashti pointedly ignored everyone, aggressively polishing a small dagger with a cloth. The other priestesses were waiting patiently, and Nessa was staring out the window with a grim look on her face.

And at the far end of the room, the chair that Damika had sat in the day before—the chair that was so clearly meant for the High Priestess of the Danrayen Temple—sat empty and waiting.

Damika made herself cross to it and sit down without hesitation. It would do no good to allow others to witness the depth of her insecurities. Those were for her alone.

"How are these meetings usually run?" she asked before anyone could say anything.

Mamá's eyes were devoid of tears today, though they were still red, with puffy bags under her lower lids. Damika felt a pang of guilt. She knew that she should have checked on her after the last meeting. She knew that High Priestess Adira had been her best friend, her childhood friend, a sister to her as much as if they had been true kin. If Damika's grief threatened to drown her, she couldn't fathom what it was that Mamá was feeling.

And yet, she had not gone to her. She was afraid that Mamá would want to talk, not about Adira, High Priestess of Danray, but about Jesadirany, the woman who was Damika's mother.

Damika wasn't ready to explore all of that. There was too much to do. And yet, when Mamá cleared her throat, which was clearly hoarse from crying, the guilt only deepened.

"We have them once a week, unless it is a time of great turmoil, such as now," she explained. "We discuss the war, how many Danrayens are at the Borders, and where we believe the rest to be on their assignments. We consider new assignments for Danrayen Warriors and Riders and allocate them and our resources accordingly. And I give updates from my messengers, if any are of note."

She looked over at General Vashti. "We also take formal requests for Summonings."

Vashti snorted. "There have only been *two* official Summonings since I have been on this council, which is longer than you have been on it, Sofia. It is not a practice commonly done."

"But there is precedent," Damika cut in. They had learned about it in their classes. Any full Danrayen Warrior could request the full force of the Danrayen Order to come to their aid, if they felt their cause was true enough.

"Yes, but we also need a High Priestess to make the final ruling!" Vashti argued, and Damika waved her arm.

"We will get to that," she said, knowing full well that she could not delay forever.

Damika turned back to Mamá. "What do we know about the increased Night Wood attacks?"

Mamá nodded, and Damika watched in amazement as the plump and friendly mother-figure of her youth transformed into a hardened warrior right before her very eyes. The changes were slight, a straightness to her posture, a strength in her arms. Her face slipped into the mask of a spy, giving away no emotion. If Damika hadn't known they were there, she wouldn't have even noticed the red eyes or tired gaze.

"We have been receiving various reports since last fall, and they all remain consistent. Night Wood creatures are no longer tied to the boundaries of the Night Wood. Not only can they venture out from the dark forest, but they can survive indefinite periods of time doing so. Since late winter, we have received reports that both, the number of monstros has increased, as has the distance they have traveled. We have even had word of some reaching as far as the coast."

Damika fought the urge to recoil in her chair. Her mission of finding the missing Name-Bearer had taken her and her team far across Tierramadri, so she had not been unaware of the attacks. She found it unimaginable that the monstros had made it as far as the coast. Up until last year, Night Wood creatures remained restricted to the boundaries of the eastern forest's shadows. Too much time out from under its dark protection meant death. It was terrible to consider that the monstros could now venture further, and survive longer, outside their confines.

"There is more," Mamá continued. "As of late, the reports have been changing. There are still the increased attacks, of course, but the monstros seem to all be heading south."

Priestess Sinchi bolted up. "You mean they are not attacking randomly?"

Mamá shook her head. "If they once were, they are not anymore. They are all moving towards a specified point." She crossed to the large map and began replacing the black pins, which were clearly meant to represent the monstro sightings. When she stepped back, the silence in the room was deafening.

"The Andalan capital," Nessa finally whispered, as startling as a shout.

"An organized attack?" General Vashti asked, leaning her thick forearms on the table. "You cannot have us believe that these creatures are capable of organizing themselves for something like that!"

Mamá shook her head. "We don't believe so. Any and all creatures encountered have been as unpredictable and vicious as the worst of rabid animals."

"But they are all moving towards one general area?" Axchel asked, and Damika felt a twinge of annoyance at his deep voice. She was not well accustomed to the company of men, and even less so in a temple that was meant to be free of them.

"Are they being attracted to something there?" he continued.

"We believe that they are being summoned," Mamá answered.

Instead of silence, this time, the room exploded in argument.

"That is not possible,"

"Absurd!"

"Who would be summoning them?"

"Who would have the power to?"

"Kichka." While the rest of the voices layered over one another in a tangled jumble, Nessa's voice was loud and clear. Slowly, everyone settled enough to look at her. Her face was pale, and there was a light sheen of sweat just below her hairline.

Kichka. The magia-user and would-be Danrayen initiate that tormented Nessa during her early years at the temple. Kichka, Damika and Nessa later learned, was the illegitimate daughter of Lord Guerro. Apparently, her dismissal from the Danrayen Temple had not stopped the girl from gaining power elsewhere.

"I know that she was powerful, but surely not powerful enough to control Night Wood creatures," Priestess Ianuaria said, her voice almost pleading.

"And yet it is her magia signature that we have been able to observe on the creatures," Mamá answered, to which Mage Nuna nodded.

"The same signature that I detected on the wounds she had inflicted on Phanessa when they were girls," she added.

Damika was certain that no one else in the room noticed Nessa's almost imperceptible flinch, but she knew her friend well. Then she saw Axchel shoot her a worried glance, and inwardly scowled. So, she hadn't been the only one to notice after all.

"What do your spies in Andala say?" Ianuaria asked Mamá, who was still standing by the map. "Do they have any news of the monstro activity in the capital?"

Mamá frowned. Damika thought it might have been the first time in her life that she had seen the woman do so.

"Reports from the city stopped just as soon as the reports of the monstros moving south began. It cannot be a coincidence," she answered.

"We need to move quickly then," Nessa said. "We need to beat as many of those creatures as possible to the city. We need to get Churan to the Flowers. It is the only way we know to stop this."

"If we are sending Danrayens to the capital, it will be to protect the people of the city," General Vashti argued. "If monstros are making their way there, we need to be ready to defend our realm against them."

"Surely we can do both," Nessa insisted. "If we are going anyway, you can help me get Churan to the palace!"

"My strategies are not dependent on a girl who never finished her training, or a child that I do not know!" the general argued.

"We haven't even decided that we are going at all! It was you, Vashti, who reminded us that there are people here, in the temple, that we need to protect," Priestess Ovidia cut in. "If the creatures are indeed moving south, then more will pass through this area to do so. More people from neighboring towns may come to seek refuge behind our walls as well. We have a duty to them!"

"We have a duty to all the people of the realm!" the general argued.

Ovidia glared accusingly at her. "You yourself were arguing for us to remain here in our last meeting!"

"That was before I learned that dioses-damned monstros of the Night Wood were making their way to our capital!" Vashti harshly retorted.

"I agree with Ovidia." Priestess Ianuaria offered. "There are far too many wounded and ill here already. We need to protect our resources. Rushing off to battle an enemy that we are unsure of will not do us any good."

"But we do know the prophecy! The one that says that if I deliver Churan to the Flowers, it will usher in a reign of peace! How can you just ignore that?" Nessa cried out.

"No one is ignoring that, Nessa," Damika assured her friend softly. "But we need to be smart about this."

Nessa glowered at her, and suddenly Damika worried that all the progress they had made the night before had evaporated in an instant.

"I agree with Phanessa," Mamá said. "We do not know how many creatures are venturing to the capital, or for what purpose. We do not know how Kichka is controlling them, or if it is a ploy by her father, Lord Guerro. We know nothing of what his final aim is. But we do know that the prophecy promises peace."

"She was the only one in the room when the so-called prophecy was uttered," Vashti argued, pointing a gnarled finger at Nessa. "How can we be sure that what she claims is true? Why is everyone so eager to trust her?"

"Because Adira trusted her," Mamá cut in so sharply that Damika could feel the coolness of her words like the edge of a blade.

"Because our Goddess came to her and forewarned her of the day that a child of prophecy would need her aid, and she trusted both in Danray and in Phanessa. Because she passed the Trial of Danray herself just yesterday, proving to us all that she is truly one of us," she continued. "Do you doubt her?"

Even seated, General Vashti was large, imposing, and powerful. Her muscles bunched underneath her tunic, veins protruding where the cloth did not cover her flesh. Her neck was wide and thick, her hands large and heavily calloused. Despite her age and injuries, Damika knew the woman could leap out of her chair and cut an enemy down in the time it took them to blink. It had been years since Damika had been under her tutelage, but even now, her deference to the woman bordered on a healthy fear.

But Mamá stared the larger woman down as if she were an unruly child, throwing a particularly ridiculous tantrum. Even more amazing was the way that Vashti caved under the look. A sheepish expression flickered across her face, and Damika watched, amazed as she lowered her gaze.

"No, of course not," Vashti grumbled.

Mamá turned back to the table. "I know that you are eager to act, mija. But we need more information. We need to know how many monstros are being compelled to travel south, and perhaps glean more about Guerro and his plan. We need to be as certain as possible about what is waiting for us at the capital."

Nessa bit her lip, then exchanged a glance with Axchel over Churan's head. Damika hated how much she resented the quiet conversation.

"I do not want to delay any longer than we already have," Nessa finally answered, standing. The boy and the soldier stood with her. "I never expected the aid of the Danrayens, and though it would be of great service to us and our quest, we are prepared to continue without it if we must."

Churan and Axchel both nodded.

"Well, that's settled then," Vashti said, sounding satisfied.

"It is not settled," Damika growled at her, feeling the tightness of her scowl over her brows. She whirled to pin Nessa with the same look. "Don't be foolish," she told her.

"We have other allies," Nessa argued stubbornly.

"Like who?" Damika challenged, watching as Nessa's face flushed with anger.

"The mages," she replied. "Alric told me that Archwizard Auberon had been rallying them to our cause for years. He said that most of the Mage University are supporters of the Unnamed Prince."

"You really think that they will ally with you? Even as their leader rots in the palace dungeons?" Damika asked.

Nessa's chin jutted out defiantly. "Yes," she asserted. "If Alric said that they are true, then I believe him."

Damika felt the scowl that had crept its way onto her face soften with pity. "And if Alric is dead? If he has succumbed to his madness, what then? Who will the mages follow then?"

For a terrible moment, Nessa looked like she would crumble to the floor. The worst agony Damika had ever witnessed fell over Nessa's face, and she was already lurching forward to catch her should she fall. But as quickly as it appeared, the look was gone, and Nessa straightened, pressing her lips into a thin line.

"They will follow him," she said firmly, placing a hand on Churan's shoulder. The boy was as quiet as ever, but his chest swelled at her words. "So will the Padir. Many of them are followers of the Flowers as well."

"That is how you will fight your way into a city being overrun with monstros?" Damika asked incredulously. "With forest-folk and the handful of mages who might actually honor a promise from years past?"

Nessa didn't answer, but Damika could see the resolve in her eyes.

"Por favor," she begged her friend. "Just wait. Wait until we can get more information. Once we do, you can request a Summoning, and we can make an informed decision. Don't be rash!"

"How? Mamá just said no reports are coming back in. How will we get any new information? We don't have time to wait and hope a missive comes through!" Nessa demanded.

"I will go."

They were the first words Taruka had uttered since the council meeting had started. As everyone around her had fought and argued, she had been wide-eyed and quiet, simply taking it all in.

"You can't," Damika said immediately, shaking her head. Taruka simply smiled softly.

"We are no longer on mission, Dami," she told her friend. "Which means you are no longer my commander. You cannot forbid me."

Damika's heart felt leaden. Taruka was right, she had no right to command her friend. And yet—

"It is too dangerous for you to go alone," she told her pleadingly.

"We cannot afford anyone else," Taruka insisted. "Ianuaria is right. There are too many refugees here to leave defenseless. I am quick, and I am quiet. I am certain that I can get through any large throngs of monstros. I don't even need to get all the way to the city, just close enough to hear the news and gossip."

"It's too dangerous," Damika argued.

Taruka smiled at her slyly. "I know full well that if you did not have to stay to fulfill your role as High Priestess, you would have been the first to volunteer this exact same thing."

Dioses-damn it, Taruka was absolutely right. It already burned her that she couldn't offer herself instead.

"Go to the Mage University," Mamá interjected. All heads turned to look at her. "If Phanessa is right, and there are allies to be found there, we would be remiss not to gather them to our cause. We can at least begin preparations should we need to launch a full-scale attack on the city."

More than one head nodded.

"All right?" Damika asked Nessa. "Will you at least wait for Taruka to return?"

Nessa sucked in a deep breath and looked at Churan and Axchel.

"*A bundle of flowers must be picked, draw their forces close,*" the boy whispered to her cryptically, and Damika frowned at the strange words. Before she could ask about them, Nessa nodded, and let the air expel from her lungs with a whoosh.

"Agreed," she answered Dami, then turned to address Taruka.

"If Alric," Nessa's voice broke, but she swallowed deliberately and tried again. "Alric will know how to rally the mages. And you can ask Rawl where we can find Leader, of the Padir."

"The leader of the Padir?" Taruka asked.

Nova shook her head. "The leader of the Padir is named 'Leader.' But as the Padir are nomadic, I do not know where we could find them at this time of year. But Rawl would know. We can also try to ask them for aid."

"Very well," Taruka said, nodding. Then she looked at Dami. "I can leave tomorrow?"

Despite her earlier claim that Damika was no longer her commander, her statement came out as more of a question.

There were no objections from the room, so Damika nodded. "It is worth a try, but be careful," she stressed.

"Well, we have the beginnings of a plan, at least," Mamá said, her tone positive, if not cheerful. "Now, before we adjourn, we have two more matters to resolve. Important ones."

She looked first at Nessa.

"We need a celebration to officially welcome Phanessa into the Danrayen ranks." Then she turned to look at Dami.

"And we need a High Priestess Ascension Ceremony."

Chapter 12

Rawl

The bottom levels of the Mage University were both ample and sparsely furnished. The day that Rawl had first arrived, he had been so worried about Alric's Mage Madness and reconnecting with his sister again that he had barely noticed his surroundings. But after Mila and Andu's commitment to doing everything that they could to help Alric, Rawl had finally been able to relax enough to notice where, exactly, he was.

The small sanctuary resembled the rest of the tower, in that its construction was of the same stone. The floors, walls, and ceilings were all fashioned of the same rocky material from the outside of the tower. Despite that fact, the rooms were neither cold nor damp, thanks to a type of magia infused into the building itself to always keep its occupants comfortable. In their hidden basement, there were several workshop-type rooms spread evenly apart and accessible through a corridor that was always lit by wall sconces. There was also an indoor washroom, complete with running water; more magia, they informed Rawl.

The first room off the corridor was where they were keeping Alric. The stiff wooden chair that they had tied him to the first day, replaced with a plush and ample couch that Andu had carried in single-handedly. Alric was still bound, of course, but the aim was to make him more comfortable.

Alric neither seemed to notice or care.

They fashioned the second room for Rawl. At first, he had argued, saying that he would not be parted from Alric, and that he would sleep on the floor if needed. His sister, in a ferocious fit of passion, swore she wouldn't help Alric at all if Rawl did not begin taking care of himself as well, which included regular meals, daily walks, allowing her to re-bandage and treat his wound, and a room to himself where he could properly sleep without the worry of being blasted by madness magia.

Rawl had relented.

The third room was where Mila and Andu discussed theories, mixed potions, and conducted experiments on how to vanquish Mage Madness. They were absent much of the day, attending their regular lessons, which Rawl learned included controlling water magia (known as Drowning), wind magia (Flying), earth magia (Growing), and fire magia (Burning). There were other types of classes, of course, spell-work, casting, history of spellcraft, and more, but Mila and Andu had advanced to the more hands-on instruction appropriate for their age and level at the university. Luckily, that also meant that their free time was their own, and they made their way back down to the workrooms as often as possible.

Mila told him that there were official university underground rooms not far from their own, including one deep below the coastline, made up entirely of glass where the students could stare out at the vast expanse of ocean. There were more workshops and even classrooms where quieter, subtler types of magia were practiced. The more volatile magias, Mila informed him, they conducted either out of doors or in the highest points of the tower, where an accident or mistake was less likely to destroy the entire building.

Mila and Andu, however, had stumbled across a separate section of the underground sometime during their second year. They did not discuss the nature of the event which introduced them to the space, or how they had stumbled across the door, but it was clear that the rooms laid abandoned for many years prior to their rediscovery, and if anyone still knew about their existence, they simply did not care.

Whatever the case, it was a blessing from the dioses to Rawl, a secret spot where they could hide both himself and Alric effectively while conducting their trials and experiments unimpeded.

So far, nothing had worked.

They had gathered as many magical stones as possible, placing them all over Alric's body, attempting to draw out the corrupted magia from his blood to no avail. Andu concocted several potions, tinctures, tonics and medicines to purge the illness from the inside out. Getting Alric to swallow the liquids was even more difficult than it had been for Rawl on their journey. It seemed that the longer the madness flowed through Alric's blood, the stronger he became. With every day that passed, Rawl felt the man he loved slipping further and further away from him.

Three days into their experiments, Rawl was frantically pacing the workroom, the cat following his footsteps to swat at his pant legs.

Since the animal had decided to stay at the university, Mila had found it a home with a feline-loving professor who readily took him in after falling victim to the very heartwarming, and, of course, completely fabricated story of how she discovered and rescued him. He was now a very spoiled animal, but still, he slipped down to the under levels of the tower from time to time to seek out Rawl.

"This isn't working," he growled in frustration, nearly tripping over the wiry body of the cat.

Neither Mila nor Andu looked up at him, now accustomed to his outbursts.

"We did warn you this was a losing battle," Mila said, not unkindly. It still hurt.

"We won't stop trying," Andu promised, finally looking up from his work. His cheeks had several scabbed-over scratches, the result of the wayward magia that poured out of Alric anytime one of them was in his immediate vicinity. In an unspoken agreement, Rawl and Andu never allowed Mila to venture too close to the mad mage.

"The problem is, I'm not sure what else to try," Mila confessed. "Everything we have been doing must have been done before," she admitted, scrolling through the thick leather-bound book in front of her. "There are entire library sections dedicated to Mage Madness and what has been done to counteract its effects. None of which has ever worked."

"I still think that if we had enough stones, or a powerful enough stone like a Dragonstear, the magia would be so drawn to it, the corruption would naturally bleed from his body," Andu said, not for the first time.

"Yes, but Andu, we only know one person in the realm with a Dragonstear stone, and he is currently locked up in the palace dungeons. So, unless you are suggesting we raid the palace dungeons, then we are back to zero."

"A Dragonstear is not the only magical item with enough power," Andu said churlishly.

Mila looked at him, confusion pinching her face. Then she threw her head back and laughed.

Rawl startled, looking between the two of them.

"What?" he asked. "What is it?"

"You don't have to laugh about it," Andu grumbled, which only made Mila laugh harder.

"I don't understand what's going on," Rawl complained.

Mila wiped her streaming eyes and grinned at her brother.

"Andu here is talking about an item we learned about in class last month. One he hasn't been able to stop thinking about since."

"It's an object of great power!" Andu argued.

"Oh sure, of course it is," Mila agreed. "It also doesn't exist!"

"You don't know that!" Andu insisted.

"I do know that! Of course I know that! Andu, it is a children's story! A folktale! The Goldenshell is not real!"

"The Goldenshell?" Rawl interrupted before the two could continue their fight.

"It's a myth," Mila said simply, the smile sliding off her face as she watched the sullen determination on Andu's.

"I've been doing research on it," Andu began.

"Of course you have," Mila muttered, rolling her eyes.

"There is a reason why they tell us that story in class," he insisted. "Why would they tell us about an object of great power if there wasn't some basis in reality?"

"Andu," Mila said gently.

"And they said that if it were to exist, it would be here. In this part of the world. Off this very coast."

"Andu!" Mila said more firmly.

"And I think I found it," he went on, fishing a rolled-up parchment from his pack.

Rawl crossed to the two of them at the table, intrigued despite himself.

"What is that?" he asked.

"This," Andu said, unrolling the paper with a flourish, "is a map!"

"Please don't tell me you want us to follow a silly treasure map!" Mila cried.

Andu hugged the old parchment to his chest, hurt clouding his face.

"It's not silly," he grumbled softly, stroking the paper as if it were a scared kitten.

"Where did you find it?" Rawl asked. "Do you think it is legitimate?" At this point, he was willing to try anything.

"Of course!" The warmth flooded back to Andu's face, and he smiled brightly at Rawl while placing the map across the table. "First, I read everything I could about the Goldenshell story."

"Myth," Mila interjected, but the men ignored her.

"Then, based on recurring themes within the story, I managed to narrow down the time of year and season. It was the start of the rainy season, in fall. An important element involves a solar eclipse, immediately followed by a raging tempest storm. So, I traced back all the documented eclipses over the last few centuries, and cross-referenced whether any overlapped with a particularly tumultuous storm. As fate would have it, there were two. But only one happened during the fall. So then, I had a year!"

Rawl stared at Andu incredulously. He knew that if the big man was at the university, then he had the aptitude for magia, and an ability to learn and study well. But given the man's size and appearance, he had thought that he would be more apt for the war magias, rather than research.

I once accused Alric of prejudice, Rawl thought, *while here I am doing the same.*

"Andu is particularly skilled in research," Mila said grudgingly, as if reading Rawl's thoughts. "He is more brain than brawn, if you can believe it!"

Andu clearly took the statement as a compliment, as the big man flushed pink from the tips of his ears to the collar of his shirt.

"Well," he said, coughing a little as he continued to blush furiously, "Once I had the year, I found accounts of treasure hunters searching for the lake in which the Goldenshell was lost. I began reading as many treasure-hunters' journals and ledgers as I could get my hands on. Captain's logs, merchant ledgers, even mercenary reports. Until finally, I found something. An account from the man who had found the lake where the Goldenshell was lost."

Rawl realized that he was leaning over the desk, as if trying to get physically closer to the story Andu was telling—and the hope that it was offering. He grasped at it like a lifeline.

"He found it," Andu told them proudly.

"Do you believe it?" Mila asked, a little breathlessly. It appeared that even she felt drawn into the tale.

"I do. That's why I went looking amongst the archives until I found his original written account. And in the false back of his leather journal, I found the map," Andu finished proudly.

"You defaced a historical artifact?" Mila squeaked, clearly scandalized.

"What?" Andu jumped, looking like he was a child who had just been caught with his fingers in a honey pot. "No! Of course I didn't!" he argued. Then, he looked down at the map on the table, then shifted from foot to foot. "Oh, well, I suppose that I might have, actually."

"If he found it, why haven't we heard of it as more than myth then?" Mila asked, back to skepticism.

"Because his intentions with the shell were not pure," Andu claimed, pulling another document from his pile. "The man was a pirate, and the first mate of the ship claimed his captain only wanted the shell in order to infiltrate the palace and seize Andala for himself."

"What is it with men and always wanting to rule?" Mila grumbled.

"So," Andu continued over Mila, "the captain took the shell onto his ship with the intention of attacking Andala from the sea. But the dioses were unhappy with his ambitions, especially given why the Goldenshell was formed. So, they sent a storm and sunk his vessel. The first mate was the only survivor, and he marked on the map where their ship was lost to the sea."

"Where is it?" Rawl interrupted, not caring if a hundred historical artifacts became damaged so long as it could help Alric. "On the map, can you tell where it is?"

Andu nodded. "Here," he said, pointing to a tiny, almost imperceivable star towards the bottom center of the map. "About six miles off of the coastline, southwest, at the bottom of the ocean."

All the hope that had built in Rawl's chest burst, knocking the air from his lungs.

"So, it's hopeless, then," he said, dropping his face into his hands. His skin felt hot. "Even if we could get a boat to take us out six miles, there is no way we could make it to the bottom of the ocean."

"That would normally be true, yes," Andu admitted. Something in his tone of voice had Rawl looking up.

The big man grinned at him.

"But we have a *Drowner*."

Chapter 13

Nova

Nova walked out of the council room, flanked by Churan and Axchel. With them by her side, she felt protected and supported. While she was feeling more comfortable with Damika after their talk and tentative truce in the garden, Nova was beginning to realize that Damika's first priority would always be the Danrayen Order.

Which was right. She was a Danrayen Warrior, after all, and very soon to be the High Priestess of the temple. It was only fitting that it should be her priority.

But Nova's priority was delivering Churan to the Flowers safely.

Although, she too was officially a Danrayen Warrior now. And while it made her smile to think about it, she knew that her goddess understood her mission, and didn't think Danray begrudged her quest. Its aim was peace, after all, and the goddess had assured her that peace was her objective as well.

"You should have accepted the Danrayen welcome celebration," Axchel muttered as they walked out towards the training grounds and the tents that now occupied the space. Nova was anxious to check in on the people of Pelgar, and Churan's magia lessons were not until sunset.

Nova shook her head. "There was a time that I dreamed of my ceremony and celebration. I imagined what it would be like to have an event as beautiful and lavish as Dami's and Raidea's had been, or Taruka and Petra's joint celebration. To stand by my friends and know myself to be an equal of them."

She sighed deeply. "At the time, I believed them to be nothing more than childish fantasies. And now, when I have passed the Trial, and have a right to a ceremony, all I can think of is how that time and effort would be better served by caring for the displaced people of Pelgar."

She looked at Axchel thoughtfully. "I think that Mamá knows that too, but she wanted me to know that they would extend every same courtesy to me that they did my Danrayen sisters, should I want them."

"She wants you to know that despite the uncertainty of your time here, that they regard you no less than any other Danrayen Warrior," Axchel supposed. Nova nodded.

"And they would do it, too, despite the frivolity. They would consider it only fair."

"But since you said no, they will not concern themselves further with it," Axchel finished for her.

"So, we are not going to have a fiesta?" Churan asked, his voice echoing disappointment. "Que pena! I love fiestas. I met you two at a fiesta!"

"Wasn't that a peace council?" Axchel asked him, grinning.

"Well, yes, but it was also a fiesta! There was music, and food, and drinks. Wasn't there?" he insisted. "You two danced," he added slyly.

Nova felt the back of her neck warm at the memory. She didn't bother asking Churan how he had known that they had danced. She refused to think about it any further, lest the blush creep to her cheeks as well. She heard Axchel let out an awkward cough.

Churan continued, oblivious to their discomfort. "The best part of fiestas is the food. Why is it that we only eat the best food at special occasions? Why can't every day be a special occasion?" he mused.

"I suppose because if you had it every day, it would no longer be special," Axchel responded, but Churan would not be deterred.

"But every day is special!" he insisted. "Especially for people like us. You were a Cassalain soldier. Nova was the Name-Bearer, and now a Danrayen Warrior. And I am a sorcerer, the Warrior Child, and the Unnamed Prince. I don't think people like us are promised tomorrow, so we should enjoy our small comforts while we can."

Nova shot Axchel an alarmed look over Churan's head. He replied with a quiet grimace. How was it that Churan could continually straddle life as a young child and old soul? Here he was, lamenting the loss of sweet cakes, while at the same time examining his own fragile mortality. It was unsettling.

"Well, you will be happy to know that you will likely have a fiesta after all," Nova said quickly to distract him. Churan stopped and whirled around to her happily.

"You will accept your Danrayen welcome ceremony?" he asked, joyously.

"No, I still believe that to be far too frivolous," Nova answered. "However, we will need a High Priestess Ascension Ceremony. The other priestesses cannot continue denying her the position. We are in a state of too much instability to not have a leader. And once they agree, Damika cannot ascend to the position quietly, as much as she would like to. There needs to be a clear message of support, the Danrayens need to rally around her to show both our enemies and our allies that we are as united as ever. That we may have lost Adira, but we still have a powerful High Priestess in power."

Axchel nodded. "Warriors need direction, and our enemies need someone to fear."

Nova inwardly smiled at his understanding. He was ever the soldier.

"Will there be food, and drinks, and music, and dancing?" Churan asked in a rushed tone.

Nova grinned. "Oh yes. And feats of magia, and barriletes gigantes, and the Dance of Danray. It will be a spectacle, with guests who come from far and wide. And for the first time, the citizens of Pelgar will be invited to attend, since they are all here, anyway. I think that will serve to bolster their spirits, especially since Danrayen ceremonies were always the talk of the town whenever they happened. To be here for an Ascension Ceremony will be quite the honor."

As they drew closer to the fields, the dull noise of human activity and conversation sharpened and grew louder, until they could grasp the sounds of low moans and snippets of conversation. Nova recognized the calm but authoritative instructions of the temple healers as they made their rounds, the soft weeping of men and women contrasting sharply with the giggles of nearby playing youths. Nova almost smiled to see the resilience of children.

She could smell sweat and blood mixed with the sharp, sweet scent of infection, as well as the more ordinary odor of too many bodies crowded in too small of a place.

The three of them busied themselves quickly. Churan and Nova held basins of water for the healers, mixing fresh poultices, and fetching clean bandages. They employed Axchel to help lift and carry some of the injured to more comfortable dwellings indoors. Other times, they asked him to hold others down as the healers did their work on particularly difficult wounds. He did so resolutely and unflinchingly, his words and demeanor soft, even as his actions radiated strength. His actions reminded Nova once again of the duality of his nature—of the trained soldier who was more a healer than a fighter at heart.

As Nova was scrubbing her hands of some dried blood, a young initiate of about twelve years scampered up to her, eyes bright with purpose.

"Priestess Damika would like you to meet her at the library," she informed Nova, her voice slightly breathless as she mentioned Damika's name. It amused Nova, both that Dami's reputation preceded her, and that the young girls were already calling her "priestess," although she had yet to accept the title.

She thanked the girl, then hesitated only long enough to tell Axchel that Damika had summoned her. He nodded at her but did not move to join her.

"Churan and I will clean up at the guest baths and go to his lesson," he told her, and it surprised her to find that she would regret his absence.

Nova examined those feelings as she made her way to the library. She supposed that it meant she still felt somewhat apart from the other Danrayens, even being able to claim herself as one now. She still felt love for them all, particularly her old friends, but the memory of their anger and resentment towards her would not quickly fade. It would not do to have such division. The goddess had stressed she should mark well who both her allies and her enemies were, and she could never consider her Danrayen sisters as enemies.

So, I must work harder to accept them as my allies, Nova resolved within herself.

As soon as she opened the door of the library, she immediately recognized the reason that Damika called for her. A small, compact body hit her around the middle, half-knocking the breath from her lungs.

"Petra!" she gasped out, delightedly throwing her arms around the smaller woman. Then she pulled back, scanning her friend. She had traveled long and far from Tureene, and all on her own. She was rumpled and dirty, but she seemed uninjured.

"How are you?" she asked her softly. Petra had stayed behind to bury both Raidea and her father.

The smile that she returned was sad. "My body is well," she told her, squeezing her hands. "Though my heart still bleeds."

"As do ours," Nova replied sadly. Damika, standing in the corner, nodded at them both in agreement.

Petra sighed, then looked around the room. "Though I would feel better if I could see my wife!" she said, her voice adopting a livelier tone.

As if conjured by magia, Taruka stepped through the door. "Wife?" she questioned with a raised eyebrow.

"What, have I not married you yet?" Petra asked, a grin lighting up her features.

Taruka rolled her eyes and opened her mouth to reply, but Petra reached her in two quick strides, dipping her low to kiss her soundly. Petra's romantic gesture impressed Nova, as Taruka was significantly taller than her small friend.

"Close the door, Taru," Damika said as soon as Petra released her. Taru stumbled a bit, looking dazed and flushed, but did as Dami bid her. Together, they all sat in the assortment of mismatched chairs the library offered, bringing them together in a haphazard circle near the hearth.

Slowly, Petra told them all about the funeral rites, and the aftermath of the attack in Tureene. She had stayed long enough to lend her aid where she could, then set out a few days after the rest of them had.

"I moved surprisingly fast," she told them, a puzzled frown creating many small straight lines on her brow. "After the attack, I thought that I would encounter much more monstros on the way here, but while I saw many signs of them, it was as if they had moved on just as I caught up to them."

The rest of them exchanged glances.

"Moving south," Damika muttered.

Then it was her turn to relay the events which had transpired since they had parted. Petra began to cry, quietly, as they reached the part about the attack on Pelgar, and all the lives lost, both of townspeople and of Danrayens. Her tears continued as she heard of Adira's passing, then gasped when the truth of Damika's parentage was revealed. Taruka held her hand through it all, and once Damika had finished her account, Petra was quietly contemplative. The rest of them waited patiently as their friend processed their news.

Finally, she looked up at Damika.

"I am sorry for your loss," she told her, voice raw with emotion. "I do not remember much of my mother, but having just buried my father," she swallowed. "I know well that there is never enough time."

"I did not know her as my mother," Damika confessed helplessly.

"And so, you mourn twice, for the woman you loved as your priestess, and for the mother you never knew," Taruka answered, and Damika closed her eyes so tightly that Nova could only see where the wispy ends of her lashes met.

Then Petra turned to Nova.

"And I owe you an apology as well, Nessa," she said. "I had already decided that I believed you. I had a long way to travel alone with my thoughts. I was going to ask for your forgiveness. Adira's confession of her part in your secrets means little. I already knew in my heart that you were the same Nessa of our youth. I'm sorry it took so long to see that."

Nova had not realized the ice that she had held around her heart until Petra's words caused some of it to melt. She nodded at her with a sniffle.

"I'm sorry, too," she said.

They sat quietly for a long moment, each lost in their own thoughts.

"What now?" Petra finally asked.

"Well," Damika slowly answered. "Tomorrow, Taruka will leave for the Mage University."

"I will go with her," Petra declared, but Damika shook her head. Petra, who had always been quick to anger, scowled in her direction, but Damika held a hand up to cut her off.

"Tomorrow, I also begin preparations to ascend as High Priestess of this order," she continued. "Something that half of the priestesses here believe to be a very bad idea. And I can't say that I don't agree with them."

Nova tisked at her, but Damika continued. "They can't all know about our mission, not yet. We do not know how many will be loyal to the crown, and how many to the Flowers. I will need people around me that I can trust."

"So, you expect Taru to travel alone? South? In the direction that you just told me all the monstros are headed?" Petra demanded angrily.

"Amor, I will be fine," Taruka said, stroking her arm. Petra practically vibrated with fury.

"Yes," Damika answered. "I would not send her if I didn't have faith in her abilities."

"I volunteered, actually," Taruka grumbled, but they ignored her.

"And, because when she makes it to the university, she can send word to us regarding Leader of the Padir. If the Padir can be recruited as allies, I will need someone that I trust to leave in search of them."

Nova nodded to herself, understanding the wisdom in Damika's plan. The fewer people who knew of their true intentions at the moment, the better. If Rawl could direct them to Leader, one of their party would need to go to convince the Padir to join them. It needed to be someone who knew everything that was at stake. She could not go, because she needed to keep Churan safe. Axchel's oath to the child to do the same prevented him from going. Damika would be accepting the role and responsibility of High Priestess and would need to remain in the temple under Mamá's tutelage.

That left only Petra.

Nova watched as her friend went through the same information in her mind, and recognized the moment when she came to the same conclusion Nova had. The anger drained from her face, and she slumped back in her chair, looking defeated.

"I understand," she acquiesced.

"That is tomorrow," Damika said, standing suddenly. "Tonight, we drink."

The rest of them looked at her as if she had gone mad. Perhaps she had. Perhaps the strain of recent events had been too much. Damika, like the rest of them, had drank the occasional ale and ron since they were young women. But never, in all her time at the temple, had Nova *ever* heard her suggest it first. That had always been Petra or Raidea's role.

"For Raidea," Damika clarified, noting their confused faces. "Up on the rooftops, where we took our first bottle of stolen alcohol as children and drank ourselves sick."

They all grinned at one another. It was after the first Danrayen welcome ceremony that they had been allowed to attend. Nova realized that they had not had a moment to mourn the loss of their friend together. In fact, she suspected that they had all been pushing her death from their minds, as Nova had. With the exception of Petra, of course, who had conducted her Danrayen last rites. It was important that they say goodbye to her as they were meant; together.

"We drink," Petra echoed, rising.

"For Raidea," Nova agreed.

Chapter 14

Rawl

"So, this Goldenshell, it is like one of your stones? One powerful enough to absorb even great amounts of magia?" Rawl asked Andu. He still wasn't sure how the item was meant to help Alric, but "an object of great power" sounded promising.

Andu shook his head. "It is not *quite* like our spell stones," he confessed, but before Rawl's spirits could sink, Andu added, "It is much, much more powerful."

"How?" Rawl asked, confused.

"Now you've done it," Mila grumbled, but sent Andu an indulgent smile, and he flushed from the attention.

"Well, to understand that, you need to understand how both magia and spell stones work," he answered.

"As you know, magia does not come from within us. We mages simply have the ability to create magia from the energy around us. We convert that energy into our spellwork, and that is what creates magia, but every time that we do so, it poisons our blood. Unless purged, that corruption infects more and more of our bodies, until it is impossible to remove."

Rawl nodded. Mila had explained much of this to him before leaving for the Mage University, and Alric had furthered his education during their travels.

"Sorcerers, which are exceedingly rare, are able to pull energy and convert it into magia without poisoning their own blood," he recited to Andu, who nodded.

"Because they have an Affinity for magia," the big man added. "It makes them immune to the corruption. Most people with Affinities—or 'gifts from the dioses,' as we often say—are unaware of their own Affinity. It can be as simple as an Affinity for music, an ease in playing instruments, or voices that sound sweeter than anyone else."

Rawl nodded again. He remembered this.

"For those of us who do not have an Affinity for magia, spell stones, like the Griffonstalon that your sister has, or my Wolfang, are able to absorb the corruption in our blood that occurs when we use magia. Some stones are stronger than others."

"Alric said that his Phoenixeye was very powerful," Rawl said. "How did it break?"

"It's very rare for a stone to break, or shatter," Mila admitted. "Unless you are using a very weak stone, that is unable to absorb a lot of magia." She flicked her wrist and a candle near them ignited with a spark of flame from her fingertips. "That bit of magia, for instance, took almost no effort from me," she continued, tapping her Griffonstalon stone, which sat snugly in a leather cord around her neck. "The stone would have absorbed the corruption just by being in contact with my flesh. Any weaker stone would have been able to absorb it, then purify the energy without an issue."

Mila rummaged around a small pouch that sat at her hip.

"Here," she said, placing a small, almost translucent rock on the table and taking off her Griffonstalon necklace. She handed it to Andu. She blew out the candle, then lit it again. "My body now has a slight amount of corruption, likely not enough to kill me, but enough to make me ill for a few days if it's not dispelled. New mages, before they learn of their abilities, are often prone to sickness because they don't realize that they are performing small acts of magia."

Rawl remembered Mila as a small child, constantly bedridden with fevers. He had just assumed that she had been a sickly child, and never would have imagined that it was an early sign of her mage-gift.

Mila placed a gentle fingertip on the stone, and it flashed quickly before fading. "The Cloudrop stone, despite being a very weak stone, was able to absorb the corruption without issue. If I left it alone for an hour or two, it would cycle the energy back into the world, purifying it so that no corruption remained. Then I could use it again without an issue."

Mila repeated her act of blowing out the candle, but this time relit it along with several more on the table with her magia. The flames blazed to life, further illuminating the room.

"But if I were to funnel more corruption into the stone than it was able to hold." She tapped the stone, and it shattered. Andu handed her back her Griffonstalon.

"Stronger spells require stronger stones, or more stones," she said, fastening the necklace in place once more. "Certain stones have little risk of becoming overwhelmed like that," she added, jerking her chin towards the remnants of the Cloudrop. "Your friend's Phoenixeye should never have failed him. They are capable of absorbing massive amounts of corruption, and they are capable of purifying very quickly. For it to have gotten overwhelmed as it did ..." she hesitated. "He must be a very powerful mage."

Rawl swallowed past the lump that had grown in his throat, re-membering the day the madness had begun. "He was protecting me," he said quietly. "He saved us, both of us, but I think he was protecting me."

"This isn't your fault," Andu cut in softly.

Rawl nodded. "I know," he said. "It is the fault of whatever is allowing creatures from the Night Wood to venture into our lands. Those monstros are the reason why Alric had to expend as much magia as he did." Swiping away an errant tear, Rawl faced Andu.

"So, this Goldenshell," he started. "It is more powerful than most stones? As powerful as a Dragonstear?" he asked.

Andu shook his head. "The Goldenshell isn't a spell stone at all. It is an object of power," he explained.

Rawl felt his forehead crease. "I don't understand," he admitted.

"Spell stones are purifiers. They only absorb remnants of magia long enough to purge the corruption and release the cleansed energy back into the world. But objects of power are objects that can absorb power and then keep it."

"They maintain the power?" Rawl asked, beginning to understand.

Andu nodded. "They absorb remnants of magia, or corruption, and turn it into pure power, now housed within the object."

"That is possible?" Rawl gaped, mind reeling.

"In theory," Mila interjected, her voice skeptical. "There are many myths about objects of power, but no one has ever found one that we know of. We can't be sure that they actually exist." The last part directed sternly at Andu. "The object itself would have to be incredibly powerful; like, 'blessed by the dioses' powerful."

"Which the Goldenshell was," Andu insisted.

"If the story is more than a myth," Mila argued.

"I think," Rawl interrupted, "that I would like to hear this story."

Chapter 15
Legend of the Goldenshell

Many, many years ago, around the shore of a vast and bountiful lake, lived two warring tribes…

An old and powerful king ruled the Ixbint tribe, the last in a long line of monarchs who had established trade routes and allies far and wide across the lands. As a result, his people were wealthy, their city opulent, and their people happy.

A mighty and fierce warrior queen ruled the Hunhan tribe. She trained all her subjects in the art of battle, defense, and strategy. They were the best hunters and trackers of the land, and they filled their city with the finest meats, furs, and bonework of anyone around. Despite their strength in fighting, the Hunhan were a peaceful tribe—with one exception.

For decades, the Ixbint and Hunhan tribes were at war with one another. The Ixbint resented the fine goods that the Hunhan were able to procure, coveting the coin it would bring them, had they had such goods for themselves.

The Hunhan resented how the Ixbint cleared more and more of the forests for their roads and trade routes, driving away the game which was their livelihood.

The two tribes battled fiercely and often. It wasn't until the loss of life on both sides was too much to bear that the fighting began to dwindle. Instead of continuing the bloodshed, the tribes finally decided on a truce. They created a very firm boundary that separated one side of the great lake from the other. They even went so far as to mark how far each tribe could venture out on the water with their fishing boats.

The center of the lake remained unclaimed out of respect for the dioses of the lake.

And so, the two tribes lived in relative peace for many years. And while both tribes respected the boundaries, both sides remained ever wary, convinced that someday the other would break their oath and attack once more.

None dared, however ...

Until Untik and Zena.

Untik was a young and strong warrior of the Hunhan tribe. He was a promising youth, rising among the ranks with great speed and fervor. The warrior queen herself had noticed him and promised him a spot within her own guard if he continued to advance.

This promise pushed Untik to train harder and longer than all others in his endeavors, arising earlier than his peers and training until late in the evening.

It was on one such night that Untik was running along the edge of the lake when he found himself dangerously close to the boundary. Just as he was about to turn back, however, he saw a figure emerge from the gentle fog that always seemed to caress the water's surface.

This was the moment that Untik first saw Zena.

Zena was the daughter of the Ixbint king, and therefore the princess of her tribe. Untik did not know this, of course. He only knew that she was the loveliest woman that Untik had ever seen.

As she stepped from the water, clothes clinging to her body, Untik averted his eyes in respect.

The moon saw this and approved.

Zena noticed the young man right away and knew that she should fear. He was, after all, a warrior of the Hunhan tribe. Not only was his clothing made from very fine leather and furs, but he was also standing within Hunhan territory. They were her people's sworn enemies. But she saw how he had turned his back on her to give her privacy, and she recognized the vulnerability in that action.

Too shy to speak, Zena gathered her things before moving away from the boundary. Desperate to preserve any connection with her, Untik turned.

"Por favor," he pleaded in a soft voice. "I am Untik. Please, if you would give me your name?"

Zena hesitated, casting a startled look over her shoulder. Her heart softened at the pleading in his eyes, and she found herself responding.

"Zena," she answered. "I am Zena."

After a breathless moment, Zena broke their stare and went home.

For the next two moons, Untik found Zena there every night. Slowly, they began to know one another. Zena explained that, because of the strictness of her father, the nights were the only times that she was able to be on her own. That she only came so close to the border because she was sure that none of the Ixbint patrols would venture so far, for, if she was discovered, they would surely tell her father.

Untik explained to her his ambitions of rising to be the guard of the warrior queen, and how his training had led him to her that fateful evening.

Night after night they shared their lives with one another, and soon, their hearts. After every passing moon, they both strayed closer and closer to the invisible wall that separated them.

The wind saw this and approved.

Finally, one night, unable to contain the depths of his feelings any longer, Untik knelt in front of the princess at the very edge of the boundary and confessed his love for her.

"I know well that I am only a lowly warrior, and that I am no one in the presence of a kind and beautiful princess," he said. "But if I were to die tomorrow, I would praise the dioses, for I have been able to know your spirit, even a little." He looked up at her, staring back at him, quiet and stunned.

"You have my heart, princesa, forever."

At his words, Zena knelt on her own side of the boundary and tentatively reached her hand forward. Untik immediately mirrored her action, until their flesh met, breaking years of truce and trust for the privilege of touching one another.

The lake saw this and approved.

In that moment, a wave rippled on its surface, pushing a shiny shell towards them both. Untik picked it up and presented it to Zena as his token.

She accepted it, and with it, his proposal.

"You have my heart as well," Zena confessed to Untik. "And my hand, should you desire it."

Together, Untik and Zena formed a plan. Zena was hopeful that if her father, the king, learned of her love for a Hunhan warrior, he would recognize the strategic alliance such a union could provide.

Hunhan begged Zena to run away with him instead, fearful that the king would not view their match favorably, but become enraged that his daughter, the princess, had fallen in love with a warrior from an enemy tribe.

"Let me try," Zena begged him, desperate for peace among their people.

Untik, who could deny his love nothing, conceded. They agreed to meet the very next night at their spot, so that Zena could share with him the news.

But the next night, Zena did not come.

For the following three days, Zena did not come.

Driven to desperation, Untik decided to break the boundary, and their tribe's truce, to find his love. However, on the day he had chosen to leave, word came to the Hunhan tribe.

"The Ixbint! They are declaring war!" one of the warriors cried.

"Their armies come! They approach the boundary!" another yelled.

The warrior queen herself appeared, speaking to her subjects.

"The Ixbint prepare to battle us," she confirmed. "We have received word that they believe we have stolen their princess from them, and come to retrieve her,"

Untik's heart lifted as cries of "lies!" and "liars!" broke around them.

If the princess was missing, then perhaps …

Without waiting to hear what more his queen was saying, Untik broke away from the crowd and began sprinting from his people towards the spot where he and Zena met. He was very strong and very fast from his training, and so was not easily followed. He made it to the boundary, heart hammering and breath short in his lungs.

But his vitality returned when he saw Zena there, waiting.

They crashed into one another, unsure and uncaring of which side of the boundary they stood upon, just relieved to be in each other's company once more.

"You were right," Zena cried to Untik, clinging to him. "My father did not understand. I tried to deliver us peace, and all I have done is bring about more war."

Untik shook his head. "This is no fault of our love," he assured her. "We will leave our people to their hate, and start our lives somewhere else, anew."

But it was already too late. Both tribes had tracked the couple to their spot by the lake. Soon, they were surrounded with nowhere to go.

"Please," Zena cried out, attempting to shield her love from her people. "He is not the enemy! Nor are the Hunhan! We—"

But Zena never finished her plea, for in that moment, an arrow embedded itself deeply into her belly. Untik did not know if the first attack had come from his tribe or hers, but as the crimson blood spilled from her perfect brown skin, he found it did not matter.

"No!" Untik roared, sinking to his knees with Zena's weight upon him.

The moon saw this and despaired. She traveled across the sky, blocking the sun in an effort to return her favor to the young lovers. Members of both tribes cried out in fear over the sudden eclipse.

He saw her people advancing before him, scared and enraged, and knew that his were coming just as surely from behind. Untik knew, with sudden clarity, that death would separate them. The Ixbint would take her body back to the king, to have a royal burial, and his body—for he was determined to die there with his love—would be taken back with the Hunhan.

He could not allow that to happen.

With all the strength left to him, Untik dragged Zena to the lake, submerging them both. He swam with Zena under one arm, her still face resting against his shoulder. Untik swam and swam, but his strength began to waver.

The wind, who had seen this, blew hard and fast, creating a tempest storm above the waters of the large lake. Her winds pushed Untik and

Zena until they reached the middle of the lake, which belonged to no one but the dioses themselves.

"Dioses," he pleaded, "Allow us to stay here, with you, unbothered and undivided for all of eternity. Por favor, use your magia to make sure that no tribe ever finds us and divides us again."

Then Untik finally allowed his strength to falter, sinking under the water with Zena.

The dios of the lake saw this and grieved for the love and life lost. He felt the token of his love, the simple, humble shell he had bestowed upon them, cradled in a chain against the dead princess's throat. In it, she had placed all of her hope for a new life, and it brimmed with power. Not magia, but the true power of love and hope. With it, the dios of the lake released a burst of great magia, the wind and the moon aiding in his efforts. Together, the dioses turned both the souls of Untik and Zena into the swirling night currents of the lake, free to dance and play over its surface for all of eternity.

In that moment of great magia, it is said that there was a burst of golden light from the center of the lake, a glowing shell suspended above the water before sinking down into its depths. A shell imbued with the love of two youths, and the magia of the gods. A magia that need not dissipate back into Tierramadri, but free to remain harnessed within the object forevermore.

CHAPTER 16
NOVA

The next morning, Nova felt like she had head-butted an orcuyo. There was a burning pressure behind her eyes, her temples throbbed, and even her hair seemed to hurt. Every step she took felt like it reverberated from the soles of her feet, up her ankles and shins, shooting up her spine to rattle her teeth. She smacked her lips a few times, trying to unstick her tongue from the roof of her mouth, fighting the dryness that no amount of water seemed to quench.

She knew she was far too old to overindulge, but once they had begun, it had been hard to stop. They had told stories of their past, reminiscing over their years growing within the temple walls. They had laughed. They had cried. They had embraced. Petra and Damika had even tussled for a moment, arguing over ... something.

The details were fuzzy.

Taruka had been the only sensible one, likely because she was the only one that needed to travel come morning. She had broken up the fight before the women had a chance to fling themselves from the roof to their deaths. She had retained the sense to cut off their ron and insist they get at least a few hours of sleep.

Nova had woken in between a very warm Damika and a lightly snoring Petra. Already dressed and packed, Taruka threatened to pour water over the lot of them if they did not see her off.

Together, they headed towards the secret temple exit that they had come in from during the Pelgar attack. There were scouts above the main temple entrance, so they would know if any monstros made their way to their home, but all agreed that they best not open the doors, just in case. Taruka could easily slip out of the passage, and most would be none the wiser.

As they rounded a corridor into an outdoor courtyard, Nova heard quiet weeping. At first, she assumed that it was Petra, drink-weary and emotional over Taruka's departure. But as they continued, the source of the tears became clear. It was a young Danrayen initiate, no more than six years old, dressed in her training gear. She sat against a stone wall, knees drawn up to her chest, a mass of tangled dark hair obscuring her features.

"Are you all right?" Taruka asked her softly as they approached.

The girl sprang up, the sound of her sobs having muffled their approach. She hastily swiped the tears from her cheeks with the sleeve of her tunic and gave them all a jerky bow.

"Why do you cry?" Taruka continued.

The girl shook her head furiously. "I am not crying," she declared, voice wobbling, her face splotchy and damp.

Damika leveled a look at her, and her bottom lip trembled. Suddenly, she threw herself on the ground and began crying once more, louder than before.

Nova winced at the noise, then instantly felt guilty for it. Though, the way that Petra held her fingers to her brow, she knew she was not the only one who was affected.

"Stand, soldier," Damika commanded, kindly but firmly. Nova started, remembering hearing those exact words from the same voice during her Trial. It seemed to work as well on the child as it had for her in the sanctum, because training and custom had the girl hauling herself up and facing Dami at attention. Tears continued to trail down her cheeks, but she sniffed hard and stopped wailing.

"Now," Damika continued, satisfied, "What is your name?"

"Graciela, Priestess," she answered. Damika twitched at the title but did not correct her.

"What ails you, Graciela?" she asked instead.

Graciela's lip began trembling once again, more furiously than before, but she kept her tears at bay.

"I am not a warrior," she admitted, shame clouding her face. "I thought I could be, but I was wrong." She took a deep breath before continuing, "It's so hard," her little voice cried. "I am so much littler than all the other girls and I am bad at everything. I can't hold the weapons, even the practice ones! I'm tired." Her tiny shoulders slumped. "I wanted to be brave and strong, but I can't do it."

"You are capable of doing anything, little warrior," Damika corrected her, but Graciela shook her head.

"I can't! I can't do it," she argued sulkily.

"If you want to do it enough, you can," Damika corrected.

"But I'm too small," the girl repeated, her voice whining.

"So? Petra is tiny. In fact, she is almost as small as you and she's way older," Damika answered.

"Hey!" Petra protested indignantly, but Nova grinned. Now that she looked at them, Dami was right. Petra wasn't all that much taller than the child.

"She's also the least flexible person I've ever met," Nova added, not being able to resist teasing her friend.

Petra shot her a fierce glare, but the rest of them laughed.

"Very true," Damika agreed. "Even if she were taller, her kicks wouldn't extend past her opponent's thigh. As it is, she can probably just kick someone's ankles."

"I'll kick your ankles," Petra grumbled.

Another laugh erupted around them, and even the girl's mouth twitched a little.

"But she is incredibly strong. She could lift me up and toss me clear across this courtyard if she wanted to," Damika finished.

The little girl turned to stare at Petra, her eyes like two round moons in her dirty, tear-smudged face.

"I'd be happy to give a demonstration," Petra growled, moving towards Damika.

"Nessa here is totally uncoordinated," Damika continued, not even sparing a glance at Petra.

"Oye, what did I do?" Nova argued, bemused.

"She's pretty good at hand-to-hand combat, but never did learn to make a sword an extension of herself," Damika continued, swinging her own around in her hand. "But she has incredible accuracy with throwing knives. She could clip a feather off the top of a bird's head from fifty yards away."

The girl was looking at her curiously now, a glimmer of respect in her eyes.

"I'm not very strong," Taruka interjected. When the rest of them turned to argue with her, she lifted a hand. "I'm not *physically* strong. My body doesn't allow it. No matter how hard or long I trained, I was never able to create enough muscle to make my punches or blows very effective." She smiled coyly. "However, my arms are plenty strong enough to string a bow, and my aim with my arrows is as good as Nessa's is with her knives."

"Better," Nova admitted without resentment.

The girl's gaze swept back towards Damika, and Nova realized that she was waiting for Damika to confess a weakness as well. Which was a problem, since Damika was the most skilled warrior Nova had ever known. She was tall, and strong, and agile, and capable, and had deadly accuracy and precision. She even excelled in research and strategy. She had an Affinity for battle, blessed by the goddess Danray herself. She was exactly what was expected of an elite warrior.

Nova leaned forward to continue encouraging the child and hopefully distract her from the unspoken question, when, to her surprise, Damika spoke.

"I am often stubborn. Too set in my own ways. I was the best for a long time, better than most of my peers at weapons and combat and battle. That made me weak in other areas. Because I always thought that since I was best at everything, that meant that I knew best for everyone." Damika sighed softly, then ran a hand through the girl's tangled hair, smoothing it away where it stuck to her wet cheeks. "That isn't the case. I had to learn to trust others, to trust in each of their unique strengths. Because no matter who you are, or how skilled you may be, we are always stronger together."

She looked straight into Nova's eyes, and her breath stuttered.

"We are better together," she said. They stayed that way for a long moment, before the girl clapped her hands and jolted them back to reality.

"I am going to train so hard! And be one of the best Danrayen Warriors, and find myself friends just like you," she gushed, beaming at all of them. The women grinned at one another at her quick transformation.

The resilience of children, Nova thought again as the girl scampered away, presumably back to training.

"You were good with her," Nova told Damika as they continued on. "You will make a wonderful High Priestess."

Damika's shoulders tensed, but she did not reply.

"Of course she will," Petra answered easily. "She was always meant for that path."

Damika regarded her thoughtfully but remained silent. Eventually, they reached the hidden door, and she pulled Taruka in for a hug.

"Be safe, be careful, be smart," she told her. "Be *you*," she added with a smile.

Nova hugged her next. "Give Alric and Rawl my love," she said, refusing to believe that Alric would not be there to receive the message. Taruka nodded, her chin tapping the top of Nova's head as she did so.

Damika and Nova walked back down the corridor to give Taru and Petra some privacy. There were the sounds of murmured words and soft promises, then the grating of stone against stone. After a few moments, Petra joined them, surprisingly dry-eyed and stoic.

"Let's go," she told them both, walking past them. "We have an Ascension Ceremony to plan."

Chapter 17

Rawl

A lric did not look good.

Rawl knew that the mage hadn't looked good in weeks, but seeing him against the rich opulence of the Mage University furnishings, freshly cleaned and clothed in proper robes, somehow made him look *worse* than he had before. Perhaps it was the juxtaposition of the fine, clean tailoring and the sallow, hollow gauntness of his face and body. The bruising and corrupted veins seemed to stand out even more harshly against it all.

Rawl sat on a stool close enough to Alric to be able to talk to him, but not so close that the mage's errant magia could strike him. Even now, watching Rawl, the sparks of power began flying from him. They were worse when the mage was mad. And these days, he always seemed mad.

Undeterred, Rawl shifted his position on the stool and showed Alric what he was holding. It was a charango. His sister had found the small stringed instrument for him, likely hoping it would help distract him from the mage's illness. Instead, he had taken it straight to him. Alric, the *real* Alric, had always loved Rawl's songs and stories. If that Alric was still in there somewhere, he hoped that he'd be able to hear him.

"Any requests?" Rawl asked, regretting the question as soon as it left his lips.

Alric grinned a predatory smile at him and repeated, "*Requests?*"

His voice was like the grinding of boots over cobblestones.

"Yes, I have some *requests*," he drew out the last word, creating a sibilant hissing sound.

"I *request* that you let me out of these bonds," he said conversationally, his red eyes burning a path through Rawl's skin and squeezing around his heart.

"I *request* that you let me splice the tongue from your mouth," he continued. "So that I may never have to hear your wretched singing again. I *request* that you then cut your hands from your body. I will help you with the second one, since you won't have a hand left to hold the ax."

Rawl suppressed a shudder.

"I then *request* we nail your eyelids to your forehead so you can watch while I kill that pretty little sister of yours, and her giant friend, too."

Rawl kept his face as impassive as possible, even though inside his heart was hammering, pieces of it breaking each time it beat.

This isn't him. This isn't him, he repeated to himself. *I will fix this.*

"The story of the squirrel it is!" Rawl said as cheerfully as he could. "That was one of your favorites, if I recall correctly." And then he launched into the song as quickly as possible to keep Alric from saying anything more.

It wasn't his best performance. Alric did not say anything more or interrupt, but he stared at Rawl the entire time, his face slack and unblinking. At one point, a small bit of drool leaked from the mage's mouth and dribbled onto his robes, and for some reason the sight of his fastidious mage allowing himself to be soiled so was grotesque to Rawl. So, he faltered, just a little, and his voice cracked more than once, but he made it to the very end of the song.

In the quiet that followed his performance, Rawl tilted his head back, eyes closed, and allowed himself to mourn. He mourned for the friend that he had lost. He mourned for the other friends they had left behind, abandoning them in a time of need to pursue this likely fruitless dream that Alric could be cured. He mourned for Churan, who had found in Alric the type of teacher and mentor that the child had always wanted. He mourned for Nova, who he knew loved Alric like a brother.

And he mourned for himself. For the life, and love, that he would never get a chance to know with Alric if they didn't find a way to save him.

"You won't win," Alric's voice cut through the dark. "You will die."

The matter-of-fact tone was like a dagger to Rawl's heart.

"You," Alric started again, but Rawl quickly interrupted him.

"Do you remember your brother?" he asked him, opening his eyes and forcing himself to meet Alric's crimson gaze.

A small twitch fluttered on Alric's brow, but he didn't continue speaking, which Rawl took as a good sign. Emboldened, he leaned forward.

"Your younger brother, Lionel. You loved him very much."

Alric's brows pulled down lower, two dark slashes of paint over a pale, rough canvas.

"He joined the Andalan army and went to fight in the war. You promised your mother you would try to find him," Rawl insisted. "You tried, for many years, to find him."

"It is the young who die in war," Alric murmured darkly. Despite the nature of the words, Rawl's heart lifted.

"Yes! That is what you told me! That is what you said that night in the red canyon as we fought our way back to Rojya—Nova. We were laying there, talking across a bonfire in the middle of all that red rock and dust, under a night sky full of stars. It was the first time we had a proper conversation."

"It is the young who die in war," Alric repeated, firmer. A look crossed his face that made Rawl's veins feel like the mage had doused them in ice water. Alric grinned at him, and Rawl noticed that his gums had started turning a dark red color as well, the color of his magia, corrupted.

"And Lionel is long dead," he continued, straining against his bonds. "He died, young and bloody and full of misplaced youthful optimism. He died alone, in pain, for a war he understood nothing about. He died a *hero*," he said, spitting out the last word as if it were poison. "The way you will die. The way everyone that you love will die. You will share the little lion's fate."

"The little lion!" Rawl repeated, grasping now. "That is what you called him. I carved a lion token for you, in his honor."

Rawl let his voice trail away, defeated. The knot in his throat was painfully tight, but it didn't matter. His mouth was so dry he had no spit to swallow, anyway. He didn't know why he continued trying to find the old Alric inside the creature he had become, but he didn't know how to stop.

"Peruda's day," he heard a soft voice say.

Rawl jerked his head up, staring at the mage. He could scarcely believe the quiet, thoughtful voice was coming from the same person who had been threatening to destroy him and everyone he cared about just moments ago.

"Qué?" he asked, confused.

"You carved the token for Peruda's day," Alric repeated.

Rawl leaped from his chair.

"Yes, that's right," he wanted to yell it, but it came out as a hoarse whisper. A single tear traveled the length of his cheek, remaining suspended under his chin. "It was a token of affection, for Peruda's day."

He had worked long nights for weeks, by the light of their fires, alone, to sculpt the perfect lion figurine; its mane full and waving, muscles bunched and ready to pounce. The face had been the hardest. Rawl had wanted it to look mischievous and cocky rather than frightening, just the way that Alric had described his brother. He hoped that by giving it to Alric, the mage would recognize the depth of his affection.

It hadn't quite worked out that way.

"I carved one for Nova, as well, do you remember?" Rawl asked, but Alric merely stared off into the distance, looking dazed. "Do you remember Nova? I call her Rojya, for her red hair. Do you remember?" he pressed. "She was—she *is*, your friend."

Alric did not answer.

Rawl knew he should not hold to hope that their interaction meant anything. It could be the corruption messing with Alric's mind. It could be a horrible game that the mage was playing, to give him hope and then tear it apart. The cruelty that resulted from the Mage Madness truly knew no bounds.

But as he stared at the man he loved, immobile, bound, and so, so broken, Rawl allowed himself to hope.

Chapter 18
Churan

Churan sat cross-legged in front of Mage Nuna.

A Danrayen initiate had led him and Axchel to a small structure just outside the horseshoe-formation of buildings that made up the bulk of the temple grounds. As far as Churan could tell, it was built almost completely out of stone, rather than the mixture of wood and other materials that the guest quarters employed. Once they had entered the building, Nuna led them through a narrow, straight hallway until they reached the main room, which was a curved dome-shape. If he could look at the building from above like a bird, Churan imagined that the structure would resemble a capped mushroom. Deep blue tile made up the floor of the room, with a large white circle in its center.

Mage Nuna had not wanted Axchel to sit in on the lesson, but the soldier had insisted. Churan was glad, as he wouldn't have wanted to be left alone in that cold, strange room with the equally strange mage.

She was a nice enough lady; he supposed. She was older than both Axchel and Nova, with light bits of gray hair peppering her scalp and fine lines that were etched around her eyes and mouth, even when her face was relaxed. Her skin had a looseness about it that older people seemed to get, hanging off bone like overfilled pockets. Despite her age, he could tell that she was as much of a warrior as any of the other women he had seen in the temple.

It amazed him, the variety of strong and powerful women housed in the Temple of Danray. He had heard of Danrayen Warriors, of course, even before meeting Nova. He imagined that there were few people in Tierramadri who hadn't. There were reports of the fearsome women battling at the Borders in the south, the whispered rumors of their feats and deeds. There had even been some ballads sung about them that had reached him all the way up in the Northern Tribes area. But tales of their strength and prowess had not done them justice.

They were incredible.

So, Churan knew that he should feel fortunate that the head temple mage herself had offered to train him. Churan was sure that there were likely few people in the realm that could match her knowledge in magia. He should have felt elated.

Instead, he felt nothing but resentment.

He knew what his old guardian, Kallpa would have said. He would have told him that one should give thanks to the dioses for all those who were willing to aid him in his journey.

He would be right, Churan thought to himself.

Kallpa took Churan in shortly after the boy first lost control of his magia; the magia which confirmed Churan as a sorcerer. It had happened when he was very young, during a battle amongst two warring tribes. During that battle, magia had instinctively exploded from Churan, killing the intruders and saving most of his town.

Unfortunately, his blast had also killed many members of his own tribe in the process, including the grandparents that had been raising him.

Kallpa took him in when others were too frightened to lend their aid. He realized the difficult path that Churan would walk, but also recognized the potential of his abilities. The rareness of his magia made him special, someone that others would follow. Kallpa began rallying others from varying tribes to come meet the young sorcerer that stopped a village raid single handedly. Slowly, news of the "Warrior Child" spread. Kunaq and Lucia joined them from separate tribes as Churan's counselors, and Churan became a beacon of hope and a symbol of peace for his people. He was proud of that.

However, no matter how many shamanes, brujos, or brujas that they brought to him, he had yet to learn to control his magia. He tried, and he trained, but his skills were erratic at best. So, Churan knew that every single one of his counselors would have reminded him that the path of the Warrior Child was to bring peace to the realms, and that anyone who could teach him more about his magia was worthy of his respect.

And, at the very least, his attention.

But sitting there with the Danrayen mage, Churan couldn't keep his mind from wandering to Alric.

Alric had understood him better than anyone that he had ever met. Before him, his training was limited to etiquette and customs of varying tribes, of political strategy and diplomacy. As a vessel for peace, he was told that he should have manners beyond reproach. His companions in the Northern Tribes had not thought of teaching him the ways of combat or battle and were further ill-equipped to educate him in his magia.

Alric had been training him in both.

It wasn't much, as they hadn't had time for extensive lessons. But when the mage would pull Churan away each evening for their sessions, he would patiently explain the intricacies of magia, helping him practice basic control. Churan wasn't very good at it and would often get frustrated with his lack of progress. When he was ready to give up, Alric would have him rise and teach him how to properly throw a punch or dodge a blow. They would practice that instead, tiring his body until the anger at his own failures burned away from him.

Then, they would work on magia some more.

His progress had been slow, but Alric had never let him feel discouraged. A feeling Mage Nuna had provoked in him not five minutes into their first session.

"What is it that you can do already?" Nuna asked him.

He shrugged, which seemed to irritate her.

"Were you taught the basics? Can you move stones? Swirl water without touching it?" she pressed.

Churan began shrugging again, then caught Axchel's disapproving glare. He stopped the movement midway and cleared his throat.

"Only sometimes," he answered.

"How about fire magia?" she asked him. "Burning? Are you able to light fires?"

"Not consistently," Churan admitted, trying not to grind his teeth.

"Candles? Can you light a single candle flame?" she asked, placing a fat cream-colored candle in the center of a circle in front of them.

Churan took a deep breath and attempted to clear his mind, as Alric had taught him. He imagined what he wanted—lighting the single wick. He pulled energy from the surrounding air, imagining the invisible power as strands of light that he could shape with his mind. He pulled at it, layering each bit on top of the other, holding it in his mind's eye. Then, thinking of the blaze of light he wanted, he mentally flicked the power out towards the wick.

The candle exploded with a resonating crack, flinging burning blobs of melted wax every which way around them. They sizzled when their hot surfaces splattered against the cool stone floor, and Mage Nuna yelped and flung off some errant globs from her arm.

Churan could feel his cheeks burning in embarrassment.

"Not consistently," Churan repeated, wiping some stinging wax off his chin.

"I see," Nuna replied, scooting back from him. He didn't think she even noticed that she had done it, but it hurt.

"I did think that a sorcerer would have more control over his power," she admitted, ringing a bell. A young, pretty girl of around Churan's age entered the room and began cleaning the wax as soon as Nuna motioned to the mess.

"Even young magia users are able to light a single candle," Nuna continued, and Churan's ears burned as the young girl's eyes flickered to and away from him.

"I did light it," Churan answered sullenly, pointing towards a curled piece of wick that had detached from the exploding candle, now burning and smoking in an inelegant pile near them. He was fairly certain that he heard Axchel laugh at that, but he quickly disguised it as a cough.

"Hmm," was all the mage answered. Churan waited as the girl put out the small fires around the room, then finished cleaning. He realized, with a start, that she needn't touch the wax to peel it off the ground, but that it was being pulled from the floor by her magia. When she exited once again, Churan turned to Nuna.

"It's always like that," he said. "Sometimes the magia is barely enough to rustle a feather. In other moments, it is ten times more powerful than I intend. I don't know how to control it," he admitted ruefully.

"You must learn," Mage Nuna replied seriously.

Churan resisted the urge to roll his eyes.

If only I had thought of that, he thought to himself.

"I am trying," he answered instead.

"No, I don't think that you are," Nuna replied, almost dismissively, and anger prickled beneath his skin.

"I have been training as best I can since I was a child," he responded.

"You are still a child, so that means very little," she retorted. "You need more discipline."

"What do you suggest?" he asked through gritted teeth.

"You need to focus, for one thing. Not let your mind wander to playtime, or games, or sweets. You must fully decide to embrace your magia, then dedicate as much of your spare time to meditating and studying as possible."

Churan stared at her incredulously. "Do you think I am not dedicating myself to my training?" he asked.

"Clearly not well enough," Nuna responded, motioning towards the area where the candle had once been.

"I have known that I am a sorcerer and the Warrior Child for as long as I can remember," Churan answered angrily, practically vibrating with the unfairness of her words. "Magia users across the Northern Tribes were found and brought to train me. I have read every scroll and text we could find on the nature of magia users and sorcerers before me. I have tried to master my powers!"

"Not hard enough," Nuna insisted.

Churan sprang up to his feet, looming over the mage with every inch of his twelve-year-old frame.

"I am trying!" he yelled at her. "I am working as hard as I can! Alric saw that. Why can't you?"

"I am not Alric," Nuna replied cooly.

A stiff wind suddenly picked up in the room, spinning erratically around them and raising the strands of hair which had escaped Nuna's bun. They whipped violently across her face.

"No, you're not Alric!" Churan yelled at her, the wind increasing in pace. He saw Axchel jump to his feet. "You aren't half the mage that he is! I wish I had never come here! I wish I had gone with him instead!" The winds began picking up, and somewhere a shutter flew open, bouncing off the stone wall with a startling *bang*. Several more followed suit, but Churan barely noticed them.

It's not fair, he railed to himself. *How dare she talk to me like this! She doesn't know me at all.* He was in a new land with new people that were determined to judge him before even knowing him. His blood boiled with the injustice of it all.

"Niño!" the mage cried out as her body began sliding across the floor with the force of the winds. "Calm yourself!"

For a brief second, Churan was pleased to see her distress.

Good, he thought. *That is what you get.*

Then the boy looked up and saw that Axchel too was battling against the cyclone of wind, trying to reach him. The man did not look angry, or reproachful. Instead, he looked worried.

For me, Churan realized. Axchel wasn't just worried about what his errant magia was doing to the room or to Mage Nuna, but he was worried for *him.*

Just like that, the strength of his anger burst like a soap bubble. Shame flooded his body instead, and before he could face either of them, Churan turned and ran out the door and into the cool evening air. He panted, feeling, rather than seeing, the winds behind him dissipate. He didn't turn to see if they were all right, but began running towards the maze of the temple gardens. Faintly, he could hear the calls of Axchel and Nuna, but he ignored them, weaving between plants and ducking under low branches. He ran back towards the extensive temple gardens, hoping to find a quiet place where he could be alone, just for a while. Eventually, he found a thick old tree and made his way up the trunk, pulling himself from limb to limb until he was higher even than the temple walls.

Churan sat with his back against the rough bark, panting quietly. He embarrassed himself with his outburst, and even more by his lack of control over his magia. It wasn't the first time that a strong emotion triggered a burst of magia, and it seemed like his emotions were getting more and more unpredictable. Alric had talked to him about it a little, something about growing up and changes within his body. The conversation had made him blush without fully understanding why. Alric had told him they would talk about it more, that magia-users needed to always be aware of their feelings, especially when they were still learning restraint. It was dangerous for him to lose control like that. *He* was dangerous, and Churan knew that all too well.

Mage Nuna had been right. He wasn't working as hard as he could. Alric had recommended meditation as well, and he had tried. He really had! But he didn't like what came up when he did. Memories that he would prefer remained buried would surface, and he didn't want to think of them. So, for a while, he just pretended to meditate, trying not to fall asleep. He was pretty sure that Alric knew he had been faking it, but he hadn't confronted him about it.

Churan missed Alric.

If only I had more control over my magia, he thought bitterly, *then maybe I could have helped him.*

He ducked his head remorsefully, his black hair swinging forward to cover his eyes and cheekbones. He had gone over that day so many times. Alric lying unconscious and in pain, his skin swirling with the markings of magical corruption. Churan was a *sorcerer*. He was, by all rights, supposed to be the most powerful person in all the realms. At the very least, the most magically gifted one. He should have been able to draw the madness from him, somehow.

He should have been able to save him.

I must do better, he thought to himself. *If I couldn't help Alric, I must be ready to help the next one of my friends who may need it.* Churan was still a boy, but he was not so naive as to think that they all wouldn't face grave danger by the time they saw their quest through. It was up to him to keep them safe.

Nuna may not be Alric, but she can help, he decided. *And I will do better.*

Feeling determined—and oddly hungry after his outburst—Churan promised himself that he would be more mindful of his emotions and dedicate himself more fully to learning his magia.

He wondered to himself if his new resolve was as much a desire to get out of the tree and look for some food as honest repentance but decided that, as long as he truly resolved himself to change, it didn't matter as much what his true motivations were.

He just wouldn't tell Axchel the real reason for his return.

Thinking of Axchel, a knot of tension clenched in his chest. He dreaded facing him, and even more so Mage Nuna. He knew he had been childish. He decided that he would apologize to both her and Ax over his outburst, no matter how uncomfortable it would be. He would agree to meditate more, to do whatever other tasks Nuna believed would help him manage his magia better. He would get his power under control.

Decided, Churan lifted his chin and prepared to climb down. As he did so, he noticed a lone figure in the east, headed towards the town of Pelgar. He squinted, trying to bring the vision into better focus.

Monstros, he thought, terror gripping his throat. *The monstros were coming!* He needed to warn someone!

But as quickly as the terrifying thought came, it vanished, as he realized the figure was not moving toward the temple but, instead, was making its way into Pelgar. His shoulders relaxed ever so slightly, only to tense again.

Why would anyone head towards a town overrun with creatures from the Night Wood?

CHAPTER 19

RAWL

It had taken Rawl and Andu an entire two days to convince Mila that their plan was not "too reckless to be contemplated." Then, it had then taken them the better part of the week to work out all the logistics of how the quest would be handled.

"You can't go with us, Mila. As the Drowner, you need to be somewhere safe and quiet to keep us safe in turn," Andu was arguing with her again.

"I can manage from the water!" she argued … again.

"But it is easier and takes a lot less of your strength if you are not fighting the sea and the waves and performing the Drowning magia all at once!" he stressed.

"I don't like it," she grumbled for the hundredth time.

Rawl folded her up in his arms, still amazed that his younger sister was of the same height as him. He pressed his cheek against hers and her curls tickled his chin.

"Do you know how lucky I am?" he asked her. She tried to pull away to look him in the eye, but he held on to her. "Do you know how lucky it is that my hermanita, my baby sister, of all people, is the most promising mage of her year? Of this university? And that out of everyone in Tierramadri, I not only happen to know the person who holds the best chance for Alric, but that she just so happens to love me?"

"The best chance for Alric is the Archwizard Auberon," she muttered.

"The best un-imprisoned chance, then," he conceded, and she elbowed him in the ribs. With a chuckle, he finally released her.

"I know you don't like this," he said, schooling his laughter to look at her seriously. "But can you do this?"

Mila straightened and lifted her chin. "I can do this," she said.

"Then we go tonight."

A few hours later, Rawl, Mila, and Andu ended up in the one place Rawl never wanted to go—the submerged glass chamber in the underpart of the university tower. When they stepped into the room, with only glass separating them from the unrelenting and immeasurable expanse of the ocean, his skin prickled and his shoulders tensed. His entire body tensed, in fact, and he had to work hard to will his clenched fists to relax.

How am I meant to relax, he thought, *when all that keeps me from a watery grave is the same material as the cup Alric broke just this morning?*

He knew that there was magia involved as well, but it did little to ease his mind as he stared out into that great nothingness. A large hand landed on his left shoulder, nearly toppling him to the ground.

"If this is making you uncomfortable," Andu said with his characteristically cheery grin, "then you really aren't going to like it when we're out there," he finished, motioning to the dark sea.

"I'm trying really hard not to think about that part," Rawl admitted, which Andu seemed to find amusing. He laughed heartily and patted him on the back, sending Rawl stumbling a few steps forward before Andu caught him.

It was very late at night, or very early morning, depending on how one looked at things. The room was abandoned, which was good. Mila would need a quiet, secure spot to do her work.

"We are directly beneath the overlook ledge on the western side of the tower," she told them, though Rawl and Andu already knew. They had discussed their objective at length. But if it made Mila feel more confident to repeat their plan again, Rawl wasn't about to stop her.

"When you leave this room, I will wait exactly ten minutes and then begin shifting the water down to these windows. You'll be pretty wet until I can see you, but when I do, I will form an air pocket around the two of you that will move with your motions."

Rawl and Andu nodded. Andu looked excited by the prospect. Rawl thought he might be sick.

"The pocket will last about three hours, which should give you enough time to reach the ocean floor and walk the six miles to the artifact's area. When you find it, you need to start swimming up. The air pocket will understand your movements and bring you towards the surface, but it will take you more energy and, therefore, more oxygen, so try not to make any swimming motions before you absolutely have to."

They nodded again, Rawl feeling bile rise up in his mouth. He did his best to school his features so that Mila wouldn't know just how frightened he was.

It's for Alric, he told himself. *You're doing this for Alric.*

He swallowed back the gurgling acid in his throat and forced himself to stand straight.

"There will be a boat waiting for you to take you back once you surface," Mila said, and then turned very serious. "If you don't find the Goldenshell within the three hours, you *need* to surface."

She looked sternly at Andu, and then at Rawl. "Once the three hours are up, you only have a few minutes to swim up before the air runs out. So, no lingering, no waiting, no dawdling. If you can't find it, it's over and you come back. Do you understand?"

Rawl and Andu nodded once more.

"Of course, Mila," Andu assured her softly.

She took a deep breath.

"All right. Let's get started."

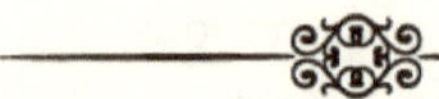

Rawl's breath was coming hard and fast, his chest constricting painfully with the effort of trying to keep up his pace. His heart was thundering against his ribs, and his legs were burning.

Andu was ahead of him by several strides, bounding up the winding tower stairs as if he were simply taking a leisurely stroll along a flowery meadow. It was hard to hear over his own wheezing inhales and ragged exhales, but Rawl was pretty sure that the giant wasn't even breathing hard.

Bastard.

Rawl's calves were cramping painfully, and the backs of his thighs were on fire. Even his glutes had begun burning, but he'd be damned if he asked Andu to stop or slow down. He knew they only had a certain amount of time to reach their designated location before Mila began Drowning.

They had left her on the floor of the submerged room, on top of a pile of blankets and pillows and furs. She would need to remain in a deep trance to keep her connection with them for the duration of the magia. Ordinarily, Andu had explained to him, she would be in the ocean itself, her feet, ankles, and even sometimes legs submerged to maintain the best possible connection. But there was a reason that the Drowning happened in groups. While the ocean was wonderful, it was also duplicitous and wild, and could never fully be trusted. Someone would have needed to stay with her, to ground her and pull her back from the waves if the tides decided to change.

There was no-one any of them trusted enough to pull into their plan, and together they decided that it was more important to have two people under the water. It was safer that way, in case one of the air pockets faltered.

So, Mila was the closest she could be to the sea without putting herself in unnecessary danger. Although Rawl remained skeptical about just how safe an underwater glass room could possibly be.

Which is how he and Andu found themselves on a large, jutting platform just above the ocean's edge, staring out into the indigo sea. Rolling waves struck the stones just below them, misting Rawl's face and clothing with a salty spray. It felt good against his flushed skin, and he briefly thought how nice it would be to submerge his aching limbs into that cool water. But then he realized just how volatile the waves were, and with how much force they were slamming against the rockface.

We're supposed to get into that? Rawl wondered. *We'll be killed, and this will all have been for nothing.*

"Any moment now," Andu said, staring intently at the violent, crashing water below them.

Rawl couldn't tell what he was looking for. At what moment were they meant to jump to their deaths? He opened his mouth to express his concerns to Andu when he noticed something in the space below the overlook.

Snapping his mouth shut, he leaned further against the banister.

Almost directly below them, the waves were slowing down. They were no longer crashing against the side of the tower with such force. They seemed to be suspended in time, still moving, but thickly and languidly, like the pouring of honey. After a moment, there was a section of water the size of a pond that was completely still, like a placid pool in the center of a raging storm.

"Quickly now!" Andu said happily, vaulting over the ledge with a single hand and dropping into the water below.

Rawl, who would have considered himself a very active, very fit individual, hauled himself over the ledge and dropped into the sea with all the grace of a baby fawn.

I have climbed trees my entire life, he thought to himself as he fell. *Mila and I have been performing acrobatics since we were children. How is this man so much stronger?* But, before he could finish his thought, the ocean reached up to meet him in a liquid embrace and the coldness of the water stole both his grumblings and all conscious thought away.

Rawl's body became completely submerged, his hair and clothing immediately clinging to his flesh. He kicked his already burning legs hard, internally laughing at himself for thinking that being in the water would somehow be soothing to them. His head broke the surface not a moment too soon. He had an instant to view Andu's sandy hair, pushed away from his face with a sunny smile lighting his features, before they began to sink.

It was as if they were ants floating on the top of a wineskin, and someone had poked a hole in the bottom of the leather. The water pulled them down, down, down, but Andu and Rawl remained at the top of that gentle pool, watching as a wall of water surrounded them on all sides. Rawl had a brief moment where he imagined whatever was holding the torrent of water at bay snapping and releasing, and how all of that violent turbulence would engulf him and Andu.

He quickly shoved those thoughts aside as they continued to descend. Finally, they slowed, and Andu swam over to him.

"Look," he said, turning Rawl slightly to his left.

Rawl gasped, then sputtered as he inhaled a small amount of water with the motion.

Directly in front of them was the submerged room. The glass stretched from their calm section of water, far to either side of the rolling sea. Mila had illuminated the lamps, powered by magia, of course, which lit both him and Andu, and the room within. Rawl could see his sister reclined on her mess of clothes and pillows. Her eyes opened into half slits. He could just make out the curve of her lips into a small grin when she saw them, and it looked like she tried to lift her hand to wave at them, but it only raised a small way from the cushion before flopping back down again. She then closed her eyes and Rawl could see the rise of her chest as she sucked in a deep breath.

Rawl knew that she was creating the air pockets for them, but it was a few minutes before he felt any change. It started small. He was suddenly more aware that he was wet. Which seemed silly to him. Of *course* he was wet, he was in the water. But he hadn't *felt* wet. Not until he noticed that there was a small space of air between his body and the water which had once fully encapsulated him. The clinging, dripping clothes suddenly felt cold and clammy against his skin in a way that they hadn't just moments before.

He looked up and saw that the pillar of air, created in their descent, was being slowly swallowed up again by the water. The starlit night sky slowly faded from view until nothing but the deep purple-black of the ocean remained. Rawl moved his arms, and saw that he was, in effect, at the center of a bubble. He could spread out his arms and the air warped around him, keeping him protected from the water. On instinct, he took a deep breath, just to ensure that he could. Andu, he realized, was in a bubble of his own, though his was much larger due to the man's size.

Then, once more, they began to descend. Rawl watched as the submerged room, along with his sister, was swallowed by darkness above him. Once they had lowered far enough that the light from the room dissipated completely, Andu did something which illuminated the area around their pockets of air. Finally, after what seemed like an eternity, their feet hit the ocean floor.

Andu motioned for Rawl's attention, then held up three fingers in front of him.

Three hours. They had three hours.

Rawl nodded his understanding, and Andu grinned, spreading his arms wide and turning in a circle. Rawl didn't need to hear him to understand what the big man was saying.

Isn't this incredible?

But Rawl was a man of the woods. He had been born and raised on solid ground, and he felt deeply and intrinsically connected to the earth. The ocean was beautiful, but unfamiliar to him. When he, Nova, Alric, and Axchel had traveled back from Cassalain to Andala on a ship, his feelings towards the sea had shifted from dazzling admiration to a healthy and respectful fear. When Alric had succumbed to sea illness, he had been more than happy to stay below deck with the man, rather than contemplate the seemingly endless expanse of unknown that was the ocean. Even cleaning out the sick bucket and mopping sweat away from the mage's brow had seemed better than staring out into its haunting depths.

The thought of Alric cut through Rawl's hesitation. It was on that trip that he and the mage had gotten closer. The fact that the man had allowed him to care for him, had wanted him by his side ... It was the moment Rawl began to have hope that the mage could feel what the archer felt for him.

He couldn't lose that.

With another deep breath, Rawl faced the ocean head on, and began walking towards his fears—and his salvation.

CHAPTER 20

NOVA

The following days were a flurry of planning and preparation for the High Priestess Ascension Ceremony. Since the battle of Pelgar, young initiates had been pulled from classes to help with building long barracks to house the displaced refugees. Slowly, the makeshift encampment, hastily erected to deal with the influx of civilians, had dissipated, leaving the training grounds empty once more. Instead of resuming combat practice, however, the space was quickly turned over to house the hundreds of people that would be in attendance for the ceremony.

The council meetings continued to be a contentious mess of differing opinions, with half of the priestesses supporting Damika's new role, with the others resenting it. As none of those opposed could figure out a better solution, the ceremony was proceeding as planned; but not everyone was happy about it.

General Vashti had been the most vehemently opposed to Damika's ascension, and so, Nova had thought for a while that the priestess hoped for the title herself. However, when someone suggested she take the position, Vashti had looked shocked and horrified.

"I am a soldier. A Warrior of Danray. I lead my girls in battle, not in the full path of Danray and all she has to offer," she had said. "No, not me. It should never be me. But nor should it be *her*."

The last sentence was, of course, directed at Damika. As always, Damika had neither defended herself nor argued. In fact, Nova couldn't help wondering if she didn't partially agree.

She needs to accept her new role, Nova thought to herself as she walked towards the temple infirmary. *She needs to embrace it, but acceptance would be a good first step.*

Despite the new housing for the Pelgar refugees, many were still being held in the infirmary. Most could care for their injuries on their own, or only came by to have the healers change bandages or to collect healing tinctures and ointments. Unfortunately, however, the monstro attack had left many people with far more serious wounds, external as well as mental and emotional. The priestesses were doing their best for each person, but there were many who needed care.

Stepping into the sickroom, Nova caught the sweet and woodsy scent of cinchona bark tea right before the scent of astringent, menta, and arnica burned the insides of her nostrils. She smothered a series of sneezes in succession against her sleeve, and when she looked up, she saw a clean cloth hanging in front of her watery eyes.

"Gracias," she told her benefactor, wiping her eyes before blowing her nose. It was only after she finished that she was able to see that the owner of the cloth was Axchel.

"Oh," she started, shoving the fabric deep into her pants pocket. There was no way she would return that to him! "Como estás?"

Axchel smiled at her, and she relaxed. "I should be asking you that, don't you think?"

The priestesses had given Axchel an unofficial place among the temple healers, spending much of his free time in the infirmary. He had earned the trust of the healers by routinely showing up in the encampment, and helping in whatever way he could, whenever he could. The priestesses had appreciated his consistency, as well as his acceptance of performing any tasks deemed necessary, no matter how difficult, strenuous, or off-putting they might be.

Nova was proud of his ability to carve his way into a small portion of Danrayen life, and how he did so in a way that earned him acceptance and respect among her sisters. Nova had thought that more would have their reservations about him, being not only a man but a former Cassalain soldier. However, his arrival with her and Damika had seemed to be enough to assuage the others.

Still, Nova found—to her surprise—that she missed spending time with him. There was not a lot of free time in war, and that seemed to be what it was that they were all preparing for. Even still, she rarely saw him outside of the council meetings, which were hardly conducive to a private conversation. Which is why she had stolen the time to seek him out now.

"Thank you," Nova answered him, motioning to the pocket which now held the soiled cloth. "But I am well. My nose just had to get used to the scents."

Axchel nodded. "We have spent the better part of the afternoon creating more salves and tonics, and the ingredients are strong. I don't smell anything anymore, which would have been useful back at my post at the Borders." He leaned in conspiratorially. "Soldiers are not best known for their impeccable hygiene."

Nova grinned at him. "I am well aware," she confessed. Then she looked around. "Are you busy? Is there somewhere you need to be?"

"No," Axchel said quickly. "Most of the pressing tasks are done. The new shift has already come in to relieve us. I was just finishing up some of the salves, so as not to let any materials go to waste."

"And Churan?" she asked, not having spotted the boy.

"Meditating in the temple gardens," he replied. "He has been much more diligent about it since, well, the incident."

Axchel had told her about how Churan had lost control of his magia in his first lesson with Mage Nuna. Axchel thought that Churan might be missing Alric, and that it had heightened his emotions. Nova's heart bled for him, as he wasn't the only one that missed the mage.

"I'm surprised you left him alone to do so in peace," Nova joked. In many ways Axchel had turned into a mother hen around the young sorcerer. A very large, very muscular mother hen.

As if sensing her thoughts, Axchel flushed. "I may have been a bit overprotective," he admitted sheepishly. "I am bound to him, to protect him. And I will, until my dying breath. But I also need to realize that may not mean shadowing the boy every hour of every day. That would not go well; for either of us."

His lips twitched in a rueful grin. "Besides, where could be safer than the interior of the Danrayen Temple?"

Nova grinned. "This is true."

"Did you need me for something?" he asked, and suddenly Nova felt shy. She resisted the urge to tuck down her chin.

"I thought, if you'd like, we could take a walk together?" she asked, feeling pleased when her voice did not waver. "Much has happened, and much continues to happen. We haven't had a lot of time ..." she let her voice trail off.

Time for what, exactly?

Luckily, Axchel saved her. "Of course!" he answered, washing his hands in a water basin. With his back turned, Nova quickly threw away the cloth she had blown her nose in and washed her own hands. She would feel better without having to think about the rag in her pocket.

"Vámonos?" Axchel asked, motioning to the door.

They walked aimlessly, neither of them speaking, but content to wander in quiet contemplation. The temple was as busy as always, young women dashing to and fro while priestesses taught lessons or congregated in small groups. Nova saw a group of Pelgar children playing with some of the younger Danrayen initiates. They rounded the small cottage that had been Mamá's home since Nova was a child. As they continued through a wide field of grazing horses, one came bounding up to them.

Nova gasped, feeling her heart flip over in her chest. "Azucar!" she cried out, opening her arms wide to let the mare nuzzle into her chest. The force of the horse's greeting nearly knocked her down, and she laughed, tears of joy leaking from her eyes.

"Y quién es esta belleza?" Axchel asked, rubbing the mare's forehead with his large hand.

"This is Azucar," Nova answered, feeling dazed. "She was my horse—well, not mine. Not really. But she was my favorite, and the one I chose every time I had a lesson. I didn't think she would still ..." Nova let her voice trail away.

"She's a fine old lady," Axchel murmured appreciatively. Azucar sniffed at their pockets for treats, and when she found none, she galloped back to the herd without so much as a backwards glance.

Nova laughed again. It was so typical of the mare. She was exactly as Nova had remembered.

"It's funny," she said, watching the horses graze. "I spent so long here. Lived so much of my life here. And I thought that it felt like home. It was more of a home than any other I had ever known. But I always held something of myself back from it. From my friends, and from this place. I was so convinced at the time that I didn't belong. And I knew that someday I would have to leave. So, I always had one foot out the door."

She stopped, but Axchel didn't interrupt her, seeming to understand that she had more yet unsaid.

"Now, I am back. My friends know the truth about me, and so do some of the priestesses. I took the Trial, and the goddess Danray herself accepted me as her own. This is, more than anywhere else, the place that I belong." Nova continued.

"But you don't feel it," Axchel said softly.

She turned to look at him. After a while, she shook her head.

"No," she finally admitted. "No, I still don't feel like I belong. I am Danrayen, but I was the Name-Bearer first. And my path should be that of Danray, but I first follow the Flowers. I feel ..."

"Divided?" Axchel suggested, and the tension in Nova's shoulders released.

"Yes."

Axchel nodded.

"I understand," he started, then frowned. "No, that isn't true. I couldn't possibly understand your situation. But I can understand what it feels like to be divided. Being half-Condori and half-Cassalain, I have never felt like I was enough of either. But when we found Churan, and his guardians allowed me to take the protective oath for him, I finally felt like there might be a place for me among the Northern Tribes."

He sighed. "And yet, even after receiving that confirmation, I am too much of my other half to feel fully at home there, even if I was finally welcomed to it."

Nova bit her lip. "Do you think that we will ever feel fully at home anywhere?" she asked him.

"No," he responded, meeting her gaze. "But I do think we will feel at home with the people we choose."

She thought of Alric and Rawl, of that last night in Tureene with Petra's family. She remembered watching Churan play with children his age, gossiping with Raidea and sharing ron with Axchel. A warmth blossomed in her chest at the memory.

"I think you are right," she finally responded.

"Is that why you sought me out today, rather than your Danrayen friend?" Axchel asked.

Nova slid her gaze away from him. "Which friend?" she asked. "I have several—"

"Damika," he cut in. "I have seen the way that she looks at you." He smiled ruefully. "I have seen the way she looks at *me*."

Nova had noticed it, too. Whenever Damika looked at Axchel, her face would scrunch as if she had bitten into a lime. Worse, in fact. Nova had seen Damika bite into limes after a shot of tequila, and she had far too much self-control to betray her expression. Yet she couldn't help it when it came to Axchel.

"I'm sorry," she told the man, though she wasn't quite sure what she was apologizing for.

His hand lifted to brush her cheek with the back of his fingers, and Nova shivered at the touch.

"Do you think it bothers me that she cares for you?" he asked softly. His fingers slipped back into her hair. "How could I fault her for the same feelings I possess?"

"I—" Nova started, then swallowed. She didn't know how to say what she felt, but luckily Axchel seemed to be able to read the pleading in her eyes. His own softened.

"Do you think that it bothers me that you care for her as well?" he continued, stepping closer to her. "I am Condori, meft royan. We do not believe in possessing a person, even your partners. Especially your partners," he explained.

Axchel ducked his head, and Nova could feel his breath tickling her lips.

"I don't ask you for all of your heart," he said. "Only a piece of it, if you care to gift it."

At that moment, Nova wanted that very much. Quieting the voices in her head for once, she raised up on to her tiptoes and closed the space between them, pressing her lips against his.

Chapter 21
Rawl

Rawl was not sure just how long he and Andu had been walking, but his best guess was that they were not too far from their three-hour deadline. And still, Andu showed no signs of stopping. Somewhere, high above them, the sun would start to rise soon, Tz'ola's rays illuminating and warming all the creatures on the surface.

Rawl couldn't wait to be among them.

The dampness of his clothing and the coldness of the sea floor had caused him to begin to shake. What had started as small, intermittent shivers had now turned into body-wracking shudders, his teeth chattering within his skull. He couldn't tell if Andu was experiencing the same, but he had seen the big man's lips change to lilac, then blue against his pale skin.

Worse than the cold, however, were the air pockets. As they had traveled, the space between their bodies and the water surrounding them had grown thinner and thinner.

They were running out of air.

Finally, Andu made a motion with his arms, and Rawl snapped his attention over to him.

Here, he mouthed. *We're here.*

They had made it! Rawl, who had been doing his best to not take in his surroundings during their long walk across the sea floor, suddenly began to really notice where they were. The floor below them consisted of compacted sand, rocks and vegetation. Rawl never thought of what kinds of plants could grow this far underwater, but had he done so, he didn't expect them to look as pretty as they did.

The men passed schools of fish and solitary creatures as they walked, but Rawl ignored them all as best as he could.

Fish, he decided, *were best served on a platter with limon, sal, y aji.*

Now that he was paying more attention, however, he found himself captivated by the variety of different sizes, colors, and patterns on each creature. The way they moved was fascinating as well, in undulating motions, or quick darts across the water. Turning in a slow circle, he took it all in, trying at the same time to find the promised sunken ship.

Andu, he saw, was making a slow scan of the ocean floor as well. Without speaking—because they couldn't anyway—they swept the floor in alternating rows, pacing back and forth and crisscrossing one another every so often. After a while, Rawl began to worry. After all, wouldn't a wrecked ship be immediately apparent to them? He did his best to hold out hope, but the longer that they scanned the seemingly infinite space, the more Andu's cheery smile began fading from his face. And more worrisome, the closer the air pockets got to their bodies.

They were running out of time.

The crushing weight of defeat began to relentlessly overtake Rawl. He had failed. This had been the best chance for Alric, his last chance, his only chance, and Rawl had failed him. He resisted the urge to sob, fearing that he would waste his last breath and find himself drowning in the heady mixture of the ocean's salty waters and his own tears.

Rawl's foot caught on something, and he stumbled, expelling a curse that was lost in the underwater silence. Andu was by his side in a flash, but Rawl waved him away. It had simply been a bit of uneven ocean floor, or a rock, or ...

The sandy ocean floor gave way beneath him.

Rawl didn't know one could fall while underwater, and yet there he was, tumbling down an underwater ridge. He found himself less concerned about his landing, since he *was* floating. But, for an instant, he felt panic bubble up in his chest at the rate of his descent. Briefly, Rawl wondered if he would be able to swim all the way back up to the surface by the time their hours were up. Then, with a jolt, he stopped falling, and he felt something solid beneath his feet once more. Looking down, he saw that he'd landed on a large piece of broken wood.

Rawl's eyes widened, and he looked up in time to see Andu following him down, but in a much more dignified way than Rawl had descended. When the man was finally standing beside him, they looked at one another in shock. Andu blinked several times in rapid succession, his mouth parted, looking much like the fish that swam around them. When they both looked back down at the wood, Rawl felt his jaw drop open as well.

It was a ship. It was a sunken ship. It had to be the one from the ledger Andu had found!

They hadn't seen it before, since the ocean floor crevasse hid it from their view. Had Rawl not fallen, they might have bypassed it altogether.

It was a medium-sized vessel, not as large as a trading ship, but larger than a fast transport one. Rawl thought it was rather the perfect size for a small pirate vessel, but of course, could not be sure.

Rawl spun in a slow circle, taking it all in. Submerged at an angle, sediment engulfed one-third of the vessel's hull. Once composed of solid wood, saltwater and age deteriorated and decayed the planks.

Parts of the deck and hull collapsed, and missing segments of the ship were now lost to time and the sea. More apparent was the abundance of corals, sponges, and algae that obscured the original shape of the ship. Rawl stepped carefully, afraid that even his floating form would be too much for the relic.

A part of him couldn't believe that it was really there. He had hoped, but also prepared for the fact that they might not find anything at all. But if the map was right about the sunken ship, then maybe Andu's letters had been right about the Goldenshell as well.

Andu waved his arms to get his attention, then pointed below. Then, mimed steering a large ship's wheel, and pointed below again.

Ah, the captain's quarters, Rawl thought. *Of course.* If the Goldenshell really was there, it would likely be in the captain's room.

He nodded to Andu, and together they looked for a safe way to descend to the lower decks.

It took longer than he hoped, as they had to move extremely carefully. More than once, Rawl felt the wood buckle beneath his feet, pulling his weight back before he could get injured. Finally, however, Andu found a set of stairs leading down. Marine life covered the steps, but they seemed solid enough to bear their weight.

Their air pockets grew even thinner.

Together, Rawl and Andu moved through the expanse of the ship. Rawl was not well-versed in ships, but he knew enough to guess that a captain's quarters would likely be in a strategic location that would provide easy access to the helm for quick command, but far enough away from common areas and other crew's quarters for privacy. Therefore, they should head towards the quarterdeck of the ship, close to the ship's wheel.

Andu seemed to have the same thought, for he moved past the long corridor of closed doors towards the ship's stern, ignoring all rooms clumped close together. It was all the better, as debris obstructed many of the doors, while rust ate at the hinges of others. Rawl would not have liked forcing their way into room after room and wasting valuable time just to check their contents.

Eventually, the corridor split, leading to the left and right of the vessel. Rawl and Andu shared a look. Rawl knew neither of them were eager to split up, but since their time was short, they both reached a wordless agreement with a terse nod. Andu went left, Rawl right.

Rawl passed another set of stairs leading even further down as he prayed to the dioses that he would not have to descend even further into the wretched ship. He continued forward instead, rounding a corner when the path demanded it.

And was almost hit right in the face by an enormous animal.

It came right for him, its long, sinuous body undulating side to side and almost whacking Rawl with its long tail. Rawl stumbled and fell onto his rear, heart hammering hard, his breaths expelling in frantic pants. He could almost see the air pocket diminishing round him.

The sea creature turned around in the hallway, a cumbersome feat as its body was long and wide, and the space small in comparison. It still managed it quicker than Rawl would have liked, before it began advancing towards the archer once again. Its mouth opened as it swam, baring rows of jagged, and extremely sharp-looking, teeth. Rawl managed to temper his panic long enough to mark the thing's movements, making quick mental calculations.

Not yet, not yet, he said to himself. Even his inner thoughts became difficult to hear over his hammering heart.

Then, when the creature was close enough that Rawl could swear he could smell its acrid, fish-rot breath, he whirled, pressing himself against the wall of the corridor, forcing it to continue a few strides before maneuvering its awkward turn once more. With the creature occupied, Rawl scanned his surroundings, looking for something, anything, that would keep him from becoming the animal's next meal. He saw a section of particularly rotted wood underneath what was once a glass porthole. He lunged for it, grasping the wood and prying it up with great effort. It strained and buckled but did not fully snap.

Rawl felt the movement of water behind him but refused to turn around to see how close he was to death. Instead, he braced his feet against the wall and pulled with all his might.

A piece of old wood broke from the old window. It was not very large, but at least it was sharp. Rawl used the momentum of the break to swing his arms around, directly into the face of the sea creature.

The spiky end of his makeshift weapon landed with near-perfect accuracy, just under the creature's left eye. It was not enough to kill it, or even blind it, but Rawl thanked Padir that it was enough to distract the beast. It shook its head violently and dashed further down the corridor, escaping to the open ocean through a large gap in the ship's wall.

Rawl stumbled backwards, knocking open a door and falling into the room. Bracing his hands against the floor, he worked to steady his breathing, sucking in quick gasps through his mouth. It took longer than he liked to regain composure, but when he finally felt like he wasn't on the verge of passing out, he hauled himself up and took in where he was.

Directly in front of him, the large door he had knocked into had fallen from its hinges, and he found himself in a large and once opulent room.

He had found the captain's quarters.

Chapter 22

Rawl

Rawl walked into the room, careful not to trip over the tumbled ottoman. Or the fallen chair. Or the overturned desk.

There were ragged scraps of what might once have been books scattered around the room, as well as an impressive amount of rusted weapons. Rawl's initial thought, that the vessel would have made a good pirate ship, suddenly seemed to have more merit.

There were wooden frames on the ground, but whatever art they once displayed had long withered away. Algae and a thick coating of barnacles covered what was once a bed. He scanned the space slowly, searching for some sort of safe or lockbox. None was readily visible, but this didn't deter Rawl.

As best he could, he began shifting items in the room, searching for Alric's last hope. It was slow, but he refused to be deterred. Finally, he reached the remnants of what appeared to be an old bookshelf that had toppled after a plank of wood had collapsed from the ceiling. Squatting to peer under it, the edge of a chained lockbox suddenly became visible.

Rawl's heart surged in his chest, and he reached forward, gripping the chains. He tugged at it, but the heavy wood beam kept the box firmly immobile. He turned, placing his back against the fallen bookshelf and pushing with all his might, but it didn't even wobble.

A flash of motion caught his eye and Rawl turned in time to see Andu stepping into the room. Apparently, after not having found anything on his end of the ship, he had come to seek out Rawl. The archer motioned wildly, pointing to the lockbox underneath the shelves and heavy wooden beam.

Andu's eyes shone, and he made a triumphant motion with his arms, crossing over to help Rawl retrieve it.

Together, Rawl and Andu attempted to lift the wood, straining and heaving with all their might, but not even with the giant could they manage to lift it. Desperately, Rawl began scouring the area for something that they could use for a lever, when suddenly the light that had been surrounding their air pockets flashed three times.

Andu jerked his head towards Rawl, his eyes full of panic. He motioned up towards the surface.

We need to ascend, Rawl knew he was saying. *Now!*

Rawl stubbornly shook his head. He knew that he was being stupid and reckless, but they almost had it! He wasn't going to leave now, not when they were so close. They couldn't just leave and return for it later. Mila would take days to recover after this bit of magia, and Alric did not have days.

Rawl found a length of metal, possibly a staff, or a weapon of some kind? Whatever it was, Rawl slid it free from where it lay, half under the bed. Then he maneuvered it underneath the larger plank of wood and began to push.

Andu tugged on his arm, but Rawl shook him off.

Help me, he mouthed, pointing at the lever.

Andu froze for a moment, looking up towards the collapsed roof of the room. Then, with a look of pure determination, he, too, grasped the plank. As Rawl pushed down, he pulled from underneath. Slowly, the wood began to shift. It was almost imperceptible at first, so subtle that Rawl thought it was just wishful thinking. Then it moved.

As the plank slid off the bookshelf, it seemed to collapse on itself, relieving the buried box. Andu dove forward to dig it out of the sediment that had collected around it. As he tried to jerk it loose, Rawl clasped the chains in his hands, grunting silently as he strained to unearth the thing. It came away in a moment, launching Rawl backwards, where he floated through the water for a breathless moment. Then, Andu's hands were clasping the fabric behind his neck, and they were moving through the long corridor once more.

They reached the stairs just as the air pockets' light flashed again, twice this time, and Rawl could see the space between the ocean and his skin was less than a fingers-width apart. They sprinted up the steps, far less worried about their integrity than they were on their way down. Once they were on the upper deck of the ship again, they began to swim upwards as quickly as they could.

Rawl kicked his legs desperately, the pain of climbing the university's stairs long forgotten as a new, burning pain enveloped him from foot to thigh. He refused to use his arms, worried that if he slackened his grip on the lockbox for even a second, their prize would slip and sink back to the bottom of the sea. But the weight of the thing pulled him down, and he had to work twice as hard to move half as much distance as the bigger man.

Andu noticed, grabbing on to him and helping him to maneuver up. Once they moved far enough away from both the ship and the ocean floor, it was difficult to determine just what was up and what was down, so Rawl was grateful for the bigger man's guidance. He kicked and kicked and kicked, and tried not to panic when the light flashed, a single, solitary time. The space of air between him and the water was like the skin of an apple, the rind flush against his skin.

Then the light extinguished.

Rawl had time for one last little gasp of breath before the water was over him, on him, all around him. At the first icy onslaught he almost screamed, remembering only at the last second that he needed every bit of air he had left. He no longer felt the weight and pressure of Andu's hand, and without the light, he could not see a thing. His eyes burned with the sting of salt, and he squinted against the pain, against the dark, continuing to kick. He could only hope the big man was doing the same.

His lungs burned, they ached, they screamed. His throat constricted, the apple in his throat bobbing with desperation to breathe. Just breathe, he needed to breathe! He struggled, holding the box tight against his chest, moving and moving and praying to all the dioses that he was moving in the right direction. He had no idea how close the surface was. For all he knew, they hadn't even made it halfway up before the air faltered. For all he knew, he was swimming back down to the ocean's depths.

He could use his arms to speed up his ascent, but he knew he would sooner die than let it go again.

His kicks slowed, and so did his heartbeat. It was as if his body knew that the end was near.

Just breathe, he thought again. *It'll be over soon.*

He opened his mouth ...

And his head broke through to the surface. Rawl sputtered, half of the seawater already making it down his throat and into his lungs. He hacked and coughed and spat, still kicking to keep his head above water. He turned, still wheezing, and to his great relief, saw Andu swimming towards him.

"Thank the dioses!" he said hoarsely, his wet hair plastered against his forehead. "Come on, the boat is just behind you."

Rawl whirled, and sure enough, not far from their location was the small fishing boat Mila had bribed to meet them out here. Rawl would have expected the fisherman to look horrified at their sudden appearance, but living near the Mage University must have desensitized him to the eccentricities of mages, for he simply threw them a rope and helped them haul their way onto his boat. When Rawl and Andu were both on, sprawled over one another like a heap of puppies, he calmly began rowing back to shore.

The sun was just peeking above the distant tree line.

"You kept it?" Andu said suddenly, his voice full of awe.

With an effort, Rawl turned his neck to look at him, but he wasn't looking at Rawl at all. He was staring at the chest.

"Oh," Rawl said dumbly.

"You held on to it, even when you needed to swim up?" Andu asked incredulously.

Rawl waited until he met his eyes.

"You would have, too," he said simply, knowing it in his heart to be true.

Andu opened his mouth, then closed it. Finally, he nodded.

"I would have."

The rest of the trip back to the shore was quiet, both men too exhausted to do anything more than lie there. Rawl thought he might have even fallen asleep for a moment, the type of sleep fueled by exhaustion where you think that you are still awake, but your body shuts down to preserve you as best it can. The fisherman seemed unbothered by neither the state the men were in nor their silence, and luckily ignored them for the duration of the trip. He broke his silence only when they were near a small wooden dock south of the university tower, when he made a low grunt.

Rawl and Andu took that as a sign to lift themselves from the fishing boat's floor. Rawl absently noticed that it, and now he and Andu, smelled heavily of fish. It spoke to the level of his exhaustion that he hadn't noticed until then.

As the fisherman was tying off the boat, a figure emerged from the main road, turning down the path towards the dock. It was just a dark blur at first, but then revealed itself to be Mila, flushed and wild and panting from running. She reached Rawl first, throwing her arms around him. His own arms became pinned between them as he still clung to the box.

"Oh, thank the dioses," she breathed. "Thank the dioses that you're all right!"

She let him go abruptly and vaulted onto Andu, legs wrapped around his thick waist. One hand clasped her on the back of her thigh, the other cradled the back of her head.

"We're fine, Mila mia," he murmured into her hair. "We're all right."

Rawl looked away, swallowing against the lump in his throat at the sight of them. He still wasn't sure what was between his sister and the large man, but the easy intimacy between them made his heart ache for the person who he wished he could hold in that way.

When Andu finally released Mila, she turned back to Rawl, and her eyes widened like two big Tinamou eggs.

"Did you—" she gaped at the chest. "Is that?" she asked.

"We did it," Rawl said, a sliver of hope breaking through his exhaustion. "We got the box."

"Should we?" Andu started, but Mila shook her head.

"Not here," she said. "Let's get back to the university."

Andu and Rawl looked at one another in alarm, then to the path that led to the main road, the university tower jutting out proudly in the distance.

"Walking?" Rawl asked in horror, then watched Andu's face fall as Mila sheepishly nodded.

With a long-suffering sigh, they began their trek back.

CHAPTER 23
DAMIKA

The night was dark, and the moon hid shyly behind floating smudges of clouds. Damika knew that she should be wary of the salta-sombras—Night Wood creatures hidden in shadow—but on nights like these she found she feared nothing.

Damika knew that wasn't normal. She knew it probably wasn't right. But the cool lack of emotion helped her stay sharp and alert, and, where she was going, she needed to be both. There would be time for emotion once she made it to her destination.

Her footsteps fell softly, the grass and foliage under her feet wet enough that they sprang back quietly, rather than crinkling beneath her. She slipped like a wraith from tree to tree, sometimes crouching and stretching her long legs in lunging steps close to the ground. When she reached the river which marked the edge of Pelgar, she stopped.

The monstros were apparent from where she stood.

Every day, more and more left, always heading south, but the village was still overrun. Damika wasn't sure when the people of Pelgar could safely return, but even when it was empty of the creatures, rebuilding would be a long and arduous process.

From a distance, Damika could hear growls and hisses, high pitched keening and grunts. She saw the shadows of the demon dogs, noticed a low slithering mass of something that looked like an enormous snake.

The snake-like monstros of the Night Wood, known as culebretos, could range in size from a standard garden snake, to a massive being that resembled the dragons of elder lore. She looked up towards the sky, and in the tiny slivers of moonlight that were allowed to peek through, she could see winged creatures circling the buildings above. The stench reached her even there, sickly sweet rot and sweat, coppery blood and the undeniable aroma of death. She made herself inhale shallowly at first, then deeper and deeper until she could take a normal breath. The scent remained, but she shoved it away to the back of her mind, where it could not affect her. It was incredible what the human body could become accustomed to. Once she could breathe without a pang of nausea, she began preparing herself.

Now, she thought. *Now.*

Damika allowed all the walls she built around herself to drop. Some were easy to discard, like her pretense that she didn't begrudge the Cassalain who had come into their midst. She knew that Axchel's presence was not something that she should be angry about. That compared to the other, sharper griefs in her life, his mere presence was an inconvenience at most. But she didn't have to be Sensible-Damika, here in the dark. Here, at the edge of a monstro-ridden village, she could feel everything that she held at bay during the day. So she allowed herself to hate him, at least for the moment. To resent his presence and his closeness to Nova.

She thought of all the people of Pelgar. Of all the villagers who were not fast enough, or just lucky enough, to have escaped to the temple. She thought of them being taken down by the Night Wood creatures, screaming and crying, their loved ones forced to watch. She imagined the young Danrayen women—warriors, priestesses, and initiates alike—who risked their lives to help them, battling through the throngs of people and monstros to slay as many as possible. She thought of the eight girls who hadn't made it, who returned to their goddess.

She thought of Nessa. Of their tumultuous reunion, and the shaky new ground on which their relationship stood. She internally railed at the Flowers, messengers of the dioses and proclaimers of prophecy that had done nothing but ruin lives for decades. Probably longer.

She thought of Raidea. She imagined her as she had last seen her friend, stretched out on a kitchen table, her usually lively, light-filled features dull and devoid of emotion. Empty and lifeless.

And Damika thought of Adira. She thought of her High Priestess, abandoning the safety of the temple walls to aid in the fight. She remembered her as she last saw her, the woman's skin tinged with purple poison. She thought of her long ago, as Jesadirany, the young, scared girl that had fallen in love with a boy, down in that very town. She thought of the baby she had created with that boy.

And how she had decided to give her away rather than raise her.

Damika allowed the rage to fill her, swelling her heart with thick, hot ire that bubbled from her chest to her belly and thighs. It rose up like water in a well until it overflowed, saturating her body with its force. She let the anger spread, warming her biceps and forearms, clenching her hand around the hilt of her blade so hard that her fingers became white.

By the time she strode purposely down the path to the Pelgar bridge, her anger had her by the throat, gripping her with stinging dark talons. So, when a creature jumped out from behind the cover of a tree, Damika didn't even pause, but simply cut it down with a deep, guttural growl. Burning, sticky blood spattered on her cheek, but she barely felt it. By then, her limbs had a mind of their own, propelling her towards the town. She didn't even pause to look at what sort of monstro it had been. It didn't matter, because it was dead now.

A reptilian creature lunged from the inky darkness of the river, snapping at her with a protruding snout and needle-sharp teeth, but Damika vaulted above it, slicing a long gash across the thing's back. It screeched as she twisted in the air, landing to face it. She had an impression of a mutated cayman before she plunged her blade deep in and out of its right eye.

The lizard's call attracted more creatures, as two demon dogs sprinting out from the cover of Pelgar's outermost buildings. They ran up to her, snarling, long strings of drool dripping from their grotesque snouts. Damika pulled two daggers from the harness on her left thigh, twirling her Danrayen blade in her right palm. She threw both knives simultaneously, flicking her fingers so that one would veer left, the other right. The dog on the left yelped in pain as the blade struck and lodged itself in the creature's neck. The one of the right dodged, its clawed paws sliding on the tiled pathway, Damika's blade narrowly missed its leathery flesh.

The distraction was enough. Damika ran, coming around the first demon to her left, rolling over its back, sliding her blade underneath its head to slit the thing's neck in the process. Her momentum carried her over its falling body, and she rolled towards the one that remained. By then, it had regained its balance, raising up on its hind legs to bellow at her. Damika jumped forward, sprinting at it head on. At the last moment, before its swinging arm could slice through her chest, she slid, gliding under it as it lunged towards her. The tip of her blade found its mark, just below the creature's ribs, dragging it down to open its belly. She was back on her feet before the flesh could open, missing the spilling blood and entrails she left in her wake.

Damika picked up one of the discarded knives as she assessed her surroundings. More monstros were coming now, slinking from dark alleyways, jumping down from rooftops and balconies. Above her, the moon peeked through her veil, only to be obscured again by dark, flapping wings. She could see several creatures rounding her as they all attempted to surround her.

Damika readjusted her grip on her weapons, and smiled.

Chapter 24
Rawl

Rawl wanted to open the lockbox right away, of course. If it did, in fact, contain an item that could help counteract Alric's Mage Madness, he wanted them to attempt it as soon as possible.

Andu, affable as ever, conceded, even though Rawl could see just how exhausted the big man was. Still, he knew how important this was to Rawl, and the archer suspected that Andu would sacrifice much of his comfort for those he cared about. He felt guilty for pushing, but the need to confirm whether the box contained the Goldenshell eventually won out.

In the end, it was Mila who convinced him to wait.

"You are both dead on your feet," she chided. "I have seen dried seaweed with more life than you."

When Rawl opened his mouth to argue, she held up a hand.

"And I am just as drained. Do you think that box will be simple to open?" she demanded. "Do you think, after all of that, we will not require magia to discover its secrets?"

Rawl glanced down at the lockbox, secured tightly with silver chains, sitting on top of their workroom table.

"I have no more magia to spare today. Neither does Andu," she added. "And, last I remember, you don't have magia at all."

Rawl's shoulders slumped, and he gave an acquiescing nod.

"So, we eat, and we rest," she continued firmly. "And the two of you, for the love of all dioses, bathe. You smell like a fish market."

Rawl hadn't believed that the excitement over the success of their quest would allow him to sleep, but after a warm bath and a hearty meal, he fell into a heavy, dreamless sleep before his head hit the pillow. He awoke sometime in the late afternoon feeling dizzy and groggy, confused as to where he was.

When he was finally able to drag himself from his pallet and into the hall, the hope and emotion over their find began bubbling back in his chest.

We found the box, he thought giddily. *We found the shell.*

Calma, another voice chided inside his head. *Nothing is confirmed yet.*

But by the time he reached the workroom, the hope had spread, warming him from heart to limb.

Andu and Mila were already awake, Mila pouring over some old scrolls, and Andu staring at Mila. He wasn't awkward about it, or obtrusive. He simply gazed at her with a quiet reverence. As if he could not imagine anything else in the world more pleasing than to simply look at her.

Rawl cleared his throat.

Mila looked up from her scrolls, and Andu snapped out of his revelry, shooting Rawl an easy smile.

"How do you feel?" Mila asked him, her tone all worried older sister, despite her being several years younger than him.

"Fine," he said. "Better," he amended ruefully. "Have you two been up long?"

"Just woke up myself, not five minutes before you did!" Andu told him happily, tossing him an orange. Rawl managed to catch the fruit, but not before it hit him in the chest, forcing a pained grunt from him. Andu didn't seem to notice.

"Gracias," he said, fishing a knife from his boot to cut it into slices. "Have you ..." he said, angling his head towards the chest.

"No," Mila said, shaking her head. "We thought we'd wait for you."

"Gracias," Rawl repeated, feeling relieved. He wanted to be there if, *when* they managed to open it.

Excitement had him abandoning the cut up fruit and crossing to the table in a few quick strides.

The box was about the size of a vegetable crate and made of some sort of metal, with fat studs sealing piece to piece against one another. Small barnacles and tiny shells clung tight to its smooth planes, thickly clustered on two sides with a spattering of smaller seashells across its top. Idly, he tried to pry one away with his fingernail, but it clung on tightly. Tentatively, Rawl lifted the entire thing and turned it in his hands, noticing it felt less heavy than it had in the water, which was strange. He hadn't thought of it as he desperately swam for his life, but it was almost as if the box hadn't wanted to leave its watery home. When he flipped it to look at the bottom of the box, he noticed that it had similar fastenings on the sides, making it impossible to pry open.

It will have to be opened from the top, then, he thought.

As he maneuvered the box in his hands, the chains that held it closed together slid and rattled gently. They were tight enough that they only slipped a little bit at a time, staying fairly flush to the edges of the case. After hours on land, it was dry, but still felt cold to the touch and smelled heavily of seawater and marine life.

"How do we start?" Rawl asked, looking at his sister as he set the chest down again.

Mila chewed on her lower lip as she regarded him. "There is a complex opening spell that requires a lot of energy and quite a few materials, but Andu and I can collect them all from the classrooms upstairs after the instructors have retired for the evening. We are free to take materials without asking permission, but it would be best that they didn't ask too many questions about what, precisely, we needed them for. We'll have to wait a few more hours, of course, but it seems the best course of action. If that doesn't work, then I suppose—"

A loud, crunching noise interrupted her musings, and both she and Rawl jumped. They turned their attention to Andu, who stood with a pair of large pliers in hand, a length of chain broken off and trailing across the wooden table. He moved to a second chain, placed it into position between the two large pieces of metal, and then squeezed the handles shut. The loud, grinding sound assailed them again, Rawl wincing at the way the noise seemed to scratch at the inside of his brain. Another chain fell free.

"Abuelo always told me that, when faced with a problem, you should always try the simplest things first, then work your way up to the harder ones," he said, squeezing down on the handles once more. When he released them, the chain he had snipped slithered down the box and off the table, landing with a heavy clinking sound on the floor.

"That way, you save your energy. And a lot of things require simpler solutions than we place on them," he continued.

There were only two chains left. Rawl watched in rapt silence as he snipped one, and then the last.

The box lay bare on the table.

Rawl glanced at Mila. "Surely it can't be so easy as lifting the lid?" he asked uncertainly.

"Most definitely not!" Mila gasped, scandalized. "We have no idea what is inside it, or if the box itself is cursed! What if the person who opens it dies on the spot? Or their hands turn into dust? Or they are doomed to turn everything they touch forevermore into barnacles or sand? What if—"

Andu opened the lid of the box, and both Rawl and Mila sprang back as if struck by lightning.

Andu examined his hands. "They haven't crumbled to dust yet!" he remarked genially.

Mila sprang forward and punched the big man on the biceps. He leapt back with a yelp, clutching his arm. Rawl imagined it was more from surprise than pain, as he wasn't sure that a boulder launched from a catapult could penetrate the man's enormous muscles.

"What was that for?" Andu asked Mila, pouting.

"For being a complete, utter, estupido. Quien te crees? Te crees invencible?" she threw up her arms and stalked away from him, only to whirl back and shove a finger into his face. She had to reach her arm up pretty high to manage it, but she made it happen.

"Never do that again. Do you understand me? You have to *think*, Andu!"

"Um, amiges?" Rawl said.

"When will you learn that sometimes you need to think before you act?!" Mila continued, ignoring Rawl.

"Mila, Andu," Rawl tried again, stepping closer to the table, his eyes fixed on the box.

"And all right, I will admit that opening the box did not, in the end, use the great amounts of magia that I originally thought that it would, but dammit Andu you didn't know that you wouldn't blow us all up by what you just did!"

"OYE!" Rawl yelled, making Mila and Andu startle.

He pointed to the inside of the open box.

"Is that it?" He was unable to hide the disappointment in his voice.

Mila and Andu joined him at the table, peering down at their treasure.

Inside the box lay a single oyster shell. Not a golden oyster shell, or a glowing clam shell, or an oyster shell with iridescent, pulsating magia. Just a plain, simple, regular oyster.

Rawl's knees buckled, and he landed hard on the floor, knocking some of the wind from his body. It didn't matter to him, not when the sight of the simple shell robbed him of any hope.

"Don't try to convince me that that shell has magia," he said, his voice tired. "Don't tell me that that is the Goldenshell. I won't believe it."

"Rawlly," Mila started softly, but Rawl drew up his legs and buried his face against his knees.

"All that work. All that effort, wasted." Then, quieter, he added, "He's going to die."

"Maybe not," Mila said, with enough conviction in her voice that Rawl lifted his head reluctantly. She held the oyster in her hands.

"Pass me your knife," she told him, and he grabbed it from his boot again by the hilt, flicking it towards her in an easy, practiced motion. She caught the blade between her fingertips like she had done hundreds of times in their childhood. Andu gasped, one hand fluttering to his throat in horror, the other reaching out to Mila. She waved him off.

"What if it wasn't the shell itself?" she asked, more to herself than to them. "That's the thing about myths, right? They are old. They are passed on orally over time." Carefully, she wedged the knife tip into the narrow crack of the shell. "What if it wasn't the shell at all? What if the shell was just the protection?"

She strained, continuing to wiggle the knife carefully. "After all, don't you think a shell is a strange proposal token? It wasn't a simple token of affection, but a marriage request. What if —" and with a soft crack, the oyster shell split open. Removing the knife, she wedged the pads of her fingers against the sharp edges and pulled them apart. A burst of light emerged from the parted sides, moving like smoke and curling over Mila's hands before dissipating. As the smoke faded, the inside of the shell became clear.

In its center lay a perfectly round, perfectly smooth, perfectly golden pearl.

Chapter 25

Rawl

Rawl found himself standing in the middle of the great Andalan forest.

After spending so much time journeying away from it, it felt strange to be back. The forest had always been his domain, his joy, his refuge. The tree canopies were as lush and verdant as ever, and his boots rested on top of a carpet of springy moss. Toucans grunted in the distance, and the rustling of the leaves in the thick undergrowth was so familiar it should have been comforting. Instead, standing there, while Alric continued to wither away in the bowels of the Mage University, it suddenly didn't feel much like home anymore.

Rawl, Mila and Andu stood in a small clearing, facing each other in an uneasy triangle. Andu held the pearl, swallowed up in his meaty fist. Despite Mila chastising him for not taking caution when handling the lockbox, he had still reached forward and plucked the golden pearl from the open shell the moment Mila had uncovered their treasure. She had gritted her teeth in exasperation, but when Andu hadn't melted, or turned into solid gold, or disintegrated, she had merely expelled a long-suffering sigh.

"Not here," she had said. "We don't know what it does. We best not be in the university when we try to figure it out."

Which is how they found themselves in the middle of the woods, staring down at the pearl, looking impossibly small in the vast width of Andu's palm.

"It's pretty," Andu remarked. "I could fashion a chain for it, and you could wear it around your neck," he told Mila with a shy smile.

Mila looked at him incredulously. "It's an item of power, tonto! Not a pretty trinket. We need to know what it's capable of!"

"Oh," Andu mumbled, the sides of his neck going red under the day's growth of stubble. "Of course."

"It is pretty, though," Rawl admitted, taking pity on the big man. Andu flashed him a grateful smile.

"So, what should we do?" he asked, turning back to his sister.

She frowned at the pearl, then opened her pack and pulled out a small leather journal. "I checked out the Olmo Scroll from the university while you two were sleeping. It details all of the steps for getting an object to reveal its power. The scroll is ancient, and not in the best condition, and the librarian swore she'd turn me into a bookshelf if I damaged it, so I copied it all down."

Andu looked horrified. "Can she do that?" he asked her, his voice barely more than a whisper.

Rawl could see Mila struggle to keep from rolling her eyes. "Andu, you are a mage in training. You know that you cannot turn a living being into an inanimate object."

"Trees were once living beings, but they get turned into wood for bookshelves all the time," Andu countered.

Rawl barked a laugh. "He has you there, hermana!" he said.

"Not by magia," she seethed at them, glaring. "Now, can we get to work?"

Mila had Andu place the pearl in a small earthenware bowl that also came from her pack. It sat, fat and glimmering in the sun, the light bouncing off its surface as it moved between the leaves above them.

"Stand back," Mila whispered, and Rawl and Andu hastened to obey. Then she extended a trembling hand, pointing her index and middle finger towards the bowl and the item inside. Then, without warning, she yelled out an unintelligible word, so loudly that several birds flew from their tree perches and flapped frantically into the air, as large crashes were heard in the dense forest around them. Andu startled and moved towards Mila, tripping over a raised tree root and falling on his face. Rawl reached for his bow, forgetting for a moment that he had left it behind, and grasped nothing but air.

Then, the forest was quiet again, and Mila looked between the two of them, eyebrow raised.

"Perdon," she murmured evenly, but Rawl knew her well enough to hear the amusement beneath her tone. "Perhaps I should have warned you."

"Perhaps," Rawl replied through gritted teeth. He reached an arm out to help Andu back up, but the giant pulled so hard that he almost tumbled Rawl to the ground with him. Somehow, they managed to right themselves and stand once more.

Rawl looked expectantly at the pearl, but it lay unaltered in the bowl. He glanced at his sister, but before he could ask, she spoke.

"Well, that didn't work," she said. "But there are a lot more steps to try."

And try they did.

There were more words hurled at the pearl, but they did nothing but further disturb the peace of the forest. There were more complicated spells involving leaves and powders and tonics, rubbed on Mila and Andu, then on the bowl or sprinkled on the pearl itself; but to no avail. One potion released a noxious green vapor that had the three of them coughing and sputtering, making them move away from the clearing and drink deeply from their water skins before returning to their work. One spell cracked the earthen bowl but left the pearl unmarred and untouched on a curling brown leaf, its secrets intact. The sun began falling on the horizon, and still they had no answers.

"We will try again tomorrow," Andu told Rawl kindly as he helped Mila pack away their materials.

Rawl felt too numb to answer.

"There are still things left on the list to try, aren't there, Mila mia?" Andu continued, looking towards Rawl's sister.

She didn't respond, only pressed her lips closed into a tight line. Rawl couldn't find it in him to care.

Is this what it feels like to give up? he thought, emotionless.

Mila was bending down to scoop up the pearl when Andu suddenly grabbed her by the arm, hauling her backwards. He swept out an arm to keep Rawl back as well.

"Ow, what are you doing?" Mila demanded, shoving against him. She might as well have been pushing a mountain. Rawl looked up at the absolute terror on the man's face. Finally, he felt something. A cold chill of fear trickled up Rawl's spine.

"What is it?" he whispered to the man.

Wordless, Andu pointed at a long shadow.

Rawl and Mila exchanged confused glances.

"The shadow?" Rawl asked, his voice a little louder this time.

"Look at the other shadows," Andu said breathlessly.

Rawl looked. The sun had been steadily sinking throughout the long hours, and all the tall trees surrounding their clearing were casting dark, lengthened shadows pointing to the left of them.

The shadow that Andu was referring to, however, was stretching straight towards them.

Rawl jumped backwards, but Andu grabbed him, shaking his head.

"It's a salta-sombras!" Rawl hissed, gripping the man's forearm. On Andu's other side, Rawl caught a glimpse of Mila's deathly pale face.

"Exactly," Andu replied. "A salta-sombras. A monstro capable of hopping from shadow to shadow. Look at where we are."

Carefully, Rawl twisted his neck around, taking in the elongated circular clearing. There were trees surrounding every side of them, which meant that there were shadows on every side of them.

And the sun continued to set.

"What do we do?" Mila asked.

"We cast a light spell," Andu said, his voice steadier than the Padir's had been. "We cast it back towards where we came, and we run."

"We're both drained," Mila argued, but Andu cut her off.

"First-year students can handle a simple light spell. You and I can manage it until we are on the main road."

Mila didn't seem convinced, but she nodded. "All right," she agreed.

Rawl swallowed hard, but his mouth was dry, and he felt as if he was choking on his own tongue.

"Ready?" Andu asked them, and Rawl could see Mila's terse nod.

"Now!" Andu yelled, and the clearing was lit up like the dawn, cutting a clear path through a patch of woods towards the Andalan main road. Andu gripped Rawl's arm, but he had a sudden, terrible realization.

"The pearl!" he cried out, twisting away from Andu's grasp. He moved so quickly, and so suddenly, Andu didn't have a chance to readjust his grip.

"Rawl, no!" he heard Mila scream as he lunged towards the pearl—and the shadow.

Then it was as if time slowed. A bird took flight in the distance, wings opening so, so slowly, pushing against the force of the evening wind. He noticed the almost imperceptible motion of the grass bending underneath his feet and felt the languid motion of his muscles in action. He saw the pearl, golden and beautiful, still within his grasp. As if outside of himself, Rawl witnessed his outstretched fingers, fingertips almost touching the smooth roundness of the gem.

And then he saw the shadow. At first, it looked just like a regular shadow, but a moving one. Then, from the infinite darkness of the shadow's center, black tendrils began to unfurl. He watched in horror as they lifted, expanded, and rolled out further and further from the inky darkness, stretching far and high; reaching for him.

Rawl's blood froze in his veins, and he saw his death coming for him from a deep, unending well of evil. A tendril, studded with rows and rows of barbed spikes, descended upon him just as his fingers clasped around the pearl.

Then the world righted itself once more, as an enormous wave of glistening golden light shot forward from the pearl, warming Rawl's fingers and pushing against him with the force of the magia. In fact, the wave was so powerful it bent not only the grass below his feet, but the trees outlining the clearing. They bowed backwards, righting themselves after the crest broke with a snapping swing.

The shadow burst apart in front of Rawl's eyes, not even dust remained. It was there one moment, and in the next, simply was not.

Rawl stumbled backwards, panting hard. He stared at the empty clearing, the golden glow fading slowly and leaving them in darkness once again, only the lingering scent of saltwater remaining. He looked down at his clenched fist, holding the lightly pulsating pearl. As his heartbeat slowed, so did the pulsations. Wearily, he turned to make sure his sister and friend were all right.

They both stared at him, shock and disbelief written across their faces.

"Well, we know what it does," Rawl croaked.

Mila and Andu exchanged a glance, and Andu's expression fell. Mila shut her eyes tightly, and Rawl saw a tear leak from the corner of her eye, barely noticeable in the fading light.

"What?" Rawl asked, suddenly concerned. "What is it? I'm all right, see?" he continued, motioning to himself. "And we know what the pearl does now. Isn't that a good thing?"

"Let's get to the main road," Andu said softly, but the tone of his voice put Rawl on edge. He took a defensive step backwards.

"What is it?" he demanded. "What aren't you telling me?"

"Rawlly," Mila said softly, reaching out for him.

Rawl shook his head.

"What is it?" he yelled. Then, his shoulders slumped, and all the fight escaped his body.

"Mila, que?" he pleaded.

"It's defensive magia," Mila finally answered, more tears escaping her green eyes. "Powerful, defensive magia," she continued. "More powerful than anything I have ever seen."

"What does that mean, Mila?" Rawl begged.

She sighed, then wiped her eyes with the back of her hands. "It means that if we bring the object around Alric, and he becomes threatening, the pearl may destroy him. It can't help him," she added.

"It will only kill him."

CHAPTER 26
DAMIKA

Damika didn't react as a flash of pain stabbed her into her right side. It was deep enough to bleed, she knew, but she also knew that reacting would only make the situation worse. So, she gritted her teeth and prepared to face the rest of the torture that awaited her. Despite her inner resolve, she couldn't help but flinch as the next sharp instrument embedded itself into her flesh.

"Hold still," the seamstress grumbled, shifting the fabric around Damika's frame.

Dami bit the inside of her cheek. "You are poking me with pins," she said in an even voice.

"I wouldn't poke you if you didn't move so much!" the woman responded in complaint.

Damika refrained from pointing out that it was, in fact, her stabbing that made Dami move in the first place. She didn't think that the woman would listen. So, she stayed soldier-still as gnarled hands shifted, pinched and pulled on her flesh.

"You are so bruised!" the woman muttered. "Black and blue, and black and blue! We could leave your stomach bare, but no! More bruising. You have lovely, toned arms, but covered in scratches. And your legs!' the seamstress snorted. "Don't let me get started on your legs!"

Let her get started? Damika asked herself, almost amused. *This was her showing restraint?*

"I am a Danrayen," she said out loud through gritted teeth. "Bruises and injuries are common. I am a warrior."

"Not a very good one, if you are getting this injured just from training exercises," the woman scoffed.

Damika looked down at her incredulously.

"I am about to be named High Priestess of our order," she said. "Only the most elite warriors become priestesses, let alone High Priestess!" The woman only snorted and pulled the fabric tighter.

"Let us see if we can make it look like you deserve it."

An excruciating forty minutes later, Damika stumbled out of her fitting.

Thank the dioses that was the last one, she thought to herself.

She made her way out of the guest wing, through the quarters which the priestess had hastily fashioned into a tailor shop. The old Pelgar woman had been a seamstress in the village for decades, and Mamá had given her the room and employed her to create the outfits for the Ascension Ceremony.

"We have to look the part," she had said when Damika protested.

It wasn't that Damika didn't understand the need for the spectacle and ceremony. She knew that the death of Adira had rocked the order, especially in the wake of the increased monstro attacks. She also knew that the uncertainty in the realm meant that their enemies would be looking to them for weaknesses. They could not afford to show any.

And yet, she desperately wished that the Ascension Ceremony was not necessary. She wished that Adira had not placed this burden at her feet. Further still, she wished that there had never been a prophecy regarding her birth or her Affinity. Then, she could have earned her place at the head of the order slowly, organically over time, rather than being thrust into it before she felt ready for it.

And yet here she was, being fitted for her ceremonial outfit.

The truth was that Damika had never thought it would get this far. She had truly believed that one of the other priestesses would have put a stop to this madness long before now. She had hoped that General Vashti would have amassed supporters to challenge her. She assumed someone else would have suggested a better alternative. That another priestess would lay claim to the honor herself.

None had.

And so, preparations had begun to ascend Damika into the position, despite the fact that she had never fully accepted it. Now, it was too late to stop it.

Damika made her way through the temple grounds, taking in all the preparations for the upcoming fiesta. The priestesses had wooden posts taken from storage and set deep in the ground, colorful hanging lanterns strung in between them. They'd pulled out long tables from the meal hall and placed them in several straight rows on the freshly smoothed training grounds. There was a platform where she and the other priestesses would dine, just under the stairs leading to the main Danrayen doors. She knew that, by the evening, the tables would house brightly colored tablecloths strewn with flowers. There would be pitchers of wine and sangria, bottles of ron and more. Food, special to this occasion, would cover the banquet tables.

Guests coming to witness the Ascension had already started trickling in, and with the increased monstro sightings, the temple dispatched their Danrayen girls to escort travelers and their convoys to the safety of the temple walls. Damika had wanted to be among them, but the look on Mamá's face when she had volunteered had given her the answer.

While they'd informed the guests about the refugees from Pelgar, and that accommodations would be more rustic than in other years, it didn't stop them from coming to witness the youngest Danrayen initiate to take the Trial now ascend to the youngest Danrayen Warrior to become High Priestess.

Damika sighed.

She was hungry, but she knew that the kitchens were busy preparing a meal worthy of the event, and didn't want to get in anyone's way. More so, she didn't wish to be roped into yet another conversation about the ceremony, her new role, or how dioses-damned excited everyone was for her to "take her rightful place."

Instead of the kitchens, she made her way to the orchards. It was late in the season, but there was a chance some apples remained on the boughs. She suddenly wished that Nessa were with her. She had always been the best at foraging.

Instead, as she approached the most promising cluster of trees, she found Petra. She was in the middle of a series of training exercises, swinging her morning star with greater and greater strength. Damika stopped to watch, admiring both her friend's strength and her form. After a while, however, her movements became more and more fierce, and she swung the weapon with wild abandon, breaking from the careful technique she had started with.

When she slammed the spiked ball down hard into the soil, leaving it wedged in the ground, Damika cleared her throat.

"Anyone I know?" she asked lightly.

Petra spun to regard her, then looked down at the ball with a sigh. With a hard jerk that had the muscles in her arms bulging, she dislodged it with a cloud of dust.

"We should have heard something by now," she all but growled.

Taruka. It was the same conversation that they had had for days.

"I know you are worried about her—" Damika started, but Petra interrupted quickly.

"Worried? Of course not. Why would I be worried? Because she is traveling through the realm alone, unaided, and surrounded by monstros? Or because she just so happens to be heading in the direction all those monstros are also traveling towards?" Petra railed, every word dripping with sarcasm.

"Petra," Damika started, only to be interrupted again.

"Why would I worry, Dami? Because you sent her to the Mage University, and to the company of a man who was last seen suffering in the grips of Mage Madness? Why on Tierramadri would I be worried about my wife?" she demanded.

Damika did her best to restrain her smile. "You do know you have to actually marry her before you can claim that title, right?"

"Do not mock me, Damika!" Petra yelled in frustration, her short hair wild around her face as she raked her hands through it impatiently. "She is out there, alone, and I have to be here, waiting for word!"

"I know, I know," Damika agreed, instantly sobering. "Lo siento, I wasn't trying to mock you. I was just teasing, but I realize that this isn't the time."

Petra put her back to a tree and slid down to sit on the ground.

"I know why I couldn't go with her," she said quietly. "I even agree with the reasons. But it doesn't make it any less difficult to bear."

Damika found a patch of grass beside her friend and sat down next to her.

"I know," she said. "For what it's worth, I am sorry for it."

Petra made a noncommittal grunt.

"You know as well as I do that Taru is fine. That she is strong, capable, and cunning. We will hear from her soon." She didn't say any more. There was nothing else that she could say that Petra didn't already know. She stood long enough to pick two apples from the tree, then sat back down and offered one to her friend. She crunched through the crispy skin, wiping a dribble of juice that trickled down her chin. After a few moments, she heard Petra begin to eat as well.

Once they were done, cores thrown back into the field from where they came, Petra finally spoke again.

"Gracias," she said.

Damika turned her head to look at her in surprise. "For what?" she asked.

"For always knowing what to say, but more importantly, knowing when not to say anything at all. You've always been so solid, Dami. Someone that everyone else can depend on." She sighed, leaning her head back against the tree trunk.

"You will make a wonderful High Priestess."

A knot formed in Damika's stomach at the words. She dropped her gaze to her bent legs. "What if," she hesitated. "What if I don't want to be High Priestess?" she asked.

Petra laughed ruefully. "A little late for that, isn't it?" she joked, but the words felt like she had doused Damika in icy cold water. She curled her knees tighter to her chest. Concern crossed Petra's face at the action.

"Hey," she said, placing a small hand on Damika's shoulder. "This is just nerves. You know that. Of course you would be nervous, it's a tremendous honor. But one you deserve. You were meant to do this, Dami. You'll be fine!"

I won't be fine! Damika screamed in her head. *This isn't what I want! Not like this. Not now. Why does it have to be now?*

Damika nodded. "Of course," she said out loud. "Just nerves."

Petra nodded, looking relieved. "You'll see, after the Ascension Ceremony ..." she leapt up to her feet with unnatural speed. "Coño,

Dami!" she yelled, grabbing her friend's arm and hauling her up with all of her strength. Which was quite a bit. "Your ceremony is tonight! We need to go get you ready, now!"

Damika rubbed at her arm where Petra had gripped her as she trailed after her friend.

It was time to become a High Priestess.

CHAPTER 27
RAWL

R awl sat in front of an unconscious Alric, pearl in his pocket.

Like he had suggested, Andu had fashioned a golden wire and chain necklace that held the orb in place, but Rawl refused to wear it. Firstly, because it didn't feel like his. He had offered it to his sister, knowing that an item of power was better in the hands of a mage, and he would sleep easier knowing she had protection around her, especially in these uncertain times of war and monstros. But Mila had refused. She said it was his need that had made them search for the pearl in the first place, that he had carried the box up to the surface, and that it was he that had first reignited its powers.

"The first person in centuries to do so," she had said.

So Andu had fashioned the necklace and given it to Rawl, who had pocketed it. The second, and most important reason that he refused to wear it was because it apparently needed skin contact to be activated. And being this near Alric, well, Rawl didn't want any accidents happening.

Alric did not have long for this world, and Rawl knew it. Soon his spirit would slip from the broken shell of the person he once was, and out of Tierramadri entirely, to dwell amongst the dioses. Rawl wanted to be glad for him. To be happy that his suffering would end, because he knew his friend was suffering. Instead, he could only feel the terror and dread of knowing a deeper, more terrible suffering would soon pass down to him—the suffering of being the one left behind.

Tears leaked from his eyes freely, here with no one near to witness him. Not that Mila or Andu would judge him, he knew them both better than that. But they would try to make him feel better, and there was nothing either could do or say that would make the passing of the man he loved better.

"I should have told you," Rawl said to Alric, watching the ragged breaths lift and fall in the mage's frail chest. His closed eyelids were spider-webbed with tiny veins, so dark-red that they appeared black.

"I should have told you that I loved—that I love you. I've known it for a while now." Rawl clenched his hands into fists. "I thought that we'd have more time."

Rawl reached into his pants pocket—not the one holding the pearl, but the other one—and drew out a small vial. The drafts that Mila had been concocting to keep Alric pliable, and more manageable, had been working, but the doses were getting too high. They had weakened him.

"This has enough of the dosage to put him into a very, very deep sleep," Mila had said, pressing the glass container into his hand. "He won't wake up from it."

A few weeks ago, Rawl would have been enraged by the insinuation. He would have yelled and cursed at his sister, smashing the vial at their feet between them. He would have raged, yet again, that Alric was still alive. That Rawl was going to save him.

Instead, he had taken the offering from her silently. He knew that what was to come wasn't pretty. That Alric would continue to wither away, his corrupted magia becoming more and more volatile, until it ate away at his very flesh, boiled the blood inside his veins. It was a terrible and unfathomably painful way to die.

Or he could sleep, Rawl thought. He loved him enough to give him that.

He pulled his stool as close to Alric as he could, allowing himself to look. There was not an inch of the man's skin that was not mottled, or blotchy, or streaked with burgundy-colored veins. His once dark, thick hair was thin and greasy, hanging in oily strands around his face. The mage's lips remained perpetually chapped and bleeding, as were his gums, forever staining his teeth red. And he was so, so thin. He hadn't had much weight to lose in the first place but managed to continue fading away before Rawl's very eyes.

Rawl ran his fingertip over Alric's brow, then trailed it down his cheek. Angry sparks of magia crackled and burned his fingertips, as if he were pressing his skin into open flame. Even when unconscious, his body rebelled and struck out against his imagined enemies. The magia hurt, but Rawl ignored it. He would deal with the burns later.

"Lo siento," he whispered, cupping the sleeping mage's cheek. "I'm so, so, sorry that I couldn't save you," he choked out, then gripped the edges of Alric's fraying shirt, burying his head against his chest. The magia slashed and stabbed out at him, but Rawl couldn't feel it over the pain of his breaking heart.

"I'm not going to keep you waiting any more, amor," he said, unstopping the cork from the vial. "I'm sorry I kept you here for so long," Rawl whispered.

He pressed a burning kiss to Alric's forehead, then felt a sharp pinch of magia slice open his lip at the action. When he pulled away, there was a smear of Rawl's blood on Alric's skin.

With shaking hands, Rawl tilted up Alric's chin, moving to open his mouth. Just as the mage's lips parted, he heard a commotion outside of the door.

Coño, he thought. *Can I not even do this in peace?*

At the thought, the door flew open with such force that it slammed against the room's back wall and bounced forward again and would have hit Andu in the face if Mila had not stopped it.

"You haven't given him the draft yet, have you?" Andu asked, oblivious. He hurried inside. "Is he … gone?"

"Not yet," Rawl replied testily. The decision to give Alric the sleeping tonic at all wasn't something that he had come to lightly. He didn't appreciate the interruption, now that he had finally decided to go through with it.

"What are you two doing here?" he demanded. They had offered to be with him when it happened, and Mila had even offered to feed Alric the liquid. But he had refused them, wanting one last moment alone with Alric. Why were they here now?

"Mila had an idea," Andu said quickly, practically bouncing on his heels.

"Not a good idea!" she admonished him, her eyes full of pain. When she looked at Rawl, he thought he understood why. She didn't want to give him any more hope that she could not deliver on.

"I have no hope left," Rawl reminded her, lifting up the uncorked vial as proof. "If there is one final thing to try, it cannot hurt."

"It might hurt," Mila said softly.

Rawl chuckled humorlessly. "Any more than he is already being hurt?" he asked, motioning towards Alric.

"Not him," Mila clarified. "You."

Rawl frowned. "What do you mean?"

"Magia is … strange. It comes in so many forms. In Affinities, in brujeria, in mage work. Some people can't control it at all, and others don't even realize that they have it. But Mage Madness only ever affects mages powerful enough to call on the energy of Tierramadri and refocus it into something else."

"Yes," Rawl said slowly. Alric had once explained something similar to him and Rojya once.

"But the thing about mages is, the knowledge of the power makes it susceptible to corruption. People with Affinities rarely know they have Affinities. They simply think that they are particularly skilled or blessed in a thing. And brujas and brujos have magia, but not enough of it for the corruption to be attracted to them. Sorcerers have more magia than anyone, but their Affinity for magia makes them immune to the corruption."

"What are you saying, Mila?" Rawl asked, exasperated.

"I am saying that knowing you are a mage with power leaves you open to corruption. If you had magia, but didn't know it, the Mage Madness could not seek you. And it is possible to forget your magia."

"It's true," Andu interrupted. "Two years ago, a young mage in training tried a spell far too advanced for his level. The force of the power blew him backwards and down a flight of steps. He survived but was badly injured. When he awoke, he didn't remember who he was, why he was at the Mage University, or that he had magia at all. And because of that, he was never able to access magia again."

"So, you think that if Alric forgets he is a mage, then what? The madness will just stop?" Rawl asked them, scratching at the back of his head.

"Magia can't be corrupted if it can't be accessed. The madness would have nothing to latch itself to," Mila confirmed.

Rawl stared at the vial in his hand for a long, deliberate moment. He slowly plugged the cork back into the vial and placed it back into his pocket.

"Do you think you can make him forget that he is a mage?" he asked Mila.

"No," she answered.

"But you just said—"

"He would have to forget *everything*," she finished.

Rawl froze. "What do you mean, 'everything?'"

"Magia is so tied into who Alric is as a person. He showed signs of it so young. He spent so many years studying here, in the university. It is too interwoven into his life to make him forget it."

"So then, it's hopeless?" Rawl despaired.

"Not if he forgets who he is entirely," Andu told him, his voice full of pity.

"If he forgets ... everything?" Rawl asked.

Mila nodded.

"His family, his brother, Nova, me?" his voice cracked. "He will forget me?"

"But he will live," Andu reminded him.

"He won't be Alric," Rawl argued.

"Not the one you knew, no," Mila conceded. "But he will have a chance to live the rest of his life as someone new. And the rest of his life would be longer than a few hours," she said, pointedly looking at the unconscious mage bound to a chair.

Rawl drew in a trembling breath. There was no decision, not really. He loved Alric. The Alric he was before the madness. But Mila had been right from the beginning—that Alric couldn't be saved. Maybe something of him could live on.

"How?' he finally asked.

"There is a spell, a complicated one, but it's successful. It wipes all the memories of a person's past life, and allows them to start a new one, without wondering about the missing gap in their memory," Mila told him.

Rawl frowned. That sounded familiar.

"That is the spell they use on the families of Name-Bearers," he finally gasped. "So that they don't go looking for their children!"

Andu looked ashamed, but Mila tilted her chin up and stared back at him defiantly.

"Yes," she said simply.

But he would be alive, Rawl thought. *He could live a new life.* One not wrapped up in court intrigue, considered a traitor to the throne for supporting the Flowers, and Rojya, and the Unnamed Prince. Churan, Rawl reminded himself, his heart contracting hard in his chest. He wouldn't remember Churan either. It would devastate the boy. Rojya too. But maybe, just maybe, they would understand.

"Is he strong enough for it?" Rawl asked Mila softly, not meeting her gaze.

"If he isn't, he'll die either way," she responded. Rawl knew she didn't say it to hurt him. It was simply the truth.

"You are a fool," a voice said, and Rawl looked over, into eyes which were a swirling mist of red haze and lightning. Alric had woken.

"Your death is inevitable. You will not strip my power from me," he said, baring his blood-stained teeth. "It is a *part* of me. It is *mine,* and I will use it to burn the flesh off of your bones. You cannot take my magia, fool." Alric's voice rasped, the cracks in his lips splitting as he spat out his vile words. "*It is impossible,*" the mage seethed.

Furiously, Rawl stalked over to the chair, slamming both of his hands down over Alric's bound arms. It was like placing his hands over lit candles and his palms burned with the contact. Deliberately, he brought his face down to Alric's, so close that their noses were almost touching. Crackles of electric magia spat from the mage's skin and singed his face, but Rawl barely noticed the pain. A particularly violent spark swept over his brow and down his cheek and he could hear his own skin sizzling, could smell the blood that ran freely down to his chin. He heard Mila gasp, but he was beyond being able to feel physical pain. Rawl searched Alric's eyes, trying to find some semblance of his old self behind the crimson haze.

"It is the age for impossible things," he hissed at the man that looked like the person he loved, before backing away once again. Filomila tutted at him when he returned, lifting a hand to his cheek. He brushed her off, crossing the room away from them all.

He wouldn't leave, he couldn't leave if these were Alric's last moments on Tierramadri. But he wouldn't stand beside them while they wiped away the identity of a man that he loved.

He threw himself on a chair and bent over at the waist, trying not to vomit. "All right," he mumbled. His voice sounded strange to his ears, as if he was back underwater, and trying to speak through the air pocket.

"Do it."

Chapter 28

Rawl

"Rawlly," his sister started, her voice laden with concern, but Rawl didn't look up.

"Just do it," he repeated.

After a moment, he heard shuffling. "Listo?" He heard Mila ask Andu.

There was no answer, but Rawl imagined the giant nodding.

Then there were sounds of movement, packs opening, papers rustling. At one point, there was a smell that reached him from across the room. Not unpleasant, but not one Rawl could identify. After what seemed an eternity of waiting, with his heart lodged in his throat and his stomach threatening to rebel the entire time, Mila and Andu began speaking.

No, chanting, Rawl realized. Despite himself, Rawl lifted his head. Across from him, Andu and Mila stood on either side of Alric, their hands linked in a circle around his prone form. At some point, Alric's head had slumped forward, his hair covering his face. An intense, burning rage suddenly filled Rawl.

Why hadn't they pushed his hair away from his face? Why had they not made him comfortable?

He stood without planning to, the instinct to rush across the room and stop the spell overwhelming every inch of his body. It trembled with the need to just make it stop.

But the desire to keep Alric alive, any part of him alive, was just too great.

The chanting intensified and, in an instant, Alric's body snapped up, bending backwards like a bow, straining against his magical bonds. His dark hair whipped back from his face, and Rawl saw his eyes; completely red now, open and furious. Alric's hands curled into the arms of the chair, clawing into the fabric like the talons of a great bird. His mottled veins bulged against his skin, and Rawl could see the corrupted magia rippling through them.

Alric let out an inhuman howl, the kind an animal makes when in undefinable pain.

"No," Rawl rasped, but Alric's own wailing drowned out his voice. Alric began to thrash. "No!" he cried out again, stumbling forward.

Mila and Andu raised their voices, shouting their chants over the screaming and convulsing mage.

"Stop it!" Rawl yelled, rushing towards them more quickly. He wasn't sure what he intended to do, only that he needed to do something.

Just before he could reach his sister, Alric's wailing abruptly stopped. The silence in the room was somehow more terrifying than the cacophony had been, and Rawl paused, suddenly unsure. Then he watched, horrified, as Alric's eyes rolled up into the back of his head, and his body seemed to lift off of the chair, as far as the bonds would allow. Slowly, a thick red mist began floating up and around, slinking from his body. When Rawl looked closer, he saw that it seemed to be coming from Alric. The bulging veins and ancient, magical glyphs seemed to burn from his skin, a black-tinged, crimson vapor, the remnants of it. Burning, boiling, lifting from underneath his flesh, and disappearing into the ether.

Alric's body, ravaged by the process, began convulsing. But Rawl dared not stop it now. Wide-eyed and gaping, he could see parts of Alric's flesh uncovered for the first time in weeks—paler perhaps than usual, but unmarred and whole as the vapors dissipated. His once scarlet veins began settling back down under his flesh, no longer bulging and pushing up against his skin. The bruises and mottling faded, leaving sweat-damp but ordinary skin in its place.

After a few moments, the red mist vanished completely, and Mila and Andu stopped chanting. Alric's body slammed back down onto the couch, whole and so like the man he once was that Rawl felt his heart lighten with hope.

They had done it. Alric was no longer plagued with Mage Madness.

Rawl darted forward to remove the bindings, to let him loose, to get him comfortable, to set him free, to hold him, but before he could reach the mage, Andu grabbed him roughly, pulling him back. Rawl looked up at the big man, confused, and in his face found nothing but sorrow.

"Qué?" Rawl asked, then whirled towards his sister when Andu didn't respond. "Qué?" he demanded more forcefully.

"Rawl," Mila said, tears streaming down her cheeks, flushed with exertion. "It didn't work."

"What are you talking about?" Rawl asked incredulously. "Of course it worked, you did it! Look at him, there's not a trace of the corruption on him!"

Rawl beamed at Alric, still slumped in the chair, his body new again, whole again. Of course, he was skinnier than he once had been, and weaker, no doubt, but it was nothing that a few weeks of steady meals and light exercise couldn't fix. Rawl would help him to heal, and soon he would be back to normal. Everything would be all right again.

He grinned stupidly at the mage, who looked peaceful for the first time since his Phoenixeye had broken. When he woke up, he would need water, food, and rest. A proper bath, too! Rawl would take care of him.

"Rawl," Mila said again, crying harder.

Rawl was confused. Why was she crying? They had done it! Alric was all right. He was cured. The spell had worked.

The spell—something about the spell had formed a knot of tension in the center of Rawl's forehead. There was a strange pressure in his heart. There was something that he hadn't liked about the spell, but what was it?

It didn't matter, Rawl decided. Alric was better, and that was all that was important. He moved towards Alric once more, but again, Andu held him back.

"Let him," Mila said quietly. "Let him go to him."

Andu slowly released his grip on Rawl's tunic, and the archer patted the big man heartily on the back to show him that there were no hard feelings. He had helped save Alric, after all.

Rawl crossed to the still mage, kneeling in front of him. He held one of his hands, which felt chilled and clammy.

"He's cold," Rawl muttered, more to himself, rubbing his hand between his own. Rawl gently tilted Alric's head back, smoothing the hair from his face the way that he wanted to do earlier. It hit the back of the chair and lolled to the side. Quickly, Rawl removed the magical bindings.

"Mago?" he said softly to the mage, trailing his fingers across his cheek. "Alric, you can wake up now."

Rawl heard a small sob catch in Mila's throat behind him, and he frowned at the sound.

"Amor?" he continued, confused.

He pressed a hand against Alric's chest.

And realized the mage was not breathing.

CHAPTER 29
CHURAN

Churan let warmth flood his body. He imagined that he was outside, sprawled on a patch of grass, in a field devoid of any trees, with nothing to shade him from the rays. He imagined those rays tickling first his toes, then moving up the tops of his feet, and circling his ankles. He could feel it, the warm flush of his skin as the rays crept up his calves and knees, his thighs, pelvis, and lower back. By the time the comfortable heat traveled up his tummy, through his chest and arms, caressed his neck, and then engulfed his head, Churan felt completely relaxed. Once his body felt fully encapsulated in warmth and security, he felt the usual shift of perception, which left him falling backwards into deep meditation.

Some part of him, waiting patiently in the back of his mind, knew that he was neither outside nor under Tz'ola's bright rays. He knew that he was inside of the temple mage building, in the main room and sitting on the cold tile floor, his legs crossed in front of him.

Lessons with Mage Nuna had been going better as of late, and he found himself in the building more and more, his interest in the lessons slowly growing over time. It helped that the mage had been more patient with him as well. Apparently, after his outburst, Axchel had confronted the woman, admonishing her for treating Churan the way she had in their first lesson.

Nuna confessed that she had been unconvinced that Churan was, in fact, a sorcerer, and that, even if he was, it didn't mean that he was the Unnamed Prince. She told Axchel that, as much as she wanted to believe in a child destined to bring peace to their realm, she had been living in a world of war for too long to count on it.

"Prophecies," she had said, "are all well and good. But how can we know which ones to believe?"

Churan was sure that the mage had expected Axchel to keep her confession in confidence. She likely never imagined that an "adult conversation" would be shared with Churan. But Axchel didn't believe in keeping things from him, especially when they involved his own life. He had asked the boy seriously if he wanted to abandon his lessons with the mage altogether.

Churan had considered it. It was, if he was honest, very tempting. If he didn't work on his magia, it would remain unusable. And if he couldn't access it, perhaps he could better protect others from it.

But he knew better. He had already hurt people with his magia, but also come close to doing so again. Not having control of his magia was more dangerous than mastering it.

He also realized that Mage Nuna's concerns were, regrettably, valid. It was the first time Churan had considered what a person would think of a prophecy when they weren't actively living in it.

It would be a difficult thing to accept, Churan had thought.

So, he had continued with his lessons, determined to do his best. Remarkably, it seemed that Mage Nuna recognized his efforts. She was still strict and firm, but Churan thought she was also fair. And even when he was exhausted and frustrated, he couldn't fault her methods.

The hardest part, however, was that the mage had asked him to "find the source of his magia."

When the mage first uttered those words to Churan, he was sure that she might be mad. After all, everyone knew that magia was fashioned from the energy of Tierramadri, not harnessed from within a single person. Nuna had explained that it didn't matter, that she was sure there was something in Churan's mind that was blocking him from accessing his full power. As long as his mind and emotions were working to keep it at bay, he would never be able to have full control over it.

It had taken several meditation sessions for him to visualize anything in his mind other than clear light. Nuna had remained patient, quietly talking to him outside of his meditation, guiding him to the innermost recesses of himself. Slowly, images had begun to appear.

Deep in his meditation, Churan waited for the clean white light of nothingness to dissipate. He focused on where he wanted to go, more comfortable now with the colors and shapes and sounds of the vision. Slowly, the visage around him began to change, fashioning his surroundings into a now-familiar scene. Churan stood outside once more, in a field of endless green, spattered with wildflowers. No matter how he turned, he saw nothing but the lush foliage of his mind, a thick, inviting wood at its edges. He didn't move towards the far away trees, but instead focused on where he was standing.

Churan looked down at his feet, and at the bank of a deep channel. It looked like it had once been a passage for a great and rushing river, but now the land was dry and arid instead. Only a tiny trickle of water was visible, soaking into the thirsty ground faster than it could flow. Churan had found the channel during his last session, but had tumbled from his meditation at the realization that the water was the source of his power. This time, he schooled his breathing and began following the channel against the meager flow, walking, and walking, and walking, until finally, the water moved with a bit more strength.

It was there that he found the dam.

The dam was enormous, far taller and wider than Churan's small frame. It was an impressive structure, made of fallen trees, rocks, dried mud, and filled with grass. Some pieces were mere pebbles, others were the size of ceiba trees. Water was escaping from small gaps, but that was nothing compared to what was being held back.

Churan gaped at it, the mental representation of everything that had gone wrong with his magia, with his power. His own body had built that dam within his own mind, denying him access to his gift.

And that meant that he was the only one who could undo it.

"Good," Mage Nuna's voice found him over the raging water behind the blockage. "Do not try to move too much," she cautioned. "Your mind has fashioned this for a reason, it will not easily be parted with it."

Churan nodded to himself, then stepped into the small flow. Instantly he felt a spark of magia, moving from his feet, up his legs, and shooting across the rest of him. His breath caught, momentarily stunned by the touch of his raw power. When he felt in control once more, he crouched near a cluster of large boulders, finding a stick no larger than his hand wedged between the stones. He gripped it and pulled.

The stick would not budge.

He frowned, gripping it tighter, and pulling with more strength.

The stick slid free a fraction, enough that he could wiggle it to-and-fro. Wrapping both hands around the wood, he pulled with all his might. It became more loose, but continued to be stuck between the large rocks.

Churan knew that this was all happening in his mind, but he swore he could feel the roughness of the bark in his hands, the stinging splinters that embedded themselves into his palms. He lifted a leg from the stream, bracing it against one of the boulders. Then, with every bit of strength he possessed, Churan *pulled*.

The stick gave way, and with it, a tiny bit more water came through. But the force of his pull and the stick dislodging caused him to fall backwards, landing on his back on the hard ground, the wind knocked out of him.

Churan peeled his eyes open, wheezing with the effort to draw in a breath. When his vision focused, he saw that he had flung himself from his meditation and was now sprawled on the cool tiles of the mage room. Nuna peered down at him, but instead of concern on her face, he saw pride.

"Muy bien," she said, a ghost of a smile on her lips. "Tomorrow, we try again."

CHAPTER 30

DAMIKA

T z'ola had finally bowed her flaming crown and set its rays beyond the far horizon, but the temple grounds blazed with their own light, illuminated with lanterns, candles, and a happily blazing bonfire. Damika stood at the entrance building of the Temple of Danray, right behind its closed and well-secured main doors. No monstros had, as of yet, dared to approach the temple, and Damika wondered if the warrior women believed that the creature's limited brains could understand that nothing but death would meet them there—or that the dioses were favoring them and the civilians they protected behind their walls. She hoped that they never learned the truth. That Damika was out there every night, making sure none strayed too close. Either way, the doors remained locked and barred.

She had on soft fabric trousers which billowed the closer they reached her feet, giving her the illusion of a layered skirt with all the comfort of pants. Her top was tight around her toned stomach and reached high up her chest and even wrapped around her neck, with a horizontal slit that revealed only a glimpse of her clavicle. The top's sleeves billowed just as the pants did, the cloth framing her toned biceps, and then opening out after hitting her elbows. The entire outfit was a luxurious cream-color that showed off the richness of her warm umber skin.

Mamá was with Damika, ready to descend the steps before her and announce her to the guests. They had practiced the ceremonial speech countless times over the last few days, the simple words that, when recited under the goddess Danray's statue, would proclaim her as the next High Priestess.

Damika wasn't sure if the nausea that was swirling in her gut was due to her fear of stumbling over the words, or the prospect of finally becoming the leader of the Danrayen Order.

Likely both.

She did her best to take slow, steadying breaths and to unclench her muscles, which were stiff with tension. Her palms itched with the desire to unlock the doors, draw a sword, and slay any monstros that stood in her path. She knew it would be a much more effective stress relief than a few deep breaths.

Instead, Damika focused her attention back to Mamá, who had been speaking to her.

"And you will have to make sure to formally acknowledge General Hector. He journeyed all the way from the Andalan capital. I know that means he is likely under Lord Guerro's thumb, but we cannot judge anyone too quickly, or blame the army for following orders. That is, after all, a soldier's job, and Hector has always been a good soldier."

Damika nodded, feeling numb.

"We will see where their allegiance lies when we finally make our move to the capital. Speaking of generals, it would be good to take a moment to reiterate that you won't be making any changes to the Danrayen priestesses for the time being. I know that she has not been your biggest supporter, but it would be wise to reassure General Vashti that she will continue to function as the Danrayen general. We cannot afford to replace her now, not in so turbulent a time, and so close to battle."

"Of course!" Damika gasped, shocked that Mamá would even mention it. She had no intention of changing the order of the priestesses. Not only had the thought never crossed her mind, it was something she hadn't even realized that she could do.

Just more proof that you are not worthy of this position, a voice inside her whispered.

"Several of my 'friends' are in attendance tonight," Mamá continued. Damika knew that "friends" meant her non-Danrayen spies.

"They will distribute themselves around the fiesta and listen to the chatter. By the end of the evening, we will know who supports you, who needs persuading, and who we can consider among our enemies."

Damika felt as though a bucket of icy cold water cascaded over her. She was a Danrayen Warrior. She had always wanted to be a Danrayen Warrior. She knew full well that enemies had always been a part of that life. But she had always assumed that they would be enemies that she could meet head-on; in battle. She was unprepared for the prospect of political enemies, hidden and treacherous adversaries who would smile to her face while plunging a dagger deep into her back.

I am not ready for this! the voice in her head screamed. But instead of crying it out loud, she merely nodded at Mamá.

"That will be useful," she said.

The music from the marimba and drums suddenly stopped, and Mamá regarded Damika with a look of fierce pride.

"It is time, mija," she said, gripping her upper arms under her strong fingers. Damika didn't flinch as she squeezed fresh bruises. She was used to the aches and pains of her body by now.

Damika did her best to smile at the woman who had been more of a mother to her than anyone else in her life had ever been.

"I'm ready," she lied to her face.

With one last squeeze, Mamá turned and made her way down the long steps.

Once she was alone, Damika turned to face the barricaded doors of the temple.

You could run, she thought to herself.

She didn't have her Danrayen blade strapped to her back, like she did when she was first welcomed into the order. Once a Danrayen girl passed her Trial, they presented her in whatever garment she pleased but was usually decked out, head to toe in her finest weapons. It was a symbol of her beginning her new life as a full warrior.

During a High Priestess Ascension, however, she was devoid of any weapons, save for a single dagger strapped to her calf. As a leader, Damika was meant to be presented as more than a warrior, as a leader, and a symbol for peace.

She felt the pressure of the dagger against her flesh, the metal already made warm from the heat of her skin. It wasn't much in the way of protection, but she could make do. There would be many discarded weapons in Pelgar. She could pick some up there and disappear, battling monstros across the realm like she was meant to do.

Almost reflexively, Damika raised her arm to lift a beam from the door, when out of the corner of her eye she caught a glimmer of light. Pausing, she twisted her arm to look at the ornamental band adorning her biceps.

It was the same leather armband that Adira had gifted her when she passed her Danrayen Trial. It was a pretty piece of work, elegant and practical. It was lightweight enough to not encumber, but could deflect a poorly aimed blow, or be used to block the swing of a blade. It wasn't armor, and wouldn't completely save her from harm, but could buy her time. Furthermore, it contained a secret.

Damika traced the mixed metal detailing with the pads of her finger until she felt the tiny catch. Digging her nail underneath it, she pried up a silver spike, a piece whose tip was meant to be coated in poison. A last resort, to take out an enemy—or oneself.

It threw Damika back to the day Adira had presented her with the gift. She had been so proud. The High Priestess herself, giving her, of all people, a gift! And one as finely made as the armband. She had glowed with pleasure and pride at the sentiment. Damika had thought that Adira was recognizing her efforts, congratulating her on all of her hard work. She hadn't known then that it was not just a gift from a High Priestess to her warrior ... but from a mother to her daughter.

Damika slipped the weapon back into place and straightened. She hadn't known Adira as her mother, and she could very well resent the decisions which that woman had made for the rest of her life. But she had been her High Priestess, too. Further, she had been a woman that Damika had loved and respected. She owed it to that version of her to fulfill her dying wish.

Resolved, Damika turned away from the doors and towards the stairs.

Towards her destiny.

CHAPTER 31

RAWL

"No," Rawl said softly, calmly. His body was a block of ice, incapable of feeling anything. Ice did not feel.

"No," he repeated, watching for the rise and fall of Alric's chest that never came.

His fingers searched, gripping the mage's dirty shirt, shaking his shoulder, pressing his fingers against the side of his neck, searching vainly for a pulse that was not there.

"No!" Rawl shouted this time, gripping the mage and shaking him so hard that his body slid from the chair and landed in a crumpled heap on the floor. Rawl followed him, his limbs no longer able to support his weight. The ice was still there, keeping most of his emotions at bay. But one burned through, hot enough to carve a path through the cold stone in his heart and heat his very blood.

Rage.

"Wake up!" he shouted, gripping Alric's arms and slamming him against the floor. "Now, mago, no estoy jugando!"

He felt Andu's strong hands around him once more, lifting him back and away from the broken body on the floor below them. Rawl tried to kick out, to land a blow on Alric's side, anything that would cause a reaction from the still mage.

"Mago, I swear to all the dioses, if you don't wake up right this moment, I will follow you to the afterlife and plague you for all of eternity!" he raged.

Andu finally succeeded in hauling him back, and immobile in his iron grip, the heat of the anger finally succeeded in melting the ice that held his other emotions at bay. He collapsed into Andu's grasp, the big man somehow able to sustain all of his dead weight. A keening wail tore from his chest, which collapsed in on itself, crumbling like old firewood reduced to ash. He could taste it, the ash on his tongue. No tears escaped his eyes, but his throat let out small, whimpering cries as he tried to draw in breath. He didn't have enough air. Dioses, he was going to suffocate and die too...

But that would be all right, a part of him thought. He would be with Alric, and that wouldn't be so bad.

It was a wild thought, a ridiculous thought, and if he was capable of feeling anything but pain, he might have felt ashamed of it.

His eyes found Alric's form on the ground. "Please, mago," he begged, his voice barely more than a whisper.

And then he saw Alric's finger twitch.

"He's not dead," Rawl gasped.

Rawl's body found new strength, and he railed against Andu, trying to escape the giant's grasp. He held him in a practiced grip that was impossible to break.

"He's not dead!" he yelled again, twisting and pushing against the unmovable wall that held him.

"Oh, Rawl," Mila sobbed, but Rawl saw Alric's fingers curl.

"Look," he cried, pointing at the mage. "Look at him! Just check, please Mila, just check!"

Mila met Andu's gaze above Rawl's head. He wasn't sure what she saw there, but it seemed to convince her. Pressing her lips into a thin line, she crossed to Alric's body, kneeling next to him. Slowly, she placed her fingertips against the side of his neck, just like Rawl had done. After a moment, she frowned.

"Wait," she mumbled, bending her head to place her ear next to Alric's nose and mouth.

"He's breathing," she gasped, voice incredulous. She looked at Andu in shock, then Rawl. "Dioses, he's alive!"

Rawl was too ecstatic to gloat. Andu's grip slackened, and he launched himself from the man's grasp and threw himself on the ground next to his sister. Carefully, he cradled Alric's head in his hands and placed it on his lap.

"Alric?" he said gently, hoping to coax the mage awake. "Mago? How do you feel?"

Rawl watched as Alric's eyes flickered behind closed eyelids, moving the thin skin this way and that. His eyelashes—those impossibly long eyelashes—fluttered, and suddenly Rawl was looking into Alric's eyes once more.

His big, beautiful brown eyes. Not a trace of red left in them, not even the thin red veins that sometimes happen after a poor night's sleep.

"Hola," Rawl breathed, and just like that, all the ash in his chest re-solidified, and he felt like his heart grew ten times larger in his chest. A tear finally escaped him, but it was a tear of profound gratitude and joy. All he could do was grin stupidly down at his friend.

"Como te sientes?" Mila asked gently, and Alric's eyes snapped to hers. He tried to sit up, and Mila helped to steady him. "Easy," she said. "How are you feeling?" she repeated.

Alric frowned at her, then turned to Rawl, staring at his long pale fingers, trapped between Rawl's tanned palm. He licked his chapped lips, wincing.

"What happened?" he asked, his voice gravelly and hoarse, but empty of the rage and malice Alric had assailed Rawl with when the Mage Madness contorted his being. He felt his grin stretch even more foolishly across his face.

"You were ill," Mila told him, avoiding the topic of magical corruption. "Very ill. You are at the Mage University, because no healers were able to help you."

Alric looked confused. "But you did?"

"They did," Rawl answered, his voice tight with emotion. Alric looked back at him, then at their hands. Slowly, he moved his away from Rawl's grip.

"And ... who, exactly, are all of you?"

The next few days were torturous for Rawl.

On the one hand, Alric continued to improve in leaps and bounds. His health improved, his weight began increasing, and, with his daily walks on the beach, the color had begun returning to his skin.

On the other hand, he had no idea who he, or Rawl, was.

The mage was told that his name was Alric, and that he had been ill. He was "introduced" to Rawl, Mila, and Andu. He had no memory of his life before waking up on the university floor, and even more strangely, seemed to have no interest in it. He didn't ask questions about where he had come from, whether he had family, how he had come to be at the university, or even what his mysterious illness had been. He remembered all the basic things about language, social cues, manners, and modality, but besides those things, his life may as well have started right there in that dingy workroom. And he seemed completely content with it.

Mila told Rawl that it was part of the spell, that it wouldn't do, to have full-fledged adults acting like infants, having to retrain and reteach them all the basic necessities of life. So those memories remained, vaguely, as more of a muscle memory. But the rest of his life, his family, his friendships, his conversations, and accomplishments were all wiped away.

Forever.

So Rawl watched from a distance as his friend and once-love continued to improve, not having the slightest clue of who he was to him.

It was a torture far beyond anything Rawl could have imagined.

If it were up to him, he would have left Mila and Andu to nurse the man back to health. He would have kept his distance, if only to protect what was left of his heart. But for some reason, the new Alric seemed to cling to him.

He searched for Rawl in every room, visibly relaxing when seeing him. He didn't eat, unless Rawl was there eating too, sometimes saving his snacks until he could split them with the archer. He was hesitant to venture outdoors unless Rawl was with him. And although he never asked what they had been to each other prior to his illness, he did ask many questions about Rawl and his life. He was, in many ways, like a helpless child, or a puppy, endlessly following Rawl around.

Rawl hated it.

He hated that the madness had reduced his once strong, capable, fierce friend to this insecure man that clung to him like a child.

That didn't mean he was cruel. He smiled back at Alric when their gazes met, though he could see none of the old Alric in the man's eyes. He sat with him, shared his table and his food, and took walks with him on the misty, salt-soaked mornings by the shore.

Some days, Rawl felt nothing but gratitude. Alric was alive, he was healthy, and he was whole. He might not remember him, or his life, but there he was, sweetly seeking him out, wanting to be in his company. Alric now had his entire life ahead of him, to make with it what he wanted.

But other days, there were moments when it grew to be too overwhelming, when the desperation hit Rawl so hard that it stole the air from his chest. It left him wanting to scream and rail and beg Alric to remember, to just *remember him*, when he wanted to lash out and hurt him for not being the person he once was.

On those days, Mila and Andu were there, infinitely patient and strong, taking turns checking in between their classes and practices, allowing Rawl time away from the source of both his greatest joy and worst torment. It was on one of those days when Mila sought him out. Rawl had finally found himself blessedly alone, Andu having taken Alric on a tour of the university grounds.

At first, he had been hesitant. What if the familiar territory jarred the mage's memory, and his magia returned along with the corruption? But Mila had softly assured him that the spell was infallible. That, once complete, there was nothing that could be done to return his memory. A tour of the university would be harmless. They simply avoided topics of his old life because they would only serve to confuse and trouble him, not because he was at risk of remembering.

Mila found her brother outside, sitting on the low branch of a great tree. The bark was rough and solid underneath him, as the trunk supported his back. He had one leg bent on the wood, the other dangling beneath him. He saw Mila coming from the corner of his eye but continued watching the rolling sea in the distance.

Wordlessly, Mila swung herself up next to him, accidentally knocking his elevated leg off the branch. He left it there as she straddled the wood in a mirror image of himself.

"Talk to me," she said.

Rawl sighed. What could he say? Mila waited, not speaking, as Rawl idly watched the swelling and crashing of ocean waves.

"I swore to help the Name-Bearer, and the Unnamed Prince," he said finally, speaking what had been most heavily on his mind.

He admitted that the cause had been secondary in his mind as he tried to save Alric, but now it was an ardent desire once more.

Mila nodded. They had both been supporters of the Flowers, and of the Name-Bearer since they were children. She, more than anyone, knew how important the quest was to Rawl.

"I can't bring him back to that," he confessed, speaking of Alric. "He is not who he was, he will never be—" his voice cracked, and he swallowed through the pain of the words. "He will never again be what he was," he finished. "He will only be a liability. Also, it would hurt Rojya and Churan too much."

"He belongs with you," Mila said softly, but Rawl shook his head.

"He did once," he agreed. "Not anymore."

"He cares for you. He has no idea in what way, or why, but anyone can see that he still cares for you," she said.

Rawl shut his eyes. "And I care for him. But I loved the person he once was. I don't know who this new person will become, but he will never again be my mago."

Mila opened her mouth to speak, but Rawl cut her off.

"I don't blame him for it. Or you, if you're worried about that. I am forever grateful that you were able to save him, even a part of him. In my worst moments, I resent him for it, a little. Needing me so much when he cannot be who *I* need." It shamed Rawl to admit it, but he always spoke the truth with his sister. "But I have no space for him in my life right now."

"He cannot stay here," Mila worriedly muttered. "It's true that mages are not the most organized of people, and that our instructors are more lax than most when it comes to skipping classes, or taking materials, or independent study. But he was a student here, and not that long ago. Eventually, someone will notice him, and that will just lead to too many questions that we cannot answer. Not to mention the confusion that it would cause him."

"I know," Rawl responded, feeling defeated. He didn't know what to do.

"What if we—" he started, before a whistle sang out in the distance. He twisted against the tree, straining to see who was announcing their approach. At first, all he saw was a tall dark silhouette, their figure made hazy by the sun. But then they were closer and in an instant their face came into clear focus. Rawl jumped from the branch and stalked towards them, disbelieving.

"Taruka?" he asked, gaping at the tall Northern woman, her long hair braided into intricate patterns that swung down, long past her shoulders. Her eyes lined with kohl, as usual, and her large bow was strapped to her back. Once, they had been on opposite sides, pointing their bows at one another, each ready to kill the other at the slightest provocation.

Luckily, they had found some small measure of peace between them during their long trek south. He found he liked the woman. However, the fact that they had found a tenable truce during their journey back to Andala did not mean that Rawl could count her as a friend now. He didn't think that they were enemies, but was wary, nonetheless.

Taruka nodded at him in greeting. "Alric?" she asked him in that soft way of hers.

Rawl's shoulders relaxed. He was sure that she was not there to speak solely of the mage, but the fact that her first act was to ask about him made him like her all the more.

"It's a long story, but he lives," he told her, and her answering smile was honest and sweet. "He does not remember his life before the madness, however," he finished, saying it fast. The swiftness of his words did little to dull the pain from the truth in them.

She placed an open palm against her heart, her large black eyes brimming with sympathy. "My heart sings for the life he retains, but cries for the one he has lost."

Rawl swallowed through the tightness in his throat and managed a quick nod. He heard a noise behind him and saw Mila swinging out of the tree to join them. Taruka smiled at her approach.

"Your sister," she said. It was not a question. She nodded towards Mila, then turned back to Rawl. "Is there somewhere we can talk? There is much to say."

Rawl tensed. "Is everyone all right? Did you all make it to the temple? Is Rojya—"

"Nessa passed the Trial of Danray," she said proudly. "She was always a sister, but now it is official. And she needs help. The High Priestess sent me to ask for yours."

Rawl raised his brow. "The High Priestess of the Danrayen Temple is asking for my help?"

Taruka nodded. "She thought you would be well suited to the task."

Rawl frowned, confused. "How would the High Priestess know what tasks I would be well suited for? I've never met the woman in my life."

A sly smile pulled at the corners of Taruka's mouth. "Oh, but you have," she told him.

"By now, Damika will be the High Priestess of Danray."

Chapter 32

Damika

Damika placed one careful foot in front of the other, descending the long stairs slowly and deliberately. She had never felt a day of awkwardness or clumsiness in her entire life, but she wasn't about to let her High Priestess Ascension Ceremony be the first.

Mamá waited for her at the bottom, as well as hundreds of expectant faces. Damika couldn't help but feel that they all wanted something from her. The Pelgar refugees wanted assurance of their safety. Mamá wanted her to fulfill her destiny, and in turn grant Adira's final wish. To see Damika as the High Priestess of her order. The Danrayen Warriors and initiates wanted a leader. Many of the priestesses wanted a better one than her. Perhaps what they wanted most was for her to prove them wrong. That she was worthy of the honor she was about to accept.

Damika couldn't bear to think that they were only waiting for her to prove them right, that she wasn't fit for the position.

The weight of their needs and expectations began to overwhelm her. Her top suddenly felt too snug, too tight. It was being pulled around her ribs and was crushing her lungs. She couldn't take a breath. Her mouth opened in a short gasp as she used every bit of willpower that she possessed to keep herself from reaching around and tearing the fabric in two across her chest.

Just as she thought she would collapse to her knees, she reached the bottom step and caught Nessa's eyes. They shone brightly with pride and admiration, and the look calmed some of the fear within her. If Nessa could see something within her to admire, then perhaps she could strive to be that person. Next to her, she saw Petra, the small woman's frame practically vibrating with pride. Slowly, Damika's breath returned to normal, and her heart settled within her chest.

Mamá beamed at her, then turned to address the crowd.

"Today is a day of great honor for the Danrayens. Last month, we mourned the passing of the head of our order, High Priestess Adira, sworn defender of her people, leader of the warrior women, and Daughter of Danray."

She turned to regard Damika.

"But today is not a day of sorrow, but one of celebration. We welcome one of our own into her new position as our High Priestess. She is the youngest initiate to have taken the Trial of Danray and will now be the youngest High Priestess to ascend to the title."

There were murmurs throughout the crowd.

"In a moment, I will invite you all to join us in our walk to the statue of Danray, where Damika will perform the Ascension Rite. But first, let us congratulate our sister, Damika, the next High Priestess of Danray!"

Cheers erupted throughout the crowd, along with thunderous applause. Her already frayed nerves startled at the sound, but she found Nessa's eyes once more and allowed them to ground her. Mamá began moving towards the temple gardens, to the statue of Danray, and Damika knew that she was expected to follow. However, she found herself completely and utterly frozen in place.

Move, she thought to herself. *It is time to move.*

But her body would not comply. It felt as if she had ingested a poison, one that left her limbs paralyzed, and her feet rooted to the ground. Mamá had stopped walking when she noticed that Damika was not behind her and turned to look at her expectantly.

Damika felt her eyes wide and wild in her head as she tried to open her mouth to call out a warning, to tell them all that something was wrong, that she was unable to move. But she couldn't even open her mouth, let alone form the words.

Her previously quieted anxiety returned with a vengeance, causing her heart to beat so fast and deafening within her chest and ears that she was sure that, at any moment, it would burst like a frightened rabbit or startled bird. She would collapse. There, in front of everyone. Only after they opened her up to examine her would they find her cause of death.

Fear.

She was going to die right there in front of all those people, her people, as a coward.

Then, out of nowhere, Nessa was by her side. She didn't touch her. She didn't even look at her. She just flanked her to the left, standing protectively with her in solidarity. From the corner of her eye, she could see Petra take the spot to her right. She didn't touch her, either, but Damika could feel the warmth of both of their bodies beside her, enveloping her with their strength.

A rush of calm flooded her system, and she found she was able to feel her limbs again. She didn't dare look at them, but allowed herself a tiny sigh, which she knew that they could hear. She hoped they understood that the small gesture contained all her immense gratitude. With them beside her, she felt able to move once more.

Together, they made their way towards the garden.

As they walked, people stopped again and again to greet Mamá, to shake her hand, kiss her cheeks, or whisper in her ear. Damika knew it should not have surprised her, but found herself in awe of just how many people Mamá knew, and how far her network spread. She saw Andalan generals and soldiers greet her with the same respect they would show peers, witnessed full Danrayen Warriors defer to her as they would any other priestess. Damika was certain that she saw members of the Padir, of the Northern Tribes, and nobles from the finest houses in Andala acknowledge the woman. How had she never realized her influence before?

Then, after what seemed both an eternity and a blink of an eye, they were at the base of the Danrayen statue.

Damika looked out into the crowd of people, dressed in their best, there to witness her Ascension. She recognized a few faces, but not many. Damika wondered which faces belonged to her Danrayen sisters, and which to initiates. She thought she could tell some of the people of Pelgar, if only because of how out of place they seemed in the temple, but she also wondered how many of Mamá's spies were among them, hiding in plain sight.

Mamá would know, of course. Not only her spies, but who the villagers were, and likely what their occupations had been when they had lived in Pelgar. She would know which initiates in the crowd showed the most promise on the training fields and in the classrooms. She would have intimate knowledge as to the assignments each Danrayen Warrior had left to be present for the ceremony. It would not shock Damika if Mamá—no, *Sofia*—knew the names of every person in the temple that night.

"Lista?" Mamá whispered to her when they had reached their place. She waited patiently for Damika to consent, so they could begin the ritual.

It's time, Damika thought to herself, forcing her attention back to the task. Her panic did not return. Instead, grim resolution filled her.

It is what must be done, she thought. *For the good of the order.*

Damika frowned. *For the good of the order?* she questioned herself. *Was this truly for the good of them all?*

She stared into Mamá's unwavering gaze, and a perfect, beautiful thought suddenly occurred to her.

"No," she whispered. Mamá's face was instantly concerned.

"¿Qué pasa mija?" she fretted.

Damika shook her head. "No, I am not ready." A smile began to creep its way on to her face.

Mamá glanced behind her at the enormous crowd of waiting people.

"Damika," she started, but Dami interrupted her.

"I am not ready because it is not my time!" She almost laughed at how clear everything had become. "It is not my time," she repeated.

Mamá opened her mouth, likely to disagree, or offer her reassurances, but Damika didn't let her.

"Mamá I am not ready, I'm not! I have been wrestling with this for weeks. Since I learned what was expected of me. I have been struggling so much, trying to make myself believe that this was my path. Forcing myself to swallow my reservations for the good of the order. At first, I thought that my hesitation was just regular nerves, but they aren't. It has been my heart telling me that this isn't my place."

She looked up at the goddess statue and could swear she felt her beaming her love and acceptance down on her.

This is what is right, she thought to herself.

"Damika, the order needs a leader!" Mamá whispered nervously. "We need to present a strong front. A High Priestess must ascend!" her voice tinged with panic as she tried to keep her tone low.

"We do need a High Priestess," Damika agreed, grabbing Mamá's hands. "One that knows the order, and the girls within it like she knows her own heart. Someone who understands what is needed to keep the people of this realm safe. Not a soldier, fighting on the field of battle. But a leader who can see beyond that field."

Nessa and Petra had been quiet the entire time, but suddenly Petra sucked in a deep breath of air through her teeth.

"Someone who knows the other political players on the board, and already has the allyship of many. Someone with spies throughout the realm—hell, throughout all of Tierramadri!" Petra added, staring at Mamá in wonder.

Nessa smiled. "Someone our order already trusts; initiates, Warriors, Riders, and priestesses alike." She turned to Damika. "You're right. This makes the most sense."

"Stop it, all of you!" Mamá cried out. "What you are suggesting is impossible!" Her face pulled tight with worry. "Only a Danrayen Warrior can ascend to High Priestess. And need I remind you that I am not a Danrayen? I never took my Trial! I left before my training was complete!"

"That doesn't mean you aren't a Danrayen," Nessa responded firmly. She took a deep breath. "When I took my Trial, the goddess appeared to me," she added softly.

Petra and Damika took a step back from Nessa at the same time. Talking about one's Trial was not something a Danrayen did, ever! It was worse than bad manners; it was almost vulgar. And yet, the fact that the goddess herself had appeared to Nessa was miraculous. Damika felt torn between asking her to stop speaking and demanding that she tell them more. Nessa did not give them a choice, however, and continued anyway.

"She told me that I had passed the Trial long before I had stepped into the sanctum. That she had already considered me a daughter on her path because of my actions in life. I have no doubt that you have already proven yourself to her as well."

Nessa lifted her fist, thumb out to the goddess statue, bringing it to her neck in sign of tribute.

Mamá only shook her head. "But I am not a fighter!" she argued. "I am skilled enough with blade and bow, it's true, but I haven't trained in the ways of Danray in a long time. I am no warrior!"

"Danray told me that the strength of a warrior is not measured by the sharpness of their blade, but the courage in their heart," Nessa responded, looking at Mamá with a combination of great love and pride. "If that is so, then you are the greatest warrior I have ever known."

Mamá looked stricken. "It's not …" she shook her head. "They will never accept me," she continued, subtly jerking her chin towards the group of older priestesses watching them closely.

"They will if you take the Trial," Nessa suggested.

Damika felt her face break out into an enormous grin. *Of course! Clever Nessa.* They were already there, prepared for a ceremony. They may as well have a Trial.

"Say yes, Mamá," Damika begged her.

"Your mother wanted this for you. You are meant to be High Priestess!" Mamá argued desperately.

"And so I will be," Damika declared. "One day. When I'm truly ready for it. When I have truly earned it. We both know that moment is not now."

There was a brief flicker of acquiescence in Mamá's eyes. Damika was shocked. All this time and Mamá had doubts herself. She had never let them show, not once. She felt herself grinning again. It was more proof that the leadership of the Danrayens belonged to her. The woman was *good*.

"Adira didn't know that the goddess believed us to be warriors even without the Trial," Nessa told the older woman. "I think that, had she known, she would have insisted you take yours a long time ago. And she would have agreed to let Damika grow into the priesthood on her own terms, while you kept her safe until she was ready."

Damika nodded thoughtfully. "I didn't know Adira as my mother. But I knew her well as my High Priestess. She would have wanted the best for the Danrayens." She placed her hands on Mamá's shoulders and looked the smaller woman in the eye.

"You are what's best for all of us."

Mamá's eyes watered, but she allowed no tears to fall. Instead, she gave the smallest nod of her head. A tiny jerk of her chin, but it was enough. Damika felt the weight of a thousand souls, a thousand lives, lift from her chest. She turned to the crowd behind them, who were growing ever more impatient.

"There has been a change of plans," Damika declared. "I know that you all believe you are here to witness me ascend to the title of High Priestess. But the truth is that I am not yet ready for such an honor."

Scandalized gasps and whispers rose all around them, then some shouting. Damika raised her hand as authoritatively as she could, and most of the noise died down.

"We are Danrayens," she continued, allowing her voice to boom. She was speaking directly to her people now. "We are warriors, and warriors value truth. We cannot be effective as fighters, as units, as sisters if we are not truthful with one another. And the truth is that there is someone more worthy of becoming High Priestess on this day."

Damika stepped to the side to pull Mamá to the forefront. Once again, gasps erupted from the crowd, but no one moved to shout or deny her claim. Damika stole a quick glance at the older priestesses, observing them with shock as they looked more thoughtful than upset. Where Damika assumed she would find denial, she saw pensive consideration instead. She thought she even saw General Vashti look at her approvingly.

"The goddess Danray accepts all warrior women into her fold. They can find their way to the order at any age." Damika looked at Mamá.

"Sofia found her way to us when she was young, but the dioses had a different path for her to walk first. Now she has found her way back to us, and no one can deny that she is as part of this temple as any other priestess." Damika saw many young initiates nodding their heads at her words. "Today, she takes her Trial to confirm what it is that so many of us already know."

Damika held Mamá's hand. "Sofia is a true Daughter of Danray."

The roars of the crowd were even louder than those that they had welcomed her with. Damika felt no resentment, but merely filled with an overwhelming sense of pride mingled with relief. She caught Nessa's eye, and they smiled at one another.

This was right.

CHAPTER 33

RAWL

B ack inside the under rooms of the Mage University, Taruka filled Rawl in on what had happened since they had parted ways in Tureene.

Apparently, Rawl had missed quite a lot.

Eventually, Andu and Alric returned, and Taruka was "introduced" to the mage once more. To her credit, she was gracious and kind as always, never indicating that they were familiar with one another. Once she was done with her tale about Lord Guerro, Princess Zerlina, and her half-sister, Kichka, Rawl's head was swimming.

"Have you heard any of this?" Rawl asked Mila and Andu. They lived much closer to the Andalan capital and the royal family. Surely, if there was dark magia brewing inside the palace, there would be some word of it.

Andu shrugged, but Mila bit her lip.

"Que, Mila?" he prodded.

"They're just rumors," she hedged.

"You know as well as I do that many rumors are based in truth," he told her. "What have you heard?"

"There have been stories of monstros of the Night Wood venturing further and further from their eastern border," she said.

Rawl slumped back in his chair. "We know that already," he said sullenly. "We've seen it time and again, up north with the Padir, in Cassalan, and in Tureene. Even as far as the Danrayen Temple," he added, remembering what Taruka had said about the battle waged in Pelgar. "We barely survived a salta-sombras just the other day!"

"Que?" Taruka asked, shocked. Rawl waved her away. He didn't want to get into the story of their failed attempt with the Goldenshell. Or more accurately, pearl.

"Yes, bruto," Mila shot back angrily. "But they are saying that these monstros aren't attacking people of the city. That they are gathering around the capital, and around the palace itself. As if someone was controlling them."

Rawl shot a look at Taruka, and she nodded gravely. "Those are the same reports the Danrayens are sending back to us."

Monstros under someone's control? Rawl wondered. *Taking orders?* It seemed impossible, but they had witnessed many impossible events in the last few years. The word was beginning to lose some meaning.

"Rawl," Taruka continued, "they have the Andalan army, the ones who aren't across the border in Cassalan, anyway. And now, they have an army of monstros."

"No," Rawl denied quickly. "No!" he repeated, not wanting to believe it. If it were true, their quest was doomed to fail. How could they—even with the support of all the Danrayens—hope to defeat a force that strong?

"Do you think this Lord Guerro has enough power to do something like that?" he asked Taruka.

"No," she said quickly. "He isn't powerful in and of himself, he simply surrounds himself with powerful people." She scratched her chin thoughtfully. "Kichka was fairly skilled, even from a young age, but not enough for this. If Zerlina is as powerful as she is, then perhaps, together?" her voice trailed off into a question.

"Could they be the ones who drew the monstros out in the first place?" Rawl wondered.

A quiet descended on the room, each person lost in their own thoughts. Well, Rawl, Taruka, and Mila were lost in their own thoughts. Alric was staring at them all, his gaze darting from person to person shyly. And Andu was preoccupied with what looked like a children's game on the floor.

"You said that Damika—the High Priestess," he fumbled, "had a task for me?"

"The first request is that you give me directions on how to find Leader, and the Padir," Taruka said.

"You want the help of the Padir?" Rawl asked, surprised.

"The Padir are a peaceful people," Mila argued. "We do not involve ourselves in wars."

"You no longer have the luxury of peace," Taruka said in a voice so firm it surprised Rawl. He sometimes forgot that underneath her soft and sweet demeanor, there was a warrior made of the strongest metal.

"The Padir were being plagued by the Night Wood monstros even before I left them," Rawl told Mila softly. "We had lost several members to their evil. If there was a chance to be rid of them and end the war in the North ..." he trailed off. "If we could be safe, I think Leader would at least consider it."

Mila looked upset but said nothing more. Rawl turned back to Taruka.

"I can provide you with a map to the Padir encampment where Leader will most likely be this time of year," he told her.

"Gracias," Taruka answered.

"You said that was the first thing? Is there more?" Rawl asked.

"Yes. We also need you to rally the mages to our cause," she answered.

At that, Rawl laughed out loud. "Me? How am I to convince a group of stuffy, snobbish, magia-wielders to believe in the Flowers?" he asked, and then yelped as he felt a fist collide with his arm.

"I am one of those 'stuffy, snobbish, magia-wielders,'" Mila glared at him. "Or did you forget?"

"I didn't mean you, Filomila!" Rawl argued, rubbing at his arm.

"Nessa needs to bring Churan to the Flowers," Taruka continued, as if she hadn't noticed their childish antics. "It is the only thing that will stop all of this. And to reach the palace, we will need all the help we can get."

Rawl nodded. Hadn't he already realized that the Danrayens would not be enough of a force to contend with an entire army of monstros? Taruka was right, they would need both the Padir and the mages to offer their aid as well. But ...

"But how?" he said, finishing his thought out loud.

"There are more people sympathetic to the Name-Bearer than you think," Mila said suddenly, her voice low. "The Archwizard Auberon was a regular at this university, you know, before he was imprisoned for treason against the crown."

"So, he was gathering supporters?" Rawl asked, somewhat heartened at the news.

"Yes," Mila said, stretching out the word. "I don't know much about it. It was before my time. But, even now, there are whispers. Passed down from the older students. Stories too specific to be all rumors. Stories about a secret order. That sort of thing is very appealing to mages in academia."

She paused for a moment, her lips pressed into a thin line. With a little sigh, she continued. "But after his arrest, it seems that people grew scared. If there was a secret society, they likely dissolved. No one has heard whispers of students meeting in the dark or exchanging covert messages. I wouldn't have believed that they ever existed at all, if it wasn't for a certain professor. He slipped once, basically confirming the existence of the order, but wouldn't tell me anymore when pressed."

"Do you think we could get that professor to say more?" Rawl asked. "Could we spurn this 'secret society' into action once more?"

Mila shook her head. "They're too frightened, Rawl," she argued. "It would take time, far more time than it seems we have."

"Isn't there anything that we can do to reignite their support?" Rawl asked, frustrated.

"Nothing short of the Archwizard Auberon himself showing up at the university and demanding their fealty," she quipped.

Rawl sat still, mind racing.

"Rawl, no," Mila gasped, horrified. She knew him too well. "It is impossible," she insisted.

"That word is beginning to lose meaning to me," he said, voicing aloud what he had been thinking earlier.

"No, Rawl, it can't be done!" she cried.

"I missed something," Taruka said, frowning.

"Rawl is considering breaking the Archwizard Auberon from the most heavily guarded building in the southern realm," Mila replied, in a voice that let Rawl know just how stupid she believed him to be in that moment.

"I've always been a fair hand at picking locks," he said.

"Regular locks!" Mila screeched. "Do you really think that the most powerful mage in the entire realm, perhaps in all of Tierramadri, will be incarcerated with regular, ordinary locks?"

"You are the most promising mage in an age," Rawl shot back. "You cured—" he cut himself off before saying "Mage Madness." "You cured Alric," he amended. "You are powerful. And strong. Between the two of us, we can do this. I know it."

"Three of us," Andu mumbled, still preoccupied with the puzzle-like game. Rawl beamed at him gratefully.

"Three of us, then," he amended. Mila was shaking her head. "Mila," he said softly, holding her hands. "We have to do something. We have to try. If you really don't believe we can sway the mages to our cause ..." he paused until Mila reluctantly shook her head, "then we need to get the one person who can."

"We don't even know where he is being kept!" Mila argued. "The palace is enormous, and unless you became a noble since the last time we saw each other, then none of us has ever been in the palace! We wouldn't know our way around!"

"I know my way around the palace," a surprising voice interrupted them.

All eyes turned to land on Alric, who looked as confused as they did.

"I know ..." he trailed off, frowning. Then he nodded and shrugged. "Yes, I know my way around the palace."

Rawl glanced at Mila, who looked stricken.

"I told you. Basic things don't always leave. He won't know why he knows the palace grounds, he won't even care why," she told Rawl and Taruka quietly. "But if he says he remembers, then he remembers."

"No," Rawl said quickly. "We're not taking him."

Alric's eyes were darting across from person to person, watching them whisper amongst themselves across the room. He looked anxious until his eyes met Rawl's. Then his body visibly relaxed, and a small, tentative smile pulled across his lips.

Something painful twisted inside of Rawl's body, like a knife to the gut. Alric, *his* Alric, never looked at him with such vulnerability, and he didn't know how to feel about it. If only—but no. There was no point in reminiscing about the past or wishing for a different future. That part of his life was gone.

Rawl frowned on instinct, then had a moment of regret when Alric looked down at the ground, his eyes full of hurt.

He shook his head and turned back to Mila and Taruka. "We can't bring him. He's a liability," he insisted.

"If he knows the layout of the castle, then he is anything but," Mila argued. "If you will not be persuaded out of this insane plan, then we will need him."

"He is like a newborn pup," Rawl whispered harshly. "How can we guarantee his safety?"

"If we venture into the Andalan Palace with the sole purpose of breaking out their most infamous and dangerous prisoner, then we can guarantee none of our safeties!" Mila argued.

"Why not ask him?" Taruka said, her voice quiet and even.

Rawl looked at her, exasperation tensing his shoulders. "He—" he started, but Taruka cut him off.

"He is not a newborn babe, or a pup, and to say so is completely condescending," she chastised him. "Just because he is not the man that you remember does not mean he is not a man," she continued, and the gaze she leveled on Rawl made him shrink in on himself, shame burning in his chest and throat.

"He is capable of making his own choices," she finished.

"I want to go," Alric cut in, his voice so low, Rawl barely heard it. The archer closed his eyes. He had thought that the rest of them were speaking quietly enough that Alric would not hear, or at least that he would not be too interested in their conversation to try. But Taruka was right, he wasn't a child, he was a man. He had to stop punishing him for not being the man that Rawl wanted him to be.

Alric cleared his throat and pitched his voice louder. "I understand the importance of the Name-Bearer, and the Unnamed Prince. I know that all of you," he looked at Andu, who had stopped playing his game, Mila, and finally at Rawl, "believe deeply in the quest. I want to help."

"It will be dangerous," Rawl said gruffly. "We might not succeed. We may be imprisoned with Archwizard Auberon; or be killed. You need to know that."

Alric lifted his chin. "I don't know what happened to me before I awoke here. I find I don't seem to care. Every time I try to recall, my thoughts slip away, and I lose interest." He shrugged. "I don't know if I should care, but I find that I do not. But I do care about all of you," he continued, nodding around the room. "You all have helped me, that much I know. I trust you all, that much I know as well." He looked straight at Rawl. "And I would help you all, if I could."

Mila met Rawl's eyes, tilting one shoulder up.

It's up to you, she seemed to say.

Rawl sighed, then rubbed his forehead with his right hand.

"I suppose we should start planning a dungeon heist," he said reluctantly. "And make preparations for a trip."

"Excellent," Andu beamed at them, sitting up from the floor. "Where are we going?"

CHAPTER 34

CHURAN

C huran was back at the dam.

As always, the scenery was beautiful; green and rich. He noticed that the more of the water he freed from the dam, the more wildflowers bloomed in his mind. The ground around the trickling river was becoming more abundant and less arid, and he could feel the reflection of that outside of his meditation, through the improved accessibility to his power.

"Remember," Mage Nuna's voice broke through his meditation softly. "Only remove what you feel capable of today."

Since the first time he had found the dam, Churan had been moving more and more of his inner obstruction. At first, mentally moving a single rock or stick had left Churan weak and exhausted for days. Now, he was far more adept at maneuvering the blockage, and the increasing flow of the stream was testament to that. Every time he looked at the heightened water level, he felt a rush of pride. Still, he knew Nuna was right. He didn't need to move boulders; not yet. For today, a few pieces of debris would be enough.

His work was faster and easier each time he did it, managing larger pieces with greater ease. By the time Churan finally opened his eyes within the waking plane, his brow tingled with sweat and his muscles ached as if he had really been moving rubble. He was also hungry; very hungry. He had managed to remove an entire tree branch this time, as well as several smaller stones, and he could already feel his power flowing more swiftly within him.

"Muy bien," Mage Nuna said, shifting her posture in front of him. Churan felt a shiver of pleasure at her praise.

It's working! he thought to himself. *The hard work is paying off!*

"We will return to this tomorrow, after practicing your Burning."

Churan glanced at the row of candles set out to his right. Only half of them had melted down to puddles of wax, and only one had exploded! He had managed to light the rest with just enough magia.

Improvement.

Churan thanked the mage with a small bow and turned to where Axchel was sitting in the corner. He couldn't understand how the man could sit there so quietly and patiently for hours on end. It would have bored Churan right out of his mind, but Axchel assured him that he didn't mind.

The soldier lifted himself off the floor as Churan bounded over to him.

"Let me guess, you want to eat?" Axchel asked him, his voice teasing. Churan nodded furiously.

"Si, por favor!" he answered, half jogging to keep up with Axchel's long-legged stride. "I don't know why I get so hungry after I meditate! I mean, if I was doing actual work, with my hands and my arms, or working the fields like farmers, or training like the warriors, I would understand! But I am not even moving. I am just sitting there."

"Are you not expending energy to expand your mind and consciousness?" Axchel asked him, and Churan stopped to consider it. Then had to run to catch up when Axchel didn't stop with him.

"I suppose you're right. You must be right, anyway, because it happens every time, doesn't it?" he mused out loud. "Do you think they'll have those apple tarts at the kitchen? Like last time? The ones with cinnamon and honey and all those other spices? With the crispy crust..." his voice drifted as his eyes went dreamy at the memory. "Do you think they will?" he asked again, his voice filled with hope.

"I heard say that it was the end of apple season," Axchel answered regretfully. "But I'm sure they will have something else you will like just as much."

"I'll never like anything as much as those apple tarts," Churan grumbled sullenly. Then brightened. "Unless they have that herbed bread with melted queso!"

Axchel laughed. "Whatever they have today, we must eat quickly," he reminded the boy. "There is another council meeting today, and Nova wants us there."

Churan sobered. "With the new High Priestess," he said, almost reverently.

"With the new High Priestess," Axchel confirmed.

CHAPTER 35

RAWL

"Let's go over the plan again," Rawl insisted, sitting in the back of the old horse cart with Mila and Alric. Andu was driving the wagon, and Rawl was unsurprised to find that the man was quite good with horses and other animals, likely due to his easygoing nature.

It was not Viejo pulling them this morning, as the weight of the extra people in the cart—including Andu—would have proven too much for the old boy. Instead, Andu had borrowed Montaña from the mage stables, a horse truly worthy of his name. He carried them along with ease.

"We have been through the plan a hundred times," Mila argued. "A million times! I could recite the plan in my sleep!" she said, flinging herself backwards dramatically.

Alric grinned shyly at her antics, but Rawl stayed firm. "Wonderful," he told her. "Then you can walk us all through it once more."

Mila groaned but righted herself once more. "We get to the Andalan capital, say we are from the Mage University and have traveled there to pick up supplies, so they allow us through the gates. Andu stole us some passes. You know, he's quite nimble for someone as big as he is."

Andu didn't turn, but Rawl watched as the back of the man's neck turned red. Rawl looked to see if Mila had noticed, catching her self-satisfied smirk.

What is going on between the two of them? he thought, not for the first time.

"We leave the horse and carriage at an inn friendly to the Padir, near the outskirts of the city and make our way on foot, so we are less likely to be remembered. Just a blade of grass in a glade, with how many people there are in cities."

Both she and Rawl shuddered. They were both forest people at heart, that many people all together was only good for one thing: pickpocketing. But that's not what they were going there for now.

"When we get to the palace, we keep the original story. We say we are on a supply run from the university and need a few special ingredients in the palace mage-rooms." Mila continued. "The passes aren't the special passes that would actually allow us access inside the palace, but so few mages need to go gather supplies there that we are hoping the guard, or guards, won't know the difference."

"And if they do?" Rawl pressed.

Mila rolled her eyes, and Rawl had a flash of her as an awkward little kid, complete with a splattering of freckles and two missing front teeth. "Then we complain about our instructors giving us the wrong documents but leave."

"That's right, we leave and reassess. No trying to subdue the guards or slip by them. We regroup at the inn and figure out a new plan," Rawl insisted.

"We know, Rawl!" Mila groaned. "I'm not trying to fight off some palace guards!"

"It wouldn't be the first time you tried to fight off guards!" Rawl countered.

"I was twelve! And he took my pan dulce!" Mila argued.

"The pan dulce that you *stole* from the pastelería window!" Rawl reminded her.

"That is completely besides the point!" she huffed indignantly.

"Con cuidado," Andu cautioned them suddenly. "We are approaching the gates."

The three of them in the cart turned to face forward just as the capital came into view, the palace proud and towering above the rest of the cityscape. As they got closer, Rawl noticed large, dark figures dotting the sides of the expansive city gates. He squinted to see them better. Had they added giant sculptures to the city facade since he had last been?

Then Mila gasped and clutched the sleeve of Rawl's tunic.

"Dioses," she whispered, her voice stricken. "It's true, it's all true."

Rawl couldn't understand what she was gaping at, until suddenly, terribly, it came into view. What he had thought were statues were actually monstros of the Night Wood.

Fear gripped him so fiercely that he couldn't have moved if his life depended on it. He felt rooted to the spot, watching in horror as the parade of creatures from the worst of his nightmares strolled casually around the capital city.

There were several of those demon dogs prowling the length of the gate, their ugly leathery hides slicked with oily sweat, spittle flying from their mouths as they paced. Alric had nearly lost his life battling two of those creatures, and there were at least *thirty* that he could see from his vantage point on the cart. Enough to tear each of them to shreds without so much as a thought.

There were also lizard-like creatures, and what he presumed was a yacumama, though he had never seen one before. The stories he was told as a child spoke of a giant sea serpent that could devour a full-grown man with a single snap of its jaws. The thing certainly looked the part, sinuous and scaly, with a head large enough to easily swallow him whole. Rawl was certain they were not supposed to exist outside of the water, and yet there it was.

Worst of all, however, there were at least twelve orcuyos. Their immense frames made Rawl a little ashamed of having called Andu a giant in his head so many times since meeting the man. He was an extraordinarily large man, but he was still clearly just a man. The size and bulk of the orcuyos was unnatural and terrifying. The tops of their heads almost reached the top of the gates, their bulging muscles stretching wide. Tough, nearly impenetrable skin was on display, dirty gray clothes wrapping around their lower bodies. Two tusks protruded roughly from their lower lips, fat and yellow, curving inwards.

When he and his company had been in Cassalan, seeking Axchel, a single orcuyo destroyed an entire company of soldiers, and there, in front of him, stood at least a dozen. The city would be decimated.

"They're not attacking," Andu whispered, his voice a combination of fear and wonder.

Their cart had reached a small line of other wagons and walking travelers, waiting to be admitted into the city. Most of the people looked as terrified as Rawl felt, shooting glances at the monstros flanking them on all sides. One demon dog got too close to a family on their cart, and the mother screamed, pulling her child back from the edge and wrapping herself around the crying boy. A guard called out, striding forward from his place at the gates, brandishing a long-spiked spear. But to Rawl's amazement, when he reached the family, he did not drive back the dog. Instead, he rapped the spear against the wagon and yelled at the woman to shut up, and to "keep her brat quiet as well."

He felt a warm hand slip into his own, and he squeezed automatically, assuming that it was Mila. It took him a second to realize that the hand was too large to be his sister's, and he glanced down quickly. It was Alric's hand in his own, his long-tapered fingers wrapped around Rawl's calloused palm. He looked towards the face of his old friend, but he was preoccupied with staring up at the orcuyos, his tan brow dotted with sweat.

It was a battle with monstros like these that led to Alric's Mage Madness, and Rawl wondered if they were one of those things that Alric remembered, but *didn't* remember at the same time. The mage certainly looked like he was reliving an old terror.

He's not a mage any longer, Rawl reminded himself. Unable to help himself, Rawl shifted his grip to interlace his fingers with Alric's, and Rawl could see a pretty flush creep up the man's cheeks at the action.

Rawl looked away, trying to drive the image from his mind. He didn't have time to dissect the confusing knot of emotions in his stomach; they had a mission to accomplish.

Together, their group watched as the line to enter the city became shorter, and shorter, as most people gained passage through the gates. The guards only turned one person away that they could see, for reasons unknown. By the way that the man hustled away from the gates, darting furtive glances at the monstros behind him, he didn't seem too upset about it.

Throughout the entire process, the monstros were called to heel, somehow. Rawl had no idea how it was possible, but somehow, someone had trained the monstros against attacking at random. Either that, or they were being controlled. It was unfathomable, and more frightening than he had words for.

Then it was their turn. Andu confidently wove their anxious party to the guards, passing them their stolen paperwork with steady hands. The man asked Andu a few questions, which Rawl couldn't hear over the roaring in his ears. He felt Alric squeeze his hand tighter, but found that he didn't mind the sensation. Andu must have answered their queries to their satisfaction, because once again they were moving, rolling into the city streets.

"No," Mila gasped beside him, and Rawl's heart sank, seeing what she did at the same time.

The city was completely overrun with monstros.

CHAPTER 36

RAWL

The monstros spread much further than the city gates. There were dozens more inside, stationed on corners, prowling the streets, and perched on the roofs of buildings and houses. As they continued their way through the cobbled pathways, Rawl could see that they were everywhere. The dozens he had originally seen quickly turned into hundreds of monstros. They weren't attacking the people, but lingering menacingly.

The air was ripe with the stench of both rot and fear, permeating the city streets, clinging to the buildings and alleyways. Civilians that had dared to brave the outside of their homes walked quickly and silently, their heads down, cloaks pulled tight around themselves, as if it would somehow protect them from a monstro attack, should one occur. The tension in the air was palpable, and Rawl felt it coursing through himself and his companions.

In wordless agreement, they reached the inn as fast as they possibly could, leaving the horse and cart with the stable hand. Each of them visibly relaxed once they were indoors. Which was ridiculous, because if the monstros decided to suddenly attack, being indoors or outdoors would make no difference. They were all guaranteed an ugly and painful death.

Mila left them at the doorway to talk to the innkeeper, while the rest of them shuffled awkwardly inside the great room to look warily out of the window. The inn was more crowded than expected, likely other travelers mimicking their own sentiments of feeling safer inside. People who would have once slept in courtyards or found a night's lodging in a hayloft, now crowded into whatever imagined safety that they could find.

After a few moments, Mila made her way back to them.

"They always save a few rooms for Padir, as is the code," she let them know. "Fortunately, there are no other Padir here today. Lucky for them," she continued, shuddering at the monstros outside. "So, we got two rooms."

"We should—" Rawl started, but Mila cut him off.

"The trip took longer than we expected, and it will be dark soon. We don't want to be out there when it's dark," she added, her face losing some of her color.

"Why? I mean, besides the obvious," Rawl said, motioning to the throng of monstros outside.

"There is a city-wide curfew in effect," Mila said. "Apparently *they*," she jutted her chin towards the window, "are well behaved during the day. Once the sun goes down, however, they have leave to hunt anyone, or anything, left out on the streets."

"Qué?" Andu gasped.

Mila nodded.

"And the palace isn't doing anything?" Rawl demanded, aghast.

"They are the ones enforcing it," Mila replied, her voice grim.

Rawl bit the inside of his cheek, feeling his hands curling into fists. *What kind of nobles allowed this treatment of their people? What has happened to Andala?*

"So, we rest. Isabella," she said, motioning to the innkeeper, "has sent baths up to our rooms. Andu and I will take room three. You and Alric can take room five," she finished, handing Rawl a key.

"But—me and—why," Rawl stammered, looking between his sister and the very quiet Alric.

"Well, I'm not sharing a room with you, hermano!" she scoffed. "I grew up with you. I know how badly you snore."

With that, she turned, dragging a bewildered Andu behind her.

The room suddenly felt too hot, too crowded. Rawl couldn't make himself meet Alric's eyes. He felt him shifting awkwardly beside him. Finally, Rawl cleared his throat.

"I don't snore," he muttered sullenly.

"I might," Alric answered, and Rawl caught the taller man giving him a rueful smile.

Rawl licked his lips and swallowed. "You don't," he replied without thinking.

Alric stared down at him for a long moment. Finally, it was Rawl who broke their gaze. "Come on, we should go before the bath water gets cold."

The short trip upstairs felt tense, at least to Rawl. He could feel the heat of Alric climbing the steps behind him, all the way to their room. That tension did not dissipate when they unlocked the door and entered, revealing a small chamber with a single full bed.

"Oh," Rawl said, under his breath. He noticed a still-steaming tub near the window. "You can go first," Rawl said, motioning towards it. "I will go bring us some food."

"You don't have to—" Alric began, but Rawl was practically running back to the door.

"Take your time! With so many people down there, it might take a while!" He was back in the hallway before Alric could respond. He shut the door harder than he intended, then slumped his head against it.

I will not think of Alric bathing, he chided himself, already imagining the water sliding off the planes of his body.

"Damn it," he muttered, making his way back to the first floor. When he reached the bottom of the stairs, surprise filled him at the sight of Andu, redder than Rawl had ever seen him.

They nodded at one another.

"Food?" Andu asked, as they made their way to the tavern portion of the inn.

"Food," Rawl confirmed. He wondered if he was as flushed as the big man was.

At the tavern bar, they perched on two stools, waiting for their orders.

"Your sister, is uh," Andu coughed. "She was bathing, so I ..."

"Yeah," Rawl said quickly. "Alric too. So, I also ..."

"Of course, of course," Andu replied.

When the food arrived, four heaping plates of pollo rostizado, arroz amarillo and fat, yellow and white potatoes, they both got up quickly.

"So, tomorrow?" Andu mumbled, not meeting Rawl's eye.

"Yes, uh, tomorrow," Rawl replied. They nodded to one another, then seemed to realize simultaneously that they were walking in the same direction.

The walk back upstairs was even more awkward than it had been with Alric.

Damn Mila and her meddling, Rawl thought irritably.

Knocking on the door with two full plates proved impossible, so Rawl kicked at the bottom of the door with his boot a few times. He heard some noises behind the door and when it opened, there stood

Alric, looking clean and soft in a sleep shirt, wet hair dripping onto the fabric at his shoulders.

Rawl couldn't help but stare.

"Oh, let me help you," Alric said suddenly, grabbing both plates from him before Rawl could think of anything to say. He placed them on the small table in the corner, its surface barely able to sustain both. Then he motioned to the seats.

"Do you want to, or that is, would you rather ..." his voice trailed off. "The water is still warm."

Rawl shook his head, not in denial, but to clear it. "Yes, you eat. I'll bathe first," he said, feeling the warmth creep back up his cheeks.

It seemed both he and Andu were destined to remain red-faced that day.

Deliberately, Alric turned the small stool around and sat facing the back wall, leaving Rawl a small amount of privacy. He was grateful for it. Even still, he bathed quickly, then pulled on his own clean sleep shirt as fast as he could, making it to the table before Alric was halfway finished with his meal.

They ate in silence, the room filled with a heady tension that confused Rawl. He knew that this was not the Alric he had once known, but in a way, that fact had seemed to free the Alric before him now. The mage he had known had never looked at him with such naked longing, or held his hand openly, or blushed under candlelight at Rawl's lingering gaze. They might have one day discovered those small moments between one another, but that life had been stolen from them. The Alric before him knew none of the hesitation or insecurity that his old friend had faced. It seemed that he gave himself permission to simply feel whatever it was that he felt, and it made Rawl's insides cramp with uncertainty.

On the one hand, Alric still held the lanky, regal beauty that had drawn the archer to him in the first place. He still had that mop of unruly dark hair, the least fastidious thing about him. It constantly flopped over his eyes, so deep and dark they appeared black unless in direct sunlight, when only the slightest bits of mahogany were visible. They blinked at him now, their infinite eyelashes nearly touching the low swoop of his brow. He watched patiently, allowing Rawl's slow perusal, mouth parting slightly with a deep inhale.

Quickly, Rawl looked away and stood to cross to the closed window, the rest of his meal forgotten.

He isn't him, he reminded himself. *He isn't your mago, no matter how much he looks like him.*

It hurt, but Rawl knew it would hurt much more if he allowed himself to forget that, even for a moment.

Once his treacherous heart began settling in his chest, Rawl finally began to understand the scene he was watching outside of the inn. Monstros prowled the city in throngs, some leaping from rooftop to rooftop, perched on balconies, skulked in corners. Rawl even saw a few winged shadows circling in the night sky. His skin, which had been pleasantly warm from the bath, became cold and clammy.

"It won't be enough," he murmured quietly, and felt Alric's gaze on him.

"What won't be enough?" the man asked him.

Rawl shook his head. "Even with the Danrayens, the Padir, and the mages, it won't be enough. How can we fight this?" he motioned outside. Alric moved to join him, but didn't come so near that Rawl could feel the heat of him. He appreciated that.

"We have to try," Alric said, softly but full of conviction. Rawl glanced at him in surprise.

Alric regarded him seriously.

"Forgive me," he said suddenly, rushed, as if the words were ripped from his throat.

Rawl wrapped his arms around himself, suddenly wary. "What do you need my forgiveness for?" he asked him.

Alric ran a hand through his hair, wincing as his fingers got tangled in a few unruly knots the bathwater had created. "I don't know what we were to each other, before my illness," he said.

Rawl's mouth dropped open, but he didn't speak.

"I know there is much I do not remember of that time, and I find I do not care to know. If I consider it ..." his eyes suddenly turned glassy, and his voice faded, as they did every time he tried remembering his past. Rawl's stomach turned sour. He wanted to look away, but the man's earlier words lodged into him like an arrow in a buck, striking at the very heart of him. He needed to hear what it was that Alric was trying to say.

The fog lifted from Alric's eyes, and when they refocused on Rawl, he smiled. The sight of it knocked the breath from Rawl's lungs.

"Do you ..." he hesitated. "Do you remember what you were just saying to me?" he asked hesitantly.

"No," Alric said, dashing all of Rawl's frayed and fragile hope to the ground. "What was I saying?"

Rawl turned away so that Alric couldn't see the tears that had flooded his eyes.

"Nothing important," he lied, staring back out at the monstro-filled streets.

He felt Alric step closer. "We will defeat them," Alric stated confidently.

Rawl gave a watery sniffle. "What makes you so sure?" he asked.

"You will convince the mages to join us, with or without this Archwizard," Alric continued.

Rawl whirled around, forgetting himself. "How on earth would a forest-rat of the Padir convince a bunch of stuffy mages, most of noble births, to join our cause?" he sputtered, then laughed. "You don't know me very well if you think I'm capable of it. In fact, you don't know me at all, so keep your ridiculous notions to yourself."

Alric looked hurt, but Rawl couldn't make himself feel sorry for the words. He needed to remind them both of their truth.

"I don't know what we were to each other, before," he repeated, the same phrase that had lifted Rawl high into the stars just moments before, only to dash him to pieces on the hard earth once more. He closed his eyes, not wanting to relive it.

"I don't remember," Alric paused. "I can't remember, or try to. I'll fade..." his voice trailed off, and he was quiet for so long Rawl assumed he was under the effects of the fog once more. But when he opened his eyes once more to meet his, they were alert.

"I do not remember here," he said, motioning vaguely to his head. "But I remember here," he continued, placing his hand over his heart. "I know not how, but every drop of blood in my body sings to me when you are near. And I know that we will succeed, because you are with us. I have complete faith in you, even if I do not know why."

Rawl couldn't contain the desperate, ragged inhale that caught in his throat. Alric stepped closer to him.

"I may not know you very well, as you say," he whispered. "But I think that my soul does."

CHAPTER 37
NOVA

There was a new High Priestess.

The moment that Mamá stumbled out from the inner sanctum, Nova knew that she had passed. Not that she had had any doubt. But when she emerged, glassy-eyed and dazed, Nova suspected that she too had met the goddess inside those golden walls.

There had been a quick, unanimous decision among the council members while she took her Trial, agreeing that, if and when she passed, they would grant her the title and position of High Priestess.

Damika had begun performing the Ascension Rite immediately, reciting the words that Mamá had been ready to deliver to her. Mamá, to her credit, did not miss a step, but settled into the ritual seamlessly. Within moments, it was done.

Mamá was an official Danrayen, and the High Priestess of the Danrayen Order.

The fiesta had continued on schedule, despite the change in leadership. Guests were happy to cheer, eat, dance, and celebrate the new era of Danrayen Warriors. Nova had seen the older priestesses welcome Mamá with more warmth and acceptance than she had expected. General Vashti, in particular, surprised her. She had made a speech, holding her glass of ron high in the air, welcoming Mamá into their fold.

Even so, as she stepped into the council room, Nova couldn't help but wonder if all the niceties had been simply for show. Once the council room doors shut, would the air turn resentful and angry once more?

Axchel and Churan were already in the room, the boy finishing off a crispy, sticky-looking pastry. Axchel grinned at her as he wet a face cloth with the water pitcher on the table, passing it to the young sorcerer.

Nova smiled back at them both, crossing to her usual chair.

Damika walked in, looking rested and calm. Her back was straight, shoulders pulled back and proud. There was an easy, carefree nature to her gait that Nova realized she had not seen in weeks.

It had been weighing on her more than I realized, Nova thought guiltily. *How had I not seen how much she was carrying?*

Nova had known Damika hadn't wanted to be High Priestess. At least, not now. But she, like everyone else, had assumed that Dami would accept the position and rise to the challenge. Nova still believed that, had she gone through with the Ascension, that Damika would have made a wonderful High Priestess. It would have been a blessing to the Danrayens.

But it would have been a torture to Damika.

"Buenas tardes niñas," Priestess Ianuaria said sweetly as she walked in with Priestess Sinchi.

"Buenas tardes," Nova stammered, unused to their attention. So far, the priestesses had only spoken directly to her in the meetings, and only when absolutely necessary.

"Phanessa, Damika," General Vashti greeted them with a nod, entering after them.

Nova glanced at Damika in surprise, and the woman responded with a small shrug. She apparently didn't know why the priestesses were suddenly treating them better, either.

"We have had word from Taruka," a voice interrupted, causing Nova to jump. Mamá strode purposefully into the room, Petra fast behind her.

"What?" Petra asked. "When? From where?" she demanded, practically trampling on Mamá's heels. "What does she say?"

"There is a private missive for you as well, which I will give to you after the meeting," Mamá answered, sitting in the head chair as if it were reserved for her all along. Damika sat to her right, Nova to her left.

This feels right, Nova thought.

Reluctantly, Petra found her seat as well. The doors closed behind them, and Mamá opened the letter in her hand.

"First of all, Taruka is safe and well," she said. "She found her way to the Mage University."

Nova felt an invisible hand squeeze her heart. She braced herself for the news to come.

"Your friend, Alric, is alive," Mamá continued.

A strangled croak escaped Nova's lips as air rushed from her lungs. She hadn't realized that she had been holding her breath.

"They managed to stop the Mage Madness, but unfortunately, his memories have been lost in the process. He lives but does not know who he is."

At the words, the hard, practical woman Nova had gotten used to seeing over the past weeks was replaced by the Mamá of Nova's youth. Her voice was low and compassionate, and her eyes conveyed to her all the regret she felt at delivering her the news. Nova trembled, not knowing what to feel.

Alric is alive! she thought to herself. *But he doesn't know who he is?*

"Can he—" Nova started, but Mamá cut her off.

"That is all I know at this time, and there is more to report," she said. The High Priestess was back.

Nova nodded, slumping back into her chair. At that moment, she wanted nothing more than to escape to the university and see her friend for herself, but she knew that, although it didn't feel like it in her heart, there were more important issues at hand.

"Taruka also gathered the location of Leader," Mamá continued, passing a slip of paper down the table until it reached Petra. The Danrayen scanned the parchment with a nod.

"I can make it there with this," she said.

"That, I am afraid, is all that we know thus far. Taruka says that she will be making her way to the Andalan capital. Reports from the mages confirm what we have heard, that monstros are moving south towards the city. It seems they may be gathering in even greater numbers than we first believed."

The room was quiet for a long moment.

"That is all," Mamá added, almost as an afterthought.

"If numbers are greater than we believe—" General Vashti began, "then I am unsure if *our* numbers will be enough to hold them back." She looked dazed. "I have been defending this realm from war for decades. But that is a war against men. How are we to fight both men and monstros with our resources?"

"We will have the mages," Nova insisted, though she was uncertain. Without Alric and his memories, would Rawl find a way to rally them to their cause? "And the Padir."

"That may be enough, but only just," Vashti murmured, shaking her head. "What do you think?" she asked Sinchi, their master strategist.

Sinchi had been scribbling marks and figures on a parchment in front of her, all while the others had been speaking. A harsh line had marked itself in between her brows, and a coil of honey-colored hair had escaped from its fastening to fall over her cheek.

"We will be at a disadvantage, but it may be just enough if our aim is to attack the capital," she finally answered. "In order to control the monstro problem and confront Lord Guerro."

"And deliver Churan to the Flowers," Nova interrupted stubbornly. She knew that the Danrayen Order had different goals than her, but she didn't see why they couldn't align.

"Of course," Mamá agreed quickly, and Nova relaxed.

"Is this what we have decided to do?" Priestess Ovidia asked. "Attack the capital?"

"We now have confirmation from one of our own that they are amassing monstros to them," General Vashti said. "The same monstros who have been attacking our people without restraint for months. We cannot believe that their migration, along with the presence of Lord Guerro at the Andalan Palace, is a coincidence."

"We must move against them. Before they have the chance to come into their full strength. We do not know what their intent may be, but we know it cannot be good," Priestess Sinchi added.

"What about the queen?" Mage Nuna asked. "Do we really believe that she condones this? Controlling monstros of the Night Wood?"

"We do not know the queen's intentions," Mamá answered. "We do not know if she is complicit, or if Lord Guerro has coerced her. If he has found a way into her bed, we can assume he has also found his way onto her council."

"We need to recall all of our active Danrayen Warriors," Damika suggested. "Not for a Summoning, as that now seems unnecessary. But because we will need all of our forces accounted for in order to know how best to distribute them."

"Of course," Vashti agreed, "And you will be in charge of their new assignments."

Damika raised her eyebrows at the woman, her mouth gaping.

"Don't look so surprised, niña," Vashti grumbled. "You were always my best student, and the most promising warrior the Danrayens have ever seen. Just because I didn't believe you ready to lead our order yet does not mean I do not trust you to lead at all."

Damika nodded mutely, but Nova hid a smile behind her hand.

"This will leave us vulnerable to the North," Petra commented.

"The Andalan army will have to hold back the Cassalains without Danrayen aid for a while," Priestess Ianuaria agreed.

"There will be heavy losses without them to protect the Borders," Nuna concurred.

"I can suggest ways to fortify their defenses against Cassalain soldiers crossing the Borders," Axchel said, and everyone looked at him in surprise.

He shrugged, looking directly at Nova.

"I don't want my people to die," he clarified. "But I do not want *any* more people to die because of the war! Andalan and Cassalain alike. I believe the only way to truly stop the fighting is to get Churan safely to the Flowers and fulfill the prophecy."

Mamá looked at him, considering. "That would be helpful. If you could stay after the meeting, we can write a letter to the Andalan general stationed at the Borders." She looked at Damika. "I expect you to write another one, recalling our warriors home."

Damika nodded.

"Now," Mamá said, leaning forward on her elbows to look at the map of Tierramadri. "Let's discuss strategy."

Chapter 38

Nova

Nova walked out of the council meeting and immediately twisted her body into a series of stretches. She winced as she heard multiple pops.

They had been sitting for hours, discussing various tactics, approaches, and fashioning methods of attacks. Nova had tried, many times, to redirect the conversation towards getting Churan to the Flowers, but the group had dismissed her at each opportunity. It wasn't that the priestesses were *against* her attempting to fulfill the prophecy, they just didn't seem to think it was a priority.

They don't believe, Nova thought. *Not really.*

Leaning over to touch her toes, Nova felt a shadow cross over her. She twisted her neck up to see who it was, catching Damika's amused grin. She came back to her usual posture, curving her spine slowly until she was upright again.

"I was stiff," she explained to her friend, somewhat indignantly.

"I didn't say anything," Damika replied, white teeth flashing with amusement.

"Don't you have a letter to write?" Nova asked. Axchel and Churan had stayed back with Mamá to write their own.

"I'll get to it," she answered easily. "Speaking of letters, did you see how fast Petra ran out of the room when Mamá handed her the one from Taruka?"

Nova pressed her lips together to keep from laughing. "I thought she was going to knock over Priestess Ovidia!" she answered.

"I wouldn't have minded her knocking over General Vashti," Damika admitted.

Nova glanced around quickly, as if the older woman were hiding behind a potted plant. "It seemed better with her today," she ventured cautiously.

"It did, didn't it?" Damika answered with a small frown. Without speaking, they both started walking. It was late in the evening, and no one else was in the halls. Behind the temple walls, most of the people had tucked themselves into their rooms, sleeping. They kept their voices quiet as they moved. "I don't know what changed."

"You heard her," Nova answered. "Her attitude wasn't about not liking or not believing in you. She simply didn't think that you were ready to be the High Priestess."

Damika didn't say anything, but her frown lingered. Nova looked at her incredulously.

"You agreed with her!" she reminded her friend. "You didn't think you were ready either!"

"Well, yes," Damika answered. "But I didn't want *her* to believe it, too!"

They burst into laughter at the ridiculousness of that statement. When their giggles were finally under control, Nova idly realized they'd walked towards the gardens. Towards *the* garden. Their spot.

Inexplicably, the knowledge made her think of Axchel.

When I am with him, I can't help but think of Damika. And when I am with Damika, I think of Axchel! she thought to herself.

Nova let out a frustrated breath.

"We will find a way to get them to support your plans for Churan," Damika said, misinterpreting the reason for her sigh. "We will find a way to get him to the Flowers."

"I know," Nova answered, even though she wasn't sure at all. It was all beginning to come together, the plans, the mission, the assignments. The Danrayens were determined to lead a charge on the capital. They could get her to the palace! Nova wouldn't have to go through it all alone anymore. And yet, their dismissal of Churan and the prophecy sometimes made her feel more alone than ever.

If only Alric were here, she thought.

It was the first time that Nova had allowed herself to truly think of the mage. Until the meeting where she learned that he still lived, she had effectively barred all thoughts of him from her mind. She didn't think she would have been able to do everything that needed doing if she believed him dead.

Now she knew that he lived! And yet, the knowledge brought her little comfort. If he did not retain his memories, was he truly still Alric? And what did that mean for the support of the mages? Would they still come to their aid?

A firm thumb pulled her lower lip from her teeth. She hadn't even noticed that she had been gnawing at it until Damika's cool touch.

"You'll hurt yourself," she said softly, her fingers lingering on Nova's chin for a moment.

On instinct, Nova leaned forward to bury her face against her neck. Strong arms wrapped around her as she threw her own around Damika's waist. She felt Dami's cheek press against her head and felt the tension leaving her body. She knew the feeling wouldn't last, but in that moment, she wanted to forget all her problems and worries, and just be held.

A hug, she thought dumbly. *How long has it been since I have just been hugged?*

She made a mental note to hug Churan more often. He was only a boy, far away from his family and his people. She needed to be there for him more, and not leave all his care to Axchel.

The new thoughts were enough to break the spell, and Nova disentangled herself from Damika.

"Dami, I need to get Churan to the Flowers," she told her. "I understand that we are preparing for another war. And that is important. But it is not my priority. My responsibility is to Churan. And I truly believe that his Naming will lead, not only to the end of the war with the monstros, but with Cassalan as well."

"I know," Damika answered, cupping her cheek and bending her knees slightly to look her in the eyes. Her own honey-colored ones were very bright. "Nessa, I am with you. I am with him. I was on the opposite side of you once before. I won't make that mistake again."

"But you are in charge of the Danrayen Warriors," Nova whispered. "You will be their commander. All of them."

"Except the Riders," Damika agreed, referring to the Danrayen elite.

"Except the Riders," Nova repeated, wondering how long it would be before Damika was one herself. "But you will be in charge. How can you lead them, but still help us?"

"I will figure out a way," Damika assured her. "You said that your priority is Churan. Mine is to you. You have my loyalty, and my aid, if you should wish it."

Nova placed her hand over Damika's, leaning into the touch. A bone-deep relief flooded her body. If she had Damika with her, then they truly had a chance.

Damika kissed her forehead, then released her.

"Come," she said. "Petra leaves in the early morning to find the Padir. We need to rest if we are going to see her off with the dawn.

Nova nodded reluctantly, and they began making their way to the priestess wing. Damika walked her to her door, then began heading down a different corridor.

"Wait," Nova said with a frown. "Aren't your rooms that way?" she asked, pointing in the opposite direction.

Damika glanced back and grinned. "I want to grab something from the kitchens first."

Nova nodded, then slipped into the warm comfort of her own room.

It wasn't until she was in bed, on the edge of slumber, that Nova realized the direction Damika had been moving wasn't towards the kitchens either, but sleep claimed her before she could think any more on it.

CHAPTER 39

RAWL

After Alric's soul-shattering revelation, it took every ounce of strength Rawl possessed not to throw himself into the man's arms. To forget, even for a few moments, that he wasn't the Alric that Rawl had fallen so completely for. Instead, he had fled the room. Like a coward. And now he was spending far too much time, and far too much coin, in the tavern below.

Only after he was well and properly drunk on cerveza—and then ron, when the cerveza could not do the trick of erasing Alric's pleading eyes and needy expression from his mind—did he return to their room to sleep. Alric was on the far side of the bed, closest to the wall, curled in tightly into himself, back to the room. As gently as he could, considering his state of inebriation, Rawl had crawled into bed next to him, turning his back to Alric's and trying to ignore the searing heat of his body and the additional intoxication, not of alcohol, but of having him so close.

Luckily, the liquor eventually did its duty and Rawl fell into a fitful, restless sleep.

He dreamed of Alric.

In his dream, the Mage Madness had never left him. His eyes burned red, and a thick crimson vapor lifted from his very skin. Alric grinned at Rawl as he used a long wooden pick to clean his blood-stained teeth.

"Delicious," he said to Rawl, who looked down to see the heart missing from his chest.

The next morning, Rawl woke up to an empty bed and a raging headache. The former he was grateful for, but the latter was a problem. Especially when, as he attempted to sit up, darts of light burned him behind his eyes and his stomach rolled like a restless storm with the effort.

Buen hecho, Rawl, he thought to himself, pressing the heels of his hands against his temple. *The most dangerous mission you have ever faced, and you start your day ill. Mila is going to kill you.*

The door opened softly, but even the light squeaking of hinges was a splinter of wood through his eye and into his brain. He winced and then recoiled slightly when he saw it was Alric entering the room.

Already dressed and ready for the day, Alric looked far better than Rawl knew he did. Only a swipe of purple smudges under his eyes hinted that he may not have rested easy, either. He held a steaming mug of something Rawl could not identify.

"You're awake," Alric said, walking closer to the bed, careful not to spill from his cup.

"No," Rawl grumbled. "Estoy muerto."

Alric's lips twitched, and Rawl was certain he was suppressing a smile.

"Being dead would hurt far less, I wager," he answered, then held out the mug to Rawl, who just stared at it.

"I don't think—" he groaned, stomach flipping at the thought of eating or drinking anything.

"It is a tonic. For those who ... overindulge. I had Andu make it," Alric replied.

Rawl looked at the drink suspiciously. "Andu?" he asked, and Alric nodded.

"I assumed you wouldn't want your sister to know, and Andu assured me that this particular brew was perfected many years ago. A necessity in a university where young people are not often as supervised as they should be."

Another sliver of Rawl's treacherous heart thawed for the man in front of him, and the knowledge of that cramped his belly worse than the hangover did. He didn't *want* to like the man, damn it. He wanted to keep him as a polite stranger so that he could properly mourn *his* Alric.

But he had known that Rawl would need help this morning, and instead of judging him, had gone to seek help. He had also known him well enough to know that he wouldn't want his sister involved and had managed to circumvent her. Even worse, Rawl had acted horribly to the man the night before. He knew that. And here he was, being sweet to him as if nothing was wrong between them.

Rawl accepted the drink half gratefully, half ashamed.

"Gracias," he muttered, quietly but sincerely.

"No hay de que," Alric answered.

Rawl knew better than to smell the tonic before drinking, or to take small, measured sips. Instead, he plugged his nose with one hand, gulping down the contents with the other.

The mixture was so hot that it burned his tongue and the roof of his mouth immediately, blocking out the taste until the final sips. It was only then that Rawl realized that the taste was not unpleasant at all, but more like an herbal tea mixed with wildflower honey. It was quite lovely, in fact, and soothed both his head and stomach before the cup was half empty. By the time Rawl set it down, he felt quite himself again. He looked up at Alric, surprised.

Alric was grinning at him openly now. "I told you they had perfected it," he reminded him. "You didn't need to burn your insides like a savage."

"Is that not how one drinks tea, my lord?" Rawl joked, his body feeling better than it had done in days. "Blame my manners on my poor upbringing. We didn't have a lot of tea parties in the forest."

"What was it like?" Alric asked. "Living as you did? With the Padir?"

"Well, you've—" Rawl stopped himself. *You've seen it,* he had meant to say. *You have visited our camps. You were our guest.*

But this Alric had not. He found that the fact did not anger him, as it once had. And the sadness that snuck in was like the heaviness of grave dirt sprinkled over a coffin, rather than the suffocating darkness of being buried alive, which he had grown accustomed to.

"It was nice," Rawl finally answered. "To be as connected to Tierramadri as we are. To learn the ways of the forest, and the trees, and the animals. To move with the seasons and go from town to town, creating ripples in the long river of life without stopping to settle on any bank of it. To continue floating, and learning, and experiencing; forever moving forward. Being a moment in time, a fleeting but beautiful memory to those who watch us come and go."

Alric was contemplatively staring at him. When Rawl fell silent, he nodded slowly. "It suits you, I think," he finally said. "That way of life, that motion." He ran a rueful hand across the back of his neck, ducking his head a little. "I suppose that you never thought to settle, then, anywhere? To make any one place a home?"

Rawl broke from his gaze.

"Only once," he answered, then stood up abruptly, placing the mug on the small table. He noticed that the plates from last night had been cleared and wondered just how long Alric had been up. Crossing to the window, he frowned at the sight outside the glass.

"I thought seeing them in the morning would make them less frightening," he murmured, still shocked to see so many Night Wood creatures crawling through the capital.

"No," Alric answered.

"No," Rawl agreed.

There was a knock on their door, and the men both crossed to make their way to it. The room was too small for them to maneuver comfortably together, so Rawl motioned Alric forward. He opened the door to reveal a fresh-faced Andu and sleep-tussled Mila on the other side.

"Are we ready?" Mila asked, her voice betraying the nervousness that she had kept from her face.

Rawl took a deep breath.

"Let's go rescue a mage."

CHAPTER 40

RAWL

Rawl knew that the journey across the capital was not going to be pleasant, but he was unprepared for just how horribly stressful it would be. He had known that they would be passing demon dogs, and all manner of beasts and monstros on foot, and thought that he had prepared both his brain and his nerves for the trek. But he had not anticipated just how deeply etched his sense of preservation was carved into the marrow of himself.

Years of standing alert in the forests, listening for creatures both great and small, learning to distinguish friend from foe was as a part of himself as his breathing was. Sensing threat after threat, seeing them in every shadow, in every corner, poised to strike from ahead, from behind, and even above them, had Rawl's muscles bunching and tensing every few moments. He would just manage to convince his body that they were not in danger of imminent attack when he would spot yet another fearsome and heinous beast, and then he would have to calm his thundering heart yet again.

Alric stayed close by him, but didn't attempt to hold his hand the way that he had the day prior. Rawl wasn't sure if he was relieved or disappointed. Even Andu, who was usually so affable and carefree, carried himself with an unfamiliar tension, subtly angling himself between Mila and whatever the closest threat to them was.

"I can't believe this," Mila hissed as they passed an open courtyard, an enormous orcuyo standing in the center of it, watching the people scuttle by, but not moving to attack them. By the way that the creature's eyes burned with rage, Rawl hadn't a single doubt that he would have if he could.

So, someone is controlling them, Rawl thought. *These types of monstros cannot be trained, not successfully. This is powerful magia.*

Rawl was pretty sure he could see blue glyphs on the flesh of several of the creatures. The markings were much like those which once covered Alric, when he had been in the throes of Mage Madness. But the gray skin of the more humanoid monstros, and the fur and scales of the animalistic ones, made it difficult to tell.

Rawl was not about to venture closer to them to find out.

Though horrors filled their walk, it was the city people's reactions to the creatures which was the most peculiar to Rawl. No one screamed, no one attacked. They didn't even look that frightened. They pulled their cloaks a little tighter around themselves and gave the creatures a wide berth. But they went about their day as if it was business as usual. The usual bustle and chatter of the streets was dull and muted, but it continued. Women bartered and men conversed. There was no raucous laughter from open alehouses, or pretty young flower-girls flirting with young guards, but business seemed to continue. What was most prominently missing, Rawl noticed, was the braying of livestock, and the clucks and shuffling of chickens in the streets, or caws of birds flocking around bakeries, hoping for breadcrumbs. No stray dogs wandered the paths, begging for scraps, or cats leaping from banister to banister.

Rawl didn't even see any rats, and there were *always* rats in cities.

So, we humans are the only ones foolish enough to venture out amongst this, he thought disparagingly.

Of course.

After what seemed like an age, the Andalan Palace came into clearer focus. It was expansive, creating a small city of its own among the larger Andalan capital. The outer walls were a bright, pearlescent color, and the tips of the numerous spires were gilded with gold. Brighter hues coated the archways and windows, and equally resplendent curtains spilled over from balconies. Even Rawl had to admit that it was a pretty sight. Or, it would have been, had the gates not been guarded by both soldiers and monstros, not unlike the gates they had passed to enter the city. Wordlessly, their group headed towards a side entrance, where less illustrious visitors were forced to enter. They did their best to ignore the enormous spider-like creature that lingered not too far from its doors.

"Remember," he started to say, before Mila cut him off.

"Remember the plan, yes, yes, we know," she said testily, wiping her palms on her breeches. "Let's just get this over with."

The group of them walked to the guard, and Andu presented the same papers that had gotten them past the first set of guards.

"We are from the Mage University," he said, infusing his voice with easy charm and smiling brightly at the soldier, who barely reached his chest. "We are here to collect—"

But before Andu could continue, the guard waved them forward with his spear.

"Yes, yes, go on then," he said irritably.

Rawl resisted the urge to let the shock show on his face. Only when they were well and good out of the man's earshot did he dare to speak.

"I didn't expect that," he admitted.

"I think they might be feeling a bit complacent in their duties," Mila guessed. "After all, who would dare cause trouble with all of those things around?"

Rawl had to admit she had a point, but it didn't make him feel better about the fact that they were, in fact, about to cause trouble.

Once inside the palace gates, the grounds were gloriously clear of any monstros, and Rawl felt his tensed muscles relaxing slightly, little by little. He shook out his hands, which had cramped from closing into fists. He noticed his companions doing several similar little motions, each looking slightly more at ease, despite the enormity of the task ahead of them.

"Once we get inside the palace itself, it is up to you," he whispered to Alric. "Are you sure that you know where you are going?"

A dimple appeared between Alric's brow. "I do. I do not know why—"

"Don't think of it," Rawl said quickly, not wanting Alric's gaze to cloud over again. "What is important is that you know the way."

Alric nodded, and the four of them stepped from the hot morning sun into the cool shade of the palace. Mila audibly gasped, and Rawl whistled low through his teeth. If they had thought the palace grand and imposing from a distance, it was nothing compared to its interior.

Rawl had never seen such opulence in his life. Thick, lush carpets of varying patterns and color rested over tiled mosaic floors. There were wooden staircases, evenly dispersed throughout the long corridor, going both up and down. Servants had polished the fine timber so that it gleamed in the sunlight, which poured through the largest windows Rawl had ever seen.

There were people milling about everywhere. Servants, Rawl guessed from the way they walked briskly and assuredly, as if they had a purpose. But if any one of them would have sat idly, Rawl would have mistaken them for royals, so fine were their garments. There were tunics of every color one could imagine, ranging from plain whites and blacks to pond-clear blues and mossy greens, reds like slow-cooked crabs and spilled wine, pinks like the flush of a young girl's cheeks, and sun-kissed yellows and oranges. Everywhere he looked, the palace was alive with color, in the finely woven rugs beneath their feet and the intricately embroidered tapestries hanging on the walls.

Rawl, in comparison, felt very drab and completely out of place. From the corner of his eye, he could see his sister pulling on her tunic and surreptitiously attempting to wipe some mud from her boots without anyone noticing.

"Which way to the dungeons?" Rawl asked Alric as quietly as he could without whispering. A group of whispering strangers in garb that was clearly non-palatial was bound to draw more attention than if they simply conferred normally.

The divot between Alric's brows was back, but he nodded towards their left. "This way," he answered.

They spent the next few moments in tense silence, the four of them attempting to blend into the hustle and bustle that was the inner workings of palace life. At one point, a quartet of women marched imperiously down the corridor, their arms full of freshly cut blossoms, forcing Rawl to leap to the side, nearly toppling down a curling flight of stairs. The scent of them lingered in the air as Rawl righted himself, patting the thick wooden banister that had saved him from a long tumble down the steps.

Mila rolled her eyes at him.

Soon, they approached what was undoubtedly the palace kitchens, because the scent of onions, chile, garlic, and freshly baked bread wafted through the air. Rawl leapt into the air when he heard a great rumbling growl, spinning around, sure he would see a demon dog inside the walls after all, or at least a very large guard dog who could tell that they did not belong there. Instead, he saw Andu holding his stomach, which growled loudly again.

Rawl stared at him incredulously.

"That was your stomach?" he asked him, shocked.

"It smells good," Andu replied, looking longingly down the corridor in which the smells were originating.

"No time," Mila answered tersely.

"Come on," Alric said, leading them away from the temptation. "Not too far now. We are almost there."

The "there" that Alric referred to was another long flight of stairs, tucked away from the main body of the palace. The lower they went, the cooler the air became, a chill radiating off the stone walls and floors. Sconces lit the small space, too far underground for the light from the windows to reach. Finally, they descended the final steps, and came face to face with a labyrinth of pathways and tunnels.

"Which way now?" Rawl asked Alric. When he didn't answer, Rawl turned to glance at him, his breath catching at the sight.

Alric stood, eyes cloudy and vacant, like they had been the night prior when he had tried to remember his past.

"Is he," Mila started, but Rawl waved her off.

"It'll pass. Give him a moment," he replied.

After what seemed an eternity, but was likely only a few moments, Alric came back to himself, blinking. When he saw Rawl was watching him, he smiled, and instinctively drew closer towards him. Rawl placed a hand on the dip where his shoulder met his chest.

"Alric," he said tentatively, "do you remember which way we need to go?"

Alric frowned a little, and looked around him, as if he had been completely unaware of where it was that they stood.

"Oh," he said softly, absentmindedly placing his hand over Rawl's, and dragging it to rest over his heart. The archer's own heart gave an answering kick beneath his ribs.

"Yes, of course," Alric continued. "It's—" and then the fog was back.

"No!" Mila barked, frustrated.

"What is it? What's happening?" Rawl asked, concerned. Alric's heartbeat felt steady and even beneath his palm, but why had his mind fled again?

"He doesn't remember," Mila answered, voice terse. "This only works if the memory is ingrained, stored within the muscle. If he had walked this path dozens of times, his body would remember, even if his mind did not. But he must not have come often, because his brain is trying to remember, but the spell won't allow him to."

"There is nothing we can do?" Rawl asked, panicking just a little.

"The spell is very thorough," Mila answered.

"So you've said," Rawl replied bitterly, moving his hand from under Alric's and rubbing his face with it. It was warm.

Alric shifted, then looked at all of them.

"What is happening?" he asked, when they all looked back at him glumly.

"We need another plan," Andu explained when no one else spoke.

"No," Rawl answered determinedly.

"What we need to do is get arrested."

CHAPTER 41

DAMIKA

D amika ducked beneath the claws of a particularly nasty looking monstro. It seemed to be composed of all teeth and talons and sharp, bony protrusions. At first glance, it didn't seem that the thing—with its curved back, full of spikes, and its limbs decorated with twisting blades—had any weaknesses at all. But Damika knew that every living being had a weakness.

She just needed to find a way to end it before *it* could find hers.

Damika was swinging her Danrayen blade down in a straight arc above her head when—*there*—she noticed a flickering movement towards the side of the creature's head. It was fast, but Damika was fairly certain that the creature had blinked. Changing the trajectory of her swing at the last moment, she adjusted her arms to plunge the sword into the soft flesh, rather than continuing the blow, which would have deflected off the creature's armor-like hide.

Instead, the blade met its mark with a sickening squelch. The beast thrashed a few times before collapsing in a heap.

Damika had no time to revel in her success, for already, there were two snake-like culebretos, a demon dog, and a murcieto approaching her. The murcieto provided Damika with the greatest challenge. Its bat-like appearance lent it a menacing appearance, but it was the monstro's ability to fly with great speed that Damika knew would be her greatest challenge. They were fast and dangerous.

Sweat trickled down Damika's back, sliding under the thick leather of her protective layers. She dodged a lunging dog, throwing knives down towards the slithering, oily-looking culebreto. They were both too fast, and their gait too erratic for Damika to meet her mark. Instead, they broke off from their formation, flanking either side of her as the bat-like monstro dove for her.

Damika rolled, grabbing one of the grayish dog-like demonios as she did so. The giant murcieto missed her but scooped up the animal, who trashed wildly, growling and snapping in its piercing grip.

Damika knew she had been in Pelgar for too long. She had stayed out most of the night, funneling her pain and sorrow and frustration into destroying the creatures that remained in the village. She had ventured too far, finding herself stuck in the town square as the light of a new day winked from behind the horizon. Damika knew she needed to return to the temple before the others had a chance to miss her, but she couldn't seem to make her way through the throng of creatures. Each time she dispelled one, it seemed that two more emerged to take their place.

Damika was tired.

Her muscles ached and her head throbbed from a nasty blow she had received earlier that evening. Her vision had thankfully cleared in time for her to deliver a killing blow, but now she wondered if the hit had not caused more damage than she first realized.

She raised her arm in time to use her makeshift shield—a metal pot—to deflect a glob of venom spat at her from one of the culebretos. Her right calf already bore the mark of one she had been unable to dodge in time; her pant leg burned away with much of her skin. She lobbed the "shield" at her assailant and had the satisfaction of hearing that her aim had finally been true. As the culebreto shook to remove the cooking item, a knife found its way into the creature's body.

Damika cursed as she saw the second dog barreling towards her at full speed. She braced herself for the impact, but kept her eye out for the other snake, which had mysteriously disappeared. Just as the creature was about to lunge for her, Damika prepared to use its momentum to plunge her blade straight into the monstro's guts. But before the impact, she felt a sudden searing pain in her right shoulder just as her feet abruptly left the ground.

The murcieto had, apparently, abandoned its earlier prey and returned for Damika. She kicked her legs, trying to disrupt the creature's flight as much as she could. But when that didn't work, she swung her sword above her head blindly, hoping it would hit something.

It did, and the murcieto released her with a piercing shriek. Damika hadn't realized just how high the monstro had managed to carry her as she plummeted towards the ground. No, not the ground, she realized as her body hit a thatched roof. The force of her fall caused her to crash through the straw and wood, landing on her back in the upper level of a Pelgar house. The wind was knocked out of her in a wheezing gasp.

Struggling to remind her lungs how to breathe, Damika tried rolling over to get up. But it took her more tries than she was happy with to do so.

I need to get out of here, she thought to herself, crawling towards the house's fireplace to pull herself up by the mantle. *There are too many of them.*

For the first time since she had set out to battle the monstros of Pelgar, Damika realized just how reckless her actions had become.

You would be furious if this was Petra, Damika thought to herself. *Or any other Danrayen venturing out alone.*

But that was the problem, wasn't it? Damika had always thought herself better than the other women. Not a better warrior, and certainly not a better person—simply more capable of one-on-one battles against their enemies. She hadn't worried for herself every time she stepped out from the safety of the temple. Instead, she had sought out the danger, more willing to fight the monstros of her realm than the demons in her mind.

And now, it is no longer a one-on-one fight, Damika was reminded, as she heard multiple monstros clambering up the stairs to reach her. *Now you are outnumbered, and alone.*

After hours of fighting, multiple injuries, and no clear way to escape, the rage that had kept Damika primed for battle had finally abandoned her. She was still angry. At Adira, Mamá, and Nessa for keeping secrets. Even at Raidea for dying, though she knew none of her targeted anger was fair. What remained of that anger turned inwards; at herself.

Stupid, she finally admitted to herself. *This has been reckless and stupid.*

If she died in Pelgar that morning, no one would know what had become of her. It was a good thing that she wasn't High Priestess after all. This way, at least her death would not propel the order into more chaos.

Better not to die at all, she urged herself, running out to the balcony and launching herself to the ground once more.

But if she was to die, Damika would be sure to take as many of those dioses-damned monstros with her as she possibly could.

CHAPTER 42
RAWL

It was as good a plan as any, Rawl thought. If they got arrested, the guards would take them to the dungeons. Even if it wasn't the same dungeons that housed particularly dangerous traitors to the crown, they couldn't be that far from them.

Dungeons were dungeons, after all.

"And how, exactly, do you expect to get out once you're in?" Mila seethed quietly next to him, panting heavily as they re-climbed all the stairs that they had just descended.

"That's where you come in, Mila-linda," Rawl answered, his own breaths ragged from the exertion. "You and Alric will stay back, and trail whoever it is that detains us. Once you can, you'll get us out."

"And how, *exactly*, am I supposed to do that?" Rawl knew that if she could have shrieked the question at him, she would have. Instead, it came out as a hoarse croak.

Rawl simply wiggled his fingers at her.

"Oh sure," Mila huffed. "You want me to pickpocket the Royal Guards of the Andalan Palace. Excellent plan, hermano."

"You always were light-fingered," Rawl said, hoping the flattery would help calm her mood.

It did not.

"And what if they don't decide to take you to the dungeons?" she asked. They were almost at the top of the stairs. "What if they take you and decide to feed you to one of those orcuyos outside? What then?"

"They wouldn't do that," Rawl assured her with more confidence than he felt. "The people would be horrified. They are terrified of those creatures as it is. If the guards went around feeding them this city's citizens, there would be a revolt."

"No, there wouldn't be!" Mila insisted. "No one would dare go against those things and you know it!"

"Mila," he said seriously, turning to her. They stood at the top of the landing now. "I need to do this. I need to rescue the Archwizard. Rojya—the Name-Bearer needs him."

Mila's eyes darted around at the mention of the Name-Bearer, making sure no one was within hearing distance.

Rawl continued. "I swore myself to her service. I believe in what we're doing. She needs the mages on her side, and this is the only way to make sure that is done. And if I need to get myself arrested to get close to him ..." he saw guards approaching from the servants' hallway, "then that is what I will do."

He grabbed Andu's sleeve, pulling him towards a window where they would be better viewed, then nodded at his sister, who was leading Alric to the shadows, where they could remain unnoticed. He knew that despite her arguments, she would pull through.

"Ready, big guy?" he asked Andu, who grinned.

"Are *you*?" he asked, right before punching Rawl right in the nose.

It rocked him backwards, the force of the blow bringing tears to his eyes. "Coño, hombre, not that hard! You want to make it look real without sending me to the infirmary."

"Lo siento," Andu said, panic in his voice as he approached to assess the damage. From the corner of his eye, he could see the place guards getting closer.

"You will be sorry, you giant oaf!" he roared, flinging himself on to the unsuspecting Andu.

Rawl managed to use his momentum to grasp Andu's thick neck with one arm, then swing himself around until he was clinging onto the big man's back like a particularly aggressive monkey. He wrapped both legs around his torso, momentarily aghast when he realized Andu was so wide that he couldn't lock his ankles in front of him for purchase. He then flung both arms around the man's meaty neck. He squeezed his arms together so that his muscles tightened and strained but did not put any pressure against Andu's throat. He only wanted it to appear that he was trying to kill the man.

Andu roared, his voice bouncing off the walls and rattling the inside of Rawl's skull. He heard the guards give a shout, and then there was the sound of footsteps racing towards them.

"Para, para!" one of the guards yelled, but Andu and Rawl ignored him.

Andu began flailing around, this way and that, trying to pry Rawl's arms and legs from around him. Every time he managed to peel off one, Rawl tightened the other, not allowing him to gain the upper hand. He knew that Andu wasn't fighting with all that he could, but in that moment, he couldn't help but feel like he was holding his own against the giant.

That was until Andu flung himself backwards against a wall.

The collision knocked the breath from Rawl's lungs instantly, and he gave a wheezing gasp, his breath leaving his body with such force that it tussled Andu's hair upon exiting. Rawl felt his grip slackening, his legs sliding down. Then, Andu seized him from the side, and bodily threw him towards the two guards, knocking them down like bottles at a village fair.

I know I told him to make it look realistic, Rawl managed to think, dazed, *but I didn't expect this.*

He did his best to stand, but one of the guards grabbed him roughly, pressing a blade against his ribs. Rawl instantly stilled; he wanted to get arrested, not stabbed. The second guard approached Andu with a long spear, and for a second, the man looked like he was going to charge him. Rawl's eyes widened, and he tried to shake his head subtly. He knew that sometimes some men got lost in the heat of battle and could not stop from fighting until it killed them, or their opponent. He hadn't expected Andu to be the type, but one could never be sure.

Just as Rawl was certain Andu was going to tackle the guard and wrestle the spear away from him, Andu's muscles suddenly relaxed, and he placed his palms in front of his chest passively.

"I yield," he said, the humor back in his voice.

More guards joined them then, running in from different parts of the palace, weapons at the ready.

"Take them to the dungeons," the guard who was holding Rawl said to two others, thrusting him towards them. Rawl's heart jumped in his chest. They had done it!

"Careful with the big one," the other guard said. "He is a beast."

Rawl thought that he caught a hurt look flash behind Andu's eyes, but it was gone as soon as it arrived.

Trick of the light, Rawl decided.

The guards spoke together then, quickly and quietly, while the others detained Rawl and Andu. Finally, three of them escorted them down to the dungeons.

"Lo siento, chicos," Rawl told the new guards as they ushered them to a new part of the building. "Simple misunderstanding, really. No need to take us in!" He knew that other men in his position would do their best to barter their way out of their punishment. "I don't have much in the way of coin, but surely you have more important things to do than waste your time over a little scuffle?"

"The way we heard it, you two were trying to kill one another," one of the younger guards said, frowning in what was a clear attempt to appear older and tougher than he was.

"Nah," Rawl answered jovially. "Like I said, we just had a misunderstanding. Isn't that right, big guy?" he directed towards Andu, who remained silent. "We will let it go and be on our way, we promise."

To Rawl's horror, the guards actually started slowing down.

No, he thought, desperately. *This isn't actually supposed to work!*

"We do have a busy day," the guard behind Rawl said thoughtfully. "And it is such a long way down to the dungeons..."

"Do you swear by the dioses that you will cease your fighting and return to your business?" the third guard demanded.

Rawl shot a frantic look at Andu and was met with an expression as cold as the first frost of winter.

"I will kill you," Andu said simply, then leaped forward as if to start their fight anew. For just a fraction of a second, Rawl forgot that he had nothing to fear from Andu, and his body flooded with adrenaline. Then, he remembered their objective: get sent to the dungeons.

"I'd like to see you try it, you ugly ox!" Rawl roared, lifting his fists.

The guards broke them up before they could get within an arm's length of one another, and Rawl winced as Andu received a heavy blow to his back. If the guard meant for the blow to reach his head, it could have done serious damage, but luckily, Andu was just too tall for the much shorter guard to reach. They took Rawl and Andu to the dungeons at a much faster pace than before, shoved unceremoniously into twin cells, the metal bars closing behind them with a ringing clang. The click of their locks echoed in the stone underground, and soon they were alone.

Rawl and Andu had succeeded. They were in the Andalan Palace dungeons.

It was time to free a traitor.

CHAPTER 43
LEADER

L eader was bored.

This wasn't uncommon for them. They often felt themselves in need of entertainment or stimulation. As the head of the nomadic people of the Padir, Leader wasn't accustomed to stagnancy.

What *was* uncommon was that nothing seemed to keep their attention for very long. At first, they had ordered an elegant and elaborate meal to their large rooms, then invited several of their closest friends and partners to join them in dining. When that had not been enough, they had requested the musicos and bailarines of the camp to join them, hoping the music and dancing would prove entertaining. Instead, they had felt distant, removed from the scene, as if watching it all from a very great distance.

Finally, realizing that company was not going to alleviate their apathy, Leader had sent all of them away again.

They had then raided their own closets, as fashion had always been somewhat of a passion for Leader, and they hoped that a perfectly selected outfit would lift their spirits. As a nomadic people, hauling around trunks and trunks full of elaborate clothing was perhaps not entirely practical, but luckily their people had grown used to their eccentricities.

Currently, they sat on their plush, oversized green velvet chair with their right leg kicked out to perch above the armrest, admiring the way the finely tailored fabric pulled up from their calf and slid down their thigh at the motion, revealing a leather boot which was as sturdy as it was lovely. The pants were the color of an impeccably cooked steak, warm brown with hints of faded garnet, matching their suspenders perfectly, which lay against their billowy turmeric-colored tunic.

Several rings adorned each of their fingers, flashing with fine gems as well as intricate metal work. A long white feather earring dangled from their left ear, a small dagger from their right. Their light brown hair, which hung past their shoulders not two days ago, was now cropped short at the sides of their head, leaving a curling cluster of chestnut ringlets at the center of their skull. The cut was also a result of their growing restlessness, and a decision that they only slightly regretted.

Leader heaved out a great sigh. Now they were well-fashioned *and* bored. But bored all the same.

No, not bored, Leader thought to themselves. They felt something akin to boredom, but not quite.

Expectant, they decided. It was as if they were *waiting* for something.

But what? they pondered.

Leader was *not* a lot of things. They were neither male, nor female, neither young nor old. They were not cruel, but nor were they particularly kind. They were not overly skilled in reading, writing, or arithmetic, and they were a decent fighter, but did not show a great aptitude for either fist-fighting or a specific weapon of any kind.

What Leader *was*, was clever. Clever and sly, a person with brilliant, unexpected ideas and a manner of being that made people want to listen and follow them. It was why they were selected as the leader of the Padir.

What most people did not know, however, was that Leader was also *different*.

Not different in the ways that others could see, but there was something in them that had always been more attuned to changes. To the fluctuation of the winds, to the turning of the tides. Leader always seemed to know when the weather was about to shift, or when their group should migrate and make camp elsewhere. They knew when a member of the Padir was about to embark on a dangerous endeavor, and which gambles would be worthy of the risk.

They were also extremely adept at cards and other games of chance, so much so in fact, that no one would agree to play with them anymore.

Leader had once spoken to Sarakshi about their almost unnatural instincts, and the young seer had informed them that they likely had an Affinity for the Unveiled Sight. Not the true Unveiled Sight as she had. The one that allowed her to deliver prophecy and catch glimpses of the future with startling accuracy, but a subtler form of it that allowed them forewarning, if not clarity on what, exactly, was being forewarned.

Whatever it was, Leader was mostly glad that it honed their intuition, until moments like these. Leader knew something was coming, but they had no idea what to prepare for.

Luckily for them, they did not have to wait long.

A bell rang from outside of Leader's tents and they straightened, slamming their raised leg back down on the ground and fighting every instinct to leap forward to their hung leather door.

Leader forced a feigned nonchalance into their voice.

"Enter," they called out indifferently.

A young Padir messenger strode in. "You have a visitor, Leader," she informed them, serving them a bow along with the news.

"A visitor?" Leader allowed their voice to play, rising up to slide down once again. "What sort of visitor?"

"A woman," she clarified. "Says she's a Danrayen. She looks it too, for all that she is small."

"Interesting," Leader answered. "Is anyone else with her? A handsome young mage and one of our own, perhaps?"

"No, Leader," the messenger said. "She is alone."

"Hmmm," was their only reply.

Leader pulled at their lower lip with their fingers, deep in thought. They had no doubt that they would admit this new Danrayen guest for an audience, but would they make her wait a while first? Their mind rebelled against the thought instantly. If the presence of the Danrayen was the reason Leader had been so restless in the last week, then they wanted to see her as soon as possible.

They looked around at the remnants of the lavish meal they had requested, now strewn disorderly around the room.

"Send for people to take care of this mess. Leave only the wine, bread, and cheese. Then you can bring this Danrayen before me."

The girl scrambled to do their bidding, and soon Leader's tents were immaculately tidy, with the perfect amount of refreshment for a guest. The bell rang again, and Leader positioned themselves on their chair once more.

"Enter," they said again.

After a few moments, a young Danrayen Warrior walked in. She was surprisingly small, short in stature, and slender at first glance. However, as she strode confidently across the room to greet Leader, they could see that every inch of her small frame was covered in muscle. Her light hair, cropped to hit her chin, was currently tucked back behind both ears. Her eyes were an equal mixture of green and brown, large in her heart-shaped face.

When she reached Leader's seat, she bowed respectfully and once again, Leader could see the power in her movements. There was no doubt that this young woman was a warrior through and through.

"Leader?" she addressed them confidently. "Both in name and of the Padir?"

Leader gave a single nod of their head. "And you are?" they inquired.

"I am the Danrayen Warrior known as Petra," she responded.

"And what brings you to our camp, Petra of the Danrayens? In fact, how did you find our camp?" Leader asked.

"That is a long story," Petra replied evenly. "But the short answer is that we have a mutual friend."

"Oh?" Leader asked, raising an eyebrow.

"Rawl," she said.

"Rawl," Leader repeated, a smile tugging on their lips. So, this did have something to do with his strange visit last year. Sarakshi had told them what she had Seen for them, and Leader was clever enough to work the rest out for themselves.

"So, your visit has something to do with the Name-Bearer and the Unnamed Prince," they mused.

"No, well yes, but ... in a sense," Petra stammered, a small frown dimpling the space between her brows.

Leader smothered another smile. They always enjoyed catching someone off guard.

"Then what is it about, young warrior?" they asked.

As Petra spoke, a story began shaping itself in Leader's mind, as if watching a play. Lord Guerro and his quest for power. Brujas who kept him young. His infiltration into the Andalan Palace, and the increase in monstro attacks.

Even after Petra finished, Leader kept silent, absorbing the information. Some of it they had already gathered, but most of it was new. The Padir didn't often involve themselves with the affairs of the capital.

"Interesting," they finally replied. "But it still does not tell me why you are here, seeking an audience with me."

"We need the Padir to join us in taking up arms against Guerro and the palace," she answered. "We need numbers if we are going to defeat them, the Andalan army, and the monstros that they are somehow controlling."

Leader felt their mood sink, as if suddenly attached to an anchor and thrown overboard.

Was that all? they thought. *Was this really what I was waiting for?* How disappointing.

"No," Leader responded, bored once more.

Petra blinked at them, her frown deepening.

"No?" she repeated. "What do you mean, 'no?'"

"The Padir are a nonviolent people," Leader responded, waving their hand dismissively. "We do not concern ourselves with the wars of this realm, and we certainly do not fight."

"You no longer have the luxury of remaining peaceful," Petra argued, and Leader noticed her hands curling into fists.

"We do not fight unless first attacked," Leader said, already dismissing her and her visit from his mind. "You are welcome to stay here as long as you wish, enjoy our food, our wine, and our hospitality. My people will make sure you have everything you need."

"That is not good enough," Petra argued, and Leader raised an eyebrow in surprise. Why was she still arguing with them? Leader had already said no. They weren't used to people arguing with them.

It was ... not boring.

Petra plowed on.

"Monstro attacks are increasing throughout all of Tierramadri. Even you, tucked away as you are, cannot have been unaffected. This is a threat that affects us all."

Leader remained expressionless, but inside felt a twinge of self-doubt. The little warrior wasn't wrong. They had experienced more attacks in the last year than in all of their time as Leader combined, and the amount kept growing.

"We need to put a stop to it, which means we will need to attack the palace where the monstros are being controlled. And we cannot do that alone."

Leader knew that there was truth in her words but could not help but shake their head. Before they could speak, however, Petra continued.

"We have the Name-Bearer. We have the Unnamed Prince. If the prophecy is sound, then the only thing that will guarantee peace for Andala, for all of our people—including the Padir—is to deliver the boy to the Flowers."

"So, they did find the boy," Leader remarked, not able to hide their smile this time. "Fascinating."

"I am told that many Padir are followers of the Flowers," Petra suggested.

"Many are," Leader conceded. But we are Padir first and foremost. We do not break our vows of nonviolence easily. It is one thing to battle on a hunt, or when defending ourselves from flesh-peddlers and bandits. It is quite another to seek out a war."

"I understand," Petra replied. "Though the Danrayens are warriors, war is not our first option, either. But we are defenders of the realm. And we intend to protect our people from this threat. But we need your help."

She fell into silence once again, allowing Leader to think. It was clever to allow them to their thoughts rather than pressing the point, and they wondered if negotiations were a part of Danrayen training, or if Petra was simply good at delivering her point.

They drummed their well-adorned fingers against the armrest of the chair as they pondered.

Everything the warrior had said was true. The attacks against their people had only worsened over time. If a power-hungry man like Lord Guerro had found his way into the palace, it did not bode well for their realm.

The Danrayens were formidable warriors. For them to come to the Padir with this request meant that they viewed the situation as very dire indeed. Leader was not foolish enough to dismiss that.

And yet, Leader's people were not soldiers. They were good fighters, of course. One does not join a nomadic tribe of entertainers and sometimes-thieves without learning how to defend oneself. But to send them off to war?

And yet, Petra was right. There were many of their party who were followers of the Flowers, and believers in the prophecy. Leader was one of them, though they would never admit that to the Danrayen. If they had a chance to aid the Name-Bearer and deliver the Unnamed Prince to the Flowers, was that not a worthy cause?

It was not a decision for Leader alone, they decided. This sort of request could only be granted or denied by the will of their people.

"Very well," Leader decided, and Petra visibly brightened.

"You'll help us?" she asked.

"Not quite," they replied with a sly grin. "But you will have a chance to plead your case to the Padir. I will call for a junta."

"A junta?" Petra asked, looking puzzled.

"Yes," Leader replied. "We will send for every member of the Padir in the immediate vicinity, and for representatives from our other camps. In seven days' time, you will have your chance to address them."

"All of them?" Petra repeated, her voice faint.

"All of them," Leader replied, and grinned as they watched the color drain from Petra's face.

Finally, a little excitement!

Chapter 44

Rawl

The dungeon was cold and dark. The floors were made up of overlaying stones of different shapes and sizes. Moss and fungi grew from between their cracks, giving the area a damp, earthen smell which was far preferable to the other scents which lingered; most of which Rawl would rather not dwell on.

The guards had thrown him into the cell roughly, and he had landed on his hands and knees, scraping both. He stood up gingerly, wiping his palms against the sides of his pant legs as he did so, firmly pushing from his mind just how dirty those stone floors might be. Behind the bars that separated them, he saw Andu equally taking in their surroundings.

Other than he and Andu, this section of the dungeon was surprisingly empty of prisoners. Rawl stuck his face through the bars until the skin on his face was pulled tight, twisting to see as far up and down the long hallway of cages as he could. Most other cell doors were open, and as far as he could tell, the place was empty, save for him and Andu. Where were all the prisoners?

"Are you all right?" Rawl heard Andu ask softly, then extracted his head to watch Andu move as close as he could towards him. When he reached the portion of their cage that divided them, he wrapped his large hands around the metal bars, leaning towards him. Andu had managed to stay upright when the guards had shoved him inside the prison, a feat Rawl was both impressed and bitter about.

"Fine," Rawl answered, trying to keep his voice light. "Must be nice," he continued, gesturing towards Andu with a wave. "You know, to be big enough that no one can knock you down."

To Rawl's surprise, Andu frowned and pushed away from the bars. "I suppose so," he answered coldly.

Rawl was momentarily stunned. Both by the expression on his face, and the coolness in his voice, which were so foreign, and so unlike the normally jovial man that he just stood gaping at his turned back for a long moment.

"Are *you* all right?" he finally asked, wondering if he had missed something.

"Fine," was Andu's response. "Like you said, not much can hurt me."

Somehow, Rawl was getting the sense that was not the case.

"There are many ways a man can be hurt, and not all physical," he responded, and saw Andu's shoulders stiffen. "If I caused offense, I am sorry," he continued.

Andu stood tense and motionless for a long moment before his shoulders slumped and he turned to look at Rawl sheepishly.

"No, I am sorry, amigo," he said, crossing the space which divided them once more. "You are right, some wounds are not physical, and I sometimes find that old ones can find a way to cause pain even after much time."

Rawl nodded. "I have found that it helps to speak of them, preferably to a friend," he ventured, and Andu rewarded him with a kind smile.

"While I do consider you a friend, I do not need to bore you with my tale," he answered.

Rawl sat carefully perched on the single stone bench adorning his cell, doing his best to allow as little of his clothing to touch the cool material as possible. "We have nothing if not time," he told the big man. "There is nothing else for us to do, but wait, after all."

Andu mirrored Rawl's actions and sat on his own bench, but with less discernment of how much of it came in contact with his clothing. Rawl suppressed a wince. They would both need thorough baths after this endeavor.

"I know that I am a large man," Andu finally said. "And I understand what a blessing that can be. Not only am I tall, but I am wide and have the strength to show for both. I am also gifted at fighting. Most think that having this much bulk would slow me down, like an ox, but instead, I am quick and agile like a cougar."

"Those are many blessings indeed," Rawl answered, impressed.

Andu nodded slowly. "I have come to see them as such," he admitted. "But I did not always. When I was young, I was always seen as older than my years, for I was always so much larger than others of my age. When I was three, I already looked five or six, and was treated as such. My pare—*people* would get upset with me when my three-year-old mind and body was unable to perform the tasks of children older than I was. And I was punished for it."

"That's not fair!" Rawl gasped, indignant on behalf of young-Andu, who he pictured as a large but sweet-faced toddler, with chubby cheeks and a gap-toothed smile.

Andu shrugged. "By the time I was seven, the other families in my village had forbidden children of my age to play with me. I was so much bigger than my peers, you see, they were afraid that I would hurt them."

"But that's, that's ..." Rawl struggled.

"They weren't wrong," Andu continued. "I just wanted to play, to run, to wrestle, but I didn't know my body well, nor my own strength. There were many scrapes and bruises among my classmates, and I suppose I was lucky that their injuries weren't worse."

"But you were just a child," Rawl insisted.

Andu looked at him with the most serious expression Rawl had ever seen. He hadn't even known the man capable of it.

"I don't think that I was ever a child, not really," he mused. He didn't seem upset over the realization, merely resigned. "In any case, the older children allowed me into their ranks, youths who often forgot that I wasn't actually of their age." A flush crept over his face. "I may have grown up faster than I should have. Gotten into situations that were for those far beyond my years."

Rawl didn't interject this time. He simply allowed his heart to bleed for the young boy forced into circumstances he never should have been in, simply because of the way in which he was born.

"I remember my mother pulling me aside one day, when I was still young," Andu continued. "She warned me that I must never get angry, never be sullen. That I should always smile and appear less than what I am." He turned his head to smile at Rawl. "I know she only worried for my safety. That others would see my size and strength as a challenge. Sometimes, even as an affront. So, I resolved to always be kind, as kind as I could be. There was never much violence in my heart, anyway."

No. That was clear. Andu might just have been the sweetest person Rawl had ever met. Not once had he worried or feared for his sister's safety around the big man. Only for her heart, but that was between the two of them.

"It was a relief when I began showing signs of magia and was sent away to train. When I got to the university, I was not the only one who had been feared in their homes for their nature. We were all connected by the strength of our magia, if not our bodies. And people there were a lot less frightened of my size, as they had powers of their own to wield."

Rawl opened his mouth to respond, but then clamped it shut when he heard the hallway door swing open. He jumped up, bracing for more guards, only to see the cautious face of his sister peeking around the door.

"Mila!" Andu beamed at her, rushing to the door of his cell. "Have you come to rescue me?"

She gave a customary roll of her eyes and swung the door open wider, admitting both her and Alric into the room. Alric's eyes darted around the space, the air around him sizzling with restrained anxiety, until his gaze landed on Rawl's. Then his entire body relaxed. He nodded towards the archer, crossing towards them quickly as Mila followed more languidly.

"Come on, Mila," Rawl urged, anxious to be released. "Did you get the keys or not?"

"Did I complete the impossible task that you placed on me mere moments before executing your ridiculous plan, you mean?" Mila shot back.

"Come on, Mila," Rawl growled, rattling his cell door a little. "You did get them, didn't you? Because you're right," he added, looking down at the door lock, "there is no way we could pick these."

Smiling like a cat who had gotten into the cream, Mila lifted a heavy ring of keys from her tunic pocket. The fact that he hadn't heard them rattling was a testament to their delinquency-filled youth.

Rawl sighed in relief. "Never doubted you for a second," he said as Mila tried several keys on his door, before hearing the latch slide back and click open.

"How did you do it?" Andu asked, flashing her an impressed grin as she crossed to his door next.

"She flirted with the guard," Alric supplied. Rawl nodded. It was often the fastest and most effective method, but Andu looked shocked.

"You did what?" he asked her, remaining stunned in his cell even after the door swung open. Rawl caught Mila suppressing a smirk.

"It wasn't too bad. At least he was a young and handsome one," she said coyly.

"He ... what?" Andu stuttered, and Rawl reached into the cell to pull the big man out.

"Come on," Rawl urged them. "We need to find the Archwizard."

"I know where he is," Alric said confidently.

Rawl and Mila exchanged a glance.

"You remember now? I mean ... are you sure you know the way?" Rawl asked tentatively.

"Yes, I don't—" Alric started.

"We know you don't remember everything," Rawl snapped, tired of hearing the words and seeing the confusion on Alric's face.

"Hey!" Mila said with a hard slap to Rawl's shoulder. "He is confused! You try forgetting what you're thinking every few seconds!"

Rawl took a deep breath. His sister was right, and he couldn't keep punishing Alric for things outside of his control. He looked at the man's worried face.

"It's all right," he assured him. "You don't need to remember everything, or know why you remember what you do, as long as you can show us the way."

Alric looked at Rawl with such naked affection, the archer's heart wrung in his chest like a rag on wash-day. He hated how eager this Alric was to please him. It just made things more confusing.

"This way, then," Alric replied, leading them further down the cell-lined hall. "You'll need to bring the keys," he added to Mila.

They crossed the room quickly, opening heavy metal doors to another part of the dungeons. The floors were littered with scraps of fabric, straw, overturned buckets and splinters of wood. There were enough cells to hold dozens of men at a time, each with their own enclosure, but they encountered no one.

"Did you see anyone when you two made your way down here?" Rawl whispered to Mila, not sure why he felt the need to keep his voice hushed.

"No one but guards," she answered, equally soft.

"Hmmm," was his only reply.

"Just how handsome was this guard?" he heard Andu ask quietly before Mila shushed him.

Following Alric, the group made several twists and turns, unlocking doors and sometimes taking paths that felt as if they were doubling back. Sweat began dotting Rawl's temples despite the coolness of the air, and he was about to question Alric whether he really knew where he was going, when suddenly he stopped and whirled around.

"Here," Alric said, stepping towards a divot in the stone wall, the size of a small closet, holding nothing but an unlit sconce.

"Where?" Mila asked, confused. But then Alric grabbed the sconce, twisting it to the right. With his left hand, he found a knotted gray stone and pushed.

The wall moved.

CHAPTER 45
RAWL

Andu gasped as the stone wall slid forward, and Rawl felt his own lips part open in surprise. It was not the first hidden room or secret passage that the archer had encountered, but it was a very sophisticated one. He could have examined the twisting corridors of the dungeon for a hundred years and not figured out where this entrance was. It made him wonder how many more secrets the palace held.

"In here," Alric said, easing forward. They followed him tightly.

Once past the stone door, they found themselves in a wide rectangular room. It was brightly lit with more sconces, but each radiated an unnatural bluish light.

"Lantern spell," Mila said, and Rawl nodded. She had performed similar magia to create orbs of luz during his and Andu's trek underwater.

As their eyes adjusted to the sudden brightness, Rawl noticed the large cage in the center of the room. The back wall was stone, but the cage door, front wall, and sides were all metal bars. The bars jutted out from deep beneath the ground and extended up before impaling themselves through the ceiling.

Inside, there was a long, backless couch with worn-looking cushions and what was once a brightly colored footstool, which was now dull and tattered, embroidery frayed and tangled. There was a bed with grayish, threadbare sheets, neatly made, and what appeared to be a wooden privacy screen. On the left side of the cage, not far from the bed, was a wooden desk laden with books, scrolls, parchment, and letters. It was wide and sturdy-looking, with a solid green desk chair.

In that chair sat an elderly man, hair long and mostly gray, hanging limp and ragged across his face. His beard was equally long and liberally dabbled with gray and silver, sprouting every which way from his cheeks and chin. His skin was bronze, his eyes brown and wild.

"Ghosts," he said, when they landed on Rawl's crew.

His voice was hoarse from disuse, but despite the strain—and the strange accusation—he appeared more amused than concerned.

"Always ghosts, or apparitions. Unexpected specters. Delightful company, most of the time," he rambled. Then, jerking backwards, his hands flew to cover the bottom half of his face.

"Unless you are here to collect the tip of my nose? Or the lobes of my ears?" he asked them, scowling. "You can't have them, no matter how many times you ask!"

Rawl looked incredulously at Mila, who shrugged back.

"Sir, we are not ghosts," Andu attempted, but was cut off.

"A ghost never believes that they are a ghost." Auberon answered.

"Are you the Archwizard?" Rawl decided it was best to simply ask him directly.

The man startled, and looked at the archer, the suspicion in his eyes shifting to disorientation.

"Am I a blizzard?" he asked, sounding dazed. "No, I am a man. I am at least eighty-three percent certain of it."

Rawl shared another look of utter confusion with his sister.

"Of course, I *could* be a blizzard," the prisoner continued. "How would I know the consciousness of a blizzard, unless of course, I am one, and this has been my life all along?"

"Señor," Rawl tried to interrupt, but the man continued.

"Though, I was certain that I was in Andala, and Andala does not get blizzards. Nor snow! That is the environment of the Borders. Mountainous regions, you know, and dreadfully cold. But I am sixty-seven percent sure that I am in Andala and seventy-eight percent certain I am not at the Borders."

"What is wrong with him?" Rawl whispered to Mila, who shrugged, looking aghast.

"No se," she answered, gnawing on her lip. "Maybe he was injured when they captured him, or his imprisonment has driven him mad?"

"He has only been imprisoned a few years!" Rawl argued.

"But it looks like he has been kept solitary. Who knows what that might do to a man? Especially one of his strength and intelligence!" she answered.

"But I suppose there is always a chance that I could be a severe, cold storm," the prisoner continued to muse. "Though it is unlikely, as I mentioned, for the reasons previously stated."

"Señor!" Rawl said more loudly. "I did not ask if you were a *blizzard*, but a *wizard*. The *Archwizard Auberon*."

"Ah!" the man answered, clapping his hands loudly. "That does make more sense, of course. To be a wizard and not a blizzard." His eyes widened suddenly as they landed on Alric, who had been somewhat obscured by Andu until that moment.

"Alric?" the old man croaked, repressed emotion squeezing his words. In an instant, clarity sparked in his eyes, and he appeared more lucid than he had been since they had found him.

Alric stared at the man with confusion written all over his features. "Perdón, señor," he said politely. "But do we know one another?"

The older man's gaze darted to the rest of them quickly, more lines cutting his ancient face.

"He ..." Rawl hesitated. "He was ill. His memories ... it's best not to" he scrambled for what to say.

"He was ill and cannot remember his life prior to a few weeks ago," Mila said, her voice determined, void of hesitation or regret.

The old man's eyes were instantly a well of infinite sorrow, the pain bleeding into the corners of his mouth and the ridges of his brow. He seemed to age even further, right before their very eyes.

Rawl thought he knew how he felt.

"Are you ..." Alric hesitated. "Are you the man my friends seek? Archwizard Auberon?"

The wizard stared at him for a long moment, then nodded slowly. "My name *is* Auberon. I am ninety-four percent certain of that." Then his gaze turned somber. "But I have not been called the Archwizard in quite some time."

"My name is Rawl," the archer said, trying to take advantage of the older man's sudden lucidity. "This is my sister Mila, and friend Andu. They are both mages. And .. and Alric," he hesitated. The others nodded politely. "I am a friend of the Name-Bearer. She needs our help."

The wizard straightened his back in his chair. His eyes narrowed, and he regarded Rawl solemnly.

"The Name-Bearer lives?" he asked. "There was only a forty-nine percent chance of her not being discovered."

"She lives, and has found the Unnamed Prince," Rawl informed him.

"Sixteen percent probability," the wizard mumbled, his eyes clouding again. "But with the Prince, chances of success..." his voice trailed off.

Rawl snapped, which he knew was rude, but it seemed to help keep the man's mind from wandering too far. "She needs your help," he informed him. "They both do."

"Then I hope you have a plan for releasing me," Auberon answered.

"We have keys," Rawl started, motioning to Mila, but Auberon scoffed.

"I was not imprisoned behind an ordinary lock and key, niño. I am a mage, and a powerful one at that." His voice was more certain than Rawl had heard it since they had found him. Rawl watched as he shook his head, his hair flopping about his head.

"No, this cage is made of more than just metal," he continued. "Look closer."

They all warily approached. After a few steps, Rawl saw what the mage was referring to. Each metal bar had strange symbols carved deeply into their surface.

"Suppression runes," Mila gasped, backing away.

"Suppression," Auberon confirmed. "The repression of magia possession," he said in a sing-song tune. "And I have a confession ..." Auberon grinned. "I carved them myself! I never imagined I would lead to my own oppression. But it was my transgression, that—"

"Enough!" Rawl barked, rubbing at his head. The mage's rhyming was grating on his nerves. Worse, he wasn't sure how much of the powerful, influential wizard remained within the man that they were trying to save. He seemed to have moments of lucidity, but then would slip away into a blabbering fool.

"What do suppression runes mean?" he asked Mila and Andu.

Mila shook her head. "Nothing but the correctly corresponding key will open these doors," she answered him.

"And that key hangs on the queen's elegant neck," Auberon confirmed, wrapping a long scarf around his own neck as if to punctuate his words.

"So that's it?" Rawl asked, shoulders sagging. "Somehow, I don't think I'll be able to charm the queen of her necklace the way you did the guard his keys," he said to Mila.

"About that guard," Andu began.

"Not now!" Mila growled.

"There may be a way," Auberon said, sounding earnest. He stood slowly, crossing to the bars.

Rawl frowned at his approach, wondering how long this sudden clarity of mind would last.

"You two are mages?" Auberon directed to Mila and Andu, who nodded. "In that case, there may be enough power."

"Between the two of us? Not nearly enough," Mila answered ruefully. "Not enough for this. And you are useless behind those bars, no offense intended," she added quickly. The mage only chuckled, then seemed surprised at the sound.

"And if I did this?" he asked, stepping right up to the door and extending his arms past the bars.

Mila stared at him incredulously. "That is not how suppression magia works!" she exclaimed. "It dampens *all* of your magia. You can't just channel it only to your arms!"

"Can't I?" the mage asked.

"No! Magia lives within us, within our very blood. We pull energy from the world around us, and channel it through us. We are a conduit. We cannot limit that conduction to a certain part of us!"

"Have you ever tried?" he asked, wiggling his fingers at her.

Mila stared at him as if he were insane. Maybe he was. Perhaps the years in solitude within his cell had driven him mad. He certainly wasn't completely sane.

"No one has that much control," Mila answered, but she looked skeptical.

"Not even the Archwizard of the realm?" Auberon challenged. "I am now ninety-six percent certain that I am indeed Auberon, the Archwizard of Andala."

Mila exchanged a baffled look with Andu, then shook her head. "If you could have done this, you would have broken out already."

"Ah, but the energy I can channel through only a part of me is not nearly as much as the energy I can pull from my entire body. It is not enough to crack these runes. Believe me, I have tried. The draining of my power ..." his voice faded as he tapped a fingertip to his temple three times. "It has left damage."

Andu, Mila, and Rawl exchanged a grim look. Suddenly, the Archwizard brightened and rattled a quick merry beat against the prison bars.

"But combined..." he let his voice trail off. Mila looked at Andu again, bewildered.

"You have your stones?" the mage asked them, and they both nodded.

In the end, it was Andu who shrugged, then moved closer to the bars. He lifted one of his large hands to place it in Auberon's weathered ones, but the mage shot forward and stuck his fingers under Andu's arms, tickling him.

At Andu's incredulous look, Auberon erupted into laughter.

Andu turned to Mila, a mixture of shock and horror painted over his face.

"Oh, relax," Auberon said, sobering. "I am not *that* far gone." He rolled his eyes and reached for Andu's hand, then extended his other towards Mila.

Hesitantly, she allowed Andu to grip her fingers, then with a fortifying breath, lay her hand over Auberon's.

"Focus now," the mage said, and the three of them shut their eyes.

At first, nothing seemed to happen. The room was quiet save for the slow, steady breaths of the mages, combined with Rawl's blood, rushing in his ears to the tune of his heartbeat. Then, slowly, things began to change.

The room became warmer, the air feeling charged with static electricity. Rawl shot a tentative glance at Alric, wary of all the times he had been struck by his errant magia when he was afflicted with Mage Madness. But Alric remained still, staring raptly at the scene in front of them.

After a few moments, the exposed skin on Auberon's forearms began to glow, a deep indigo rippling across his skin. They formed glyphs and patterns, melting in and out of his flesh. Mila's skin began mimicking the symbols, hers the green of a newly budded leaf, painting her flesh with the colors of spring. Her magia was not limited to her arms, however, and Rawl could see the symbols crawling up her neck and face, then caught glimpses of jade at her exposed ankles.

Finally, more slowly, Andu also began to exhibit the same markings, his skin glowing golden. Like Mila, the magia was everywhere, painting his entire body and traveling with his blood, while the Archwizard's remained confined to his arms. The rippling movements became faster between the three of them, the temperature in the room spiking even higher. Alric took a few worried steps until he was by Rawl's side.

Rawl didn't even scold himself for taking comfort in his presence next to him.

Suddenly, the light seemed to leap from all of their bodies, mixing and melding with one another, crackling and moving towards the cage bars. They sizzled upon impact, but they did not unravel from each other, the colors braiding tightly between them. Their combined magia sparkled, traveling up and down the metal, like lightning flashing in a storm, buzzing around the cage like a hoard of wasps.

There was a deafening *crack* and Rawl saw a bar split, the metal splintering like wood.

"It's working," Alric gasped.

More cracks, booming like thunder, echoed through the room. The very air seemed to vibrate, the ground rumbling beneath their feet, and for a moment, Rawl was afraid that the earth would swallow them. But then, with a final resounding *crash*, three bars burst apart and bounced off the hard floor with a terrible clanking.

The mages opened their eyes, slowly extracting their hands from one another. The magia dissipated, melting back into their skin like oil rather than the electricity it seemed to be just moments before. Auberon pushed at the door, and it opened with no resistance at all. He lurched out, steps faltering.

Mila pulled out her Griffonstalon necklace, channeling the corruption the magia had left in her blood. Andu did the same with another gem hidden in his front pocket.

"May I?" Auberon asked, reaching for it when Andu was done. The bigger man nodded, then handed it to him.

"I once had a Dragonstear, no larger than my pinky nail," he said as he worked the magia out of himself. "Something so small, but immeasurably powerful. Ah well, no sense in reminiscing now," he finished, handing the gem back to Andu.

The tremors of the room had subsided, but Rawl felt the ripples of them still in his bones.

"We should go now," he said breathlessly. "I have no doubt that others felt that disturbance, even as far underground as we."

"Do not worry, mijo," the mage said kindly, stepping towards him. Though he spoke to Rawl, he looked at Alric appraisingly. "Now that I am released, I can use my magia. Though I will admit, channeling it to only a portion of my body was more tiring than I had expected. I am," he paused, "sixty-two percent depleted."

"Do you know the way out?" Mila asked him, and Auberon smiled.

"I know many ways."

CHAPTER 46

CHURAN

Axchel was holding the last pan dulce over his head, just out of Churan's reach.

Well, if the boy was being honest, he didn't *have* to hold it above his head to keep it out of Churan's grasp. The man was so tall he could have held it by his chest, and it would still be an impossible feat for him.

But that did not stop him from trying.

"Vamos, Ax!" he whined, gripping the man's arms to try to haul himself up. "Let me have it!"

Churan could feel Axchel's booming chuckle rattle his smaller frame. "You, mijo, have already had three!"

"But I'm still hungry," Churan protested, abandoning his attempts to climb the man in favor of dragging over a stool to perch himself on. Axchel merely moved out of range.

"Have some fruta," Axchel suggested.

"I don't want fruta!" Churan complained. The truth was, he had already had four slices of cantaloupe, a banana, and three of the small mangos that were so soft you could practically eat the peel. But he wanted the bread!

"I haven't finished my cafecito," Churan complained. "Everyone knows you eat pan dulce with cafe."

"I haven't finished my cafe either," Axchel said, and Churan looked down at their mugs, Axchel's filled with a liquid so dark it appeared black. Churan's cup held more milk than coffee.

"Por favor," Churan begged, looking up at the man with large eyes.

Axchel sighed dramatically, and split the bread in two, handing the bigger half to Churan.

"Gracias!" the boy said gratefully, dunking his piece into his milk with café, then proceeded to shove the entire thing in his mouth before Axchel could change his mind. The soldier just rolled his eyes and handed him a napkin, but Churan could see a ghost of a smile flicker on his lips.

It was early, before dawn, so the meal hall was quieter than usual. Some of the older initiates were already awake and ready for their day, those with extra morning training or chores. It would be another hour before the room filled with loud young women and the people of Pelgar.

By then, there would be more pan dulce.

Churan wouldn't usually have been there so early either, except that he had woken up with hunger pangs in his stomach. It felt like he was always hungry lately. Mage Nuna said that it was the unlocking of his abilities. Axchel said that it was his age. Churan didn't really care what the reason was, he was simply grateful that they never lacked in food.

He was just plucking a handful of grapes from the large fruit bowl in the center when he saw Nova walk in with the High Priestess. They both quickly crossed to their table.

"Buenos dias," Nova said, bending down to hug him. It embarrassed him a little when she treated him like a child, but he couldn't deny a morning hug was rather nice. He did his best to avoid marking the back of her tunic with his sticky hands. Not that he thought she'd mind. Nova was pretty great that way.

"Buenos dias," he said around a mouth full of fruit. He wiped his mouth when Nova pulled away to greet Axchel with a quick kiss on the cheek.

"Have either of you seen Damika this morning?" she asked them.

Both Churan and Axchel shook their heads, and Nova and the High Priestess exchanged a glance.

"She was supposed to meet me this morning," Mamá explained, looking concerned. "When she didn't arrive at the time we specified, I went to Nessa's room to see if she was there."

"Why would she be in your room?" Churan asked Nova curiously, then watched the girl flush red. He turned to Axchel, but noticed that he, too, was red in the face and avoided her gaze.

Churan mentally shrugged. Adults were strange.

"She wasn't, for the record," Nova said softly. "But now, we can't find her."

"There are only so many places in the temple that she could be, right?" Axchel asked.

"That's right, and while our grounds are large, we would be able to find her, unless she explicitly did not want to be found. And I cannot see why she would disappear on us right now."

"She has been acting strange lately," Nova admitted. "At first, I thought that it was because of the Ascension. But even after you took the role, she continued to act differently."

Mamá's brow furrowed. "She has been training harder than usual as well. You must have seen all the bruises and injuries she has been sustaining."

"That's just it, though. When does she have time to train?" Nova asked, chewing on her lower lip. "We are in meetings all day, or she is with Sinchi and Vashti, planning our strategy for when our sisters return. I have seen her dressed as if for a battle one evening, and the other night I noticed that she was heading towards the armory. But why would she need so many weapons just for training?"

"Has she not been sleeping?" Mamá asked, looking even more worried.

Something niggled at the back of Churan's mind.

"Maybe she has gotten overtired?" Axchel suggested. "We see it in soldiers in Cassalan sometimes. They fight too hard for too long, and their body just collapses."

"She wasn't in the infirmary," Nova answered, crossing her arms. "Oh, dioses, what if she is injured and alone somewhere?"

Alone ... Churan mused. There was something that he wasn't remembering ...

"What if a monstro found a way inside our walls somehow?" Nova cried. "A salta-sombras? We would never know if she was taken!"

That was it! Churan jerked straight up in his chair. "The monstro!" he exclaimed, and the rest of them looked at him as if he had sprouted horns on his head.

"A while ago, when I first began training with Mage Nuna, I had become upset," he explained. "I climbed a tree to be alone for a while, and from above the temple walls, I could see a monstro in the distance."

Nova gasped, and Mamá's hand flew to her throat.

"But then I noticed that it wasn't heading away from Pelgar, but towards it," Churan continued. "What if it wasn't a monstro at all?"

He looked at Nova. "You said she was dressed for a battle, not training." He shifted his gaze to Mamá. "What if all those injuries weren't from training?"

"Dioses," Mamá whispered. "She's been going to Pelgar to fight monstros?"

"Damn it, Dami," Nova growled, clenching her fists at her side.

Mamá motioned towards a Danrayen initiate, who dropped every-thing she was doing to scamper over to her.

"High Priestess," the girl greeted her with a deep bow.

"Go find Priestess Vashti and Mage Nuna. Tell them to meet us at the main temple doors. Tell them to expect battle. Then warn Ianuaria that we may have injured coming her way.

"I'm going," Nova said quickly, and Mamá nodded. "Of course. Vashti will select a few of our warriors as well."

"I'm coming too!" Churan exclaimed, jumping up, but a heavy hand landed on his shoulder.

"No," Axchel said. He delivered it simply, gently. And yet, Churan felt like he had been punched in the stomach.

"I can help!" he insisted.

"It is too dangerous, Churan," Nova said distractedly, already mov-ing towards the door of the meal hall. "You stay here with Axchel, where it is safe."

"But," Churan argued, trying to follow her, but Axchel's hand held firm. He looked up at him, but the soldier only shook his head.

"Come on," Axchel said, gently pulling on his arm so he would sit once more. Churan resisted. Axchel slid over his remaining piece of pan, but Churan wasn't hungry anymore.

"Can I be excused?" he mumbled.

Axchel looked at him pityingly. "You know we need to keep you safe," he offered by way of explanation. Churan ignored him.

"If Nuna is going to Pelgar, then I don't have lessons today. I would like to be on my own for a while," he said sullenly.

Axchel's face fell, but he nodded. "Claro. Find me later."

Churan left the hall, all of his food churning in his stomach. He made his way to the gardens and what he had now come to consider "his tree." Instead of trying to climb it again, with an aching belly, he sat with his back to its trunk instead.

It's not fair, he thought. *I was the one who told them about the person going to Pelgar. I am the one who figured out it could be Damika. I should be there to help!*

And he *could* help, he was sure of it! His magia had improved by leaps and bounds. He could now light multiple candles and sconces all at once, without exploding any wax or setting anything on fire. His air magia had improved as well, and he could move things across the entire training field; as long as it wasn't too heavy. He could swirl water and make it dance and play, could separate a cup full of it into individual, tiny droplets, then pour it back into its vessel without even breaking a sweat. Nuna hadn't begun teaching him how to use his new abilities in combat, but he was sure that he could help, anyway.

He looked at a pile of leaves by his feet, then reached for the river of power within him. The dam was still there, as always, but he had cleared enough of the debris that a steady stream of water now constantly flowed. It filled him, expanded and contracted within him like his very lungs. Churan hadn't realized how much of himself he had been denying until he unleashed it. Now he didn't know how he had ever lived without it.

Carefully, he made the leaves lift, one by one until they hung suspended in front of him. Then he made them spin, first in circles, then around one another. He made them move faster and faster, whipping them into a tiny cyclone of red and green and orange. Then, while still in the air, he flicked a tiny bit of his Burning towards them, and each ignited, raining ash down onto the garden ground.

Churan grinned triumphantly. *There,* he thought. *I can control it so much better now! I know I can help.*

And why shouldn't he? If he was going to be the catalyst for peace, shouldn't he start working towards that peace now?

I will show them, he thought suddenly. *I will prove to them that I can help.*

Churan stood. He remembered exactly where the hidden door to the outside of the temple was. He was fairly certain he could figure out how to open it. Of course, he wouldn't be able to re-enter; only Danrayen Warriors were capable of scaling that outer wall. But he would go to Pelgar, battle the monstros, and return with the group through the main doors.

He could imagine it now, the looks of pride and admiration that they would give him. Nova would hug him again, and he would let her. Damika might even thank him. She would tell him how powerful he was, and that they were lucky he had come to help.

Grinning, he made his way towards the door.

CHAPTER 47

NOVA

Nova ran across the fields, towards Pelgar, blades in hands. The priestesses ran beside her, as well as a group of full Danrayen Warriors that had remained at the temple after the Ascension Ceremony.

Shortly after the revelation that Damika might be fighting monsters in the village, they had all dressed and armored up as quickly as possible, relying on their years of training to aid their urgency. They then meet mere minutes later at the front temple doors to open them for the first time since the Pelgar attack.

Nova's heart hammered in her chest, not because of her pace as they made their way to the village, but with the fear that they would be too late.

What was Damika thinking? she thought. *How could she do this?*

But Nova knew. There was a time when she had known Damika better than anyone else in the world. And even now, she could understand her friend's motivations. Damika never was one to discuss her feelings. She would much rather work them out for herself rather than share her troubles with others. It wasn't necessarily that she was guarded, Damika was open and loving and caring with all those she cared for. But she always had the idea that her problems were her own to carry and she didn't want to burden anyone else with them. So, she found other outlets for releasing her emotions, one of her favorites being physical exertion.

Nova couldn't think of another time where Damika had been this reckless, however, but she also couldn't think of another time when her friend was so overburdened with emotion.

It's no excuse, she thought to herself. *And if the monstros haven't done it already, I'll kill her myself.*

When they reached the forest barrier between the open fields and Pelgar, they stayed on the main road, despite the fact that it would've been quicker for them to cut through the woods. Though salta-sombras were more of a risk during the night. Thanks to the increase of shadows, there was enough shade from the trees to make their presence a concern. No one wanted to lose a warrior today, especially not from an avoidable accident.

Eventually, they reached the bridge over the river that separated their land from Pelgar and paused their frantic sprint. Each of them inhaled deeply but steadily, taking a moment to catch their breath and settle their pulse. Even from there, they could hear the wild cacophony of monstros within the town limits. However, none could see any in their immediate vicinity, as the noises seemed to be coming from towards the town's center.

Those who hadn't already done so drew their weapons; Danrayen blades, bows, knives like the ones Nova held, and more. Then all the women looked to General Vashti for direction.

"I will lead on the Pelgar main road. You and you flank me," she said, pointing to Nova and another Danrayen girl. "You two," she continued, pointing at two more warriors, "follow Priestess Sinchi and take the left side of the town. Do not stray further than two blocks from the main road. That is a direct order."

Another quick turn and the jabbing of her fingers. "You two follow Mage Nuna on the right, same orders. The rest of you, stay behind me, but keep at least eight feet of distance between us at all times, unless I call for you. We all move forward, towards the center square."

The women nodded their assent and immediately broke off into formation. Nova took her spot to General Vashti's left. Wordlessly, they started forward, keeping a quick but careful pace into Pelgar. The streets were eerily empty, quieter than Nova had ever seen them, despite the noise emanating from further within.

They advanced, undisturbed for several minutes until, from seemingly nowhere, three culebretos slithered from the unkempt grass along the road to Pelgar. The creatures' long, sinuous bodies seemed to be made up of an oil-like substance, like quickly rushing black tar. Before Nova could even think of how to attack them, the general had dispatched all three with a quick slice of her sword. She then kept moving forward, as if slaying monsters of the Night Wood was but a tedious task to be accomplished.

From her periphery, Nova could see glimpses of the two other teams, making their way towards their common goal, but they were just quick flashes of motion. If they too met with any monstros on their path, they dispatched of them quietly and efficiently. Nova was starting to wonder if they had been wrong. If most of the monsters in Pelgar had already left to journey south, towards Andala like so many others before them. That Damika was not, in fact, in the village fighting them off. When suddenly, they all heard an enormous crash and piercing scream.

A scream that was most assuredly human.

Every instinct in her body screamed to run towards the noise, and to her friend, who was in trouble. Only years of relentless training held her back, waiting that split second for her general's orders.

Luckily, she did not need to wait long.

"Quickly, to me!" the general cried out, running towards the source of the sound. Her voice carried loud enough to reach the other teams, and the warriors trailing behind them. Abandoning stealth for speed, the air soon filled with the sound of slapping boots on cobblestones as they all rushed forward into the fray.

The moment the town square came into view, Night Wood monstros appeared from everywhere. They surged out of houses, lunged from alleyways, materialized from shadows. Nova could see at least two murcietos circling the sky above them, and more of the oily culebretos sliding their way.

She also saw Damika.

And she looked terrible, her clothing ripped and muddy, stained with blood, gunk, and dioses knew what else. Her white curly hair, which usually framed her scalp in a dome of curls, now lay flat on the left side, sticky and matted down with blood. Some of it had trailed down her face, crusting over on her skin from temple to chin, except over her left eye, which she had seemed to wipe away.

She was battling more than one monstro at once, several monstros, too many. More than any one person should be able to handle alone. She was holding her own, but just barely. Even from a distance, Nova could tell that her friend was tired. Her muscles strained with each movement, and she shook her head as if to clear it more than once.

The rest of them crashed into the battle, striking down as many of the creatures as they could in an effort to rescue their Danrayen sister. Nova heard a startled yelp and turned in time to see one of the warriors lifted by her braid, one of the flying creatures yanking her upwards, but an arrow from Sinchi found its mark in the monstro's eye, causing it to drop her. The girl landed on her feet in a crouch, using her surprise appearance to dispatch the beast directly in front of her.

Nova threw blade after blade, hitting creatures with skin, hair, scales, and some with forms she did not recognize. A lumbering beast barreled towards her, forcing Nova to swap her knives for the Danrayen blade strapped to her back. She ran to meet the thing head on, slicing a long cut down its fur-covered side as it roared in pain. It turned, swatting at her with its clawed paws, but Nova ducked under the swing, striking out with her blade again.

Nova wrinkled her nose as she approached it once more. Somehow, the musky, pungent aroma of wild beast was being made worse by a scent akin to burning hair. As she swung her blade once again, she noticed the reason.

The creature's fur was on fire!

It was not a flame powerful enough to do much damage. In fact, every time the creature twisted, the fire would blow itself out, only to light again. Nova didn't know where it was coming from, but used the next burst of flame, and the creature's momentary distraction, to bring her sword down hard, severing its head from its shoulders.

"Coño," she heard a small voice mutter behind her and sent a prayer up to all the dioses that it didn't belong to who she thought it belonged to.

Turning, she caught a glimpse of Churan just as a demon dog tackled the boy to the ground.

"No!" Nova shrieked, panic clawing in her chest as she grasped for another throwing blade. The dog yelped and stumbled, an arrow in its haunches before Nova threw three daggers in quick succession, embedding themselves in its hide. Another arrow from Sinchi finally brought the creature down.

Nova sprinted towards Churan, who was still sprawled on the ground.

"What are you doing here?" she demanded, hauling him up with her left arm and flinging yet another blade at a monstro heading towards them. It sunk in the thing's neck, but there were more coming.

"What were you thinking?" she yelled, resisting the urge to shake the boy. His face had gone very white.

"I thought," he mumbled, but Nova spun him around to defend them from another Night Wood creature before he could finish. One of the other Danrayen girls had seen them and joined her in protecting Churan.

Nova grasped the neck of his tunic and began dragging the sorcerer towards a crumbling building, wanting his back, at least, to remain protected. Unfortunately, a murcieto swooped down at that very moment, causing Nova to have to change their path. They stumbled even deeper into the town center, where the battle was the thickest.

The Danrayen who had joined them suddenly screamed, and Nova turned just in time to see her swept from her feet, the motion so fast she couldn't even throw out her hands to break her fall. Her face smacked against the ground with a sickening crunch, blood spurting from her nose and mouth. A long, dark green tongue wrapped around her calf, and with a snap, it dragged her backwards, into the gaping mouth of a monstro. Nova shielded Churan's eyes before the creature's jaws snapped shut, cutting the Danrayen's voice off mid-scream.

Nova kept dragging the boy forward.

"Ayudanos!" she cried out, getting Vashti's attention. When she saw Churan, her mouth dropped open.

"No!" Mage Nuna cried, seeing him at the same time the general did. The women had reached Damika and were helping hold off the monstros. But upon seeing the boy, they all gathered closer, forming a circle around him and Nova.

Monstros of all shapes and sizes quickly began to surround them. It seemed that, as quickly as an arrow or blade would take them down, two more would appear. The women fought hard, an immaculate display of Danray's finest, and still it was not enough. Nova kept her grip on Churan in the center, yanking him this way and that whenever it seemed possible that a creature could break their formation. There was a pained cry and one of the Danrayens fell. Slashes like claw marks across her back and biceps. Sinchi grabbed her and dragged her back, dropping her near Nova before returning to the fray.

"Dioses," Churan gasped, watching the blood pool from the girl's wounds, quickly soaking the ground beneath her. The girl squirmed and moaned; her body wracked with spasms. Then she was deathly still. Under her hand, Nova could feel Churan's body tremble.

There was a high-pitched screech, and then another, and another. They came so fast and so loud that Churan clapped his hands over his ears, and Nova had to fight not to do the same.

The Danrayens all looked up.

In the sky were at least a dozen murcietos. If the noise or the scent of blood attracted them, Nova did not know, but they flew straight towards their group. Three of the winged beasts were closer than the others, and without warning, one dove to grab another warrior, claws digging deep into her neck and shoulder. Nova was sure that she died before the thing even managed to lift her in the air, which was a blessing, as the other two monstros fought over her dangling body in the sky.

"How many arrows?" Vashti asked loudly.

"Not enough," Sinchi replied, looking towards the other Danrayen girl equipped with a bow. She grimaced and shook her head. She was almost out, too.

Damika, who had continued fighting through her injuries, bent her knees and looked up.

"Don't let them grab you," she grunted. "But keep an eye on the ones on the ground, too."

It seemed impossible. There was no way that they could fight the monstros surrounding them while still avoiding the grasp of the flying creatures above.

The screeching intensified and Nova shoved Churan lower to the ground, lifting her blade just as two of the bats descended on her. She had a moment to hear the screams of the Danrayens around her before talons dug into her flesh.

"No!" She heard Churan scream.

And then time suspended.

Nova knew that her feet were lifted from the ground, could feel the clutch of the creature. She could see the others being similarly lifted, but slowly, as if they all moved through water. Her eyes flickered to Churan an instant before he caught fire.

No, not fire, Nova realized. He burst with a light so bright it burned, made the air so hot that Nova was sure she would singe. Instead, she felt the creature holding her shudder and wail, before turning completely to ash.

The wave of light extended, decimating every monstro in its path. And not only the flying ones, but also the creatures surrounding them on the ground. It seemed that every monstro within Pelgar disintegrated in the blink of an eye.

As Nova plummeted back toward the ground, time righted itself, and she landed with a heavy grunt, the fall knocking the wind out of her. Around her, she could see her sisters in similar disarray, stumbling or fallen, most working to right themselves quickly, weapons still in hand, ready to continue the fight.

But the battle was done. There were no opponents left to face. Every single creature burnt, their remains blowing away with the force of Churan's magia.

Slowly, every single Danrayen eye turned to look at the small, panting boy, sprawled in the center of the Pelgar's town square.

CHAPTER 48
DAMIKA

Damika stared at Churan blearily. Her head hurt, and her vision was blurry. She wasn't entirely sure that she wasn't hallucinating. Had General Vashti and the Danrayens come to Pelgar to rescue her? Were they all there now, or was Damika dreaming?

Or perhaps she was dead after all. Surely that made more sense than what she had just witnessed. There was no way that amount of power was even possible, let alone that it emanated from the child who sat wide-eyed and trembling before them all.

"The dam," he gasped, looking at Nuna. "The dam, it burst!"

"What is he talking about?" Nessa asked desperately, crouching beside him. "What is he saying? Will he be all right?"

Mage Nuna was staring at the boy with a look Damika couldn't place. Then, softly, almost reverently, she whispered three words:

"The Unnamed Prince."

"Qué?" Vashti barked out. "What do you mean, Nuna?"

"It's true, it's all true," the mage whispered, still gaping at Churan. "I thought maybe his power was just too slight to corrupt his blood. That he was a mage, nothing more, and one with poor training at that. I believed that if enough of his power was unblocked from the defenses that he created for himself, that he would eventually need to use spell stones like the rest of us. But this ..."

She looked around at the destruction that surrounded them. "This could not have been accomplished by a mere mage. He is a sorcerer. And if that is true …"

"Then the prophecy must also be true?" Sinchi finished for her, sounding shocked.

"Of course, the prophecy is true," Nessa said, annoyance lacing her words. Damika watched as she helped Churan up, then checked him for injuries. Her own shoulders were bleeding with puncture wounds, and the sight of it made Damika grimace.

My fault, she thought to herself. *All of this is my fault.*

She made herself look, *really* look, at what her actions had wrought. Vashti had burn marks over her jaw and neck. Sinchi was favoring her right leg. A Danrayen Warrior Damika wasn't familiar with was cradling a hand with a broken wrist against her chest. Another was lying face down on the cobblestones with a set of nasty claw marks carved into her skin, unmoving. They would never be able to bury the girl taken by the bats—there was nothing left of her to bury. The survivors bore slices, cuts, breaks, and bruises; all because of her.

Worse still, people had died because of her. If the boy hadn't stepped in …

She didn't know how she would begin to apologize to them for any of it, but had a desperate need to try. She stepped forward to begin.

But darkness claimed her.

Damika awoke before she opened her eyes.

She was in no rush to see where she was. The last thing she remembered, she thought she had been battling every single monstro in the Night Wood.

And losing.

If she was dead, there was no reason to open her eyes and face her afterlife just yet. One of those bat-creatures had probably dragged her off as her Danrayen sisters watched ...

The Danrayens. She remembered that the Danrayens had been there, that they had traveled to Pelgar to save her. That people had died, and that she had almost gotten them *all* killed, had it not been for the boy. For Churan.

Damika opened her eyes.

At once, she recognized the temple infirmary. She blinked a few times as she made sense of her surroundings. She was in a private room, with a window facing the temple courtyards. Turquoise curtains fluttered beside open shutters. She was lying on a bed, and when she turned her head, she noticed that Nessa was sitting on a wooden chair beside her.

And she looked *livid*.

Shame coursed through Damika's body and she coughed lightly, preparing to speak.

Nessa held up a hand.

"You have a bruised head," she said, her voice emotionless. "You also have cracked ribs, severe burns, three broken fingers on your left hand, and more cuts and bruises than I can count."

As Nessa listed all her injuries, Damika's body began catching up to her mind. It was as if each body part woke up as Nessa mentioned them, lighting her skin, muscles, and bones on fire.

She grimaced, which Nessa noticed.

"Does it hurt?" she asked Damika, who could do nothing but nod.

Nessa leaned forward. *"Good."*

Then she leaned back and threw up her arms, clearly ready to chastise her. And while Damika knew she deserved every single second of it, she needed to know something first.

"The others?" she croaked as Nessa was taking a deep breath, likely to support her oncoming tirade. "The Danrayens, and the bo—Churan. How are they?"

Nessa glared at her, then Damika watched as all the air escaped her lungs in a deep sigh.

"We lost four Danrayens," she told her, in a tone much softer than before. Damika shut her eyes. She didn't deserve that softness. Their deaths were her fault.

"There were many injuries. Some girls are still in the infirmary not far from you," Nessa continued. "But the survivors made it back to the temple without any more trouble."

Tension radiated from Damika's stiff muscles.

"And Churan?" she pressed.

"He saved us all," Nessa answered, beaming proudly. "I yelled at him just as properly as I'm about to do to you, because it seems it is my lot to be surrounded by reckless stupidity. Although he did save us."

"And now the priestesses believe in him, and the prophecy," Damika added.

Nova nodded thoughtfully. "I would have preferred that they had trusted him, and me, from the start, but I suppose that I don't blame them for their doubts."

Guilt piled on top of the mountain of shame Damika already felt. She had been one of those who had initially doubted. And even once she believed in Nessa and her mission, how much had she tried to get the priestesses to believe them, too? She hadn't fought very hard at all.

She had been too busy battling her own demons, and the monstros of Pelgar. And now, others had died because of it.

As if she could hear her shift in thoughts, a steely resolve settled over Nessa's face once more.

"Now, *what in all the dioses' names were you thinking?*" she demanded.

Damika felt the heat of remorse race through her body, further igniting each ache and pain she harbored. She knew she deserved every sting.

"Lo siento, Nessa," she whispered, casting her eyes downwards. "I'm so, so sorry—"

"Of course, you're sorry," Nessa snapped. "I *know* you're sorry. What I don't know is why. *Why* would you be so foolish?"

"I don't know," Damika answered, but Nessa shook her head furiously.

"Not good enough," she growled.

"I don't know!" Damika cried out again. "I know I acted carelessly, and without honor. A Danrayen should never let their personal feelings affect their responsibilities, or worse, put others in danger. I did both." She hung her head.

"But why?" Nessa pressed. "Please Dami, just talk to me."

"I don't know," Damika repeated stubbornly.

"Dami," Nessa tried, but Damika interrupted with a yell.

"I don't know!" she yelled, jerking herself backwards on the bed, ignoring how her injuries screamed in protest. "I can't, I don't want to …"

"You nearly died. You did not order the rest of us to come. We went knowingly and willingly. So, the deaths of those Danrayens are not your fault, but I know you carry their burden." Nessa's voice was colder than Damika had ever heard it. "I cannot take that from you.

But this is not about them, this is about *you*. You have been slipping out, dioses-knew how many nights, *alone*, seeking out monstros of the Night Wood. And you are going to tell me why. What made that risk worth it? What is it you've been running from?"

"*She didn't want me,*" Damika cried out, mortified to hear her breath hitch with a sob.

"Oh, Dami," Nessa said, standing from her chair to perch on the edge of Damika's bed.

"Adira. She was my mother, and she didn't want me." Damika shook her head, not caring that the motion sent pins of blazing hot pain through her skull.

"I never even wanted a mother, not really," she lied. "I mean, sure, I thought about it. I thought about it every time the girls talked about the families that they had left at home. Or when Petra would see her father and brothers in Pelgar when they came to trade."

She was talking fast now. "And so, of course, I might've thought about it a little. Especially since my memories of before the temple were so hazy. I might've wondered if I had a family, and what they looked like, and if the people who got killed when Guerro's men came looking for me had loved me."

Nessa held her hand, the one without the broken fingers.

"I had no reason to believe that those people weren't my parents, and yet, even in my dreams, when I remembered them, I felt detached. I thought it was just because I was so young when they died. Or that their deaths had been so traumatic that my young brain had sought to protect me from the horrors of it."

Damika drew in a ragged breath.

"But after a while, I stopped thinking about it. I buried it down, along with the memories of my time before the temple." Tears were falling now, but Nessa made no move to stop her.

"I had everything I needed here, after all. I had the goddess. I had a purpose. I had a family. I even had Mamá, and even though she wasn't my real mother, I convinced myself that no mother would have been better than her, anyway."

Damika squeezed her eyes shut. "I convinced myself that was all that I needed, because I didn't think I could ever have anything more. But now I know the truth. Now I know that I did have a mother, not someone lost in the memories of my youth, but a real flesh and blood woman who I saw almost every day of my life in one way or another."

She looked at Nova. "She was *here*," she croaked. "The entire time, she was *here*, and she *knew* me. She knew who I was, but she let me grow up alone. Worse, I loved her. I loved and respected her as my High Priestess. I would have been so proud, and so, so happy to have her be my mother."

"Damika," Nessa said softly, squeezing her fingers.

"I know what you're going to say. You're going to say that she had no choice. That she did what she thought was best for me and for the order. And as a warrior, I understand that."

A sob worked its way from her chest.

"But as a girl, I really wanted a mother."

Nessa held her gently as Damika cried into her shirt. She held her as she fell apart, crumbled completely, emptied herself of all the pain she had been harboring for weeks. She cried until there was nothing left in her to expel.

No, she knew that wasn't true. She knew one good cry wasn't going to be enough to erase all the things she had come to learn within the last few months. But this time, at least, in Nessa's arms, she felt like she leached some of the poison that had been driving her to do all the stupid and reckless things she had been doing.

"I'm sorry," she told Nessa.

Nessa understood immediately what she was apologizing for.

"I know you are," she said. "I even know why you did it. But." She waited until Damika lifted her head to look her in the eye. Nessa removed a cloth from her pocket to wipe Damika's puffy eyes and streaming nose. "But," she continued, "never again. You can't do that ever again."

"I know," Damika whispered, chagrined.

"I don't think you do know," Nessa replied. "I don't think you understand how important you are to this order, Damika. You were almost the High Priestess. The women, warriors and initiates alike, look up to you. They respect you. And the priestesses are depending on you. It is one thing to battle for a cause. It is another to seek it out for your own gain."

Damika swallowed hard and nodded.

"If things ever get bad again, I promise you, I will find someone to talk to, instead of putting myself in harm's way," she answered. Nessa just stared at her for a long, hard minute. Something in Damika's eyes must've convinced her, because she finally nodded and kissed her forehead. She hadn't noticed how much her head was still hurting her until the small motion eased some of the pain away.

"Now rest," Nessa demanded, easing back from her. Damika clutched at her clothing.

"You aren't leaving, are you?" she asked, suddenly anxious at the thought of it.

Nessa eased back down on the bed beside her. "No," she answered, gathering her back into her arms. "Not if you don't want me to."

"Stay?" Damika asked, trying to not sound like she was begging. "Please."

Nova settled against her gently, taking care not to jostle her or make her injuries worse.

"I'm not going anywhere," she answered.

With a bruised head, three broken fingers, cracked ribs, and more cuts and bruises than she could count, Damika felt better than she had in weeks. And finally, she fell into a peaceful sleep.

CHAPTER 49

RAWL

The escape from the palace was anticlimactic compared to their entry. They did have the sense of mind to warn Auberon about the monstros in the city, which Rawl suspected that he didn't fully believe, not until he witnessed it for himself. Even then, they had to all but drag him away, as he was determined to examine the creatures more closely and ascertain just who was controlling them.

"Guerro?" he said, as they finally made it back to the inn. Rawl had just finished explaining to him what he had learned from Taruka. "He always was overly ambitious. There were rumors about Zerlina's parentage ... ninety-three percent certainty that he is the princess's sire," he grumbled. "I should have seen it. My mistake. So many, many mistakes."

At first, their journey back was tense and hurried, each of them worried that at any moment, palace guards would flood the streets, searching for the lost prisoner. Auberon assured them it was unlikely.

"Visitors?" he asked, looking both surprised and delighted. "No, no one came to see me. I would have made tea!" His mirth faded from his face. "I should have offered you all tea!" He split from the group and began wandering towards a cluster of shops. "Come, come, I've been a horrible host!"

Andu grasped his arm gently and guided him back on course. "No need for tea, señor," he told him softly. "You were saying that no one checked on you in the prison for a long time?"

Rawl watched as a fog of confusion drifted across the wizard's eyes. Once more, he couldn't help but wonder how this broken man was going to be able to rally the mages to their cause.

"Tell us about the magia used for your prison," Mila urged the older man. At the mention of "magia," his vision seemed to clear.

"The entire cage was self-sufficient, conjuring food, water, and essentials for a very long stay," he recited, as if delivering a report. "It was a clever bit of magia, if I do say so myself. If they are trying to ascertain the source of the tremors that we created when breaking the bars, it would be more likely that they would check the strength of their control on the monstros near the palace, rather than check in on me. It is what I would do."

Then he grinned and began to sing.

"Check your closets,

and under your bed,

the Night Wood comes,

and blood will run red.

Look behind your curtains,

and around each bend,

the monstros come,

and it will be your end!"

Rawl suppressed a shudder as they continued hurriedly down the road. They made their way back as quickly as they could, all of them dirty, tired, and spent by the time they reached the inn.

The mage looked especially weathered and drained as they crossed the threshold into the busy establishment. No matter how powerful the man was, it was clear that his years in the palace dungeons had weakened him. He didn't complain, but it was obvious to Rawl that even the walk from the palace to their inn on the outskirts of the city had taken a toll on him. It didn't surprise Rawl that the man was exhausted. They had kept him in a cage barely large enough to pace in, let alone exercise in.

"Why don't we sit and eat before going up to our rooms?" Rawl asked, worried that the mage would be unable to climb the stairs in his condition. Auberon nodded, and they found an empty table, large enough for all of them.

"I will order our meals at the bar," Andu said as they all sat.

Auberon looked at Alric. "There is a seventy-nine percent chance that if he attempts to bring all the plates to us by himself, our food will end on the floor rather than our bellies. Go with him to help," he said.

Alric looked surprised that the mage would single him out, but he nodded and joined Andu. As soon as he was out of earshot, Auberon whirled on Mila.

"Explain why my apprentice, and the best pupil I have ever had the pleasure of teaching, no longer remembers his life," he demanded of her.

There was a wary pause as they processed the displeasure of one of the most powerful men in the realm. Even if his mind seemed addled, it was uncomfortable, to say the least. Though the mage had directed the question to his sister, it was Rawl who finally answered. "He had Mage Madness," he told him.

"Impossible," the mage said dismissively. "One hundred percent certainty of death. Everyone knows this. There is no cure for Mage Madness."

"Mila found one," Rawl said, doing his best to keep his temper from his voice.

The mage's dark eyes found Mila's once more. "Mila, is it?" he asked, voice equal parts suspicious and intrigued. "Tell me then, Mila, how you, a child, found the answer to a problem no one else has ever been able to solve. Did you make a bargain with la ratoncita de los milagros?"

La ratoncita de los milagros, a children's story about a little mouse that could grant wishes. Rawl could not tell if the man was being sarcastic or asking the question in earnest.

Mila flushed but explained to him her theory about the magia and corruption, and her wild idea that, if Alric did not remember his magia, it would dissipate, bleeding off the corruption with it.

Auberon stared at her, shocked back into lucidity. "You didn't ..." he gasped as the color drained from his face. "For dioses' sake, please tell me you didn't do what I think you are saying."

Mila glanced at Rawl, genuine fear in her eyes.

"If he couldn't remember his magia, he wouldn't hold the energy in his body, the corruption would have nothing to grasp onto—" she tried, before Auberon interrupted her.

"He is his magia!" he bellowed. Rawl felt like the very air rattle with the force of his anger. Patrons of the inn turned to stare at them, but with a careless flick of his wrist their eyes grew glassy, and they returned to their meals, sparing no more glances to Rawl's party.

"He is a mage," Auberon continued quietly. "His gift is as much a part of him as his lungs are. And his magia is as natural to him as breathing. By removing that part of himself, you have cut out his heart." He took in a ragged breath. "No mage would ever willingly give up their magia. It is unthinkable. Deplorable. You have stripped him of his identity, carved his soul from his being."

"He would have died," Mila protested.

"He *did* die," Auberon argued, but sadly. All the ire had bled from his body. "I don't know who that man is. He may look like Alric, but my pupil is as gone as if I had buried him in the ground myself."

Another quiet descended upon them, heavy and oppressive. Rawl wanted to speak and defend his sister, but the truth was that he didn't disagree with the Archwizard. Auberon had merely voiced out loud the secret thoughts and feelings that he had struggled with for weeks.

Rawl watched as Mila batted away an errant tear from her eye, then reached out to hold her hand. He didn't blame his sister. It had been his decision as much as her power that had turned Alric into what he was now.

"I will admit that I am surprised you were able to successfully conduct the spell," Auberon grumbled. "I calculate a ninety-two percent chance of death. It is a miracle that it didn't kill him."

"It might have," Rawl mumbled, remembering that terrible day. "But he came back."

"And who are you?" Auberon asked, removing his attention from Rawl's sister, placing it on him.

He is an old man, and has been locked in the dungeons for years, Rawl reminded himself. *It's not his fault if his manners have become rusty, and his mind weak.*

Quickly, Rawl did his best to recall the last year of his life to the mage. He explained how Rojya—Nova—*the Name-Bearer* had saved his life, and how he had come to join her and Alric on their quest. He explained about Sarakshi, the Padir girl with Unveiled Sight, and how her vision had led them to Cassalan and the former king, Enrique. Auberon seemed particularly shocked to learn that the man was not dead, as their entire realm believed. He recalled their trip even further north, to the Northern Tribes, and the discovery of the young sorcerer, Churan.

"Not a sorcerer," Auberon interrupted, laughing as if Rawl had told a great jest. "My mind may be damaged, but I am not stupid. There hasn't been a known sorcerer in at least a century! And I would know. Are you certain you did not mean a 'source arrow?'"

"What is a 'source arrow?'" Rawl asked, raising his brows.

"I have no notion, dear boy, you tell me! You are the one bringing it into conversation!" Auberon answered.

Rawl shook his head. "There have been many changes, as of late," he said, recalling Rojya's words when they had been made aware of his existence. "And I promise you that Churan is, in fact, a sorcerer, and the Unnamed Prince."

He noticed that plates and mugs were beginning to arrive at the bar top across the room and hurried with his tale.

Rawl explained their battle against creatures of the Night Wood while they were in Tureene, and how Alric's stone had shattered after saving them both from monstros. "I couldn't let him die, even after it was clear he was afflicted with Mage Madness," Rawl confessed. "So, I brought him to Mila. I knew if anyone could help, it would be her," he said, smiling at his sister gratefully.

Auberon regarded Mila thoughtfully, and this time she met his gaze head on. They were interrupted by the arrival of Andu and Alric, food and drinks in hand.

Rawl leaned in towards the mage and asked him under his breath, "Is there anything that you can do?"

Auberon frowned down at his stew and ale, then met Rawl's eyes. "The spell is very thorough," he finally responded.

"So, I have been told," Rawl said irritably. "But I was also told there was no cure to Mage Madness, and yet..."

Brusquely, Auberon turned to Alric, who was sitting on the other side of him.

"Give me your hands, mijo. I need to see something," he told him. Alric shot a worried look at Rawl, who nodded encouragingly at him. Slowly, Alric lifted his long-fingered hands and placed them into Auberon's.

The mage shut his eyes, mumbling under his breath. The same indigo painting his skin before fading away and reappearing in other places. Alric closed his eyes as well, expression pained. Rawl was fairly certain he was simply confused and worried, and not in *actual* pain, but the archer tensed, ready to pull Auberon off of him if he showed any further signs of distress. Luckily, the mage's markings faded quickly, and he placed a bread roll in Alric's palm.

"Very good, boy. Very good," he said to Alric, his gaze softening. "I just needed to make sure you had properly washed your hands, even underneath your fingernails, you know!"

Rawl wanted to growl with frustration, thinking that the wizard had simply forgotten Rawl's request. But then, Auberon turned back towards Rawl and gave a subtle shake of his head.

No. Nothing to be done, it said.

Rawl hadn't realized how much renewed hope had been living with him until Auberon's casual denial burst it. Hope turned into disappointment, flooding him like a broken dam. It soaked him; he was drowning in it. He stood abruptly from the table, then fumbled as all eyes turned to look at him.

"I just—I need..." he stammered, backing away and turning over a stool. "I just need to go outside."

"It'll be dark soon!" Mila protested, but Rawl continued backing away.

"I won't be long," he promised, and rushed out of the inn's doors.

Outside, he slunk into the side alley and leaned against the building, taking great big gulping breaths. He didn't even care that there was a large culebreto slithering near the street gutters, nor a leathery murcieto perched on the balcony of the neighboring building. They both stared at him menacingly, but when they made no move to attack him, Rawl pushed them from his mind. There was too much in there to give them any space, anyway.

"Stupido," he mumbled to himself. "You knew there was no hope, you knew."

So why had he allowed himself to hope?

He braced himself against the wooden wall, closing his eyes and doing his best to stifle the darkness that grew a little larger each time he had to admit that his Alric was never coming back. He remained there, breathing steadily, until a soft hiss caused him to snap his eyes open.

The sun had nearly disappeared behind the horizon, and the fading light of day served only to illuminate several monstros that had crept into the alleyway. The air was sharp with the rancid stench of old blood and matted fur. Fear burst in Rawl's stomach as he heard the clicks of nails on cobblestones, and the shuffling of wings. Frantic, he looked around, only to find himself surrounded.

He was trapped.

"Coño," he said, heart thundering in his chest, adrenaline flooding his body and making his limbs tingle with pins and needles. They were not attacking him yet, but there was still a sliver of light against the dark night.

Rawl looked for a way around them, but they had effectively blocked off the alleyway on both sides. The murcieto had landed in front of him, crouched and ready, its eyes so black it was hard to distinguish them from the rest of its body. Rawl could see the gleam of the bat-creature's talons, able to rip his flesh from his bones, or his airway from his neck in one quick swipe.

The culebreto had slithered to striking distance, its sinuous body undulating, while fat globs of venom dripped from its fangs, sizzling as they hit the ground. While Rawl's eyes had been closed, two of the demon dogs had blocked his path back to the inn.

Rawl knew that fighting even one of the creatures would have been difficult, near impossible, without his bow. He scanned the wall behind him on either side, looking for service doors or open windows, and finding none. The light was fading fast.

He tried moving back towards the main road and the inn's door, but the dogs paced, blocking his exit. They just crowded him, but didn't touch him.

Not yet, at least, Rawl thought desperately.

He turned and tried to make his way down the other side, but the snake unfurled and stretched out, its long sinewy body extending from building to building. Rawl could have hopped over it, at least in theory. He didn't think he could rely on his body, locked in fear as he was.

The sun slipped under the horizon.

The result was instantaneous. The dogs growled and tensed their muscles. The culebreto coiled to strike. The oversized bat bared its fangs, shrieking so loudly that it momentarily deafened Rawl. He pressed himself into the wood at his back, sliding down to the ground and groping for anything that might serve him as a weapon. His hands gripped a loose stone just as the snake struck.

There was a flash of deep purple, and the culebreto was bodily flung to the other side of the alley. The dogs also burst apart, one hitting one building, the other following the snake, body tumbling in the air. The murcieto screeched again and opened its wings, lifting up into the sky before a strike of lightning singed one of its legs. It veered in the air but righted itself and continued its retreat.

"Hurry now," Auberon told Rawl, decidedly *unhurried*, as he made his way back towards the inn's entrance, Rawl fast on his heels. "There are many, many more of them, and we are but snacks to them." He paused at the entrance of the inn. "If you were a snack food, what would you be? I think I would like to be a buñuelo."

Instead of answering, Rawl shoved him through the door. The second that they were both back inside the relative safety of the building, Mila kicked his shin, hard.

"Ow!" Rawl howled, hopping on one foot.

"I told you not to go out there," she seethed, trying to kick him once more. Rawl managed to narrowly dodge her second attempt. She whirled, stalking away. "There was an open room today, and I am taking it. You four figure out your own arrangements." Then she was gone.

The men looked at each other, unsure of what to say.

"Thank you," Rawl finally ventured, breaking the silence. He patted Auberon awkwardly on the back. "You saved me."

"As you all saved me," the man replied. "And I suspect there will be more battles to come, so it would be best not to keep score."

Rawl shook his head. He couldn't keep up with the man's antics or moments of clarity.

Auberon, unaware of Rawl's confusion, turned to Alric. "Come then, mijo, show me to our room, and ask the innkeeper to fetch some bathwater, por favor. It's time we washed the stench of the dungeons off of us."

Alric shot a startled look at Rawl, then regretfully began following the mage up the stairs. Rawl felt relieved. He would sleep better without Alric next to him. He turned to Andu instead.

"Shall we do the same?" he asked the big man, who grinned.

"Thank the dioses," he replied. "I wasn't going to say anything, but you stink."

CHAPTER 50

RAWL

On their journey back to the Mage University, Rawl filled Auberon in on the political situation of Andala. They had touched on Lord Guerro and his connection to Queen Issalia, but Rawl expanded on his other daughter Kichka, her connection to the Name-Bearer, the death of High Priestess Adira, and the Ascension of her daughter, Damika, to her place.

"So, the Name-Bearer became a Daughter of Danray?" Auberon mused. "I will confess, when I sent her there, all those years ago, I only meant to protect her. There was a thirteen percent chance that she would develop into a warrior. I never imagined that she would grow into one, but I am amazed she is now a true Danrayen."

"Then you don't know her very well," Rawl answered evenly. Anyone who had ever met Rojya could see that she was a warrior, through and through.

"And you don't know Ignacio very well," the wizard retorted.

Rawl shared a confused look with the rest of their party. "No. Sorry. Who is Ignacio?"

"Ignacio?" Auberon repeated, looking just as confused as Rawl. "How do you know about Ignacio?"

"You ..." Rawl hesitated. "You just mentioned him?"

"My parrot?" Auberon asked.

"Ignacio is a parrot?" Mila asked, sounding as lost as Rawl felt.

"Ignacio was my parrot when I was a child. Why do you mention him?"

"We didn't," Andu started, but Rawl just shook his head at him. It was useless.

"So, the Name-Bearer is going to lead the Danrayens against the royal family in Andala?" Auberon continued, as if he hadn't just been speaking about childhood pets. "Bring this sorcerer child, Churan, to the Flowers? Nineteen percent chance of success."

"It is the path that you set in motion for her as a child," Rawl reminded him, a little bitterly.

"There wasn't an army of monstros at the city gates back then!" the mage retorted. "Or prowling the city to keep its citizens subjugated. I fear that the Danrayens will not be enough," he confessed. "With the Danrayens, perhaps twenty-seven percent rate of success. Even if they can convince your people to join them, that only raises to thirty-three," he continued, referencing the Padir.

"That is why we need you to convince the mages to join the fight," Rawl reminded him, but Auberon only looked thoughtful.

"We had gained many followers before my imprisonment," he said, glancing at Alric, then away just as quickly. "Followers of the Flowers. A garden!" he shouted, and Rawl and Andu jumped. "We should have called ourselves the Garden!"

"Can you rally these followers?" Rawl began, but Auberon interrupted.

"The Garden!" he yelled again.

"Can you rally the Garden," Rawl tried again, "to join the fight and assist the Name-Bearer in her task?"

Auberon frowned low, pursing his lips and looking very much like a large fish. "I have been gone many years. I do not know if they will still believe in me. I can't see the percentage."

"They're scared," Mila answered simply. "I was not at the university when you were, so I do not know the inner workings of the network you established. Just whispered rumors of what once was." She met his eyes. "But I trust that the belief in you has never faded. If you show yourself, they will come. They believe still."

Auberon sighed, his face relaxing. "Well then," he mused. "We shall have to call a meeting of the Secret Order of the Flowers."

They reached the Mage University with plenty of daylight left in the sky, and without encountering any more monstros on the Great Andalan Road.

They agreed that food and rest were much needed. After which, Auberon insisted that they bring him to the head mage. A request that Mila vehemently opposed.

"You are a traitor to the crown, and a fugitive!" she argued as Andu cleared their plates. "If word of your escape hasn't reached the university yet, it will very soon. Don Gilberto is the faculty head of this university, which is funded by the crown. He will have an obligation to report you to the authorities immediately!"

"Nonsense," Auberon responded. "Tonterias. Before I was imprisoned, I was above even Gilberto. He reported to me and was also a supporter of the Flowers. He will be delighted by my return. I am one hundred percent sure of it."

Mila looked unconvinced, and Rawl had always trusted his sister's intuition.

"Are you certain that this is wise?" Rawl asked tentatively.

"Claro, claro," the mage reassured them. "Please direct me to where I can bathe and change, and we will seek him out in his quarters."

Andu glanced at Mila, and she gave him a terse nod. Permission granted, the big man led Auberon away.

"I don't like this," Mila mumbled. Rawl rubbed her shoulder absentmindedly.

"I don't pretend to know the mage world of politics as you do, but the man was the Archwizard of the realm. Surely that still means something."

"Even if that is true, he is not the same Archwizard that Don Gilberto will remember," she replied.

"He has moments of lucidity. Maybe this will be one of them." Rawl sounded unconvinced, even to his own ears.

Mila gnawed on her lip. "I hope so," she responded.

"I have another favor to ask of you," Rawl said, and she broke out of her musings to look at him.

"Of course," she replied instantly.

"I need to send word to the Danrayens about the situation in Andala. We can't be sure that Taruka was able to get inside as we did. They need to know the threat that they face."

"Of course," she responded, leading him to the stairway. "We have a wing of the tower dedicated to sending missives with magia."

Alric, who had been very quiet since leaving Andala, stood to follow them.

"No need to come," Rawl said brusquely. "It's just a missive. You should stay and rest." Then he turned before he could linger on the hurt on his former friend's face. But he felt his stare long after he faded from his view.

Even after sending his message, Rawl avoided returning to their rooms underneath the tower. Night had come creeping in as Tz'ola's crown set in the west, melting into the endless sea. Dusk was a watercolor of navy ocean, brilliant, fading orange, and the indigo of the night. Rawl watched the blending colors until stars winked in the sky.

He knew he was a coward. That he couldn't avoid Alric forever. But he didn't know how to make peace with the loss of the man he once knew when he was always there, staring at him. He might be a different person now, but he still stared at him with the same eyes. How was he supposed to maneuver that?

With a deep sigh, Rawl decided that he had delayed enough, and went to find Archwizard Auberon.

Underground once more, Rawl knocked on the door where they had left the wizard, ready to escort him to meet with Don Gilberto. He heard heavy steps coming towards him, then felt his jaw drop open when the man opened the door.

Gone was the weak, elderly man they had rescued from the dungeons. Gone was the weathered, tired face and scraggly hair and beard.

Instead, his hair was oiled and fashioned at the back of his head, exposing a surprisingly handsome face. The streaks of salt and pepper added a distinguished, regal air to his presence. He'd even trimmed his beard back to frame a wide-lipped and full mouth. There was no doubt that the mage had the face of an older man, but not an elderly one. In fact, he was quite handsome.

"You," Rawl stammered. "You look ..."

"Yes, I rather do," Auberon preened, smoothing down the lapels of a brand-new robe. Mila must have found one for him.

Rawl grinned. He realized that the man they had rescued from the cage at the bottom of Andala's fine palace was not an accurate representation of the true Archwizard Auberon. The man in front of him now was poised, confident, even regal. He looked powerful.

This is a man people will follow, he thought to himself. They might actually stand a chance.

Auberon stepped out into the hall and instantly ruined the illusion by bursting into a whirling dance that swished the fabric of his clothing about, belting out a folk song at the top of his lungs.

In the time that it took Rawl to calm him, all his newfound hope had been thoroughly squashed.

Together, they ascended the many, many stairs to the base of the university tower. Auberon was slightly winded by the time they exited into the cool night air, but he seemed much stronger than he had the day prior. Mila, Andu, and Alric were waiting for them when they exited.

Andu looked impressed with the mage's appearance, but Mila simply nodded in satisfaction.

"He'll be in his offices," she said, and Rawl assumed that she referred to Don Gilberto. "No one else should be about this time of night, but I have placed an illusion spell on our path, just in case. Auberon nodded to her, and she began leading the way.

Collectively, their group circled the expanse of the university tower, headed for the main entrance. Rawl realized that in all his time there, he had never walked through the front doors. This wasn't uncommon, however. As a member of the Padir, and a sometime thief, he was used to entries being back doors or windows with broken latches.

This time, he walked up the university stairs and through the enormous front doors.

Inside, the university was not unlike the under rooms, walls made of the same iridescent stone as its exterior, tiles of obsidian beneath their feet. There was an elegance to the architecture, all sleek lines and sharp corners. The effect should have been cold, but instead, there was a sense of lavish comfort about the space.

Before Mila could continue to lead them, Auberon swept around her and down a long corridor. When his sister made no move to correct him, Rawl followed, assuming the mage knew his way around the university better even than she did.

They reached a set of lofty onyx doors with swirling gold overlay, the handles two curving gold rings.

Auberon did not bother to knock or announce his presence in any other way, simply grasped the handles and swung both doors open dramatically, throwing his arms out wide.

Inside the room, behind an enormous and ornate black marble desk, an older man jumped to his feet, hand extended as if to blast them all with his magia. Rawl assumed that this was Don Gilberto, the head mage of the Mage University. He had thinning, inky black hair that matched the dark and somber mood of his office, as well as a thick and well-oiled black mustache that ended in little points beneath his cheekbones. His eyes were dark and beady and appeared far too small for his face, especially against the man's large and sharp nose. While what was visible of his arms was the sunburned tan of clay before baking, his face was currently devoid of any color.

"No puede ser," the man gasped, mouth gaping open and closed like a fish flopped on dry land. "It just can't be," he repeated, voice shaking as much as the hand that still quivered in the air in front of him.

"Of course it can, and is!" Auberon boomed jovially, striding into the room as if he owned not only it, but the entire university itself.

The rest of them scurried in after him, Andu closing the large doors behind them.

Don Gilberto crossed towards the Archwizard, extending his arms to embrace the man. They met in the center of the office, hugging warmly.

"Dioses," Gilberto said, pulling back to regard the mage incredulously. "I can't believe it is really you!"

"Believe it, amigo," Auberon said, clapping his friend on the shoulder. "It must be I, for it is me. I am more and more certain of it, and the probability does not lie. Unlike donkeys." He leaned in conspiratorially. "Donkeys *always* lie."

Then he moved towards the back of the office, sinking into one of the plush chairs situated in front of the monstrous desk, swishing his robes as he lowered himself, then crossing his hands in front of him with a flourish. Don Gilberto stared at him in bewilderment.

"As you can see," he addressed the stunned head mage, "I have returned."

Don Gilberto toppled back into his seat with far less finesse than Auberon had displayed, staring unblinkingly at the Archwizard, as if he had seen a ghost.

"It is very good to see you again," Don Gilberto said, still sounding dazed. "I never imagined I would get that honor again. But how?" he asked. Auberon waved a hand in front of him dismissively.

"It does not matter how," he answered, leaning forward. "What matters is that now, our work can resume."

There was a long, uncomfortable silence.

"No," Don Gilberto answered, dark brows pulled down into a frown.

"Yes, I know it is difficult to believe. Pero vamos, hombre. Do try to keep up," Auberon admonished him.

"No, I mean *no*. No. You cannot be here," Don Gilberto said, standing again and moving around his desk. "You need to leave. You all need to leave now."

"Qué?" Auberon asked, twisting to watch the man, but not moving to stand. He didn't sound angry, merely confused.

"Why would you come here?" Don Gilberto barked, wringing his hands. "Why would you do this?"

"You seemed fairly pleased with his presence just a moment ago," Mila observed, but Don Gilberto ignored her completely.

Auberon stared at him; puzzlement written clearly on his face. "I am here," he said slowly, "to finish the work that we began. I am here because the Name-Bearer—"

"No!" Gilberto cut in quickly, his voice nearly a yell. "No," he repeated more quietly. "Things are not as they once were, Auberon. You have been gone too long, too much has changed. What you propose is far too dangerous, and I will not subject my students to your ideals any longer."

"Our path was always dangerous," Auberon said, steel lacing his words. "But we persevered nonetheless, because it was the right thing. You know that." He scanned the university head up and down. "At least you used to; once."

"Things were different then!" Gilberto argued. "There are more forces at play now! There is far too much instability in the realm, and in case you haven't realized it, there are dioses-damned monstros on our very doorstep!"

"All the more reason to aid the Name-Bearer in delivering the Unnamed Prince to the Flowers!" Auberon boomed, rising to his feet. "If we fulfill the prophecy—"

"There are no guarantees!" Gilberto argued. "How do we know that what was reported that day was true? How can we be sure that this

Name-Bearer can be trusted? She was merely a girl. And if she has found a boy to bring to the Flowers, how can we know that he is indeed the Unnamed Prince?"

"You did not have these doubts when we led the Garden together," Auberon countered, sounding disgusted.

"The Garden?" Don Gilberto asked, brows pulled down in confusion.

"He means the Secret Order of the Flowers," Mila corrected.

Don Gilberto sighed, then crossed back behind his chair to sit once more. "Perhaps I had less doubts, or perhaps they were better buried," he admitted as Auberon followed suit and sat once again. "I was more idealistic then, and you were so sure. I trusted in you, but maybe deep down ..."

Rawl, who had been watching the interchange with the rest of his party, stepped forward.

"Sir," he said with as much authority as he could muster. "I know the Name-Bearer, personally. And I was there when she found the Unnamed Prince. I can assure you that he is the boy of the prophecy. They are both ready, with the Danrayen Warriors, to fight. Not only so that the boy can reach the Flowers, but for the safety and security of our people."

"And who are you?" Don Gilberto barked. "Why should I believe in your 'assurances?'"

"He is my brother," Mila said, stepping forward. "And I don't appreciate you questioning his honor."

"Mila," Gilberto addressed her, "You are a brilliant student and wonderful mage. But you are young and cannot possibly know what this man is asking of me."

"Do you?" Auberon interrupted. "I have not yet explained our next steps. How do you know what I am asking if I have not asked it? Or have I asked it, and you have answered, but I have not heard because I have thought I have not asked?"

Don Gilberto sent Auberon a look of concern.

"You have not explained your plans yet, señor," Mila cut in quickly before the head mage could question the Archwizard's sanity.

"Amigo, I have known you for more years than these children have been alive." Gilberto answered. "And if you are here now, speaking of continuing our work and of the prophecy of the Flowers, then I know what you wish to ask. If the Name-Bearer truly believes that she has the Unnamed Prince and the support of the Danrayens, then you wish for the mages to join the fight against the capital as well."

Auberon did not answer, but Rawl could see him clench his jaw.

Don Gilberto nodded. "I thought as much. And the answer is no. The crown has grown too powerful, and they now control monstros of the Night Wood. I will not subject my students to a hopeless war. I will not allow you to endanger them."

"At least allow us to make that choice for ourselves!" Mila cried out, and Andu nodded beside her.

"My answer is no," Don Gilberto barked in a tone that bore no argument. His eyes softened when they reached Archwizard Auberon's again.

"For the sake of our friendship, I will not report your presence here. But you must leave. You have until morning."

Then, to Rawl's astonishment, he walked purposefully out of his office, leaving the rest of them in stunned silence.

"That son of a scorpion," Auberon growled, lunging to his feet. "That dundering magpie! That cowardly squirrel-monkey! Who does he believe he is, to speak to me this way? I may have been imprisoned for the last few years, but I am more powerful than that pompous academic will ever be."

The way that he said "academic" made Rawl certain he did not mean it as a compliment.

"What now?" the archer asked, turning towards his sister.

Her jaw was set in a determined line.

"Now, we do this ourselves." She looked at Auberon. "There are still people here who remember your order. How would you call a meeting in the past?"

Auberon stared at her for a long moment, then broke into a slow smile.

"It would be my utmost delight to show you, querida."

CHAPTER 51
CHURAN

Churan sat on the floor of the mage training room in front of a very angry Axchel.

The soldier paced in front of him, turning every so often as if to address him, then spinning away to stomp about once more.

Unease churned in Churan's stomach. He wasn't afraid of Axchel. He knew that, despite the man's size and strength, he would never harm him. He also knew that the reason Axchel prowled the room like a mountain cat was because he did not yet trust himself to speak. Knowing that he had disappointed the soldier was worse than any beating he could have ever received.

After his burst of magia in Pelgar, the Danrayens had acted quickly. They fashioned makeshift stretchers to bear Damika as well as another badly injured warrior, then made their way back to the temple easily, with no monstro to stand in their way.

Churan noticed the priestesses all giving him curious looks on the way, and he knew that his demonstration had proved to them that he was who he and Nova claimed him to be. They had already started acting differently around him because of that realization.

Nuna had ordered Churan to wait in the mage rooms while she assisted the others to the infirmary before sending a messenger off to find Axchel and inform him just where his charge had been.

The man had been pacing ever since.

"I promised to be your protector," Axchel finally ground out, his back towards Churan as if he were analyzing a spiderweb in the corner of the room. The boy could see that his muscles were tense underneath his clothing, his shoulders bunched up towards his ears.

"I swore an oath, and we are bonded. I do not take those words lightly," he continued, his words like thorns pricking Churan's conscience.

"I know," he answered, sounding very childish to his ears. "I am sorry."

Axchel whirled around. "You do agree that Damika's actions were reckless and misguided, do you not?"

Churan nodded slowly. Yes, it had been foolish of the Danrayen to seek out the monstros of Pelgar alone.

"Then why did you believe *your* actions would be any different?" Axchel demanded.

Churan fought the urge to fidget in his seat. "Bueno," he started, "I have magia."

"Magia you can barely control!" Axchel snapped. "Magia that was not guaranteed to protect you out there."

"I just thought—" Churan tried again, but Axchel interrupted once more.

"No, you didn't think. If you had, you would have realized that it was the worst thing that you could have done. Damika might have been reckless, but you, you were downright foolish."

To Churan's horror, moisture began welling in his eyes.

"Lo siento!" he sniffled, trying not to let Axchel see him cry. "Really! I just—I just thought that I could help."

"You will help. When we take you to the Flowers, that action will bring forth a new age of peace to your realm, and I hope, to mine.

The confirmation of you as the Unnamed Prince will serve to unite the Northern Tribes, which was your aim long before you met any of us. That is the greatest thing that anyone could do for our people!"

"But it's not the same!" Churan argued, tears finally spilling. He batted them away angrily, thinking of how he could explain. "That—the Flowers. It's a passive thing that I can do. I just show up, and somehow it makes a difference?" He shook his head. "I want to do something now. I want to help now. I don't want anyone else to end up like Alric."

Churan lifted his shirt to wipe his face, and when he lowered it again, Axchel was crouched in front of him.

"What happened to Alric was not your fault," he said, his voice much softer.

"I should have been able to help him," Churan insisted. "I should have been able to help Raidea and her father. They died because I couldn't control my magia."

"That wasn't your fault," Axchel repeated. "None of it was. Don't take that on, niño. We are at war and will see much more fighting to come. You cannot hold yourself responsible for the death that occurs around you. If you do, you will break from the strain of it."

The wetness that Churan had just wiped from his cheeks returned. "I just wanted to help," he whispered.

Axchel drew him close, his frail frame swallowed up by the man's body. He clung to his back, burying his face against his tunic.

"I am proud of you, you know," the soldier said gruffly. "I am still mad, so mad, but I am proud of your bravery. And I heard that, without you, they may not have survived."

"We would not have," Nuna's voice said. Churan lifted his face and saw the mage stride purposefully into the room. She had bathed and changed since Pelgar, and bore a few fresh injuries, but nothing serious.

"Churan released his block on his magia and saved us all," she told Axchel, who stood and stepped away from Churan so that she could look at him properly.

"You said 'the dam burst?'" she asked him. "In Pelgar, after you incinerated our enemies. You said, 'the dam burst.' Is that true?"

Churan probed inside of himself for the area where he felt his access to magia most clearly. It swirled within him, untethered and wild.

He nodded at Nuna, who smiled, slow and wide.

"Good," she responded.

Good. He knew that was what they had been working towards, and yet knowing that nothing restrained the torrent of power within him, Churan couldn't help but feel afraid.

"I could have killed everyone in Pelgar, not just the monstros," he admitted in a whisper. "I did it before, when my magia first manifested. My tribe was being attacked by another, and I killed their raiders, but many of my own people as well." He felt the color drain from his face. "If I had done that in Pelgar—"

"But you didn't," Nuna interrupted him, lowering herself to sit cross-legged in front of him. "You know that you *can*. That you have the capability to cause harm. In many instances during this life, you will have the privilege and advantage of power over others. And you will have to choose, time and again, how and when to exercise that power. You will make mistakes, but I know you will strive to make the correct choices."

"How can you be so sure?" Churan asked, still filled with doubt.

"Because you do not wish anyone harm. Because you suppressed your magia behind that dam in your mind to keep yourself from ever hurting anyone again. And because you broke that barrier in order to help the people that you care for."

Churan met her eyes.

"You are the Warrior Child," she continued, using his tribal name. "You are also a prince, and a sorcerer. You have the means to make Tierramadri a better place for all. Will you fight to make it so, or will you bury your power out of fear once more?"

Churan thought about it, truly thought about it. He hadn't overly considered his place in the world. He knew that he was all the things that she had named him and had thought that they simply *were*. He couldn't change them any more than he could change the color of his eyes or the heart that beat within his chest. But he never thought that he had a say in how he would maneuver those positions in life. That he had a part in shaping what it meant to be the Warrior Child of the Northern Tribes, Unnamed Prince of Andala, and Sorcerer of Tierramadri.

A sudden, terrifying thought occurred to him.

"What if I'm not good enough?" he asked with dread. "What if I am not smart enough, or good enough, or disciplined enough to be what everyone needs me to be?"

It was a startling question. He had always been told who and what he needed to be. Now, with Nuna revealing he had a voice, that he had choices, he suddenly worried that he would make the wrong ones. Had it merely been youthful optimism that had kept him from these concerns before?

"You will be smart enough, and good enough, and disciplined enough," Nuna stated matter-of-factly. "You will also be kind enough, compassionate enough, strong enough, and more."

"But how do you *know*?" he asked, voice bordering on a whine.

"Because you will make it so," she answered determinedly. "And most importantly, because you will not be alone. You will surround yourself with those you trust, with those who have your faith. And you will guide each other."

A tapestry began taking shape in Churan's mind. His life, with the people he chose in it. His magia, helping to stabilize Tierramadri. His friends and allies providing him counsel. His ascension to power leading to peace among the Northern Tribes, Andala, and Cassalan. The end of Night Wood creatures.

Nuna was watching his face while he thought, and something in his expression must have pleased her. She leaned forward towards him.

"Now, you tell me," she said. "Are you ready to shape your future?"

Churan grinned. "Show me the way."

CHAPTER 52

RAWL

Although Don Gilberto had insisted that Archwizard Auberon vacate the Mage University by morning, Rawl's group was fairly certain he was not going to search the tower top-to-bottom to ensure that he had complied. So, they returned to their underground rooms and made arrangements for the following day.

By dawn, Mila and Andu were up, organizing their plan.

The call for a secret meeting, Rawl had found out, was the image of a flower, burned into several subtle spaces around the university. One at the top of a stairway banister, another on the ceiling of an indoor washroom, etched on the corner of work desks, and so forth. Those who recognized the markings knew to meet at the open clearing where Rawl, Andu, and Mila had attempted to unveil the secrets of the Goldenshell. Those who did not recognize the symbol would dismiss it, or find themselves dragged along by their friends and peers.

"Is it safe?" Rawl asked Mila, thinking of the salta-sombras which had almost devoured him weeks ago.

Mila nodded. "Andu and I recruited some mages in training to erect a large protective warding around the area well before nightfall. No monstros should be able to penetrate it, so we will be able to speak freely."

"It is not only monstros we need to worry about," Andu reminded them.

By nightfall, the university was filled with a tense, expectant energy. Rawl wondered what Don Gilberto would do if he discovered their plans, and if the students were capable of keeping the secret from their instructors.

"No student here would alert their instructors, or call the authorities over a secret meeting," Mila answered confidently. "Mages are too curious by nature. They would want to see what all the fuss was about first. And I believe there are still many here loyal to Auberon, and to the Flowers."

"I hope you're right," Rawl muttered, before turning to Alric. "You need to stay here," he told him.

"Que? No, I am coming with you," he argued, confusion and a little hurt darkening his face.

Rawl shook his head. "There will be people here who knew you before … before your illness," he explained. "I know that you don't mind not remembering," *because the spell doesn't allow you to,* he thought bitterly, "but they will. They will have questions we simply cannot answer right now. You need to stay behind."

Alric set his jaw in a firm line. "No. I am not being left behind. I know that you are angry with me, for some reason, but like it or not, I am a part of this. I may not know why, or remember everything, but I know that much." An edge of panic crept into his voice. "*I am a part of this,*" he repeated.

"Of course you will come, mijo," Auberon answered, and Rawl tensed with displeasure. "You will stay by my side, and not speak to anyone, understood?" the mage continued.

Alric nodded, and Rawl let out a frustrated breath. "Very well," he agreed, stalking off, not wanting to look at either of them.

Mila caught up to him and gently guided him by the elbow, as he was heading in the wrong direction. He squeezed her hand in gratitude. They walked towards the clearing together.

"Time to build a mage army?" she quipped, and Rawl barked out a short, humorless laugh.

"If Mami could see us now," he joked softly.

"She would be so proud," Mila responded.

"Actually, she really would be, wouldn't she?" Rawl's laugh was genuine this time. After a few minutes of walking, they were close to their destination.

"They are ready," she said, turning her attention to Auberon. "We were just there. Almost the entire student body received the message." Unease flickered over her features. "And despite your words, some of the instructors as well."

Auberon flicked his wrist, as if dismissing her worry. "Only those who were once a member of the order, I am sure."

"Here we go," Andu said from behind them as they all stepped through a cluster of trees and into the open clearing.

Rawl's heart leaped into his throat, and he stopped, frozen in place. There were hundreds of people clustered around the large clearing, which now looked small, with so many bodies pressed in on one another. He suddenly realized how precarious their plans were. The fate of the realm hung in the balance, and the only thing that could sway it to their favor was an old man who would often lose himself. What if he couldn't gather his wits well enough to convince them all?

Rawl shot a desperate glance at his sister, but her lips were pressed tight as she moved through the throng. Rawl could do nothing but swallow hard and follow her.

They could hear chatter before they arrived, words melding into one another as their group approached the space. But a hush descended upon the crowd when the students began to notice who they were with.

"Is that?" someone whispered.

"It couldn't be!" another voice protested.

"Auberon! It's Archwizard Auberon!"

"No seas tonto. He is in the Andalan dungeons!"

"I heard he had been killed!"

"No, it is him! I swear it!"

"He's with Alric, is that Alric?"

"Alric! Alric!"

"Auberon!"

From the hush grew a frenzied chaos. The people began crowding in closer, trying to get a glimpse of Auberon and Alric, calling out, reaching out, trying to clasp them on their shoulders or touch their robes. The energy was excited and happy, not the suspicion that Rawl was worried about.

Auberon was clasping shoulders and shaking hands. Whenever anyone would try to approach Alric, he would gently steer them away, but he was allowing him to be seen, to be noticed. As Rawl trailed behind them, he couldn't help but feel the slow stirrings of hope. If all these people were excited about Auberon's return, then surely they would come to his aid.

Rawl could not describe the overwhelming sense of relief that gave him. He didn't want to have to tell Rojya that he had failed—twice. Once, in not saving Alric, not really, and the second by not securing the mages to their cause.

Then, in an instant, the clearing which had been lit with luz orbs was flooded with a bright flash, only to plunge them all into darkness, the moon and stars above, the only remaining light left to illuminate the gathering.

"Stop!" a voice cried out when the shock of the blaze created a moment of quiet shock. From the back of the crowd, several figures pushed through. As they approached, Rawl recognized Don Gilberto, flanked by several older looking mages.

More instructors, Rawl guessed to himself. He slipped his hand into a hidden pocket, where he carried a short blade, wondering if he would need it.

Don Gilberto reached Auberon, out of breath and sweat-soaked.

"Palace officials are here," he told the Archwizard. "They arrived this afternoon."

Rawl watched as his group tensed.

"I disavowed any knowledge of your escape, or your presence here, of course," he continued, but Rawl did not allow himself to relax. Anger simmered in the head mage's voice, and his next words only reinforced that he was right to remain wary.

"They are searching the tower and the grounds. They will be here any moment."

"We will fight them!" a voice from the crowd called out, and there were answering cheers.

"Protect the Archwizard!" another called out.

"Don't be foolish!" Don Gilberto retorted, his voice carrying above the crowd. "Word of your attack and alliance with the Archwizard will reach the capital in an instant, and your advantage will be lost."

He glowered at Auberon. "You have put me in a terrible position, and if my students come to harm this night, know that I will never forgive you.

He turned to assess the crowd. "You, you, and you," he said, pointing at Mila and two other students. "Place an ocultar spell on the Archwizard." They responded quickly, clustering around the man.

"Auberon, they are searching for your magical signature, so for dioses' sake, don't try to help them."

The head of the university turned to address the rest of the anxious mob.

"Now, as for the rest of you ..." he pulled a jagged-looking spell stone from around his neck. "It looks like a perfect night for a Lunar Ceremony, doesn't it?"

In a flash, students and instructors pulled out various looking spell stones from pockets or chains around their neck. They held them out in front of them, looking up towards the sky. Only Rawl and Alric remained motionless.

"What is happening?" Rawl asked Andu in a whisper.

"Lunar Ceremonies are a very archaic practice in which mages used to aid their spell stones purification by holding their stones under the light of the moon,." the man answered just as quietly.

"Really?" Rawl asked, surprised.

"We don't do it much anymore," Andu admitted. "It has been deemed unnecessary, as we now know that the stones are capable of purifying themselves. However, some mages keep the practice, claiming that the process strengthens their stones. We do not know whether or not that is true."

Before Rawl could ask any more questions, they heard a commotion towards the back of the clearing.

"What is the meaning of this?" a whiny voice carried across the quiet of the crowd. "I demand to speak to someone in charge!"

"Let them through," Don Gilberto called out, gritting his teeth. Rawl gripped Alric's sleeve, stepping them backwards, allowing the bodies of several mage students to obscure them while still retaining a clear view of the head of the university. With a start, he realized he could no longer see Auberon and hoped that meant that Mila's obscuring spell was working.

A short, pudgy man dressed in the bright contrasting colors of the Andalan capital made his way to the head mage, along with at least six additional Andalan soldiers. From a distance, he could see even more soldiers between the trees. They were too far to tell for sure, but Rawl wouldn't have been surprised if there was at least a full company ready to descend on them all.

"What is the meaning of this, Gilberto?" the man demanded, reaching up to poke him in the chest. Gilberto, to his credit, did not flinch.

"You're still here, Capitan?" he answered.

"Just this morning you vowed that you knew nothing of the—" he hesitated, glancing around at the attentive crowd. "Of the problem we face, and here I find you organizing some sort of assembly?"

"As I said, your problems in the capital have nothing to do with me or my university. And this is a ceremony, not an assembly. Surely you have heard of our Lunar Ceremonies?" Don Gilberto responded, looking thoroughly unbothered.

The captain, on the other hand, looked incredulous. "You truly expect me to believe that today, on the day that I arrive with my tidings, your university just so happens to be conducting a large, outdoor ceremony with all of its students?"

"Surely not all," Don Gilberto responded. "But most, yes."

The captain's eyes narrowed. "I do not believe you."

"You made that very clear this morning," Don Gilberto answered, looking from the sky to glare at the smaller man. "But as I have already mentioned, several times, I cannot help you. So, I ask that you please leave, so that I can resume leading my university in peace."

The captain looked around at all the students holding out their stones beneath the night sky. While Rawl was sure that most of them were very curious about the events happening in the center of the clearing, the majority of them kept their eyes cast upwards. They looked, for all the world, to be simply a group of mages indulging in some sort of magical ritual. Rawl saw doubt creep into the man's gaze. But then he looked up, and his jaw clenched hard.

"A Lunar Ceremony, you say?" he sneered. "*When the moon is not even full?*"

"Mage Novice Filomila," Don Gilberto barked, and Rawl's sister quickly appeared by his side. "Why do we perform a Lunar Ceremony during the full moon?" he asked, as if they were in a classroom, rather than seconds away from being arrested.

Mila straightened. "A Lunar Ceremony under a full moon provides purification and energetical cleansing of our spell stones for optimal function."

"Very good," the head mage answered. "And why would we conduct a Lunar Ceremony under a waxing crescent moon?"

"A Lunar Ceremony under a waxing crescent moon is conducted to set our intellectual and scholarly intentions for our upcoming magical examinations, as the crescent moon is a symbol for new energy and a time for building and growth." Mila responded without hesitation.

Don Gilberto turned back to the captain. "Are there any other lessons in magia you wish to learn this night, or may we return to our endeavors? I would hate to write that my students' education was adversely affected by your presence in my next report to the crown."

The captain fumed, but spun on his heels, grunting at his men to follow him. Only after he and his company were well out of range did the crowd relax once more.

With a shimmer, Auberon reappeared next to Don Gilberto. The Archwizard looked at his old friend curiously.

"So, you decided to help after all," he beamed at him. "I am so pleased, Gilly!"

Don Gilberto delivered a very unscholarly snort and waved his hand to indicate towards the large crowd. "I clearly cannot stop you," he said, still looking angry. "I don't like it, or that you went behind my back." He sighed heavily. "But I understand why you felt you had to." Then he stuck his hand out for Auberon, who clasped it firmly.

"It seems our paths align again," the head mage continued. "But I will not order any of my students or my faculty to walk it with us. If you seek their aid, you must secure it for yourself. And please, never call me 'Gilly' again!"

Auberon nodded with a boyish grin, then turned to Rawl, Mila, Andu, and Alric.

"What was it you said, niña?" he asked Mila. "Let us secure a mage army."

CHAPTER 53

RAWL

Auberon climbed the small wooden podium that Andu had hastily fashioned before their arrival, and slowly, the crowd grew silent once again, waiting for the mage to speak. Rawl felt like his heart was in his throat. What would the wizard say? Would it make any sense at all? Or would it just be nonsense?

"I am Archwizard Auberon," he said simply, and the audience *erupted*. There were claps and cheers, people embracing one another. Rawl thought he saw some wiping away tears. He regarded the mage curiously. What had the man done to gain such loyalty amongst these people? By all rights, they should be questioning him, demanding to know how he had escaped the prisons, or be calling the authorities to take him back. Instead, they had protected him from the Andalan soldiers, their loyalty seemingly directed towards him rather than to the crown.

Just how bad had the governing in Andala become if the people so easily turned away from their monarchy?

Auberon raised his hands, and slowly, the crowd quieted once more. "I have been gone too long," he started. "The work we began so long ago was unavoidably paused with my incarceration. But I hope you did not think that meant we were defeated."

There were murmurs in the crowd. It seemed apparent that several people *had* believed them all to be defeated.

"Even when I was left to rot in the bowels of the kingdom, our work continued," the mage declared. "We have set forth to fulfill the prophecy delivered to us so long ago. The Name-Bearer lives."

The crowd broke into wild cheers and frenzy once again. People jumped up and down, as if they were children, an expression on their faces that Rawl knew as well as the back of his own hand.

Hope. It was hope.

Auberon raised his arms once again, and before the roar of the excitement fully dissipated, he called out, loud and far, for all to hear, *"And she has found the Unnamed Prince."*

If Rawl had thought the temper of the crowd to be cacophonous before, it became an unrestrained frenzy of cries and screams, joyous, raucous laughter, people moving and crashing about like the waves that struck the university tower. Tears flowed freely now. Rawl could not see a single person not affected by the news.

These are Auberon's people, Rawl realized, amazed. *Mila was right, they would not have bent for anyone else but him.*

Faces turned up to the Archwizard with wonder and expectation, anxiously awaiting his next words.

"But she needs our help," he continued. The resulting silence was so deafening in comparison to the noise of before that it felt eerie and unnatural. A cold shiver crawled up Rawl's spine.

"Many of you have heard the rumors of the Night Wood creatures at our city walls," Auberon said. "I am here to tell you that not only are the rumors true, but that the truth is far worse than we could ever have imagined. The monstros have not only reached the city, but there is one inside of it that controls them."

Gasps of denial peppered the crowd, the sound of anxious feet shifting from side to side.

"The monstros guard the city gates so that none but those with the proper paperwork can enter. They prowl the very city streets, suppressing the rights and the will of the people. And they surround the Andalan Palace, so that none but those deemed worthy can pass."

He looked seriously out into the night, focusing his gaze on as many people as he could.

"The prophecy is clear. The Name-Bearer must bring the Unnamed Prince to the Flowers for a Naming. She needs aid to cross into the Andalan capital once more and deliver the Prince to his fate."

Murmurs of assent and resolve surfaced. People were glancing at one another and nodding their agreement.

"The Name-Bearer has secured aid from the Padir people, and the protection of the Danrayens."

More excitement. The Danrayens were the most respected warriors in all the realm.

Auberon was smart to include that detail, Rawl thought. It would make their impossible task seem potentially achievable. The Padir weren't yet assured, but Rawl had faith that Taruka would sway his people to their cause.

"But they need our assistance. There are too many monstros to battle alone, not to mention the Andalan army. And most of them do not have magia, as we do."

Shoulders pulled up in pride, chests puffed, and cocky smiles flitted across the crowd.

"Make no mistake, this will not be an easy task," Auberon warned them. "And each of you who agrees to it will technically be traitors to the realm, as I am considered."

Some mages looked delighted at the prospect of being anything like the Archwizard.

"And it will not be without danger. You have trained to use your battle magia against Cassalan, the enemy. Now, you would be turning it against your own people.

"Peace has been promised," he warned, "but it is not easily won. Nothing truly worth winning ever is. But we know we are capable of it. And I, for one, long for it. It has been my life's work, and many have already fought and perished to see it fulfilled." Sorrow clouded his eyes. "I cannot guarantee your safety," he said. "I cannot promise you that we will all live to see peace at the end of this war. What I can promise is that there *will* be an end to it. That our descendants can live without the fear that has held us in its grip for far too long."

Auberon paused. It was a lingering pause and held for so long that Rawl wondered if he was going to speak again at all. Finally, he did.

"I believe in the Name-Bearer. I believe in the Unnamed Prince. I believe in the Flowers, and their promise of peace. And I believe in the strong and true hearts of every person standing before me tonight. I know that, united, we can lay siege to the capital and defeat the enemy once and for all. The *true* enemy," he stressed. "Not the Cassalains. Not even the monstros of the Night Wood. But the seed of corruption that has blossomed into suffocating vines within the very heart of our realm. The relentless growth of the power-hungry greed that has blocked the light from the true citizens of Andala, strangling all that is good and just from our people. We will tear it out by its root so that what was so long buried can regrow again."

Rawl felt his heart swell with pride as he watched the Archwizard, standing tall and proud and radiating like a lighthouse of hope in a dark harbor. How he had managed to keep his thoughts in order for so long, to deliver such a powerful speech, he did not know. What he did know was that there was not one soul in the crowd that was unaffected by the force of his being.

The mage took his time, scanning the crowd, meeting as many eyes as he possibly could. Then he raised his arms up high.

"Who is with us?"

CHAPTER 54
NOVA

"We have the mages!" Nova burst into the council room, excitement evident in both her stride and her voice. "And you'll never believe how we got them."

The rest of the council members, already assembled and seated in their usual places around the large table, looked expectantly at her. Nova had only been late because of the last-minute missive from Rawl. Flinging herself into her chair, she launched into his explanation about their extraction of Archwizard Auberon from the Andalan dungeons, and the subsequent rallying of the mages at the university.

Once she finished, the mood in the room was decidedly bright. Mamá had a slight smile on her face, and Axchel regarded her proudly, as if she had arranged the feat all on her own. Churan was positively beaming. Damika was still looking battered, but she too seemed relieved at the news, as did the other priestesses.

"Have we heard from Petra yet?" Damika asked Mamá, who shook her head.

"Only that she was approaching the location of the Padir," Mamá answered, then turned back to Nova. "Did your friend say anything more?"

"I didn't finish his letter," she admitted, pulling it from her pouch. I just needed to let you all know," she finished.

Nova scanned the parchment, smiling again when she read the happy news. Then she felt as if the air had been knocked out of her lungs.

"What?" Damika demanded, leaning forward. "You've gone white. What is it?"

Wordlessly, Nova passed the letter to Mamá, who scanned it herself before handing it to Damika. Her expression didn't change, but her eyes grew hard.

Damika, however, swore so loudly and colorfully that Axchel flushed and tried covering Churan's ears. The boy swatted him off.

"Qué?" he asked nervously. "What is it?"

"The reports of monstros at the Andalan capital have been confirmed," Mamá said, addressing the room. The priestesses nodded. They had been expecting as much.

"They are in much higher numbers than we anticipated," Mamá continued.

"How much higher?" General Vashti demanded.

"Three times higher," Mamá responded.

A stunned silence fell over the room. No one spoke, no one even moved.

"No," Sinchi finally whispered. "We don't ..." her voice trailed off.

"We don't have the numbers," Damika finished for her.

Nova was shaking her head. "This can't be right. After all this time, we were so close. How can this be right?"

"Is there anything to be done?" Ianuaria asked.

"We barely had the numbers when we thought their forces were one-third their size," Vashti snapped. "It was nearly impossible then, but now ..."

"But we have a sorcerer," Priestess Ovidia insisted, looking at Churan.

Mage Nuna shook her head. "Churan is very powerful, yes. But one boy will not be enough to battle the amount of monstros that would be awaiting us."

"Not to mention the soldiers," Sinchi added.

"So that's it?" Ianuaria demanded. "Is there nothing that we can do?"

"We don't have the numbers," Vashti repeated.

"Then we get the numbers," Axchel interrupted. All heads turned to stare at him, but he was looking at Churan.

"You are the Warrior Child of the Northern Tribes. Will they not follow you?" he asked the boy quietly.

Churan stared at the soldier wide-eyed. After a moment, he nodded.

"Those who united before I left would follow," he said. "Peace for Andala and Cassalan would mean peace for our people as well. Not to mention the problem with the monstros."

"How can we contact them?" Axchel asked, turning back to the council.

"I think—" Churan spoke, then cleared his throat. "I think I could speak to them directly. With my magia." He looked at Nuna. "If you could direct me."

The mage looked shocked. "Well, yes, in theory it can be done, especially by someone with your power. But I have never attempted it before."

Churan shot her a rueful smile. "Neither have I," he answered.

Nuna blinked. "Bueno, si. Si," she repeated, looking towards Mamá. "It is possible."

"It doesn't matter whether or not it's possible!" Damika cut in. "Has everyone forgotten where the Northern Tribes are located? In the *North*. Above *Cassalan*. And, last I remember, they continue to fight. How exactly are they going to travel the entire span of Cassalan, cross the Borders into Andala, and reach the Andalan capital?" she demanded. "It cannot be done."

Silence fell over the room once more. As much as Nova hated to admit it, she was right. There was no way that the Tribes could make that kind of journey undetected. Not in the numbers that they needed.

Nova watched as defeat creeped into the room, settling over her friends and fellow warriors, weighing their shoulders and pushing down their heads. They inhaled it like a vapor, and she watched as the feeling poisoned their lungs and tightened their throats. In Damika, it looked like anger. Her friend was scowling, making her already fierce face a mask of ire. Vashti looked nearly the same. Mamá looked stunned, her eyes far away. Churan looked close to tears, Axchel doing his best to quietly comfort him.

Nova knew that she was in shock, and that the crushing sense of defeat would find her soon enough. But in that moment, she felt nothing but admiration and gratitude towards the man. He had once been her enemy, a Cassalain soldier. Had they met on the battlefield, they would have undoubtedly tried to kill one another. But since they had met as prisoners, both captured by the same band of flesh peddlers, they had somehow managed to become allies and friends instead. It was amazing what a common enemy could do.

Her eyes drifted over to the large map, focusing on the purple pins representing the Andalan army on one side of the Borders, and the clusters of red rose pins on the other side, representing the Cassalain army.

Wait, roses?

Nova squinted. Yes, the red pins that were meant to show the Cassalain forces were actually small roses. She stood, the voices of the rest of the council members fading behind her as she crossed to the map.

All around the Andalan capital were black pins, tiny black skulls to represent the monstros of the Night Wood. Above, she looked once more at the roses, then the pins of the Andalan army, purple to represent the royal color of Andala. Those pins were also fashioned to look like little flowers.

Jacarandas, Nova realized.

The Andalan army pins were small, purple jacarandas, and the Cassalain army pins were red roses.

The jacaranda and the rose, she thought to herself, straining to remember the prophecy the goddess Danray had delivered during her Trial.

The jacaranda learns to trust the rose!

Nova spun back to the council so quickly that several Danrayens reached for their weapons. Whatever discussion they had been in the middle of fell into silence.

"We make them our allies," she said out loud.

"It doesn't matter if we can make them our allies," Damika insisted. "They will not be able to reach us."

"Not the Northern Tribes," Nova answered. "The Cassalains."

General Vashti was the first to break. The woman laughed and laughed, tears streaming from her eyes. She laughed so loudly that Nova began to become concerned.

"Nessa," Damika said softly. "We have been at war with the Cassalains for centuries. They are our enemies."

"But they aren't, not really," Nova insisted, remembering the words of the goddess.

Enemy will turn friend, and friend will turn foe.

"They have been just as plagued by the Night Wood attacks as we have, haven't they?" she continued, sitting back down in her chair. "And no one is foolish enough to believe that once Guerro has secured

Andala that he will be content with one realm alone. Why would he be, when he could continue to conquer all of Tierramadri?"

"Greedy men are never satisfied," Mamá added softly.

"Exactly," Nova pressed. "We just need to convince them that we have a common enemy, and a shared goal. A promise of truce from the Danrayens would hold some sway, wouldn't it?" she asked.

General Vashti was shaking her head. "Perhaps, but likely not enough. Even if we were to entertain this madness, how would we even secure an audience with the Cassalain king to consider it?"

"We don't need the king to consider it," Axchel said. "Our monarchy is more of a figurehead. What you need is the captain of the Cassalain army. And I know his right-hand man." He looked at Nova. "He is the one who spoke for me after what happened with my old company and the bandits."

"If we managed to get a message to him, do you think he would trust you? To him, you are a traitor. You left Cassalan with the enemy," Damika asked him.

Axchel's jaw clenched, but he didn't disagree. Nova wanted to leap to his defense, but what could she say? Damika was right, if blunt.

"If the monstros are causing as much of a problem in the north as they are here, they may be willing to take a risk in order to protect our people. Though there will be no love gained once the Cassalains realize that the problem originated in Andala," Axchel finally answered.

"We'll deal with that later. We have a bigger problem. Even if we, by some miracle, find a way to convince them to broker a truce after a centuries' long war, how can we get them across the Borders without our own army massacring them?" the general demanded.

"Danrayen protection," Mamá answered. "We recall all our warriors. We meet at the border, and we vow to them, on Danray herself, that they will have our protection."

"There are hundreds of Danrayens. There are thousands of soldiers. And while any true Danrayen is worth ten soldiers, we are still vastly outnumbered," Sinchi protested.

"Perhaps the respect towards our people will lend us favor. Perhaps we can get our army to lay down their weapons," Ovidia said, sounding unconvinced.

"No," Nova said, springing forward in her chair. At once, the rest of the prophecy echoed in her mind.

The wilted crown will bloom anew when the jacaranda learns to trust the rose, she remembered. It suddenly all made sense. *The wilted crown.*

"*We* aren't enough to convince them, but we know someone who might be." She looked at Axchel.

He frowned at her for a long moment, eyes flickering as he sorted the thoughts in his head. Then Nova watched as realization dawned in his eyes.

He turned to look at Mamá.

"Someone needs to go back to Cassalan," he breathed. "Andalan, that is brilliant," he told Nova.

"What?" Damika demanded. "What is it?"

"There is something I forgot to mention," Nova replied. "King Enrique lives."

The room exploded into chaos. The priestesses fired question after question at her, too quickly for Nova to follow. Mamá raised her hand to quiet them, but it still took a few moments for the rest of them to settle down.

"How could you simply forget something like that?" she asked Nova.

Truthfully, she hadn't forgotten at all. She had simply chosen not to mention it. After meeting the man and his family, she had decided to keep his existence a secret. While she didn't agree with his choices, she did understand that his actions had been dictated by love. She wouldn't have mentioned him ever again if they didn't have such a need for him now.

Nova shrugged at Mamá. "We had other concerns," she answered dismissively. "If the captain agrees to march to Andala with the Cassalain army, Prince Enrique is the only one who can prevent a border battle. If he is the one who crosses with the Cassalain soldiers, there may be enough loyalty to the crown that the Andalan soldiers will be willing to listen."

"And if they found Danrayen support on this side ... It may just be enough," Mamá finished. She directed her attention to Vashti. "What do you think?"

Clumps of hair stood straight up from Vashti's scalp where she had been pulling at it with her hands. She blew out a long breath and looked around the room, her eyes finally locking on Churan's.

With a set jaw, she spoke, "I have never taken too much stock in prophecies. I prefer to deal with reality, not the meddlings of the dioses. But I have been a soldier for far too long, in a war that has lasted for far too long. If we have a chance for true peace, then perhaps this truce with Cassalan is the start of it." She nodded. "I say we try."

The council room turned to Mamá, who, in turn looked at Nova.

She knew that her plan was risky and unlikely to succeed. But she had promised Churan that she would do everything in her power to deliver him to the Flowers.

She grinned. "Let's go resurrect a king."

The Flowers of Prophecy Series will Return

The Flowers of Prophecy Series will conclude
May 2025

Name Pronunciation and Meanings

Name Pronunciation and Meanings

In order of appearance

Rawl: *Rah-ool* "Wise wolf"

Viejo: *Vee-eh-ho* "Old man"

Padir: *Pah-deer* Minor god; nomadic son of the River God and the Goddess of Wind

Alric: *All-rik* "Regal ruler"

Nova: *No-vah* "New"

Tz'ola: *Ts-oh-la* Goddess; of the sun

Danray: *Dan-ray* Goddess; of battle and transition

Damika: *Dah-me-kah* "Open-spirited"

Raidea: *Ray-dee-ah* "Wise goddess"

Adira: *Ah-dee-rah* "Stong, noble, powerful"

Petra: *Peh-trah* "Stone, rock"

Rojya: *Row-hyah* Animal; fox-like creature with red fur

Axchel: *Ahk-shell* "Man of peace"

Ax: *Ak-sh* (Nickname for Axchel) "Man of peace"

Taruka: *Tah-roo-kah* "Doe"

Mamá: *Ma-ma* "Mother"

Phanessa: *Fah-ness-ah* "Butterfly"

Nessa: *Ness-ah* (Nickname for Phanessa) "Butterfly"

Churan: *Choo-rahn* "Savior"

Mamajove: *Ma-ma-hoh-veh* Goddess; youngest of the three Caimen sister goddesses of the Great Andalan Rainforest

Mamamedia: *Ma-ma-meh-dee-ah* Goddess; middle of the three Caimen sister goddesses of the Great Andalan Rainforest

Mamavieja: *Ma-ma-vee-eh-hah* Goddess; eldest of the three Caimen sister goddesses of the Great Andalan Rainforest

Trucar: *Trew-car* Minor god; of trickery and deception

Ramon: *Rah-mon* "Protector"

Sofia: *So-fee-ah* "Wisdom"

Vashti: *Vash-tee* "Lovely"

Ovidia: *Oh-vee-dee-ah* "Shepard"

Ianuaria: *Ee-oon-our-ree-ah* "Healer"

Nuna: *Noo-nah* "Soul, spirit"

Sinchi: *Sin-chee* "Brave, stubborn"

Guerro: *Geh-row* "Warrior, soldier"

Zerlina: *Sehr-lee-nah* "Beautiful Dawn"

Kichka: *Keech-kah* "Thorn"

Auberon: *Aw-burr-on* "Royal bear"

Filomila: *Fee-low-mee-lah* "Beloved Miracle"

Mila: *Me-lah* (Nickname for Filomila) "Beloved Miracle"

Andu: *An-doo* "Strength"

Untik: Oon-teek "Healthy, fit"

Zena: Zen-ah "Welcoming, amicable"

Graciela: *Grah-see-el-ah* "Grace, graceful"

Lionel: *Lee-oh-nell* "Little Lion"

Peruda: *Peh-roo-dah* Goddess; of love

Kallpa: *Kall-pah* "With force"

Azucar: *Ah-soo-kar* "Sugar"

Ignacio: *Eeg-nah-see-oh* "Fiery one"

Gilberto: *Heel-behr-tow* "Bright promise"

Acknowledgements

I have a lot of people to thank, but first, let me say one thing.

I KNOW I said that this series would be a trilogy ... and here I am adding on a fourth book.

Oops!

The world, and the story, just got bigger than I anticipated. I hope you will stick around for one more journey!

I want to thank my book besties and writing partners, Michael LaBorn and Isabelle Olmo. Michael because he knew this was four books long before I did and checked in on me until I could finally admit it to myself. And Isabelle, because I could NOT have written this without all of our writing sprints. Thank you for holding me accountable, but making it fun while doing so.

Thank you to my beta reader turned alpha reader turned developmental editor, Cody Von Ruden. (Turned friend too, somewhere along the way!) Thank you for knowing the heart of this story and always doing so much to make sure that I bring it out. You have helped me make this book the best version of itself, and I appreciate you immensely.

Thank you to my copy editor and proofreader Ashley. I would apologize for all the em dashes - but I'm not sorry.

Thank you to my wenches—you know who you are. One of the best parts of becoming an author was getting to meet all of you.

A big thank you to my parents—I couldn't have gotten through this year without your help!

And most importantly, thank you to all of my readers. Your support and encouragement will never not overwhelm me with love and gratitude. You are the reason I do this, and I appreciate you all more than I could ever say.

Gracias!

Also by Natalia Hernandez

Young Adult

<u>Flower of Prophecy Series</u>

The Name-Bearer

The Follower of Flowers

Adult

<u>Pisqu Sweet and Sour Series</u>

Asiri and the Amaru